THE ASSOCIATE

ALSO BY JOHN GRISHAM

A Time to Kill
The Firm
The Pelican Brief
The Client
The Chamber
The Rainmaker
The Runaway Jury
The Partner
The Street Lawyer
The Testament
The Brethren
A Painted House
Skipping Christmas
The Summons
The King of Torts
Bleachers
The Last Juror
The Broker
The Innocent Man
Playing for Pizza
The Appeal

DOUBLEDAY

New York London Toronto

Sydney Auckland

JOHN GRISHAM

THE ASSOCIATE

DOUBLEDAY

Published in the United States by Doubleday, an imprint of The Doubleday Publishing Group, a division of Random House, Inc., New York.
www.doubleday.com

DOUBLEDAY and the DD colophon are registered trademarks of Random House, Inc.

Book design by Maria Carella

Cataloging-in-Publication Data is on file with the Library of Congress

ISBN 978-0-385-51783-6

PRINTED IN THE UNITED STATES OF AMERICA

1 3 5 7 9 10 8 6 4 2

First Edition

TO

Steve Rubin, Suzanne Herz, John Pitts,

Alison Rich, Rebecca Holland, John Fontana,

and the rest of the gang at Doubleday

THE ASSOCIATE

1

The rules of the New Haven Youth League required that each kid play at least ten minutes in each game. Exceptions were allowed for players who had upset their coaches by skipping practice or violating other rules. In such cases, a coach could file a report before the game and inform the scorekeeper that so-and-so wouldn't play much, if at all, because of some infraction. This was frowned on by the league; it was, after all, much more recreational than competitive.

With four minutes left in the game, Coach Kyle looked down the bench, nodded at a somber and pouting little boy named Marquis, and said, "Do you want to play?" Without responding, Marquis walked to the scorers' table and waited for a whistle. His violations were numerous—skipping practice, skipping school, bad grades, losing his uniform, foul language. In fact, after ten weeks and fifteen games, Marquis had broken every one of the few rules his coach tried to enforce. Coach Kyle had long since realized that any new rule would be immediately violated by his star, and for that reason he trimmed his list and fought the temptation to add new regulations. It wasn't working. Trying to control ten inner-city kids with a soft touch had put the Red Knights in last place in the 12 and Under division of the winter league.

Marquis was only eleven, but clearly the best player on the court. He preferred shooting and scoring over passing and defending, and within two minutes he'd slashed through the lane, around and through and over much larger players, and scored six points. His average was fourteen, and if allowed to play more than half a game, he could probably score thirty. In his own young opinion, he really didn't need to practice.

In spite of the one-man show, the game was out of reach. Kyle McAvoy sat quietly on the bench, watching the game and waiting for the clock to wind down. One game to go and the season would be over, his last as a basketball coach. In two years he'd won a dozen, lost two dozen, and asked himself how any person in his right mind would willingly coach at any level. He was doing it for the kids, he'd said to himself a thousand times, kids with no fathers, kids from bad homes, kids in need of a positive male influence. And he still believed it, but after two years of babysitting, and arguing with parents when they bothered to show up, and hassling with other coaches who were not above cheating, and trying to ignore teenage referees who didn't know a block from a charge, he was fed up. He'd done his community service, in this town anyway.

He watched the game and waited, yelling occasionally because that's what coaches are supposed to do. He looked around the empty gym, an old brick building in downtown New Haven, home to the youth league for fifty years. A handful of parents were scattered through the bleachers, all waiting for the final horn. Marquis scored again. No one applauded. The Red Knights were down by twelve with two minutes to go.

At the far end of the court, just under the ancient scoreboard, a man in a dark suit walked through the door and leaned against the retractable bleachers. He was noticeable because he was white. There were no white players on either team. He stood out because he wore a suit that was either black or navy, with a white shirt and a burgundy tie, all under a trench coat that announced the presence of an agent or a cop of some variety.

Coach Kyle happened to see the man when he entered the gym, and he thought to himself that the guy was out of place. Probably a detective of some sort, maybe a narc looking for a dealer. It would not be the first arrest in or around the gym.

After the agent/cop leaned against the bleachers, he cast a long suspicious look at the Red Knights' bench, and his eyes seemed to settle on Coach Kyle, who returned the stare for a second before it became uncomfortable. Marquis let one fly from near mid-court, air ball, and Coach Kyle jumped to his feet, spread his hands wide, shook his head as if to ask, "Why?" Marquis ignored him as he loafed back on defense. A dumb foul stopped the clock and prolonged the misery. While looking at the free-throw shooter, Kyle glanced beyond him, and in the background was the agent/cop, still staring, not at the action but at the coach.

For a twenty-five-year-old law student with no criminal record and no illegal habits or proclivities, the presence and the attention of a man who gave all indications of being employed by some branch of law enforcement should have caused no concern whatsoever. But it never worked that way with Kyle McAvoy. Street cops and state troopers didn't particularly bother him. They were paid to simply react. But the guys in dark suits, the investigators and agents, the ones trained to dig deep and discover secrets—those types still unnerved him.

Thirty seconds to go and Marquis was arguing with a referee. He'd thrown an F-bomb at a ref two weeks earlier and was suspended for a game. Coach Kyle yelled at his star, who never listened. He quickly scanned the gym to see if agent/cop No. 1 was alone or was now accompanied by agent/cop No. 2. No, he was not.

Another dumb foul, and Kyle yelled at the referee to just let it slide. He sat down and ran his finger over the side of his neck, then flicked off the perspiration. It was early February, and the gym was, as always, quite chilly.

Why was he sweating?

The agent/cop hadn't moved an inch; in fact he seemed to enjoy staring at Kyle.

The decrepit old horn finally squawked. The game was mercifully over. One team cheered, and one team really didn't care. Both lined up for the obligatory high fives and "Good game, good game," as meaningless to twelve-year-olds as it is to college players. As Kyle congratulated the opposing coach, he glanced down the court. The white man was gone.

What were the odds he was waiting outside? Of course it was paranoia, but paranoia had settled into Kyle's life so long ago that he now simply acknowledged it, coped with it, and moved on.

The Red Knights regrouped in the visitors' locker room, a cramped little space under the sagging and permanent stands on the home side. There Coach Kyle said all the right things—nice effort, good hustle, our game is improving in certain areas, let's finish on a high note this Saturday. The boys were changing clothes and hardly listening. They were tired of basketball because they were tired of losing, and of course all blame was heaped upon the coach. He was too young, too white, too much of an Ivy Leaguer.

The few parents who were there waited outside the locker room, and it was those tense moments when the team came out that Kyle hated most about his community service. There would be the usual complaints about playing time. Marquis had an uncle, a twenty-two-year-old former all-state player with a big mouth and a fondness for bitching about Coach Kyle's unfair treatment of the "best player in the league."

From the locker room, there was another door that led to a dark narrow hallway that ran behind the home stands and finally gave way to an outside door that opened into an alley. Kyle was not the first coach to discover this escape route, and on this night he wanted to avoid not only the families and their complaints but also the agent/cop. He said a quick goodbye to his boys, and as they fled the locker room, he made his escape. In a matter of seconds he was outside, in the alley, then walking quickly along a frozen sidewalk. Heavy snow had been plowed, and the sidewalk was icy and barely passable. The temperature was somewhere far below freezing. It was 8:30 on a Wednesday, and he was headed for the law journal offices at the Yale Law School, where he would work until midnight at least.

He didn't make it.

The agent was leaning against the fender of a red Jeep Cherokee that was parked parallel on the street. The vehicle was titled to one John McAvoy of York, Pennsylvania, but for the past six years it had been the reliable companion of his son, Kyle, the true owner.

Though his feet suddenly felt like bricks and his knees were weak, Kyle managed to trudge on as if nothing were wrong. Not only did they find me, he said to himself as he tried to think clearly, but they've done their homework and found my Jeep. Not exactly high-level research. I have done nothing wrong, he said again and again.

"Tough game, Coach," the agent said when Kyle was ten feet away and slowing down.

Kyle stopped and took in the thick young man with red cheeks and red bangs who'd been watching him in the gym. "Can I help you?" he said, and immediately saw the shadow of No. 2 dart across the street. They always worked in pairs.

No. 1 reached into a pocket, and as he said "That's exactly what you can do," he pulled out a leather wallet and flipped it open. "Bob Plant, FBI."

"A real pleasure," Kyle said as all the blood left his brain and he couldn't help but flinch.

No. 2 wedged himself into the frame. He was much thinner and ten years older with gray around the temples. He, too, had a pocketful, and he performed the well-rehearsed badge presentation with ease. "Nelson Ginyard, FBI," he said.

Bob and Nelson. Both Irish. Both northeastern.

"Anybody else?" Kyle asked.

"No. Got a minute to talk?"

"Not really."

"You might want to," Ginyard said. "It could be very productive."

"I doubt that."

"If you leave, we'll just follow," Plant said as he stood from his slouch position and took a step closer. "You don't want us on campus, do you?"

"Are you threatening me?" Kyle asked. The sweat was back, now in the pits of his arms, and despite the arctic air a bead or two ran down his ribs.

"Not yet," Plant said with a smirk.

"Look, let's spend ten minutes together, over coffee," Ginyard was saying. "There's a sandwich shop just around the corner. I'm sure it's warmer there."

"Do I need a lawyer?"

"No."

"That's what you always say. My father is a lawyer and I grew up in his office. I know your tricks."

"No tricks, Kyle, I swear," Ginyard said, and he at least sounded genuine. "Just give us ten minutes. I promise you won't regret it."

"What's on the agenda?"

"Ten minutes. That's all we ask."

"Give me a clue or the answer is no."

Bob and Nelson looked at each other. Both shrugged. Why not? We'll have to tell him sooner or later. Ginyard turned and looked down the street and spoke into the wind. "Duquesne University. Five years ago. Drunk frat boys and a girl."

Kyle's body and mind had different reactions. His body conceded—a quick slump of the shoulders, a slight gasp, a noticeable jerk in the legs. But his mind fought back instantly. "That's bullshit!" he said, then spat on the sidewalk. "I've already been through this. Nothing happened and you know it."

There was a long pause as Ginyard continued to stare down the street while Plant watched their subject's every move. Kyle's mind was spinning. Why was the FBI involved in an alleged state crime? In second-year Criminal Procedure they had studied the new laws regarding FBI interrogation. It was now an indictable offense to simply lie to an agent in this very situation. Should he shut up? Should he call his father? No, under no circumstances would he call his father.

Ginyard turned, took three steps closer, clenched his jaw like a bad actor, and tried to hiss his tough-guy words. "Let's cut to the chase, Mr. McAvoy, because I'm freezing. There's an indictment out of Pittsburgh, okay. Rape. If you want to play the hard-ass smart-ass brilliant law student and run get a lawyer, or even call your old man, then the indictment comes down tomorrow and the life you have planned is pretty much shot to shit. However, if you give us ten minutes of your valuable time, right now, in the sandwich shop around the corner, then the indictment will be put on hold, if not forgotten altogether."

"You can walk away from it," Plant said from the side. "Without a word."

"Why should I trust you?" Kyle managed to say with a very dry mouth.

"Ten minutes."

"You got a tape recorder?"

"Sure."

"I want it on the table, okay? I want every word recorded because I don't trust you."

"Fair enough."

They jammed their hands deep into the pockets of their matching trench coats and stomped away. Kyle unlocked his Jeep and got inside. He started the engine, turned the heat on high, and thought about driving away.

2

Buster's Deli was long and narrow with red vinyl booths along the wall to the right. To the left was a bar and a grill behind a counter, and a row of pinball machines. All manner of Yale memorabilia was tacked haphazardly on the walls. Kyle had eaten there a few times during his first year in law school, many months ago.

The last two booths were properly secured by the federal government. Yet another trench coat stood at the last table, chatting with Plant and Ginyard, waiting. When Kyle made his slow approach, the agent glanced at him, then offered the standard smirk before sitting in the next booth. No. 4 was waiting there, sipping coffee. Plant and Ginyard had ordered sandwich platters with subs and fries and pickles, all of it untouched. The table was covered with food and cups of coffee. Plant climbed to his feet and moved around to the other side so that both agents could watch their victim. They were shoulder to shoulder, still in trench coats. Kyle slid into the booth.

The lighting was old and bad; the back corner was dark. Pinball racket mixed with a loud game on ESPN from the bartender's flat screen.

"It takes four?" Kyle asked, nodding over his shoulder at the booth behind him.

"That's just what you can see," Ginyard said.

"Would you like a sandwich?" Plant asked.

"No." An hour earlier he had been famished. Now his digestive system and his excretory system and his nervous system were on the verge of a meltdown. He was struggling to breathe normally as he desperately tried to appear unfazed. He removed a disposable pen and a note card, and with all the nerve he could summon, he said, "I'd like to see those badges again."

The responses were identical—disbelief, insulted, then oh-what-the-hell as they slowly reached into their pockets and extracted their most prized possessions. They laid them on the table, and Kyle selected Ginyard's first. He wrote down the full name—Nelson Edward Ginyard—then his agent number. He squeezed the pen hard and recorded the information carefully. His hand shook, but he thought it wasn't noticeable. He rubbed the brass emblem carefully, not sure what he was looking for but still taking his time. "Could I see a photo ID?" he asked.

"What the hell?" Ginyard growled.

"Photo ID, please."

"No."

"I'm not talking until I finish the preliminaries. Just show me your driver's license. I'll show you mine."

"We already have a copy of yours."

"Whatever. Let's have it."

Ginyard rolled his eyes as he reached for his back pocket. From a battered billfold he produced a Connecticut license with an ominous snapshot of himself. Kyle examined it and jotted down the birth date and license data. "That's worse than a passport photo," he said.

"You wanna see my wife and kids?" Ginyard said as he removed a color photo and tossed it on the table.

"No, thanks. Which office are you guys from?"

"Hartford," Ginyard said. He nodded at the next booth and said, "They're from Pittsburgh."

"Nice."

Kyle then examined Plant's badge and driver's license, and when he had finished, he pulled out his cell phone and began pecking.

"What are you doing?" Ginyard asked.

"I'm going online to check you out."

"You think we're posted on some nice little FBI Web site?" Plant said with a flash of anger. Both found it humorous. Neither seemed concerned.

"I know which site to check," Kyle said as he entered the address of a little-known federal directory.

"You won't find us," Ginyard said.

"This will take a minute. Where's that tape recorder?"

Plant produced a slender digital recorder the size of an electric toothbrush and flipped it on.

"Please give the date, time, and place," Kyle said with an air of confidence that surprised even him. "And please state that the interrogation has yet to begin and that no statements have been made before now."

"Yes, sir. I love law students," Plant said.

"You watch too much television," Ginyard said.

"Go ahead."

Plant situated the recorder in the center of the table, a pastrami and cheddar on one side and a smoked tuna on the other. He aimed his words at it and announced the preliminaries. Kyle was watching his phone, and when the Web site appeared, he entered the name of Nelson Edward Ginyard. A few seconds passed, and to the surprise of no one Agent Ginyard was confirmed as a field agent, FBI, Hartford. "You wanna see it?" Kyle asked, holding up the tiny screen.

"Congratulations," Ginyard shot back. "Are you satisfied now?"

"No. I'd prefer not to be here."

"You can leave anytime you want," Plant said.

"You asked for ten minutes." Kyle glanced at his wristwatch.

Both agents leaned forward, all four elbows in a row, the booth suddenly smaller. "You remember a guy named Bennie Wright, chief investigator, sex crimes, Pittsburgh PD?" Ginyard was talking, both were staring, watching every nervous twitch of Kyle's eyelids.

"No."

"You didn't meet him five years ago during the investigation?"

"I don't remember meeting a Bennie Wright. Could have, but I don't remember that name. It has been, after all, five years since the nonevent did not happen."

They absorbed this, mulled it over slowly while maintaining eye contact. It appeared to Kyle as if both wanted to say, "You're lying."

Instead, Ginyard said, "Well, Detective Wright is here in town, and he'd like to meet with you in about an hour."

"Another meeting?"

"If you don't mind. It won't take long, and there's a good chance you can head off the indictment."

"Indictment for what, exactly?"

"Rape."

"There was no rape. The Pittsburgh police made that decision five years ago."

"Well, it looks like the girl is back," Ginyard said. "She's put her life back together, gone through some extensive therapy, and, best of all, she's got herself a lawyer now."

Since Ginyard stopped without a question, there was no need for a response. Kyle couldn't help but sink an inch or two. He glanced over at the counter, at the empty stools. He glanced over at the flat-screen television. It was a college game, the stands full of screaming students, and he asked himself why he was sitting where he was sitting.

Keep talking, he said to himself, but don't say anything.

"Can I ask a question?" he asked.

"Sure."

"If the indictment has been issued, how can it be stopped? Why are we talking?"

"It's under seal, by court order," Ginyard said. "According to Detective Wright, the prosecutor has a deal for you, one that the victim's lawyer cooked up, one that will allow you to walk away from this mess. You play ball, and the indictment against you will never see the light of day."

"I'm still confused. Maybe I should call my father."

"That's up to you, but if you're smart, you'll wait until you chat with Detective Wright."

"You guys didn't advise me of my *Miranda* rights."

"This is not an interrogation," Plant finally said. "It's not an investigation." Then he reached into the smoked-tuna basket and pulled out a greasy fry.

"What the hell is it?"

"A meeting."

Ginyard cleared his throat, leaned back a few inches, and proceeded. "It's a state crime, Kyle, we all know that. Normally we wouldn't be involved, but since you're here in Connecticut and the indictment is in Pennsylvania, the boys in Pittsburgh asked us to help arrange the next meeting. After that, we'll step aside."

"I'm still confused."

"Come on. Bright legal mind like you. Surely you're not that thick."

There was a long pause as all three considered the next move. Plant chomped on his second fry, but his eyes never left Kyle. Ginyard took a sip of coffee, frowned at the taste, and continued staring. The pinball machines were silent. The deli was empty except for the four FBI agents, a bartender absorbed in the game, and Kyle.

Finally, Kyle leaned forward on his elbows, and with the recorder just inches away he said, "There was no rape, no crime. I did nothing wrong."

"Fine, talk to Wright."

"And where is he?"

"At ten o'clock, he'll be at the Holiday Inn on Saw Mill Road, room 222."

"This is a bad idea. I need a lawyer."

"Maybe you do, maybe you don't," Ginyard said, leaning in so that their heads were a foot apart. "Look, I know you don't trust us, but please believe it when we say you should talk to Wright before you talk to anyone else. Hell, you can call a lawyer, or your father, at midnight. Or tomorrow. If you overreact now, the outcome could be a disaster."

"I'm leaving. Conversation over. Turn off the recorder."

Neither made any move toward the recorder. Kyle looked at it, then leaned down and said, very clearly, "This is Kyle McAvoy. The time is 8:50 p.m. I have nothing else to say. I have made no statements, and I am leaving Buster's Deli right now." He scooted off the bench and was almost out of the booth when Plant blurted, "He's got the video."

A horse kick to the groin could not have hit harder. Kyle clutched the red vinyl and looked as though he might faint. Slowly, he sat down again. Slowly, he reached for a plastic cup and took a long sip of water. His lips and tongue were parched, and the water did little to help.

The video. A fraternity brother, one of the drunks at the little party, had allegedly recorded something with his cell phone. Supposedly, there were images of the girl, naked on a sofa, too drunk to move, and admiring her were three or four or five Beta brothers, all naked, too, or in the process of undressing. Kyle vaguely remembered the scene, but he'd never seen the video. It had been destroyed, according to Beta legend. The cops in Pittsburgh had searched but never found it. It was gone, forgotten, buried deep in the secrecy of Beta brotherhood.

Plant and Ginyard were elbow to elbow again, all four eyes focused and unblinking.

"What video?" Kyle managed to ask, but it was so lame and so unconvincing that he didn't believe himself.

"The one you boys hid from the cops," Plant said, barely moving his lips. "The one that places you at the scene of the crime. The one that will destroy your life and send you away for twenty years."

Oh, that video.

"I don't know what you're talking about," Kyle said, then drank some more water. Waves of nausea crashed through his stomach and head, and he thought about vomiting.

"Oh, I think you do," Ginyard said.

"Have you seen this video?" Kyle asked.

Both nodded.

"Then you know I didn't touch the girl."

"Maybe, maybe not. But you were there," Ginyard said. "You were an accessory."

To keep from throwing up, Kyle closed his eyes and began rubbing his temples. The girl was a wild little thing who'd spent more time in the Beta house than in her dorm room. A groupie, a clinger, a party animal with an abundant supply of Daddy's cash. The brothers of Beta passed her around. When she cried rape, the brothers had instantly gone mute and solidified into an impenetrable wall of denial and innocence. The cops eventually gave up when she proved too unreliable with the details. No charges were filed. She later left Duquesne and mercifully disappeared. The great miracle of the ugly little episode was that it had been kept quiet. No additional lives were ruined.

"The indictment names you and three others," Ginyard said.

"There was no rape," Kyle said as he continued to rub his temples. "If she had sex, I promise you it was by consent."

"Not if she blacked out," Ginyard said.

"We're not here to argue, Kyle," Plant said. "That's what lawyers are for. We're here to help cut a deal. If you'll cooperate, then this will all go away, at least your part of it."

"What kind of deal?"

"Detective Wright will handle that."

Kyle slowly sat back and tapped his head on the red vinyl bench behind him. He wanted to plead, to beg, to explain that this wasn't fair, that he was about to graduate and pass the bar and start a career. His future held so much promise. His past was unblemished. Almost.

But they already knew that, didn't they? He glanced at the tape recorder and decided to give them nothing. "All right, all right," he said. "I'll be there."

Ginyard leaned even closer and said, "You have one hour. If you make a phone call, we'll know it. If you try to run, we'll follow, okay? No funny stuff, Kyle. You're making the right decision here, I swear it. Just keep it up, and this will all go away."

"I don't believe you."

"You'll see."

Kyle left them there with their cold sandwiches and bitter coffee. He made it to his Jeep, then drove to his apartment three blocks from campus. He rummaged through his roommate's bathroom, found a Valium, then locked his bedroom door, turned off the light, and stretched out on the floor.

3

It was an old Holiday Inn, built in the 1960s, when motels and fast-food chains raced to build along the highways and frontage roads. Kyle had passed it a hundred times and never seen it. Behind it was a pancake house, and next door was a large discount appliance store.

The parking lot was dark and one-third full when he backed the red Jeep into a space next to a minivan from Indiana. He turned off the lights but left the engine running and the heater on. A light snow was falling. Why couldn't there be a blizzard, or a flood or earthquake, an invasion, anything to interrupt this awful scenario? Why, exactly, was he sleepwalking through their little plan?

The video.

In the past hour he'd thought of calling his father, but that conversation would take far too long. John McAvoy would provide sound legal advice, and quickly, but the backstory had many complications. He'd thought of calling Professor Bart Mallory, his adviser, his friend, his brilliant teacher of criminal procedure, a former judge who would know exactly what to do. But again, there were too many blanks to fill in and not enough time. He'd thought of calling two of his Beta brothers from Duquesne, but why bother? Any advice they might give would be as unsound as the strategies racing through his mind. No sense ruining their lives. And in the horror of the moment he'd thought of the various schemes he could use to disappear. A mad dash to the airport. A clandestine car ride to the bus station. A long jump off a tall bridge.

But they were watching, weren't they? And probably listening, too, so all phone calls would be shared. Someone was watching at that very moment, he was certain. Perhaps in the minivan from Indiana there were a couple of goons with headsets and night-vision gear, getting their jollies as they monitored him and burned taxpayer money.

If the Valium was working, he couldn't tell.

When the digital clock on the radio hit 9:58, he turned off the engine and stepped into the snow. He walked bravely across the asphalt, each step leaving footprints. Could this be his last moment of freedom? He'd read so many cases of criminal defendants freely walking into the police station for a few quick questions, only to be charged, handcuffed, jailed, railroaded by the system. He could still run, to somewhere.

When the glass doors slammed behind him, he paused for a second in the deserted lobby and thought he heard the clanging of cellblock iron at his back. He was hearing things, seeing things, imagining things. Apparently, the Valium had reversed itself and had him ready to jump out of his skin. He nodded at the decrepit clerk behind the front counter, but there was no audible response. As he rode the musty elevator to the second floor, he asked himself what kind of fool would voluntarily enter a motel room filled with cops and agents all hell-bent on accusing him of something that never happened? Why was he doing this?

The video.

He had never seen it. He did not know anyone who had seen it.

In the secret world of Beta there were rumors and denials and threats, but no one had even known for sure if the "Elaine thing" had actually been recorded. The reality that it had, and that the evidence was now in the possession of the Pittsburgh police and the FBI, made him ponder the bridge scenario.

Wait a minute. I did nothing wrong. I did not touch that girl, not that night anyway.

No one touched her. At least that was the sworn and battle-tested version within the Beta fraternity. But what if the video proved otherwise? He would never know until he saw it.

The noxious smell of fresh paint hit him as he stepped into the hallway on the second floor. He stopped at room 222 and glanced at his watch to make sure he was not a minute too early. He knocked three times, then heard movement and muffled voices. The lock chain rattled, the door was jerked open, and Special Agent Nelson Edward Ginyard said, "Glad you could make it." Kyle stepped inside, leaving the old world behind. The new one was suddenly terrifying.

Ginyard had his jacket off, and strapped over his white shirt was a shoulder harness, with a fairly large black pistol in a black holster snug under his left arm. Agent Plant and the two others from Buster's were staring, and all three were also coatless so that young Kyle could get the full measure of their arsenal. Identical nine-millimeter Berettas, with matching holsters and black leather harnesses. Seriously armed men, all with the same scowl as if they'd be more than happy to shoot the rapist.

"Good move," Plant said, nodding now.

Actually, Kyle thought in the haze of the moment, coming here was a very stupid move.

Room 222 had been converted into a makeshift field office. The king-sized bed had been pushed into a corner. The curtains were tightly closed. Two folding tables had been hauled in and were covered with the evidence of busy work—files and thick envelopes and notepads. Three laptops were open and on, and in the one nearest the door Kyle caught a glimpse of himself, from his high school yearbook. Central York High School, class of 2001. Tacked to the bare wall behind the folding tables were eight-by-ten color photos of three of his Beta brothers. At the far end, almost to the curtains, was one of Elaine Keenan.

The room adjoined another, and the door between them was open. Agent No. 5 walked through it—same gun, same holster—and glared at Kyle. Five agents? Two rooms. A ton of paperwork. All this effort, all this work, all these men, just to nail me? Kyle felt lightheaded as he observed the power of his government in action.

"Do you mind emptying your pockets?" Ginyard said as he offered a small cardboard box.

"Why?"

"Please."

"You think I'm armed? You think I might pull out a knife and attack you guys?"

Agent No. 5 saw the humor and broke the ice with a good laugh. Kyle pulled out his key ring, jangled its collection for Ginyard to see, then put it back in his pocket.

"How about a pat down?" Plant said, already moving toward Kyle.

"Oh, sure," he said, then raised his arms. "All Yale students are heavily armed."

Plant began a very soft and quick frisk. He finished just seconds after he started, then disappeared into the other room.

"Detective Wright is across the hall," Ginyard said. Yet another room.

Kyle followed him out of the room, into the stuffy hallway, then waited as he tapped gently on the door to room 225. When it opened, Kyle entered alone.

Bennie Wright displayed no weaponry. He offered a quick handshake while spitting out, "Detective Wright, Pittsburgh PD."

A real pleasure, Kyle thought but said nothing. What am I doing here?

Wright was in his late forties, short, trim, bald with a few strands of black hair slicked back just above his ears. His eyes were also black and partially concealed behind a pair of tiny reading glasses perched halfway down his narrow nose. He closed the door behind Kyle, then waved at the appointed spot and said, "Why don't you have a seat?"

"What do you have in mind?" Kyle asked without moving.

Wright walked past the bed and stopped beside yet another folding table, this one with two cheap metal chairs facing each other. "Let's talk, Kyle," he said pleasantly, and Kyle realized he had a slight accent. English was not his first language, though there was almost no trace of his native tongue. But it was odd. A man named Bennie Wright from Pittsburgh should not have a foreign accent.

There was a small video camera mounted on a tripod in one corner. Wires ran to the table, to a laptop with a twelve-inch screen. "Please," Wright said, waving at one chair as he settled himself into the other.

"I want all of this recorded," Kyle said.

Wright glanced over his shoulder at the camera and said, "No problem."

Slowly, Kyle walked to the other chair and sat down. Wright was rolling up the sleeves of his white shirt. His necktie was already loose.

To Kyle's right was the laptop with a blank screen. To his left a thick, unopened file. In the center of the table was a fresh legal pad, white, with a black pen on it, waiting. "Turn on the camera," Kyle said. Wright punched the laptop, and Kyle's face appeared on the screen. He looked at himself and saw nothing but fear.

Wright went efficiently into the file, retrieving the necessary paperwork as if young Kyle here were simply applying for a student credit card. When the proper sheets were found, he placed them in the center and said, "First, we need to cover your *Miranda* rights."

"No," Kyle said softly. "First we need to see your badge and some identification."

This irritated the detective, but only for a few seconds. Without a word, he fished out a brown leather wallet from a rear pocket, opened it, and said, "Had this for twenty-two years now."

Kyle examined the bronze badge, and it did indeed show signs of age. Benjamin J. Wright, Pittsburgh Police Department, officer number 6658. "How about a driver's license?"

Wright yanked back his wallet, opened another compartment, fingered through some cards, and then flung down a Pennsylvania photo license. "Satisfied now?" he snapped.

Kyle handed it back and said, "Why is the FBI involved in this?"

"Can we finish up with *Miranda*?" Wright was readjusting the paperwork.

"Sure. I understand *Miranda*."

"I'm sure you do. A top law student at one of our most prestigious law schools. A very smart young man." Kyle was reading as Wright was talking. "You have the right to remain silent. Anything you say can and will be used against you in court. You have the right to an attorney. If you can't afford one, then the state will provide one. Any questions?"

"No." He signed his name on two forms and slid them back to Wright.

"Why is the FBI involved?" He repeated the question.

"Believe me, Kyle, the FBI is the least of your problems." Wright's hands were hairy, still, calm, and his fingers were laced together on top of the legal pad. He spoke slowly, with authority. There was no doubt this meeting belonged to him. "Here is my suggestion, Kyle. We have so much ground to cover, and time is slipping by. Did you ever play football?"

"Yes."

"Then let's say this table is a football field. Not a great analogy, but one that will work. You are here, at this goal line." With his left hand he striped an imaginary line in front of the laptop. "You have a hundred yards to go, to score, to win, to walk out of here in one piece." With his right hand, he laid down the other goal line, next to the heavy file. His hands were four feet apart. "A hundred yards, Kyle, bear with me, okay?"

"Okay."

He pulled his hands together and tapped the legal pad. "Somewhere in here, at about the fifty, I'll show you the video that is the source of this conflict. You won't like it, Kyle. It will make you ill. Nauseous. Sick to your stomach. But, if we are able, then we will continue your little march to the goal line, and when we get there, you will be quite relieved. You will once again see yourself as the golden boy, the handsome young man with an unlimited future and an unblemished past. Stick with me, Kyle, allow me to be the boss, the coach, the man calling the plays, and together we'll make it to the promised land." His right hand tapped the goal line.

"What about the indictment?"

Wright touched the file and said, "It's here."

"When do I see it?"

"Stop asking questions, Kyle. I have the questions. Hopefully, you have the answers."

The accent wasn't Spanish. Eastern European maybe, and at times it was so slight it almost disappeared.

Wright's left hand touched the goal line in front of the laptop. "Now, Kyle, we need to start with the basics. Just some background, okay?"

"Whatever."

Wright pulled some papers from the file, studied them for a second, then picked up his pen. "You were born on February 4, 1983, in York, Pennsylvania, third child and only son of John and Patty McAvoy. They divorced in 1989, when you were six years old, neither has remarried, correct?"

"Correct."

Wright made a check mark, then launched into a series of quick questions about family members, their birth dates, education, jobs, addresses, hobbies, church affiliations, even politics. As the list grew longer, Wright shuffled papers and the check marks multiplied. He had his facts straight, every one of them. He knew the date and place of the birth of Kyle's two-year-old nephew in Santa Monica. When he finished with the family, he pulled out more papers. Kyle felt the first signs of fatigue. And they were just warming up.

"Would you like something to drink?" Wright asked.

"No."

"Your father is a general practice lawyer in York?" It was a statement, but more of a question.

Kyle only nodded. Then a barrage about his father, his life and career and interests. After every fourth or fifth question, Kyle wanted to ask, "Is this really relevant?" But he held his tongue. Wright had all the data. Kyle was simply affirming what someone else had found.

"Your mother is an artist of some variety?" Kyle heard him say.

"Yes, and where is the football right now?"

"You've gained about ten yards. What kind of artist?"

"She's a painter."

They probed the life of Patty McAvoy for ten minutes.

Finally, the detective finished with the family and settled on the suspect. He served up a few easy ones about his childhood, but didn't dwell on the details. He already knows it all, Kyle told himself.

"Honors from Central York High, star athlete, Eagle Scout. Why did you select Duquesne University?"

"They offered me a basketball scholarship."

"Were there other offers?"

"A couple, from smaller schools."

"But you didn't play much at Duquesne."

"I played thirteen minutes as a freshman, then tore an ACL in the final minute of the final game."

"Surgery?"

"Yes, but the knee was gone. I quit basketball and joined a fraternity."

"We'll get to the fraternity later. Were you invited back to the basketball team?"

"Sort of. Didn't matter. The knee was shot."

"You majored in economics and made near-perfect grades. What happened in Spanish your second year? You didn't make an A?"

"I should've taken German, I guess."

"One B in four years is not bad." Wright flipped a page, made a note about something. Kyle glanced at his face on the laptop and told himself to relax.

"High honors, a dozen or so student organizations, intramural softball champs, fraternity secretary then president. Your academic record is impressive, yet you managed to also maintain a pretty active social life. Tell me about your first arrest."

"I'm sure you have the records in your file there."

"Your first arrest, Kyle."

"Only one. A first, not a second. Not until now, I guess."

"What happened?"

"Typical frat stuff. A loud party that didn't stop until the cops showed up. I got caught with an open container, a bottle of beer. Nit-picking stuff. Misdemeanor. I paid a fine of three hundred bucks and got six months' probation. After that, the record was expunged and Yale never knew about it."

"Did your father handle it?"

"He was involved, but I had a lawyer in Pittsburgh."

"Who?"

"A lady named Sylvia Marks."

"I've heard of her. Doesn't she specialize in stupid fraternity stunts?"

"That's her. But she knows her stuff."

"I thought there was a second arrest."

"No. I was stopped by the cops once on campus, but there was no arrest. Just a warning."

"What were you doing?"

"Nothing."

"Then why were you stopped?"

"A couple of fraternities were shooting bottle rockets at each other. Smart boys. I was not involved. Nothing went in my file, so I'm wondering how you heard about it."

Wright ignored this and wrote something on his legal pad. When he finished scribbling, he said, "Why did you decide to go to law school?"

"I made that decision when I was twelve years old. I always wanted to be a lawyer. My first job was running the copier in my father's office. I sort of grew up there."

"Where did you apply to law school?"

"Penn, Yale, Cornell, and Stanford."

"Where were you accepted?"

"All four."

"Why Yale?"

"It was always my first choice."

"Did Yale offer scholarship money?"

"Financial incentives, yes. So did the others."

"Have you borrowed money?"

"Yes."

"How much?"

"Do you really need to know?"

"I wouldn't ask the question if I didn't need to know. You think I'm talking just to hear myself talk?"

"I can't answer that."

"Back to the student loans."

"When I graduate in May, I'll owe about sixty thousand."

Wright nodded as if he agreed that this was the correct amount. He flipped another page, and Kyle could see that it, too, was covered with questions.

"And you write for the law journal?"

"I'm the editor in chief of the *Yale Law Journal.*"

"That's the most prestigious honor in the school?"

"According to some."

"You clerked last summer in New York. Tell me about it."

"It was one of those huge Wall Street firms, Scully & Pershing, a typical summer clerkship. We were wined and dined and given easy hours, the same seduction routine all the big firms use. They pamper the clerks, then kill them when they become associates."

"Did Scully & Pershing offer you a position after graduation?"

"Yes."

"Did you accept or decline?"

"Neither. I have not made a decision. The firm has given me some additional time to decide."

"What's taking so long?"

"I have a few options. One is a clerkship for a federal judge, but he might get a promotion. Things are in limbo there."

"Do you have other job offers?"

"I had other offers, yes."

"Tell me about them."

"Is this really relevant?"

"Everything I say is relevant, Kyle."

"Do you have any water?"

"I'm sure there's some in the bathroom."

Kyle jumped to his feet, walked between the king-sized bed and the credenza, switched on the light in the cramped bathroom, and ran tap water into a flimsy plastic cup. He gulped it, then refilled. When he returned to the table, he placed the cup somewhere around his own twenty-yard line, then checked himself on the monitor. "Just curious," he said. "Where's the football right now?"

"Third and long. Tell me about the other job offers, the other firms."

"Why don't you just show me the video so we can skip all this bullshit? If it really exists, and if it implicates me, then I'll walk out of here and go hire a lawyer."

Wright leaned forward, adjusted his elbows on the table, and began gently tapping his fingertips together. The lower half of his face eased into a smile while the upper half remained noncommittal. Very coolly, he said, "Losing your temper, Kyle, could cost you your life."

Life as in dead body? Or life as in brilliant future? Kyle wasn't so sure. He took a deep breath, then another gulp of the water. The flash of anger was gone, replaced by the crush of confusion and fear.

The fake smile widened, and Wright said, "Please, Kyle, you're doing fine here. Just a few more questions and we'll move into rougher territory. The other firms?"

"I was offered a job by Logan & Kupec in New York, Baker Potts in San Francisco, and Garton in London. I said no to all three. I'm still kicking around a public-interest job."

"Doing what? Where?"

"It's down in Virginia, a legal aid position helping migrant workers."

"And how long would you do this?"

"Couple of years, maybe, I'm not sure. It's just an option."

"At a much lower salary?"

"Oh, yes. Much."

"How will you pay back your student loans?"

"I'll figure that out."

Wright didn't like the smart-ass answer, but decided to let it slide. He glanced at his notes, though a quick review wasn't necessary. He knew that young Kyle here owed $61,000 in student loans, all of which would be forgiven by Yale if he spent the next three years working for minimum wage protecting the poor, the oppressed, the abused, or the environment. Kyle's offer had been extended by Piedmont Legal Aid, and the clerkship was funded by a grant from a mammoth law firm in Chicago. According to Wright's sources, Kyle had verbally accepted the position, which paid $32,000 a year. Wall Street could wait. It would always be there. His father had encouraged him to spend a few years out in the trenches, getting his hands dirty, far away from the corporate style of law that he, John McAvoy, despised.

According to the file, Scully & Pershing was offering a base salary of $200,000 plus the usual extras. The other firms' offers were similar.

"When will you select a job?" Wright asked.

"Very soon."

"Which way are you leaning?"

"I'm not."

"Are you sure?"

"Of course I'm sure."

Wright reached for the file, shaking his head grimly and frowning as if he'd been insulted. He retrieved more papers, flipped through them, then glared at Kyle. "You haven't made a verbal commitment to accept a position with an outfit called Piedmont Legal Aid, in Winchester, Virginia, beginning September the second of this year?"

A rush of warm air escaped through Kyle's dry lips. As he absorbed this, he instinctively glanced at the monitor, and, yes, he looked as weak as he felt. He almost blurted, "How the hell do you know this?" but to do so would be to admit the truth. Nor could he deny the truth. Wright already knew.

As he was lurching toward some lame response, his adversary moved in for the kill. "Let's call this Lie Number One, okay, Kyle?" Wright said with a sneer. "Should we somehow arrive at Lie Number Two, then we turn off the camera, say good night, and meet again tomorrow for the arrest. Handcuffs, perp walk, mug shot, maybe a reporter or two. You won't be thinking about protecting illegal immigrants, and you won't be thinking about Wall Street. Don't lie to me, Kyle. I know too much."

Kyle almost said, "Yes, sir," but instead managed only a slight affirmative nod.

"So you plan to do some charitable work for a couple of years?"

"Yes."

"Then what?"

"I don't know. I'm sure I'll join a firm somewhere, start a career."

"What do you think of Scully & Pershing?"

"Big, powerful, rich. I think it's the largest law firm in the world, depending on who got merged or swallowed yesterday. Offices in thirty cities on five continents. Some really smart folks who work very hard and put enormous pressure on each other, especially on their young associates."

"Your kind of work?"

"It's hard to say. The money is great. The work is brutal. But it's the big leagues. I'll probably end up there."

"In what section did you work last summer?"

"I moved around, but most of my time was spent in litigation."

"Do you like litigation?"

"Not especially. May I ask what these questions can possibly have to do with that matter back in Pittsburgh?"

Wright took his elbows off the table and tried to relax a little deeper into the folding chair. He crossed his legs and placed the legal pad on his left thigh. He chewed the end of his pen for a moment, staring at Kyle as if he were now a psychiatrist, analyzing the patient. "Let's talk about your fraternity at Duquesne."

"Whatever."

"There were about ten members of your pledge class, right?"

"Nine."

"Do you keep in touch with all of them?"

"To some degree."

"The indictment names you and three others, so let's talk about the other three. Where is Alan Strock?"

The indictment. Somewhere in that damned file less than three feet away was the indictment. How could his name be listed as a defendant? He had not touched the girl. He had not witnessed a rape. He had not seen anyone having sex. He vaguely recalled being present in the room, but he had blacked out at some point during the night, during the episode. How could he be an accomplice if he wasn't conscious? That would be his defense at trial, and a solid defense it would be, but the specter of a trial was too awful to imagine. A trial would come long after the arrest, the publicity, the horror of seeing his photo in print. Kyle closed his eyes and rubbed his temples, and he thought about the phone calls home, first to his father and then to his mother. Other phone calls would follow: one each to the recruiting directors who'd offered him jobs; one to each of his sisters. He would proclaim his innocence and all that, but he knew he would never shake the suspicion of rape.

At that moment, Kyle had no confidence in Detective Wright and whatever deal he had in mind. If there was indeed an indictment, then no miracle could keep it buried.

"Alan Strock?" Wright asked.

"He's in med school at Ohio State."

"Any recent correspondence?"

"An e-mail a couple of days ago."

"And Joey Bernardo?"

"He's still in Pittsburgh, working for a brokerage firm."

"Recent contact?"

"By phone, a few days ago."

"Any mention of Elaine Keenan with Alan or Joey?"

"No."

"You boys have tried to forget about Elaine, haven't you?"

"Yes."

"Well, she's back."

"Evidently."

Wright readjusted himself in the chair, uncrossed his legs, stretched his back, and returned to the most comfortable position with both elbows stuck on the table. "Elaine left Duquesne after her freshman year," he began in a softer voice, as if he had a long tale to tell. "She was troubled. Her grades were a mess. She now claims that the rape brought on severe emotional distress. She lived with her parents for a year or so in Erie, then began drifting. A lot of self-medication, booze and drugs. She saw some therapists, but nothing helped. Have you heard any of this?"

"No. After she left school, there was not a word."

"Anyway, she has an older sister in Scranton who took her in, got her some help, paid for rehab. Then they found a shrink who, evidently, has done a nice job of putting Elaine back together. She's clean, sober, feels great, and her memory has improved dramatically. She's also found herself a lawyer, and of course she is demanding justice."

"You sound skeptical."

"I'm a cop, Kyle. I'm skeptical of everything, but I have this young woman who is credible and who says she was raped, and I have a video that is pretty powerful evidence. And on top of that, there's this lawyer who's out for blood."

"This is a shakedown, isn't it? All about money?"

"What do you mean, Kyle?"

"The fourth defendant is Baxter Tate, and of course we know what that's all about. The Tate family is very rich. Old Pittsburgh money. Baxter was born with trust funds. How much does she want?"

"I'll ask the questions. Did you ever have sex—"

"Yes, I had sex with Elaine Keenan, as did most of my pledge class. She was wild as hell, spent more time in the Beta house than most Betas, could drink any three of us under the table, and always had a purse full of pills. Her problems began long before she arrived at Duquesne. Believe me, she does not want to go to trial."

"How many times did you have sex with her?"

"Once, about a month before the alleged rape."

"Do you know if Baxter Tate had sexual relations with Elaine Keenan on the night in question?"

Kyle paused, took a deep breath, and said, "No, I do not. I blacked out."

"Did Baxter Tate admit to having sex with her that night?"

"Not to me."

Wright finished writing a long sentence on his legal pad as the air cleared. Kyle could almost hear the camera running. He glanced at it and saw the little red light still staring at him.

"Where is Baxter?" Wright asked after a long, heavy pause.

"Somewhere in L.A. He barely graduated, then went to Hollywood to become an actor. He's not too stable."

"Meaning?"

"He comes from a wealthy family that's even more dysfunctional than most wealthy families. He's a hard partier, lots of booze and drugs and girls. And he shows no signs of outgrowing it. His goal in life is to become a great actor and drink himself to death. He wants to die young, sort of like James Dean."

"Has he been in any films?"

"Not a single one. Lots of bars, though."

Wright suddenly seemed bored with the questions. He had stopped his scribbling. His hard stare began to drift. He stuffed some papers back into the file, then tapped a finger at the center of the table. "We've made progress, Kyle, thank you. The ball is at midfield. You want to see the video?"

4

Wright stood for the first time, stretched, and stepped to a corner where a small cardboard box was waiting. It was white, and in a neat hand someone had printed, with a black marker, the words "IN RE: KYLE L. MCAVOY et al." Kyle McAvoy and others. Wright fetched something from the box, and with the steady purpose of an executioner preparing to pull the switch, he removed a disc from its sleeve, slid it into the drive on the laptop, punched a couple of keys, then took his seat. Kyle could barely breathe.

As the computer clicked and hummed, Wright began talking. "The phone was a Nokia 6000 smartphone, manufactured in 2003, with ETI Camcorder software installed, one-gigabyte memory card that holds about three hundred minutes of compressed video, megapixel quality at fifteen FPS, voice commands, voice activated, state of the art for the time. A really nice cell phone."

"Owned by?"

Wright shot him a smart-ass grin and said, "Sorry, Kyle."

For some reason, Wright thought it would be helpful to show the phone itself. He punched a key, and a still photo of the Nokia appeared on the screen. "Ever see this?" he asked.

"No."

"Didn't think so. Here's the scene, Kyle, in case you're a little fuzzy on the details. It's April 25, 2003, last day of classes, final exams start in a week. It's a Friday, unseasonably warm for Pittsburgh, high of eighty-five that day, almost set a record, and the kids at Duquesne decide to do what all good college kids do everywhere. They start drinking in the afternoon and have big plans to drink all night. A crowd gathers at the apartment complex where you rent a place with three others. A party materializes by the pool. It's mostly Beta brothers and a few girls. You go for a swim, get some rays, drink some beer, listen to Phish. The girls are in bikinis. Life is good. Sometime after dark, the party moves inside, to your apartment. Pizza is ordered. The music, Widespread Panic by this time, is loud. More beer. Somebody shows up with two bottles of tequila, and of course this is consumed as fast as possible. Remember any of this?"

"Most of it."

"You're twenty years old, just finishing your sophomore year—"

"Got that."

"The tequila gets mixed with Red Bull, and you and the gang start doing shots. I'm sure you've had a few shots."

Kyle nodded, his eyes never leaving the screen.

"At some point, clothes start coming off, and the owner of the cell phone decides to secretly record this. Guess he wanted his own little video of the girls without their tops. Do you remember the apartment, Kyle?"

"Yes, I lived there for a year."

"We've examined the place. It's a dump, of course, like a lot of college housing, but, according to the landlord, hasn't changed. Our best guess is that the guy with the cell phone placed it on the narrow counter that separates the small kitchen from the den. The counter seems to be a catchall for textbooks, phone books, empty beer bottles, pretty much everything that passed through the apartment at one time or another."

"That's correct."

"So our man pulls out his cell phone and sneaks over to the counter, and in the midst of a wild party he turns it on and hides it next to a book. The opening scene is pretty wild. We've studied it carefully, and there are six girls and nine boys, all dancing and in various stages of undress. Ring a bell, Kyle?"

"Some of it, yes."

"We know all the names."

"You gonna show it to me or just talk about it?"

"Don't be so anxious to see it." With that, Wright punched another key. "It's 11:14 p.m. when the video begins," he said, then hit another key. The screen suddenly exploded into a frenzy of loud music—Widespread Panic playing "Aunt Avis" from *Bombs and Butterflies*—and gyrating bodies. Somewhere in the back of his brain Kyle had hoped for a dim, grainy, fuzzy clip of a bunch of Beta idiots drinking in the dark. Instead, he gawked at a remarkably clear video shot from a tiny phone camera. The angle chosen by the unknown owner of the phone provided a view of almost the entire den at 4880 East Chase, apartment 6B.

All fifteen hell-raisers appeared to be very drunk. All six girls were indeed topless, as were most of the guys. The dance was a group grope with no two partners moving together for more than a few seconds. Everyone held a drink in one hand; half had a cigarette or a joint in the other. All twelve bouncing breasts were fair game for the guys. In fact, all exposed flesh, male or female, was available to everyone. Touching and clutching were encouraged. Bodies came together, hunching and lurching, then parted and moved to the next one. Some of the guests were loud and rowdy, while others appeared to be fading under the flood of alcohol and chemicals. Most appeared to be singing along with the band. Several locked lips in long kisses while their free hands searched for even more intimate places.

"I believe that's you with the sunglasses," Wright said smugly.

"Thank you."

Sunglasses, yellow Pirates cap, off-white gym shorts drooping low, a lean body with pale winter skin in need of sunshine. A plastic cup in one hand, a cigarette in the other. Mouth open to sing along. A drunken fool. A twenty-year-old lunatic on the verge of another blackout.

Now, five years later, there was no nostalgia, no longing for those rowdy and carefree college days. He didn't miss the hell-raising, the hangovers, the late-morning wake-ups in strange beds. But at the same time, there was no remorse. Kyle felt a little embarrassed that he'd been caught on tape, but it was a long time ago. His college days had been pretty typical, hadn't they? He'd partied no more and certainly no less than virtually everyone he knew.

The music stopped for a moment, between songs, and more shots were prepared and passed around. One of the girls fell into a chair and appeared to be done for the night. Then another song began.

"This goes for about eight more minutes," Wright said, glancing at his notes. Kyle had no doubt that Wright and his gang had analyzed and memorized every second, every frame. "As you will note, Elaine Keenan is not present. She says she was next door, drinking with some friends."

"So she's changed her story again."

Wright ignored this and said, "If you don't mind, I'll fast-forward a little, to the point where the police show up. Remember the cops, Kyle?"

"Yes."

The video scrambled forward for a minute or so, until Wright pressed a key. "At 11:25, the party comes to an abrupt halt. Listen."

In mid-song, and with most of the fifteen still in view, dancing and drinking and yelling, someone off camera clearly yelled, "Cops! Cops!" Kyle watched himself as he grabbed a girl and disappeared from view. The music stopped. The lights were out. The screen was almost completely dark.

Wright continued: "According to our records, the police were called to your apartment three times that spring. This was the third time. A young man by the name of Alan Strock, one of your roommates, answered the door and chatted up the officers. He swore that there was no underage drinking. Everything was fine. He'd be happy to turn off the music and keep things quiet. The cops gave him a break and left with a warning. They assumed everybody else was hiding in the bedrooms."

"Most of them fled through the back door," Kyle said.

"Whatever. The cell phone video was on voice activation, so it clicked off after sixty seconds of near silence. It was at least twenty feet from the front door. Its owner ran off in the panic, forgot about it, and in the melee someone knocked things around on the counter, the cell phone got bumped, so the picture got adjusted. We can't see as much as we could before. About twenty minutes pass and all is quiet. At 11:48, there are voices and the lights come on." Kyle moved closer to the screen. About one-third of the view was blocked by something yellow. "Probably a phone book, the yellow pages," Wright said. The music started again, but at a much lower volume.

The four roommates—Kyle, Alan Strock, Baxter Tate, and Joey Bernardo—were walking around the den, in shorts and T-shirts, and holding drinks again. Elaine Keenan walked through the den, talking nonstop, then sat on the edge of the sofa, smoking what appeared to be a joint. Only half of the sofa was visible. A television, unseen, was turned on. Baxter Tate walked over to Elaine, said something, then put his drink down and yanked off his T-shirt. He and Elaine fell into a pile on the sofa, obviously making out while the other three watched television and milled about. They were talking, but the music and

TV drowned out their words. Alan Strock walked in front of the camera, pulling off his T-shirt and saying something to Baxter, whose view was blocked. There were no sounds from Elaine. Less than half of the sofa was visible now, but a tangle of bare legs could be seen.

Then the lights were turned off, and for a second the room was dark. Slowly, the glare from the television focused and bounced off the walls to provide some illumination. Joey Bernardo came into view, also pulling off his shirt. He stopped and stared at the sofa, where some manner of frenzied activity was under way.

"Listen," Wright hissed.

Joey said something that Kyle could not understand.

"Did you get that?" Wright asked.

"No."

Wright stopped the video and said, "Our experts have studied the audio. Joey Bernardo says to Baxter Tate, 'Is she awake?' Tate is obviously having sex with Elaine, who's passed out drunk, and Bernardo stops by, takes it all in, and wonders if the girl is actually conscious. You want to hear it again?"

"Yes."

Wright reset the video, then replayed it. Kyle leaned down, and with his nose six inches from the screen he watched hard, listened even harder, and heard the word "awake." The detective shook his head gravely.

The action continued, with the music and the television as a backdrop, and though the den of their apartment was dark, figures could be seen in the shadows. Baxter Tate finally got off the sofa, stood, appeared to be completely nude, and walked away. Another figure, Joey Bernardo, quickly took Baxter's place. Some of the sounds could barely be heard.

A steady clicking arose from the scene. "We think that's the sofa," Wright said. "Don't suppose you could help on that one?"

"No."

And before long there was a high-pitched heaving sound, and the clicking stopped. Joey moved from the sofa and disappeared. "That's pretty much the end of the movie," Wright said. "The video goes on for another twelve minutes, but nothing happens. If the girl, Elaine, ever moved or got off the sofa, then it's not on the video. We're almost certain that Baxter Tate and Joey Bernardo had sex with her. There's no evidence that either you or Alan Strock did."

"I did not. I can assure you of that."

"Any idea where you were during the rapes, Kyle?" Wright asked the question, then pressed a key and the screen went blank.

"I'm sure you have a theory."

"Okay." Wright was again armed with his pen and legal pad. "Elaine says she woke up several hours later, around three in the morning, naked, still on the sofa, and suddenly had a vague recollection of being raped. She panicked, wasn't sure where she was, admits she was still very drunk, eventually finds her clothes, gets dressed, sees you fast asleep in a recliner facing the television. When she sees you, she realizes where she is and remembers more of what happened to her. There's no sign of Strock, Tate, or Bernardo. She speaks to you, shakes your shoulder, but you do not respond, so she hurries from the apartment, goes next door, and eventually falls asleep."

"And doesn't mention rape for four days, right, Detective, or has she changed her story again?"

"Four days is correct."

"Thank you. Not a word to anyone for four days. Not to her roommates, her friends, parents, no one. Then suddenly she decided she was raped. The police were very suspicious of her story, right? They finally showed up at our apartment, and at the Beta house, and they asked questions and got very few answers. Why? Because there was no rape. Everything was consensual. Believe me, Detective, that girl would consent to anything."

"How could she consent if she was unconscious, Kyle?"

"If she was unconscious, how could she remember being raped? There was no medical exam. No rape kit. No evidence whatsoever. Just the blacked-out memory of a very confused young woman. The cops dropped the case five years ago, and it should be dropped now."

"But it's not. It's here. The grand jury believed the video proves there was a rape."

"That's bullshit and you know it. This isn't about rape; this is about money. Baxter Tate's family is filthy rich. Elaine has found herself a greedy lawyer. The indictment is nothing but a shakedown."

"So you're willing to risk the spectacle of a trial, and a conviction? You want the jury to see that video? You and your three roomies drunk out of your minds while a young woman is taken advantage of?"

"I didn't touch her."

"No, but you were there, very close by, less than ten feet away. Come on."

"I don't remember it."

"How convenient."

Kyle slowly got to his feet and walked to the bathroom. He filled another plastic cup with tap water, drained it, refilled it, and drank it. Then he sat on the edge of the bed and buried his head in his hands. No, he did not want the jury to see the video. He had just seen it for the first time and prayed it would be the last. He had a visual of himself and his three pals sitting in a crowded courtroom, lights dimmed, judge frowning, jurors gaping, Elaine crying, his parents stoic in the front row as the video is played to a rapt audience. The scene made him sick.

He felt innocent, but he wasn't convinced the jurors would agree.

Wright ejected the disc and placed it carefully back into a plastic case.

Kyle stared at the industrial-grade carpet for a long time. There were sounds in the hallway, muffled voices, feet shuffling, maybe the Fibbies were getting restless. He really didn't care. His ears were ringing and he wasn't sure why.

Each fleeting thought was chased away by the next, and he found it impossible to concentrate, to think rationally, to focus on what should and should not be said. Decisions made at this ugly moment could reverberate forever. For a moment he settled on the three Duke lacrosse players who were falsely accused of raping a stripper. They were eventually cleared of everything, but only after an excruciating trip to hell and back. And there was no video, no link whatsoever to the victim.

"Is she awake?" Joey says to Baxter. How many times would that question echo around the courtroom? Frame by frame. Word by word. The jurors would have the video memorized by the time they retired to consider the verdicts.

Wright sat patiently at the table, hairy hands folded again and motionless on his legal pad. Time meant nothing. He could wait forever.

"Are we at midfield?" Kyle asked, breaking the silence.

"Past midfield, around the forty and driving."

"I'd like to see the indictment."

"Sure."

Kyle stood and looked down at the folding table. The detective began a series of movements that were immediately confusing. First, he pulled his wallet out of his rear left pocket, removed his driver's license, and placed it on the table. He produced his Pittsburgh PD badge and laid it on the table. From a box on the floor he pulled other cards and other badges and began arranging them in line on the table. He reached for a file, handed it to Kyle, and said, "Happy reading."

The file was labeled "INFORMATION." Kyle opened it and removed a stack of papers stapled together. The top one looked official. A bold title read: "Commonwealth of Pennsylvania, Allegheny County,

Court of Common Pleas." A smaller heading read: "Commonwealth versus Baxter F. Tate, Joseph N. Bernardo, Kyle L. McAvoy, and Alan B. Strock." There was a docket number, file number, and other official markings.

Wright produced a pair of kitchen scissors and methodically cut his driver's license into two perfect squares.

The first paragraph read: "This prosecution is in the name of and by the authority of the Commonwealth of Pennsylvania against the above-named defendants—"

Wright was cutting some of the other plastic cards, all of which appeared to be either driver's licenses or credit cards.

"Who, within the jurisdiction of this court—"

Wright ripped his bronze badge from its leather wallet and bounced it on the table. "What are you doing?" Kyle finally asked.

"Destroying the evidence."

"What evidence?"

"Read page two."

Kyle, who was at the bottom of page one, flipped to page two. It was blank, not a word, letter, period, anything. He flipped to page three, then four, then five. All blank. Wright was busy removing other badges. Kyle held the bogus indictment and gawked at the detective.

"Have a seat, Kyle," Wright said with a smile as he waved at the empty folding chair.

In an effort to say something, Kyle managed only a dying whimper. Then he sat down.

"There is no indictment, Kyle," Wright proceeded as if it all made sense now. "No grand jury, no cops, no arrest, no trial. Nothing but a video."

"No cops?"

"Oh, no. This stuff is all fake." He waved his hands over the pile of destroyed identification. "I'm not a cop. Those boys across the hall are not FBI agents."

Kyle rolled his head back like a wounded boxer, then rubbed his eyes. The indictment fell to the floor. "Who are you?" he managed to grunt.

"That's a very good question, Kyle, one that will take a long time to answer."

In disbelief, Kyle picked up one of the badges—Ginyard's, FBI. He rubbed it and said, "But I checked this guy out online. He really works for the FBI."

"Yes, these are real names. We just borrowed them for the night."

"So, you're impersonating an officer?"

"Certainly, but it's just a small offense. Not worth your trouble."

"But why?"

"To get your attention, Kyle. To convince you to come here and have this little meeting with me. Otherwise, you might have run away. Plus, we wanted to impress you with our resources."

"We?"

"Yes, my firm. You see, Kyle, I work for a contractor, a private one, and we've been hired to do a job. We need you, and this is how we recruit people."

Kyle blew out a chestful of nervous laughter. His cheeks were getting warm, the blood was beginning to circulate. There was a rising thrill at the relief of not being prosecuted, of having been rescued from the firing squad. But the anger was beginning to boil.

"You recruit by blackmail?" he asked.

"If necessary. We have the video. We know where the girl is. She does indeed have a lawyer."

"Does she know about the video?"

"No, but if she saw it, your life could get very complicated."

"I'm not sure I follow you."

"Come on, Kyle. Rape has a twelve-year statute of limitations in Pennsylvania. You have seven years to go. If Elaine and her lawyer knew about the video, they would threaten criminal prosecution to force a civil settlement. It would be, as you say, nothing but a shakedown, but it would work. Your life will go much smoother if you play along with us and we keep the video buried."

"So you're recruiting me?"

"Yes."

"To do what?"

"To be a lawyer."

5

With a crushing weight suddenly lifted from his shoulders, and with his breathing somewhat normal again, Kyle glanced at his watch. It was after midnight. He looked at Wright, or whatever the hell his name really was, and he wanted to smile and even hug the man because he wasn't a cop from Pittsburgh and he didn't deliver an indictment. There would be no arrest, no prosecution, no humiliation, and for this Kyle was euphoric. But at the same time he wanted to bolt across the table and punch Wright's face with as much violence as he could generate, then knock him to the floor and kick him until he didn't move.

He vetoed both ideas. Wright was fit and probably trained and could take care of himself. And he certainly wasn't the type anyone would want to hug. Kyle leaned back in his chair, placed his right ankle on his left knee, and relaxed for the first time in hours.

"So what's your real name?" he asked.

Wright was preparing a new legal pad for a fresh round of note taking. He entered the date in the top left corner. "We're not going to waste time with frivolous questions, Kyle."

"Oh, why not? You can't even tell me your name?"

"Let's stick with Bennie Wright for now. It doesn't really matter, because you'll never know the real name."

"I like this. Real cloak-and-dagger shit. You guys are good. Really had me going there for about four hours. Had a knot in my colon as big as a pumpkin. Already thinking about finding a nice bridge to wing it from. I hate your guts and don't ever forget it."

"When you shut up, we can get down to business."

"Can I walk out right now?"

"Sure."

"And no one will grab me? No more fake badges and phony FBI agents?"

"None. Go. You're a free man."

"Oh, thank you."

A minute passed without a word. Wright's fierce little eyes never left Kyle's face, while Kyle, hard as he tried, could not return the stare. His foot twitched and his eyes darted and he drummed his fingers on the table. His mind raced through a hundred scenarios, but he never once thought of leaving the room.

"Let's talk about your future, Kyle," Wright finally said.

"Sure. Now that I won't be arrested, the future has certainly improved."

"This job you're planning to take. Piedmont Legal Aid. Why do you want to waste a couple of years saving the world?"

"Don't really see it that way. There are a lot of migrant workers in Virginia, many of whom are illegal, and they're subjected to all sorts of abuse. They live in cardboard boxes, eat rice twice a day, work for two bucks an hour, often don't get paid for backbreaking work, and so on. I figure they could use some help."

"But why?"

"It's public-interest law, okay? Obviously you don't get it. It's lawyers giving their time to help others. They still teach this in law school. Some of us believe in it."

Wright was not impressed. "Let's talk about Scully & Pershing."

"What about them? I'm sure you've done your research."

"They offered you a job?"

"Correct."

"Beginning when?"

"September 2 of this year. I take the bar in July, and would start working in September."

"As an associate?"

"No, as a full-fledged partner. Or how about a secretary, or a copy clerk? Come on, Bennie, you know the routine."

"Don't get angry, Kyle. We have a long way to go."

"I see. And we should cooperate now, and be pals, because we're striving for a common purpose. Just you and me, right, Bennie? A couple of old friends. Where the hell is this going?"

"It's going to Scully & Pershing."

"What if I don't want to work there?"

"You have little choice."

Kyle leaned on his elbows and rubbed his eyes. The folding table was narrow, their faces were two feet apart.

"Have you said no to Scully & Pershing?" Wright asked.

"I'm assuming you already know the answer to that question. I'm assuming you've been listening to my phone conversations for some time."

"Not all of them."

"You're a thug."

"Thugs break legs, Kyle. We're much too smart for that."

"No, I have not said no to Scully & Pershing. I've informed them that I'm giving serious thought to public-interest law for a couple of years, and we've even discussed a deferment. They've given me extra time, but I need to make a decision."

"So they still want you?"

"Yes."

"At a starting salary of $200,000?"

"Something like that. You know the numbers."

"One of the largest and most prestigious law firms in the world."

"The largest, at least that's what they tell everybody."

"Big firm, important clients, wealthy partners with contacts everywhere. Come on, Kyle, it's an offer most law students would kill for. Why not take it?"

Kyle jumped to his feet and paced to the door and back. He glared down at Wright and said, "Let me make sure I follow you. You want me to take the job at Scully & Pershing, for reasons that I'm sure will be against my best interests, and if I say no, then you'll blackmail me with the video and the rape allegations. Right? Is this where we're headed, Bennie?"

"More or less. 'Blackmail' is such an ugly word."

"Wouldn't want to offend anyone, Bennie. I'm sure you're very sensitive. But it's blackmail, or extortion, or whatever you'd like to call it. It's a crime, Bennie. And you're a thug."

"Shut up and stop calling me a thug!"

"I could go to the cops tomorrow and bust your ass. Impersonating an officer, attempted blackmail."

"It won't happen."

"I can make it happen."

Wright slowly stood and for one horrible second made a motion as if he were about to throw a nasty punch. Then he casually pointed a finger at Kyle and in a firm and steady voice said, "You're a kid with a snoot full of law. You want to run to the cops, go ahead. Work up your little textbook theories about who's right and who's wrong, and you know what will happen, Kyle? I'll tell you what will happen. You'll never see me again. The boys across the hall, the FBI agents, are already gone. No trace whatsoever. Vanished, forever. Before long, I'll have a visit with the attorney for Elaine Keenan, show her the video, look once again at the net worth of Baxter Tate, provide her with the current addresses and phone numbers and e-mails for you, Alan Strock, and Joey Bernardo, prod her to have a chat with the prosecutor in Pittsburgh, and before you know it things are out of your control. Maybe charges will be filed, maybe not. But, trust me, I will destroy you."

"Where's Elaine? You got her in a bunker somewhere?"

"It doesn't matter. We have reason to believe she feels strongly that she was raped in your apartment."

"Please."

"She's a ticking bomb, Kyle, and the video would set her off. You have seven more years to worry about it." With that, Wright returned to his chair and made some notes. Kyle sat on the edge of the bed, facing the mirror.

"It could get really ugly," Wright continued. "Think about it, Kyle. Yale Law's brightest student arrested on rape charges. The women's groups screaming for all eight testicles. The video leaked onto the Internet. A brutal trial. Chance of conviction, prison. A career ruined."

"Shut up!"

"No. So if you think I'm worried about your two-bit threats, please rest assured that I am not. Let's talk business. Let's take the video and lock it away so that no one will ever see it. How does that sound, Kyle?"

It sounded pretty damned good at the moment. Kyle scratched his stubble as he said, "What do you want?"

"I want you to take the job at Scully & Pershing."

"Why?"

"Now we're getting somewhere, Kyle. Now we can talk business. I thought you'd never ask why."

"Why? Why? Why?"

"Because I need information."

"Great. That really explains things. Thank you so much."

"Bear with me for a few minutes, Kyle. You need a little background here. There are two gigantic corporations who compete with each other. Both are ruthless competitors, both are worth billions, and they really despise each other. There have been lawsuits, nasty ones, big public spectacles with no clear winner or loser. So, over the years, they have tried to avoid the courtroom. Until now. Now they're about to square off in the mother of all lawsuits. It will be filed in a few weeks in federal court in New York City. At stake is something in the neighborhood of $800 billion, and the loser might not survive. Nasty, vicious litigation. A bonanza for the attorneys. Each uses a huge Wall Street law firm, and guess what? The two law firms hate each other."

"I can't wait to get in the middle of that."

"That's where you're headed. One firm is Scully & Pershing. The other is Agee, Poe & Epps."

"Otherwise known as APE."

"Yes."

"I interviewed there."

"Did they offer a job?"

"I thought you knew everything."

"Only what I need to know."

"I didn't like the firm."

"Attaboy. Now you can really dislike them."

Kyle walked into the bathroom, ran cold water in the sink, splashed it on his face and down his neck, and for a long time stared at himself in the mirror. Don't get tired, he told himself. Ignore the fatigue and the fear. Try to anticipate what's coming. Try to throw him a curve, mess with his timing, knock him off course.

He sat down across the table from Wright. "Where'd you find the video?" Kyle asked.

"Kyle, Kyle, such a waste of time."

"If the video is used in court, then the owner of the cell phone camera will have to testify. You can't protect his identity at that point. Does he know this? Did you explain it to him? He's one of my fraternity brothers, and I'll bet he'll refuse to testify at trial."

"A trial? You're willing to go to trial? A trial holds the possibility of a conviction, which means prison, and prison for cute little white boys convicted of rape is not pretty."

"I'll bet she won't press charges."

"You have nothing to bet with. She needs money. If she can squeeze it out of Mr. Tate, and a few bucks from you and the other two, she'll do it. Trust me."

"I wouldn't trust you with my dirty laundry."

"Enough of the insults. We'll go to her lawyer and show her exactly how to do it. Or, maybe we won't. Maybe we'll just release an edited version of the video on the Internet tonight. Cut out the rape and let everyone see the party scene. We'll e-mail it to all your friends, family, prospective employers, the whole world, Kyle. See how it plays. Then maybe we'll edit it some more, maybe include some of the rape, post it again. When Elaine sees it, your face is in the newspaper."

Kyle's mouth actually dropped open, and his shoulders slumped. He could think of no quick response, but the one thought that hit him hard was that of being shot. Mr. Wright here was a ruthless little cutthroat who worked for some group with unlimited resources and great determination. They would ruin him. They might even kill him.

As if reading his mind, Wright leaned in a little closer and said, "Kyle, we're not Boy Scouts. And I'm tired of this bantering back and forth. I'm not here to negotiate. I'm here to give orders. Either you follow my orders, or I call the office and tell my pals to destroy you."

"I despise you."

"So be it. I'm just doing my job."

"What a miserable job."

"Can we talk about your new one?"

"I didn't go to law school to become a spy."

"Let's not call it spying, Kyle."

"Then give it a name, Bennie."

"Transferring information."

"Oh, bullshit. It's nothing but spying."

"I really don't care what you call it."

"What kind of information?"

"Once the lawsuit gets cranked up, there will be a million documents. Maybe ten million, who knows? Lots of documents and lots of secrets. We expect each of the two law firms to commit fifty lawyers to the case—maybe as many as ten partners, the rest associates. You'll be in the litigation section of Scully & Pershing, so you'll have access to a lot of material."

"Security at these firms is extremely tight."

"We know that. Our security experts are better than theirs. We wrote the book, Kyle."

"I'm sure you did. May I ask what these two big companies are fighting over?"

"Secrets. Technology."

"Great. Thanks. Do these companies have names?"

"Fortune 500. I'll give you more information as we progress."

"So you're going to be part of my life for a while?"

"I'm your official handler. You and I will spend a lot of time together."

"Then I quit. Go ahead and shoot me. I'm not spying and I'm not stealing. The moment I walk out of Scully & Pershing with a document or a disc I'm not supposed to have and give it to you or anybody else, I've broken the law and violated half the canons of ethics. I will be disbarred and convicted of something."

"Only if you get caught."

"I'll get caught."

"No. We're much too smart, Kyle. We've done this before. It's our business."

"Your firm specializes in stealing documents?"

"Let's call it corporate espionage. We do it all the time and we're very good at it."

"Then go blackmail someone else."

"No. It's all you, Kyle. Think about it. You take the job you've always wanted, at an obscene salary, living the fast life in the big city. They try to work you to death for a few years, but they reward you. By the time you're thirty, you're a senior associate making four hundred grand a year. Nice apartment in SoHo. A share of a weekend house in the Hamptons. A Porsche. A circle of friends who are all smart and rich and moving up as fast as you are. Then one day the lawsuit is settled. We disappear. The statute runs out in Pittsburgh. The video is finally forgotten, and at the age of thirty-two or thirty-three you're asked to join Scully & Pershing as a full equity partner. A million or two per year. The pinnacle of success. A great career ahead of you. Life is great. And no one there will ever know about the transferring of information."

A headache that had been smoldering for the past hour finally matured and hit hard in the middle of his forehead. Kyle stretched out on the bed and massaged his temples. He closed his eyes, but in the blackness managed to keep talking. "Look, Bennie, I know you don't care about morals or ethics and such things, but I do. How, exactly, am I supposed to live with myself if I betray the confidences of my firm and its clients? Trust is the most important thing a lawyer has. I learned that from my father when I was a teenager."

"All we care about is getting the information. We don't spend too much time pondering morality."

"That's about what I figured."

"I need a commitment, Kyle. I need your word."

"Do you have any Tylenol?"

"No. Do we have an agreement, Kyle?"

"Do you have anything for a headache?"

"No."

"Do you have a gun?"

"In my jacket."

"Let me have it."

A minute passed without a sound. Wright's eyes never left Kyle, who was motionless except for his fingers pressing gently on his forehead. Then Kyle slowly sat up and asked in a whisper, "How much longer are you planning to stay here?"

"Oh, I have lots of questions."

"I was afraid of that. I can't keep going. My head is splitting."

"Whatever, Kyle. It's up to you. But I need an answer. Do we have an agreement, a deal, an understanding?"

"Do I really have a choice?"

"I don't see one."

"Neither do I."

"So?"

"If I have no choice, then I have no choice."

"Excellent. A wise decision, Kyle."

"Oh, thank you so much."

Wright stood and stretched as if a long day at the office were finally over. He reshuffled some papers, fiddled with the video camera, closed the laptop. "Would you like to rest, Kyle?"

"Yes."

"We have several rooms. You're welcome to take a nap if you'd like, or we can continue tomorrow."

"It's already tomorrow."

Wright was at the door. He opened it and Kyle followed him out of the room, across the hall, and into room 222. What had once been an FBI command center had now been converted back to a regular $89-a-night motel room. Ginyard and Plant and the other fake agents were long gone, and they had taken everything—files, computers, enlarged photos, tripods, briefcases, boxes, folding tables. The bed was back in the center of the room, perfectly made up.

"Shall I wake you in a few hours?" Wright asked pleasantly.

"No. Just leave me alone."

"I'll be across the hall."

When Kyle was alone, he pulled back the bedspread, turned off the lights, and soon fell asleep.

6

Contrary to his best intentions, Kyle awoke several hours later. He desperately wanted to sleep forever, to simply drift away and be forgotten. He awoke in a warm, dark room on a hard bed, and for a second wasn't sure where he was or how he had managed to get there. His head was still hurting and his mouth was dry. Soon, though, the nightmare returned, and he had the urgent desire to get away, to get outside, where he could look back at the motel and convince himself that the meeting with Detective Wright had not really happened. He needed fresh air, and maybe someone to talk to.

He eased from the room and tiptoed down the hall, down the stairs. In the lobby some salesmen were gulping coffee and talking rapidly, anxious for the day to start. The sun was up, the snow had stopped. Outside the air was cold and sharp, and he inhaled as if he'd been suffocating. He made it to his Jeep, started the engine, turned on the heater, and waited for the defrost to melt the snow on the windshield.

The shock was wearing off, but the reality was even worse.

He checked his cell phone messages. His girlfriend had called six times, his roommate three. They were worried. He had class at 9:00 a.m. and a pile of work at the law journal. And nothing—girlfriend, roommate, law school, or work—held the slightest interest at the moment. He left the Holiday Inn and drove east on Highway 1 for a few miles until New Haven was behind him. He ran up behind a snowplow and was content to putter along at thirty miles an hour. Other cars lined up behind him, and for the first time he wondered if someone might be following. He began glancing at the rearview mirror.

At the small town of Guilford, he stopped at a convenience store and finally found some Tylenol. He washed it down with a soft drink and was about to drive back to New Haven when he noticed a diner across the street. He had not eaten since lunch the day before and was suddenly famished. He could almost smell the bacon grease.

The diner was packed with the local breakfast crowd. Kyle found a seat at the counter and ordered scrambled eggs, bacon, hash browns, toast, coffee, and orange juice. He ate in silence as the laughter and town gossip roared around him. The headache was fading fast, and he began plotting the rest of his day. His girlfriend might be a problem: no contact in twelve hours, a night spent away from his apartment—highly unusual behavior for someone as disciplined as Kyle. He certainly couldn't tell her the truth, could he? No, the truth was a thing of the past. The present and the future would be a life of lies, cover-ups, thievery, espionage, and more lies.

Olivia was a first-year law student at Yale, a Californian, UCLA graduate, extemely bright and ambitious and not looking for a serious commitment. They had been dating for four months, and the relationship was far more casual than romantic. Still, he did not look forward to some stuttering tale of a night that simply vanished.

A body closed in from behind. A hand appeared with a white business card. Kyle glanced to his right and came face-to-face with the man he had once known as Special Agent Ginyard, now wearing a camel hair sport coat and jeans. "Mr. Wright would like to see you at 3:00 p.m., after class, same room," he said, then disappeared before Kyle could speak. He picked up the card. It was blank except for the handwritten message: "3:00 p.m., today, room 225, Holiday Inn." He stared at it for a few minutes as he quickly lost interest in the remaining food in front of him.

Is this my future? he asked himself. Someone always watching, following, waiting in the shadows, stalking, listening?

A crowd was waiting by the door for seating. The waitress slipped his bill under his coffee cup and gave him a quick smile that said "Time's up." He paid at the cash register and, outside, refused to scan the other vehicles for signs of stalkers. He called Olivia, who was sleeping.

"Are you all right?" she asked.

"Yes, I'm fine."

"I don't want to know anything else, just tell me you're not hurt."

"I'm not hurt. I'm fine, and I'm sorry."

"Don't apologize."

"I'm apologizing, okay. I should have called."

"I don't want to know."

"Yes you do. Do you accept my apology?"

"I don't know."

"That's better. I expect some anger here."

"Don't get me started."

"How about lunch?"

"No."

"Why not?"

"I'm busy."

"You can't skip lunch."

"Where are you?"

"Guilford."

"And where might that be?"

"Just down the road from New Haven. There's a great little place for breakfast. I'll bring you here sometime."

"Can't wait."

"Meet me at The Grill at noon. Please."

"I'll think about it."

He drove back to New Haven, refusing every half mile to glance at his mirror. He slipped quietly into his apartment and took a shower. Mitch, his roommate, could sleep through an earthquake, and when he finally staggered out of his bedroom, Kyle was sipping coffee at the kitchen counter and reading a newspaper online. Mitch asked a few vague questions about last night, but Kyle deflected them nicely and gave the impression that he had bumped into a different girl and things went extremely well. Mitch went back to bed.

COMPLETE FIDELITY had been agreed to months earlier, and once Olivia was convinced Kyle had not cheated, her attitude thawed a little. The story he'd been working on for several hours went like this: He'd been struggling with his decision to pursue public-interest law instead of taking a big job with a big firm. He had no plans to make public-interest law a career, so why go there to begin with? He would eventually work in New York, so why delay the inevitable? And so on. And last night, after his basketball game, he decided he had to make a final decision. He turned off his phone and took a long drive, east for some unknown reason, on Highway 1, past New London and into Rhode Island. He lost track of time. After midnight, the snow picked up and he found a cheap motel where he slept for a few hours.

He had changed his mind. He was going to New York, to Scully & Pershing.

He spilled this over lunch, over a sandwich at The Grill. Olivia listened with skepticism but did not interrupt. She seemed to believe the story about last night, but she was not buying the sudden change in career plans. "You must be kidding," she blurted when he hit the punch line.

"It's not easy," he said, already on the defensive. He knew this would not be pleasant.

"You, Mr. Pro Bono, Mr. Public Interest Law?"

"I know. I know. I feel like a turncoat."

"You are a turncoat. You're selling out, just like every other third-year law student."

"Lower your voice, please," Kyle said as he glanced around. "Let's not have a scene."

She lowered her voice but not her eyebrows. "You've said it yourself a hundred times, Kyle. We all get to law school with big ideas of doing good, helping others, fighting injustice, but along the way we sell out. Seduced by big money. We turn into corporate whores. Those are your words, Kyle."

"They do sound familiar."

"I can't believe this."

They took a couple of bites, but the food was not important.

"We have thirty years to make money," she said. "Why can't we spend a few years helping others?" Kyle was on the ropes and bleeding.

"I know, I know," he mumbled lamely. "But timing is important. I'm not sure Scully & Pershing will defer." Another lie, but what the hell. Once you start, why quit? They were multiplying.

"Oh, please. You can get a job with any firm in the country, now or five years from now."

"I'm not so sure about that. The job market is tightening up. Some of the big firms are threatening layoffs."

She shoved her food away, crossed her arms, and slowly shook her head. "I don't believe this," she said.

And at that moment Kyle couldn't believe it either, but it was important, now and forever more, to give the impression that he'd carefully weighed the issues and had arrived at this decision. In other words, Kyle had to sell it. Olivia was the first test. His friends would be next, then his favorite professors. After he'd practiced the routine a few times and the lying was finely tuned, he would somehow muster the courage to visit his father and deliver the news that would lead to an ugly fight. John McAvoy detested the idea of his son working for a corporate firm on Wall Street.

Kyle's selling job, though, did little to convince Olivia. They traded barbs for a few minutes, then forgot about lunch and went their separate ways. There was no goodbye peck on the cheek, no hug, no promise to call each other later. He spent an hour in his office at the law journal, then reluctantly left and drove back to the motel.

THE ROOM HAD changed little. The video camera and laptop were gone, no sign of electronics anywhere, though Kyle was certain every word would be recorded in some fashion. The folding table was still ground zero, but it had been moved closer to the windows. Same two folding chairs. The setting was as stark as a police interrogation room somewhere deep in the basement.

The headache was back.

Kyle flipped the card Ginyard left behind onto the table and began with a pleasant "Please tell this son of a bitch to stop following me."

"We're just a little curious, that's all, Kyle."

"I'm not going to be followed, Bennie, do you understand?"

Bennie gave a smart-ass smile.

"The deal's off, Bennie. I'm not going to live my life with a bunch of goons watching everything I do. Forget the surveillance, forget the wiretaps and hidden mikes and e-mail snooping, Bennie. Are you listening? I'm not walking down the streets of New York wondering who's behind me. I'm not chatting on the phone while thinking some bozo might be listening. You've just wrecked my life, Bennie, the least you can do is allow me some degree of privacy."

"We have no plans—"

"That's a lie and you know it. Here's the new deal, Bennie. We agree right now that you and your goons stay out of my life. You don't eavesdrop, you don't follow, you don't hide in the shadows or stalk or play your little cat-and-mouse games. I'll do what you want me to do, whatever the hell that is, but you have got to leave me alone."

"Otherwise?"

"Oh, otherwise. Otherwise, I'll take my chances with Elaine and her bogus rape charge. Look, Bennie, if my life is going to be ruined, then what the hell? I get to pick my poison. I have Elaine on the one hand, and I have your goons on the other."

Bennie exhaled slowly, cleared his throat, and said, "Yes, Kyle, but it is important for us to keep up with you. That is the nature of our work. That is what we do."

"It's blackmail, pure and simple."

"Kyle, Kyle, none of that now. That doesn't move the ball."

"Please, can we forget about the ball? That's so tiring now."

"We can't just turn you loose in New York."

"Here's my bottom line—I will not be stalked or watched or followed. Do you understand this, Bennie?"

"This could pose a problem."

"It's already a problem. What do you want? You'll know where I live and where I work—they're basically the same place for the next five years anyway. I'll be at the office eighteen hours a day, if not more. Why, exactly, will it be necessary to keep me under surveillance?"

"There are procedures we follow."

"Then change them. It's not negotiable." Kyle jumped to his feet and headed for the door. "When do we meet again?"

"Where are you going?" Bennie asked as he stood.

"None of your business, and don't follow me. Do not follow me." Kyle had his hand on the doorknob.

"Okay, okay. Look, Kyle, we can be flexible here. I see your point."

"When and where?"

"Now."

"No, I have things to do, without being watched."

"But we have so much to talk about, Kyle."

"When?"

"How about six, tonight?"

"I'll be here at eight, and for only one hour. And I'm not coming back tomorrow."

7

At the New Haven train station, Kyle boarded the 7:22 for Grand Central. He wore the better of his two suits, a plain white shirt with an utterly boring tie, and black wing tips, and he carried a handsome leather attaché case his father had given him last Christmas. He also carried the morning's editions of the *New York Times* and the *Wall Street Journal*, and he was indistinguishable from the other sleepy-eyed executives hustling off to the office.

As the frozen countryside blurred by, he ignored the papers and let his mind wander. He asked himself if he would one day live in the suburbs and be forced to ride a train three hours a day so his children could attend fine schools and ride their bikes down leafy streets. At the age of twenty-five, that was not very appealing. But now most of his thoughts about the future were complicated and dreary. He'd be lucky if he didn't get himself indicted and/or disbarred. Life in the big firms was brutal enough, and now he would have the impossible chore of grinding through the first years while stealing confidential information and praying daily that he didn't get caught.

Maybe commuting wasn't such a bad deal after all.

After three days and many hours of talking, haggling, bitching, and threatening, Bennie Wright had finally left town. He had receded into the shadows but, of course, would soon materialize again. Kyle hated his voice, his face, his mannerisms, his calm hairy hands, his slick head, his confident, pressing manner. He hated everything about Bennie Wright and his company or firm or whatever it was, and many times during the past week he had changed his mind in the middle of the night and told them all to go to hell.

Then, in the darkness, as always, he could feel the handcuffs, see his mug shot in the newspapers, see the looks on the faces of his parents, and worst of all he could see himself afraid to glance at the jurors when the video was played to a hushed courtroom.

"Is she awake?" Joey Bernardo asks while Baxter Tate has Elaine down on the sofa.

Is she awake? The words echo around the courtroom.

The countryside vanished as the train sped through suburbs and towns, then it went underground, at some point dipped under the East River and entered Manhattan. Kyle strolled through Grand Central and hailed a cab at the corner of Lex and Forty-fourth. Not once had he looked over his shoulder.

Scully & Pershing leased the top half of a building named 110 Broad, a sleek glass edifice with forty-four floors, in the heart of the financial district. Kyle had spent ten weeks there the previous summer as an intern—the typical big-firm seduction routine of socializing, lunching, barhopping, watching the Yankees, and putting in a few light hours of work. It was a joke of a job and everybody involved knew it. If the wining and dining worked, and it almost always did, the interns became associates upon graduation and their lives were basically over.

It was almost 10:00 a.m., and the elevator was empty. The lawyers had been at their desks for hours. He stopped at the thirtieth floor, the firm's main lobby, and paused for a second to admire the massive bronze lettering that informed all visitors that they were now on the hallowed turf of Scully & Pershing. Attorneys-at-law, all twenty-one hundred of them, the largest law firm the world had ever known. The first and still the only firm to boast of more than two thousand lawyers. Counsel to more Fortune 500 companies than any other firm in the history of American law. Offices in ten U.S. cities and twenty foreign ones. A hundred and thirty years of hidebound tradition. Magnet to the best legal talent money can buy. Power, money, prestige.

He already felt like a trespasser.

The walls were covered with abstract art, the furniture was rich and contemporary. Some Asian whiz had done the decorating, magazine quality, and there was a brochure on a table that went into details. As if anyone who worked there had the time to stop and ponder the interior design schemes. A gorgeous little receptionist in stiletto heels took his name and asked him to please wait. Kyle turned his back on everything and became entranced in a work of art so bizarre he had no idea what he was looking at. After a few minutes of mindless gazing, he heard the receptionist call, "Mr. Peckham is waiting. Two floors up." Kyle took the stairs.

Like many Manhattan law firms, Scully & Pershing spent money on the elevators, reception areas, and conference rooms—the places clients and other visitors might actually see—but back in the bowels of the firm where the grunts worked, efficiency ruled. The halls were lined with file cabinets. The secretaries and typists—all women—worked in tight cubicles within reach of each other. The copyboys and other gofers worked on their feet; New York real estate was simply too expensive to provide them a spot or a nook of any significance. The senior associates and junior partners were awarded small offices on the outer walls, with a view of similar buildings.

The rookie associates were stuffed in tight windowless spaces;

three or four of them wedged together in cramped cubicles, nicknamed "cubes." These "offices" were tucked away and kept out of sight. Lousy accommodations, brutal hours, sadistic bosses, unbearable pressure—it was all part of the blue-chip law firm experience, and Kyle had heard the horror tales before he finished his first year at Yale. Scully & Pershing was no better and certainly no worse than the other mega-firms that threw money at the brightest students, then burned them up.

At the corners of each floor, in the largest offices, the real partners anchored things and had some say in the decor. One was Doug Peckham, a forty-one-year-old litigation partner, a Yale man who had supervised Kyle during his internship. They had become somewhat friendly.

Kyle was shown into Peckham's office a few minutes after 10:00 a.m., just as a pair of associates were leaving. Whatever the meeting was, it had not gone well. The associates looked rattled, and Peckham was trying to calm down.

They exchanged greetings and pleasantries, the usual banter about good old Yale. Kyle knew that Peckham billed $800 an hour, at least ten hours a day, and therefore the time that Kyle was now wasting was quite valuable. "I'm not sure I want to spend a couple of years doing legal aid," Kyle said, not too deep into the meeting.

"Don't really blame you there, Kyle," Peckham said in a quick, clipped voice. "You have too much potential in the real world. This is your future." He spread his arms to take in his vast empire. It was a nice office, large by comparison, but not a kingdom.

"I really would like to work in litigation."

"I see no problem there. You had a great summer here. We were all impressed. I'll make the request myself. You know, though, that litigation is not for everyone."

That's what they all said. The average career of a litigator is twenty-five years. The work is high pressure, high stress. Peckham may have been forty-one, but he could easily pass for fifty. Completely gray, dark circles, too much bulk in the jowls and around the waist. Probably hadn't exercised in years.

"My deadline has passed," Kyle said.

"When?"

"A week ago."

"No problem. Come on, Kyle, editor in chief of the *Yale Law Journal.* We'll be happy to cut you some slack. I'll talk to Woody in personnel and clear it. Our recruiting has gone very well. You're joining the best freshman class in years."

The same was said about every freshman class at every major firm.

"Thanks. And I'd love to work in the litigation practice group."

"Got it, Kyle. Consider it done." And with that Peckham glanced at his watch—meeting over. His phone was ringing, there were hushed voices just outside his door. As Kyle shook his hand and said goodbye, he decided he did not want to become another Doug Peckham. He had no idea what he wanted to become, or if he would in fact become anything other than a disbarred lawyer, but selling his soul to become a partner was not in the plans.

Associates were waiting at the door, sharply dressed young men not much older than Kyle. Smug, harried, nervous, they stepped into the lion's den, and as the door closed, Doug was raising his voice. What a life. And this was an easy day in litigation. The real pressure was in the courtroom.

On the elevator down, Kyle was struck by the absurdity of what he was expected to do. Upon leaving the offices of Scully & Pershing, and riding the elevator like hundreds of others, he was expected to have hidden somewhere upon his person or within his effects top secret information that belonged not to him but to the firm and especially to its client. And he would give this valuable data to Bennie with the hairy hands, or whatever his real name was, who would then use it against the firm and its client.

Who am I kidding? he said to himself. There were four others on the elevator. Sweat popped out above his eyebrows.

So this is what my life boils down to. A chance of prison for rape in Pennsylvania or a chance of prison in New York for stealing secrets. Why not a third option? Four years of college, three years of law school, seven rather successful years, all the potential in the world, and I'll become a highly paid thief.

And there was no one to talk to.

He wanted out. Out of the elevator, the building, the city. Out of this predicament. He closed his eyes and talked to himself.

But there was evidence in Pennsylvania, and none in New York. Yet. He was certain he would get caught, though. Months before any crime was committed, he knew he would get caught.

Two blocks away, he found a coffee shop. He sat on a bar stool in the window and for a long time looked rather forlornly at 110 Broad, at the tower that would soon become his home, or his prison. He knew the numbers, the statistics. Scully & Pershing would hire 150 new associates worldwide, 100 in the New York office alone. They would pay them a nice salary that would amount to about $100 an hour, and the firm would in turn bill their well-heeled clients several times that rate for the associates' work. Kyle, like all rookie grunts on Wall Street, would be expected to bill a minimum of two thousand hours a year, though more would be required to make an impression. Hundred-hour workweeks would not be uncommon. After two years, the associates would begin dropping out and looking for more sensible work. Half would be gone in four years. Ten percent of his freshman class would survive, claw their way to the top, and be awarded with a partnership after seven or eight years. Those who didn't drop out along the way would be squeezed out by the firm if they were not deemed partnership material.

The work had become so awful that the trend was for firms to market themselves as "quality of life" firms. The associates were expected to bill fewer hours, have more vacation, and so on. More often than not, though, it was simply a recruiting gimmick. In the workaholic culture of every big firm, the greenest associates were expected to bill almost as much as the partners, regardless of what the recruiters mentioned over lunch months earlier.

Sure the money was great. At least $200,000 to start with. Double that in five years as a senior associate. Double it again in seven years as a junior partner. Well over a million bucks a year at the age of thirty-five as a full partner with a future filled with even higher earnings.

Numbers, numbers. Kyle was sick of the numbers. He longed for the Blue Ridge Mountains and a nonprofit's salary of $32,000 without the stress and pressure and hassle of life in the city. He yearned for freedom.

Instead, he had another meeting with Bennie Wright. The cab stopped in front of the Millenium Hilton on Church Street. Kyle paid the driver, nodded at the doorman, then took the elevator four floors up to a room where his handler was waiting. Bennie motioned to a round table with a bowl of bright green apples in the center, but Kyle refused to sit or remove his jacket.

"The offer is still good," he said. "I'll start in September with the other associates."

"Good. I'm not surprised. And you'll be in litigation?"

"Peckham thinks so."

Bennie had a file on Doug Peckham, as well as files on all of the litigation partners and many of the firm's other lawyers.

"But there's no guarantee," Kyle added.

"You can make it happen."

"We'll see."

"Have you thought about an apartment here in Manhattan?"

"No, not yet."

"Well, we've done some homework, looked around."

"Funny, I don't recall asking for your help."

"And we've found a couple of places that will be ideal."

"Ideal for who?"

"For you, of course. Both places are in Tribeca, fairly close to the office."

"What makes you think I would even remotely consider living where you want me to live?"

"And we'll cover the rent. Pretty pricey real estate."

"Oh, I see. You'll find an apartment for me, and pay for it, so I won't need a roommate. Is that it, Bennie? One less person for you to worry about. Helps to keep me isolated. Plus the rent means that we're financially joined at the hip. You pay me, I give you secrets, just a couple of shrewd businessmen, right, Bennie?"

"Apartment hunting is a bitch in this city. I'm just trying to help."

"Thanks so much. No doubt these are places that can easily be watched, maybe even wired or bugged or compromised in ways I can't even imagine. Nice try, Bennie."

"The rent is five thousand bucks a month."

"Keep it. I can't be bought. Evidently I can be blackmailed, but not bought."

"Where are you planning to live?"

"Wherever I choose. I'll figure it out, and I'll do so without any involvement on your part."

"As you wish."

"Damned right. What else do you want to talk about?"

Bennie walked to the table, picked up a legal pad, and studied it as if he didn't know what he'd already written on it. "Have you ever seen a psychiatrist?" he asked.

"No."

"A psychologist?"

"No."

"A counselor or therapist of any type?"

"Yes."

"Details please."

"It was nothing."

"Then let's talk about nothing. What happened?"

Kyle leaned against the wall and folded both arms across his chest. There was little doubt in his mind that Bennie knew most of what he was about to explain. He knew far too much. "After the incident with Elaine, and after the police finished their investigation, I talked to a counselor in student health services. She referred me to a Dr. Thorp, a specialist in drug and alcohol addiction. He roughed me up, got under my skin, forced me to take a long hard look in the mirror, and he convinced me the drinking would only get worse."

"Were you an alcoholic?"

"No. Dr. Thorp didn't think so. I certainly didn't either. But there was too much drinking, especially of the binge variety. I seldom smoked pot."

"You're still sober?"

"I quit drinking. I grew up, found some different roommates, and have never been tempted. I've yet to miss the hangovers."

"Not even an occasional beer?"

"Nope. I never think about it."

Bennie nodded as if he approved of this. "What about the girl?" he asked.

"What about her?"

"How serious is the relationship?"

"Not sure where you figure into this, Bennie. Can you help me here?"

"Your life will be complicated enough without a romance. A serious relationship could pose problems. It's best if you postpone it for a few years."

Kyle laughed in frustration and disbelief. He shook his head and tried to think of an appropriate retort, but nothing came to mind. Sadly, he agreed with his tormentor. And the relationship with Olivia was going nowhere fast. "What else, Bennie? Can I have some friends? Can I visit my parents occasionally?"

"You won't have the time."

Kyle suddenly headed for the door, yanked it open, then slammed it as he left.

8

There is a student lounge on the first floor of the Yale Law School, and on the walls outside its door are posters and notices advertising internships and even careers in public-interest law. The students are encouraged to consider spending a few years helping battered women, neglected children, death row inmates, immigrants, runaway teens, indigent defendants, the homeless, asylum seekers, Haitian boat refugees, Americans sitting in foreign jails and foreigners sitting in American jails, First Amendment projects, innocence projects, conservation groups, environmental activists, and on and on.

A belief in public service runs deep at Yale Law. Admission is often determined by the applicant's record of volunteerism and his or her written thoughts about using a law degree to benefit the world. First-year students are inundated with the virtues of public-interest law and are expected to get involved as soon as possible.

And most do. Around 80 percent of all freshmen claim that they are attracted to the law by a desire to help others. At some point, though, usually about halfway through the second year, things begin to change. The big firms arrive on campus to interview and begin their selection process. They offer summer internships, with nice salaries and the prospect of ten weeks of fun and games in New York, Washington, or San Francisco. Most important, they hold the keys to the lucrative careers. A divide occurs at Yale Law, as it does at all prestigious schools. Many of those so enamored with righteous dreams of aiding the downtrodden suddenly switch gears and begin dreaming of making it to the major leagues of American law, while many are turned off by this seduction and cling to their idyllic notions of public service. The divide is clear, but civilized.

When an editor of the *Yale Law Journal* takes a low-paying job with legal services, he is a hero to those on his side and to most of the faculty. And when he suddenly caves in to Wall Street, he is viewed less favorably by the same people.

Kyle's life became miserable. His friends on the public-interest side were in disbelief. Those on the corporate side were too busy to care. His relationship with Olivia was reduced to sex once a week and only because they needed it. She said he had changed. He was moodier, gloomier, preoccupied with something, and whatever it was he couldn't tell her.

If you only knew, he thought.

She had accepted a summer internship with an anti-death-penalty group in Texas; thus she was full of zeal and big plans to change things down there. They saw less and less of each other but somehow managed to bicker more.

One of Kyle's favorite professors was an old radical who'd spent most of the 1960s marching for or against something, and he was still the first one to organize a petition against whatever he perceived to be the latest injustice on campus. When he heard the news that Kyle had flipped, he called and demanded lunch. Over enchiladas at a taco bar just off campus, they argued for an hour. Kyle pretended to resent the intrusion, but in his heart he knew he was wrong. The professor railed and hammered and got nowhere. He left Kyle with a disheartening "I'm very disappointed in you."

"Thanks," Kyle retorted, then cursed himself as he walked to campus. Then he cursed Bennie Wright and Elaine Keenan and Scully & Pershing and everything else in his life at that moment. He was mumbling and cursing a lot these days.

After a few rounds of ugly encounters with his friends, Kyle finally found the courage to go home.

THE MCAVOYS DRIFTED into eastern Pennsylvania in the late eighteenth century, along with thousands of other Scottish settlers. They farmed for a few generations, then moved on, down to Virginia, the Carolinas, and even farther south. Some stayed behind, including Kyle's grandfather, a Presbyterian minister who died before Kyle was born. Reverend McAvoy led several churches on the outskirts of Philadelphia before being transferred to York in 1960. His only son, John, finished high school there and returned home after college, Vietnam, and law school.

In 1975, John McAvoy quit his job as a lowly paid pencil pusher in a small real estate law firm in York. He marched across Market Street, rented a two-room "suite" in a converted row house, hung out his shingle, and declared himself ready to sue. Real estate law was too boring. John wanted conflict, courtrooms, drama, verdicts. Life in York was uneventful enough. He, an ex-Marine, was looking for a fight.

He worked very hard and treated everyone fairly. Clients were free to call him at home, and he would meet them on Sunday afternoons if necessary. He made house calls, hospital calls, jail calls. He called himself a street lawyer, an advocate for clients who worked in factories, who got injured or discriminated against, or who ran afoul of the law. His clients were not banks or insurance companies or real estate agencies or corporations. His clients were not billed by the hour. Often, they were not billed at all. Fees were sometimes delivered in the form of firewood, eggs and poultry, steaks, and free labor around the house. The office grew, sprawled upstairs and down, and John eventually bought the row house. Younger lawyers came and went, none staying more than three years. Mr. McAvoy was demanding of his associates. He was kinder to his secretaries. One, a young divorcée named Patty, married the boss after a two-month courtship and was soon pregnant.

The Law Offices of John L. McAvoy had no specialty, other than representing low-paying clients. Anyone could walk in, with an appointment or without, and see John as soon as he was available. He handled wills and estates, divorces, injuries, petty criminal cases, and a hundred other matters that found their way to his office on Market Street. The traffic was constant, the doors opened early and closed late, and the reception area was seldom empty. Through sheer volume, and an innate Presbyterian frugality, the office covered its expenses and provided the McAvoy family with an income that was in the upper-middle class for York. Had he been greedier, or more selective, or even a bit firmer with his billing, John could have doubled his income and joined the country club. But he hated golf and didn't like the wealthier folks in town. More important, he viewed the practice of law as a calling, a mission to help the less fortunate.

Patty had twin girls in 1980. In 1983, Kyle was born, and before he started kindergarten, he was hanging around his father's office. After his parents divorced, he preferred the stability of the law office to the strains of joint custody, and each day after school he parked himself in a small room upstairs and finished his homework. At the age of ten he was running the copier, making coffee, and tidying up the small library. He was paid $1 an hour in cash. By the age of fifteen he had mastered legal research and could hammer out memos on basic subjects. During high school, when he wasn't playing basketball, he was at the office or in court with his father.

Kyle loved the law office. He chatted up the clients as they waited to see Mr. McAvoy. He flirted with the secretaries and pestered the associates. He cracked jokes when things were tense, especially when Mr. McAvoy was angry with a subordinate, and he pulled pranks on visiting lawyers. Every lawyer and every judge in York knew Kyle, and it was not unusual for him to slip into an empty courtroom, present a motion to a judge, argue its merits if necessary, then leave with a signed order. The court clerks treated him as if he were one of the lawyers.

Before college, he was always around the office at five on Tuesday afternoons when Mr. Randolph Weeks stopped by with a delivery of food—fruits and vegetables from his garden in the spring and summer and pork, poultry, or wild game in the fall and winter. Every Tuesday at 5:00 p.m. for at least the past ten years, Mr. Weeks came to pay a portion of his fee. No one knew exactly how much was owed or how much had been paid, but Mr. Weeks certainly felt as though he was still in debt to Mr. McAvoy. He had explained to Kyle many years earlier that his father, a great lawyer, had pulled a miracle and kept Mr. Weeks's oldest son out of prison.

And Kyle, though only a teenager, had been the unofficial lawyer for Miss Brily, a crazy old woman who'd been run out of every law office in York. She trudged the streets of the town with a wooden file cabinet on wheels, boxes of papers which she claimed proved clearly that her father, who had died at the age of ninety-six (and she still suspected foul play), was the rightful heir to a huge tract of rich coal deposits in eastern Pennsylvania. Kyle had read most of her "documents" and had quickly concluded that she was even nuttier than most lawyers suspected. But he engaged her and listened to her conspiracies. By then he was earning $4 an hour and worth every penny of it. His father often parked him in the reception area to screen those new clients who at first glance showed the potential to waste a lot of his time.

Except for the usual adolescent dreams of playing professional sports, Kyle always knew he would be a lawyer. He wasn't sure what kind of lawyer, or where he would practice, but by the time he left York for Duquesne, he doubted if he would return. John McAvoy doubted it, too, though, like any father, he often thought of the pride he would have if the firm name became McAvoy & McAvoy. He demanded hard work and excellent grades, but even he was a little surprised at Kyle's academic success in college and at Yale Law School. When Kyle began his interviews with the big corporate law firms, John had plenty to say on the matter.

KYLE HAD CALLED and told his father he would arrive in York late Friday afternoon. They had agreed on dinner. As usual, the office was busy at 5:30, when he arrived. Most law firms closed early on Friday, and most lawyers were either in bars or at the country club. John McAvoy worked late because many of his clients got paid at the end of the week, and a few stopped by to write small checks or see about their cases. Kyle had not been home in six weeks, since Christmas, and the office looked even shabbier. The carpet needed replacing. The bookshelves sagged even more. His father couldn't stop smoking; therefore smoking was permitted, and a thick haze floated near the ceiling late in the day.

Sybil, the ranking secretary, abruptly hung up the phone when Kyle walked through the door. She jumped to her feet, squealed, grabbed him, and thrust her gigantic breasts at him. They pecked on the cheeks and enjoyed the physical greeting. His father had handled at least two divorces for Sybil, and the current husband would soon be on the street. Kyle had heard the details during the Christmas break. The firm currently had three secretaries and two associates, and he went from room to room, downstairs first, then upstairs, where the young lawyers were kept, speaking to the employees as they packed their briefcases and purses and tidied up their desks. The boss might enjoy staying late on Fridays, but the rest of the firm was tired.

Kyle drank a diet soda in the coffee room and listened to the voices and sounds of the office as it wound down. The contrasts were startling. Here, in York, the firm was filled with co-workers who were friends who could be trusted. The pace was busy at times, but never frantic. The boss was a good guy, someone you would want as your lawyer. The clients had faces and names. The lawyers across the street were old pals. It was a different world from the hard streets of New York City.

Not for the first time he asked himself why he didn't tell his father everything. Just spill it all. Start with Elaine, her allegations, the cops and their questions. Five years earlier he had come within minutes of hustling home and asking his father for help. But then it passed, and then it went away, and John McAvoy was never burdened with the ugly episode. None of the four—Kyle, Joey Bernardo, Alan Strock, and Baxter Tate—had told their parents. The investigation ran out of steam before they were forced to.

If he told his father now, the first question would be, "Why didn't you tell me then?" And Kyle wasn't prepared to face it. Many tougher questions would follow, a regular cross-examination by a courtroom brawler who'd interrogated his son since he was an infant. It was much easier for Kyle to keep his secrets and hope for the best.

What he was about to tell his father was difficult enough.

After the last client left and Sybil said goodbye and locked the front door, father and son relaxed in the big office and talked about college basketball and hockey. Then family, the twin sisters first, as always, then Patty.

"Does your mother know you're in town?" John asked.

"No. I'll call her tomorrow. She's okay?"

"Nothing's changed. She's fine." Patty lived and worked in the loft of an old warehouse in York. It was a large space with lots of windows that provided the light she needed to pursue her painting. John paid the rent, utilities, and everything else she needed through a monthly stipend of $3,000. It wasn't alimony, and it certainly wasn't child support, but simply a gift he felt compelled to pass along for her upkeep because she could not support herself. If she had sold a painting or a sculpture in the past nineteen years, no one in the family knew about it.

"I call her every Tuesday night," Kyle said.

"I know you do."

Patty had no use for computers or cell phones. She was severely bipolar, and the mood swings were, at times, astonishing. John still loved her and had never remarried, though he'd enjoyed a few girlfriends. Patty had been through at least two ruinous affairs, both with fellow artists, much younger men, and John had been there to pick up the pieces. Their relationship was complicated, to say the least.

"So how's school?" John asked.

"Downhill. I graduate in three months."

"That's hard to believe."

Kyle swallowed hard and decided to get it over with. "I've changed my mind about employment. I'm going to Wall Street. Scully & Pershing."

John slowly lit another cigarette. He was sixty-two, thick but not fat, with a head full of wavy gray hair that began no more than three inches above his eyebrows. Kyle, at twenty-five, had lost more hair than his father.

John took a long drag from his Winston and studied his son from behind wire-rimmed reading glasses perched on his nose. "Any particular reason?"

The list of reasons had been memorized, but Kyle knew they would sound flat regardless of how smoothly they were delivered. "The legal services gig is a waste of time. I'll end up on Wall Street eventually, so why not get the career started?"

"I don't believe this."

"I know, I know. It's an about-face."

"It's a sellout. There's nothing that requires you to pursue a career in a corporate firm."

"It's the big leagues, Dad."

"In terms of what? Money?"

"That's a start."

"No way. There are trial lawyers who make ten times more each year than the biggest partners in New York."

"Yes, and for every big trial lawyer there are five thousand starving sole practitioners. On the average, the money is much better in a big firm."

"You'll hate every minute of a big firm."

"Maybe not."

"Of course you will. You grew up here, around people and real clients. You won't see a client for ten years in New York."

"It's a nice firm, Dad. One of the best."

John yanked a pen from his pocket. "Let me write this down, so a year from now I can read it back to you."

"Go ahead. I said, 'It's a nice firm. One of the best.' "

John took notes and said, "You're gonna hate this firm and its lawyers and cases, and you'll probably even hate the secretaries and the other rookie associates. You're gonna hate the grind, the routine, the sheer drudgery of all the mindless crap they dump on you. Response?"

"I disagree."

"Great," John said, still writing. Then he pulled on the cigarette and blew out an impressive cloud of smoke. He put down the pen. "I thought you wanted to try something different and help people in the process. Did I not hear these words from you just a few weeks ago?"

"I've changed my mind."

"Well, change it back. It's not too late."

"No."

"But why? There must be a reason."

"I just don't want to spend three years in rural Virginia trying to learn enough Spanish so I can listen to the problems of people who are here illegally in the first place."

"I'm sorry, but that sounds like a great way to spend the next three years. I don't buy it. Give me another reason." With that, John shoved his leather swivel chair back and jumped to his feet. Kyle had seen this a million times. His father preferred to pace and toss his hands about when he was agitated and firing questions. It was an old habit from the courtroom, and it was not unexpected.

"I'd like to make some money."

"For what? To buy things, some new toys? You won't have the time to play with them."

"I plan to save—"

"Of course you will. Living in Manhattan is so cheap you'll save a fortune." He was walking in front of his Ego Wall, framed certificates and photos almost to the ceiling. "I don't buy it, and I don't like it." His cheeks were turning colors. The Scottish temper was warming up.

Speak softly, Kyle reminded himself. A sharp word or two would make things much worse. He would survive this little clash, as he had survived the others, and one day soon all the harsh words would be over and Kyle would be off to New York.

"It's all about the money, isn't it, Kyle?" John said. "You were raised better."

"I'm not here to be insulted, Dad. I've made my decision. I ask you to respect it. A lot of fathers would be thrilled with such a job."

John McAvoy stopped pacing and stopped smoking, and he looked across his office at the handsome face of his only son, a twenty-five-year-old who was quite mature and unbelievably bright, and he decided to back off. The decision was made. He'd said enough.

Any more and he might say too much. "Okay," he said. "Okay. It's all you. You're smart enough to know what you want, but I'm your father and I'll have some opinions about your next big decision, and the next. That's what I'm here for. If you screw up again, I'll damned sure let you know it."

"I'm not screwing up, Dad."

"I will not bicker."

"Can we go to dinner? I'm starving."

"I need a drink."

THEY RODE TOGETHER to Victor's Italian Restaurant, John's Friday night ritual for as long as Kyle could remember. John had his usual end-of-the-week martini. Kyle had his standard drink—club soda with a twist of lime. They ordered pasta with meatballs, and after the second martini John began to mellow. Having his son at the largest and most prestigious law firm in the country did have a nice ring to it.

But he was still puzzled by the abrupt change in plans.

If you only knew, Kyle kept saying to himself. And he ached because he couldn't tell his father the truth.

9

Kyle was relieved when his mother did not answer the phone. He waited until almost eleven on Saturday morning before calling. He left a pleasant little message about popping in for a quick hello as he was passing through York for some vague reason. She was either asleep or medicated, or if it was a good day, she was in her studio thoroughly absorbed in creating some of the most dreadful art never seen in a gallery or an exhibition. Visits with his mother were painful. She rarely left her loft, for any reason, so the suggestion that they meet for coffee or lunch was always dismissed. If the meds were in sync, she talked incessantly while forcing Kyle to admire her latest masterpieces. If the meds were out of order, she would lie on the sofa with her eyes closed, unbathed, unkempt, often inconsolable in her gloom and misery. She seldom asked about his life—college, law school, girlfriends, plans for the future. She was much too absorbed in her own sad little world. Kyle's twin sisters stayed far away from York.

He left the message on her recorder as he was hustling out of town and hoped she didn't return the call anytime soon. She did not; in fact, the call was never returned, which was not unusual. Four hours later he was in Pittsburgh. Joey Bernardo had tickets for the Penguins–Senators hockey game Saturday night. Three tickets, not two.

They met at Boomerang's, a favorite watering hole from their college days. After Kyle quit drinking (Joey did not), he avoided most bars. Driving to Pittsburgh, he had hoped for some quiet time with his old roommate, but it wasn't to be.

The third ticket was for Blair, Joey's soon-to-be-announced fiancée. By the time the three of them settled into a tight booth and ordered drinks, Joey was gushing with the news that they had just become engaged and were looking at wedding dates. Both were glowing with love and romance and seemed oblivious to everything else. They held hands, sat close, even giggled at each other, and after five minutes Kyle felt uncomfortable. What had happened to his friend? Where was the old Joey—the tough kid from South Pittsburgh, son of a fire captain, accomplished boxer, all-conference high school fullback, tremendous appetite for girls, a cynical, smart-ass wisecracker who believed women were disposable, the guy who'd vowed he wouldn't marry until he was at least forty?

Blair had turned him to mush. Kyle was astonished at the transformation.

They eventually tired of their wedding plans and potential honeymoon destinations, and the talk turned to careers. Blair, a chatterbox who began every sentence with either "I" or "me" or "my," worked for an advertising agency and spent far too much time detailing some of their latest marketing maneuvers. Joey hung on every word while Kyle began glancing at the clock behind them, high above a row of windows. As she prattled on, Kyle worked hard at maintaining enough eye contact to feign interest, but his mind drifted to the video.

"Is she awake?" Joey asks as Baxter has sex with a dangerously intoxicated Elaine Keenan.

"Blair travels to Montreal quite often," Joey said, then Blair ricocheted onto the subject of Montreal and its beauty. She was learning French!

Is she awake? Joey, sitting there with his hand under the table no doubt rubbing some flesh, had no earthly idea that such a video existed. When was the last time Joey even thought about the incident? Ever? Had he forgotten it completely? And what good would it do for Kyle to bring it up now?

After the Pittsburgh police quietly closed the file on Elaine and her rape, the brothers of Beta buried it, too. During his last two years of college, Kyle could not remember a single instance when the episode was discussed. Elaine disappeared and was quickly forgotten.

If Bennie Wright and his operatives had been snooping around Duquesne and Pittsburgh in recent weeks, Kyle wanted to know about it. Perhaps Joey might have seen or heard something. Perhaps not. Joey wasn't noticing much these days except for Blair.

"Have you talked to Baxter?" Joey asked when Blair finally stopped for air.

"Not in a month or so."

Joey was grinning as if a joke was on the way. "He finally got in a movie, you know."

"No kidding. He didn't tell me."

Blair giggled like a first grader because she undoubtedly knew the rest of the story.

"That's because he doesn't want you to know," Joey went on.

"Must be a great movie."

"Yep, he got drunk one night—and by the way, the drinking is now in no-man's-land—so he called and told me he'd made his debut. It was a cheap cable flick about a young girl who finds a human leg washed up on a beach, and for the rest of the movie she has nightmares about being chased by a one-legged killer."

"Where does the great Baxter Tate fit in?"

"Well, you have to watch real close or you'll miss him. There's a scene on a boat where the cops are gazing at the ocean, presumably looking for the rest of the body, though this is never clear. The movie has a lot of uncertainties. One of the deputies walks over to the sheriff and says, 'Sir, we're low on fuel.' That's our movie star."

"Baxter is a deputy?"

"And a bad one. He has only that one line and delivers it like a frightened sophomore in the school play."

"Was he sober?"

"Who knows, but I would say yes. If he'd been drunk, as usual, he would've nailed the line."

"I can't wait to see it."

"Don't, and don't tell him I mentioned it. He called the next morning, begging me not to watch it and threatening me if I told anyone. He's a mess."

And that reminded Blair of one of her friends who knew someone "out there" who landed a role in a new sitcom, and away she went. Kyle smiled and nodded as his brain switched compartments. Of the three roommates, Joey was the only one who could possibly help, if indeed help was possible. Baxter Tate was in dire need of intensive rehab. Alan Strock was thoroughly consumed with medical school at Ohio State and, of the four, was clearly the least likely to get involved.

For Joey, the stakes were high. He was on the tape, wondering aloud if Elaine was awake and conscious while Baxter did the deed, then Joey himself took a turn. He was currently handling accounts at a regional brokerage firm in Pittsburgh and had two promotions under his belt. He was goofy in love with Air Blair here, and any hint of an old rape charge would upset their perfect lives.

On the one hand, Kyle felt as though he was taking the fall for Joey. He hadn't touched Elaine that night, yet it was his life and career now getting hijacked by Bennie Wright and his dirty little video. Shouldn't Joey at least know about it?

And on the other hand, Kyle couldn't convince himself that he should drop the bomb on Joey at this point. If he, Kyle, took the Scully & Pershing job and met the demands of Bennie Wright, and didn't get caught, there was a decent chance the video would eventually be forgotten.

Hours later, during a break in the game, with Blair off in the ladies' room, Kyle suggested they meet Sunday for breakfast. He needed to leave town early, he said, and might it be possible to get together without Blair for an hour or so? Let her sleep in, maybe?

They met for bagels at a shop owned by a chain, a place that had not existed when Kyle was at Duquesne. Blair was still asleep somewhere, and Joey admitted to needing a break. "Sweet girl," Kyle said more than once, and each time felt guilty for lying. He could not imagine a life with such a windbag. She had great legs, though, the type Joey had always coveted.

They talked about New York for a long time—life in a big firm, the grind of the city, the sports teams, other friends who were there, and so on. Kyle eventually brought the conversation around to the old Beta gang, and they played catch-up for a while. They laughed at pranks and hazing and parties and stupid stunts pulled by themselves and others. They were twenty-five now, far removed from the craziness of their early college days, and the nostalgia was fun for a few minutes. Several times, the "Elaine thing" was at the surface, waiting for a comment or a question, but Joey did not mention it. It was forgotten.

When they said goodbye, Kyle was convinced Joey had buried the episode forever, and, more important, no one had brought it to his attention recently.

He drove north to Interstate 80, then headed east. New York

was not far away, neither in time nor in distance. A few more weeks in the cozy world of academia, then two months prepping for the bar exam, and in early September he would report for duty at the largest law firm in the world. There would be a hundred associates in his class, all bright kids from the finest schools, all polished and decked out in their newest clothes, all anxious to jump-start their brilliant legal careers.

Kyle felt lonelier each day.

BUT HE WASN'T exactly isolated, not even close. His movements to, in, and around York and Pittsburgh were closely monitored by Bennie Wright and his gang. A small magnetic transmitter, the size of a man's wallet, was tucked away under some mud and dirt in the rear bumper of Kyle's red Cherokee. It was hot-wired from the left taillight and emitted a constant GPS signal that kept track of the vehicle anywhere it went. From his office in lower Manhattan, Bennie knew precisely where the Jeep was located. He was not surprised by Kyle's visit home, but the trip to see Joey Bernardo was far more interesting.

Bennie had no shortage of gadgets—some high-tech, some low-tech, and all very effective because he tracked simple civilians and not real spies. Corporate espionage was far easier than that of the military or national security variety.

Kyle's cell phone had long since been compromised, and they listened to every conversation. The kid had yet to mention his predicament to anyone on the phone. They were also listening to Olivia's chatter, as well as that of Mitch, his roommate. So far, nothing.

They were reading Kyle's e-mails. He averaged twenty-seven a day, and almost all were law school related.

Other efforts to listen were far more difficult. An agent had eaten at Victor's in York, at a table twenty feet from Kyle and his father, but heard almost nothing. Another had managed to land a seat two rows away at the Penguins game, but it was a wasted effort. At Boomerang's, though, one of Bennie's stars, a twenty-six-year-old blonde in tight jeans, managed to secure the booth next to Kyle, Joey, and Blair. She sipped one beer for two hours, read a paperback, and reported that the girl talked nonstop, and about nothing.

Bennie was generally pleased with the progress. Kyle had abruptly declined the legal services job in Virginia. He had hustled over to New York and cleared things with Scully & Pershing. He was seeing less of Olivia, and it was obvious, at least to Bennie, that the relationship was going nowhere.

But the sudden trip to Pittsburgh was bothersome. Had he planned to confide in Joey? Had he in fact done so? Was Alan Strock next? Would Kyle attempt to contact him and/or Baxter Tate?

Bennie was listening in all the right places, and waiting. He had leased two thousand square feet of office space in a building across Broad Street and two blocks down from Scully & Pershing. The tenant's name was Fancher Group, a financial services start-up domiciled in Bermuda. Its registered agent in New York was Aaron Kurtz, also known as Bennie Wright, also known as a dozen other men, with perfect identification to prove any alias he chose. From his new perch, Bennie could glance out his window and gaze down Broad Street, and in a few short months he'd be able to actually see their boy Kyle enter and leave his place of employment.

10

The lawsuit was filed in federal court in the Southern District of New York, Manhattan Division, at ten minutes before five on a Friday afternoon, a time chosen so that the filing would attract as little attention as possible from the press. A "late Friday dump." The lawyer who signed it was a noted litigator named Wilson Rush, a senior partner with Scully & Pershing, and throughout the day he had telephoned the clerk to make sure it would be properly received and docketed before the court closed for the week. Like all cases, it was filed electronically. No one from the firm was required to walk into the Daniel Patrick Moynihan U.S. Courthouse on Pearl Street and hand over a thick pile of papers to commence the action. Of the forty or so civil lawsuits filed that day in the Southern District, it was by far the most serious, most complex, and most anticipated. The parties involved had been feuding for years, and while much of their bickering had been well reported, most of the issues were too sensitive to bare in public. The Pentagon, many senior members of Congress, and even the White House had worked diligently to prevent litigation, but all efforts had failed. The next battle in the war had begun, and no one expected a quick resolution. The parties and their lawyers would fight with bare knuckles for years as the dispute crept its way through the federal judiciary and eventually landed at the Supreme Court for a final ruling.

The clerk, upon receiving the complaint, quickly rerouted it to a secure bin to prevent its contents from being exposed. This procedure was extremely rare and had been ordered by the chief district judge. A bare-bones summary of the lawsuit was ready and available to the press. It had been prepared under the direction of Mr. Rush, and it, too, had been approved by the judge.

The plaintiff was Trylon Aeronautics, a well-known defense contractor based in New York, a privately held company that had been designing and building military aircraft for four decades. The defendant was Bartin Dynamics, a publicly held defense contractor based in Bethesda, Maryland. Bartin averaged about $15 billion a year in government contracts, a sum that represented 95 percent of its annual revenue. Bartin used different lawyers for its different needs, but for the biggest fights it was protected by the Wall Street firm of Agee, Poe & Epps.

Scully & Pershing currently had twenty-one hundred lawyers and claimed to be the largest firm in the world. Agee, Poe & Epps had two hundred fewer lawyers but boasted of more offices around the world; thus, it claimed to be the largest. Each firm spent far too much time jockeying with the other and boasting of its size, power, prestige, billings, partner profiles, and anything else that might jack up its rankings.

The core of the dispute was the latest Pentagon boondoggle to build the B-10 HyperSonic Bomber, a space-age aircraft that had been dreamed about for decades and was now closer to becoming a reality. Five years earlier, the Air Force had launched a contest among its top contractors to design the B-10, a sleek bomber that would replace the aging fleet of B-52s and B-22s and serve the military through the year 2060. Lockheed, the largest defense contractor, was the expected front-runner in the competition, but it was quickly outpaced by a joint venture put together by Trylon and Bartin. A consortium of foreign companies—British, French, and Israeli—had smaller roles in the joint venture.

The prize was enormous. The Air Force would pay the winner $10 billion up front to develop the advanced technologies and build a prototype, and then contract for the procurement of 250 to 450 B-10s over the next thirty years. At an estimated $800 billion, the contract would be the richest in the Pentagon's history. The anticipated cost overruns were beyond calculation.

The Trylon-Bartin design was astounding. Their B-10 could take off from a base in the United States with a payload the same size as a B-52, fly at seventy-six hundred miles per hour, or Mach 10, and deliver its payload on the other side of the world in an hour, at a speed and from an altitude that would defy all current and foreseen defensive measures. After delivery of whatever it happened to be hauling, the B-10 could return to its home base without refueling either in flight or on the ground. The aircraft would literally skip along the edge of the atmosphere. After ascending to an altitude of 130,000 feet, just outside the stratosphere, the B-10 would turn off its engines and float back to the surface of the atmosphere. Once there, its air-breathing engines would kick on and lift the plane back to 130,000 feet. This procedure, a skipping motion much like that of a flat rock bouncing across still water, would be repeated until the aircraft arrived at its target. A bombing run that originated in Arizona and ended in Asia would require about thirty skips with the B-10 popping through the atmosphere once every ninety seconds. Because the engines would be used intermittently, significantly smaller amounts of fuel would be required. And, by leaving the atmosphere and venturing into cold space, the heat buildup would be dissipated.

After three years of intense and often frantic research and design, the Air Force announced that it had selected the Trylon-Bartin design. This was done with as little fanfare as possible since the dollar amounts were staggering, the country was fighting two wars, and the Pentagon decided it would not be wise to broadcast such an ambitious procurement plan. The Air Force tried its best to downplay the B-10 program, but it was a waste of time. As soon as the winner was announced, fighting erupted on all fronts.

Lockheed roared back with its senators and lobbyists and lawyers. Trylon and Bartin, historically fierce competitors, began sniping almost immediately. The prospect of that much money splintered any notion of cooperation. Each corralled its politicians and lobbyists and joined the fight for a bigger piece of the pork. The British, French, and Israelis eased to the sidelines but certainly did not go away.

Both Trylon and Bartin claimed ownership of the design and the technologies. Efforts to mediate succeeded, then failed. Lockheed loomed in the background, waiting. The Pentagon threatened to yank the contract and have another contest. Congressmen held hearings. Governors wanted jobs and economic development. Journalists wrote long pieces in magazines. Waste and watchdog groups railed against the B-10 as if it were a shuttle to Mars.

And the lawyers quietly prepared for litigation.

TWO HOURS AFTER the lawsuit was filed, Kyle saw it posted on the federal court's Web site. He was at his desk in his office at the *Yale Law Journal*, editing a lengthy article on his computer. For three weeks now he had been checking the filings in all the federal courts in New York, as well as the state courts. During their first wretched session, Bennie had mentioned the upcoming filing of a massive lawsuit in New York, the one that Kyle was now expected to infiltrate. In meetings since then, Kyle had repeatedly prodded Bennie for information about the lawsuit, but each inquiry had been met with a dismissive "We'll talk about it later."

Oddly, the online posting of the lawsuit revealed nothing but its title and the name, address, law firm, and bar certification number of Wilson Rush. The word "SECURE" was inserted after the title, and Kyle was unable to access the contents of the complaint. In the Southern District of New York, no other case filed in the past three weeks had been locked away in such a manner.

Red flags began to wave.

He searched Agee, Poe & Epps and studied their exhaustive list of corporate clients. The firm had represented Bartin Dynamics since the 1980s.

Kyle forgot about the law journal work piled on his desk and around his chair, and lost himself on the Internet. A search of Trylon soon revealed its B-10 HyperSonic Bomber project and all the problems it had caused, and, evidently, was still creating.

Kyle closed the door of his small office and checked the printer for paper. It was almost eight on Friday night, and though the law journal types were known for their odd hours, the crew had cleared out for spring break. He printed all available corporate info on Trylon and Bartin, then added more paper. There were several dozen newspaper and magazine articles on the B-10 fiasco. He printed them all and began reading the most serious ones.

He found a hundred defense and military Web sites, and on one for futuristic warfare there were pages of background on the B-10. He checked prior court filings to see how often Scully & Pershing had sued on behalf of or defended Trylon, and did the same for Agee, Poe & Epps and Bartin. On into the night he dug and dug, and the thicker his file became, the worse he felt.

There was a chance he was chasing the wrong lawsuit. He couldn't know for sure until Bennie confirmed it. But there was little doubt. The timing was on schedule. The law firms were in place. Billions were at stake, just as Bennie had said. Two corporations that were old competitors. Two law firms that hated each other.

Military secrets. Stolen technology. Corporate espionage. Foreign intelligence. Threats of litigation and even criminal prosecution. It was one monumental, sordid mess, and now he, Kyle McAvoy, was expected to insert himself into the fray.

In recent weeks, he had often speculated about what type of case was worth the high cost of such elaborate espionage. Two corporate rivals fighting over a pot of gold could describe any number of disputes. Perhaps it was an antitrust case, or a patent dispute, or a couple of drug companies brawling over the latest obesity pill. The worst-case scenario was the one he had just been handed—a gold-plated Pentagon procurement program complete with secret technologies, warring politicians, ruthless executives, and so on. The list was long and disheartening.

Why couldn't he just go back to York and practice law with his father?

At 1:00 a.m., he stuffed his notebooks into his backpack and for a few seconds went through the fruitless ritual of straightening his desk. He looked around, turned off the light, locked his door, and again realized that any decent operative could intrude whenever he wanted. He felt certain Bennie and his thugs had been there, probably with bugs and wires and mikes and other crap that Kyle tried not to think about.

And he was sure they were watching. In spite of his demands that Bennie leave him alone, Kyle knew they were following him. He'd seen them several times. They were good, but they had made a few mistakes. The challenge, he told himself repeatedly, was to act as though he had no clue that they were watching. Just play the role of a naive, unconcerned college kid hauling a backpack around campus and looking at girls. He never changed his routines, or his routes, or parking lots. Same spot for lunch almost every day. Same coffee shop where he met Olivia occasionally after class. He was either at the law school or at his apartment, with few diversions along the way. And because his habits remained the same, so did those of his shadows. They became lazy because he was such an easy target. Kyle, the innocent, lulled them to sleep, and when they nodded off, he caught them. One face he'd seen three times already, a young ruddy face with different eyeglasses and a mustache that came and went.

At a used bookstore near the campus, Kyle began buying old paperback spy novels for a dollar each. He bought them one at a time, kept the current one in his backpack, and when he finished, he tossed it in the wastebasket at the law school and bought another.

He assumed that none of his communications were confidential. His cell phone and laptop were compromised, he was certain. He increased, slightly, his e-mails to Joey Bernardo, Alan Strock, and Baxter Tate, but all messages were quick howdies with almost no substance. He did the same for other Beta brothers, all under the guise of encouraging his buddies to do a better job of keeping in touch. He called each of them once a week and talked sports and school and careers.

If Bennie was in fact listening, he heard not one word to indicate Kyle was even remotely suspicious.

Kyle convinced himself that to survive the next seven years, he must learn to think and act like his adversaries. There was a way out. Somewhere.

BENNIE WAS BACK in town. They met for a sandwich on Saturday at a pita place north of town, away from campus. He had promised to drop in every other week or so throughout the spring, until Kyle graduated in May. Kyle had asked why this was necessary. Bennie had offered some meaningless blather about maintaining contact.

In each of their subsequent meetings, Bennie's personality had softened slightly. He would always be the no-nonsense hard-ass handler with a mission, but he was acting as though he wanted their time together to be somewhat pleasant. After all, they would spend hours together, he said, and this always evoked a frown from Kyle, who wanted no part of any pleasant chitchat.

"Any plans for spring break?" Bennie asked as they unwrapped their sandwiches.

"Work," Kyle said. The break had started the day before, and half of Yale was now somewhere in southern Florida.

"Come on. Your last spring break and you're not headed for the beach?"

"Nope. I'll be in New York next week looking for an apartment."

Bennie looked surprised and said, "We can help."

"We've had this conversation, Bennie. I don't need your help."

Both took enormous bites and chewed in silence. Finally, Kyle asked, "Any news on the lawsuit?"

A quick dismissive nod. Nothing.

"Has it been filed yet?" Kyle asked. "Why can't you tell me about it?"

Bennie cleared his throat and sipped his water. "Next week. Let's meet next week when you're in New York, and I'll walk you through the lawsuit."

"Can't wait."

Another hefty bite and they chewed for a while.

"When do you take the bar exam?" Bennie asked.

"July."

"Where?"

"New York. Somewhere in Manhattan. It's not something I'm looking forward to."

"You'll do fine. When do you get the results?"

Bennie knew the dates and places the exam was given in New York. He knew when the results were posted online. He knew what happened to young associates if they flunked the bar. He knew everything.

"Early November. Did you go to law school?"

A smile, almost a chuckle. "Oh, no. I've always tried to avoid lawyers. Sometimes, though, well, that's what the job requires."

Kyle listened carefully for the accent. It tended to come and go. He thought of the Israelis and their talent for languages, especially among the Mossad and the military.

Not for the first time, he wondered whom he would be spying for and against.

THEY MET five days later at the Ritz-Carlton in lower Manhattan. Kyle asked Bennie if he had an office in the city, or whether he did all of his work in hotel suites. There was no response. Before the meeting, Kyle had looked at four apartments, all in SoHo and Tribeca. The cheapest was $4,200 a month for an eight-hundred-square-foot walk-up, and the most expensive was $6,500 a month for a thousand square feet in a renovated warehouse. Whatever the rent, Kyle would be handling it himself because he did not want a roommate. His life would be complicated enough without the strains of living with someone else. And besides, Bennie did not like the idea of a roommate.

Bennie and company had followed Kyle and the broker around lower Manhattan and knew precisely where the apartments were located. By the time Kyle arrived at the hotel, operatives were calling the same realtor, inquiring about the apartments, and making plans to visit them. Kyle would indeed live where he chose, but the place would be infested by the time he moved in.

Bennie had some thick files on the small table in the suite. "The lawsuit was filed last Friday," he began, "in federal court here in Manhattan. The plaintiff is a company called Trylon Aeronautics. The defendant is a company called Bartin Dynamics."

Kyle absorbed this with no expression. His file on the case and the litigants now comprised three four-inch spiral notebooks, over two thousand pages, and was growing by the day. He was sure he didn't know as much as his pal Bennie here, but he already knew a hell of a lot.

And Bennie knew he knew. From his comfortable office on Broad Street, Bennie and his tech guys kept close tabs on Kyle's laptop and his desk computer in his office at the law journal. They monitored nonstop, and when Kyle opened his laptop in his apartment to send a note to a professor, Bennie knew it. When he was working and editing a case note, Bennie knew it. And when he was monitoring the court filings in New York and digging through the dirt on Trylon and Bartin, Bennie knew it.

Sit there and play dumb, son. I'll play along, too. You're smart as hell, but you're too stupid to realize you're in way over your head.

11

As springtime reluctantly arrived in New England, the campus came to life and shook off the lingering chill and gloom of winter. Plants bloomed, the grass showed some color, and as the days grew longer, the students found more reasons to stay outside. Frisbees flew by the hundreds. Long lunches and even picnics materialized when the sun was out. Professors became lazier; classes grew shorter.

For his last semester on campus, Kyle chose to ignore the festivities. He kept himself in his office, working feverishly to finish the details for the June edition of the *Yale Law Journal*. It would be his last and he wanted it to be his best. Work provided the perfect excuse to ignore virtually everyone else. Olivia finally got fed up, and they parted amicably. His friends, all of them third-year students and about to graduate, fell into two groups. The first concentrated on drinking and partying and trying to savor every last moment of life on campus before being evicted and sent into the real world. The second group was already thinking about their careers, studying for the bar exam, and looking for apartments in large cities. Kyle found it easy to avoid both.

On May 1, he sent a letter to Joey Bernardo that read:

Dear Joey: I graduate from law school on May 25. Any chance you could be here? Alan can't do it and I'm afraid to ask Baxter. It would be great fun to hang out for a couple of days. No girlfriend, please. Correspond by regular mail at this address. No e-mails, no phones. I'll explain later.

Best, Kyle

The letter was handwritten and mailed from the law journal office. A week later, the reply arrived:

Hey, Kyle: What's with the snail mail? Your handwriting really sucks. But it's probably better than mine. I'll be there for graduation, should be fun. What the hell is so secretive that we can't talk on the phone or use e-mail? Are you cracking up? Baxter is. He's gone. He'll be dead in a year if we don't do something. Oh, well, my hand is aching and I feel like such an old fart writing with ink. Can't wait to get your next sweet little note.

Love, Joey

Kyle's reply was longer and filled with details. Joey's response was just as sarcastic and filled with even more questions. Kyle threw it away as soon as he read it. They swapped letters once more, and the weekend was planned.

PATTY MCAVOY could not be coaxed from her loft for her son's graduation, not that any real effort was made. Indeed, both John

McAvoy and Kyle were pleased with her decision to stay at home, because her presence at Yale would complicate things. She had skipped the diploma service at Duquesne three years earlier just as she had skipped the commencements for both of her daughters. In short, Patty didn't do graduations, regardless of how important they might be. She had managed to attend both daughters' weddings, but had been unable to take part in the planning of either. John simply wrote the checks, and somehow the family survived both ordeals.

Joey Bernardo arrived in New Haven Saturday afternoon, the day before the law school's ceremonies, and, as directed by the written word carried by the U.S. Postal Service, he proceeded to a dark and cavernous pizza parlor called Santo's, a mile from campus. At precisely 3:00 p.m. on Saturday, May 24, he slid into a booth in the far-right corner of Santo's, and began to wait. He was amused and quite curious, and he was still wondering if his friend was losing his mind. One minute later, Kyle appeared from the back and sat across from him. They shook hands, then Kyle glanced at the front door, far away and to the right. The restaurant was almost empty, and Bruce Springsteen was rocking through the sound system.

"Start talking," Joey said, now only slightly amused.

"I'm being followed."

"You're cracking up. The pressure is getting to you."

"Shut up and listen."

A teenage waitress paused at the table just long enough to see if they wanted anything. Both asked for diet colas, and Kyle ordered a large pepperoni pizza.

"Wasn't really that hungry," Joey said when she was gone.

"We're in a pizza place, and so we need to order a pizza. Otherwise, we'll look suspicious. In a few minutes, a thug wearing faded jeans, a dark green rugby shirt, and a khaki golf cap will walk through the door, completely ignore us, and probably go to the bar. He'll hang around for less than ten minutes, then he'll leave. Though he'll never look at us, he'll see everything. When you leave, either he or one of his teammates will follow you and check your license plates, and within minutes they'll know that I had a semisecret meeting with my old pal Joey Bernardo."

"These guys are friends of yours?"

"No. They are professional operatives, but because I'm just me and not some highly trained thug myself, they're assuming that I have no clue that they're following me."

"Great. That clears things up. Why, old buddy, are they following you?"

"It's a very long story."

"You're not drinking again, are you? Not back on the smack?"

"I never did smack and you know it. No, I'm not drinking and I'm not losing my marbles. I'm dead serious and I need your help."

"You need a shrink, Kyle. You're spooky, man. There's a glow in your eyes."

The door opened and the thug walked in. He was dressed precisely as Kyle had said, but with the addition of a pair of round tortoiseshell eyeglasses. "Don't stare," Kyle whispered as Joey's jaw dropped. The diet colas arrived, and they took a drink.

The thug went to the bar, ordered a draft beer, and from his stool could see their table in the long mirrors behind the racks of booze, but he could not possibly hear what they were saying.

"He just put on the eyeglasses," Kyle said with a large smile as if they were telling jokes. "Sunglasses would be too conspicuous in here. He added the big round ones so he can look around and not get caught. Please smile. Please laugh. We're just two old chums reminiscing here. Nothing serious."

Joey was flabbergasted and could manage neither a smile nor a laugh. So Kyle erupted in a loud cackle, then pulled off a slice of thin pizza as soon as it arrived. He was animated and smiling, and with his mouth full he said, "Eat, Joey, and smile and please utter a few words."

"What have you done? Is that guy a cop or something?"

"Or something. I've done nothing wrong, but it's still a complicated story. You're involved in it. Let's talk about the Pirates."

"The Pirates are in last place, and they'll be in last place come September. Pick another subject, or another team." Joey finally took a slice and bit off half of it. "I need a beer. I can't eat pizza without a beer."

Kyle flagged down the lazy little waitress and ordered one beer.

There was a large screen in one corner. ESPN was running baseball highlights. For a few minutes, they ate pizza and watched the footage. The guy in the rugby shirt was working on a twelve-ounce draft, and after about ten minutes it was gone. He paid in cash and left. When the door closed behind him, Joey said, "What the hell is going on?"

"That's a conversation the two of us must have, but not here. It'll take an hour or two, and then the first conversation will lead to another and another. If we do it here this weekend, we'll get caught. The bad guys are watching, and if they see us engaged in serious talk, they'll know. It's important for us to finish the pizza, walk out the front door, and not be seen together alone, until you leave town tomorrow."

"Thanks for inviting me up."

"I didn't invite you for the graduation, Joey. Sorry about that. The reason you're here is to give you this." Kyle slid across a folded sheet of paper. "Put it in your pocket, and quick."

Joey grabbed it, glanced around as if assassins were moving in, and shoved it in a jeans pocket. "What is it, Kyle?"

"Trust me, Joey, please. I'm in trouble and I need help. There's no one else but you."

"And I'm involved, too?"

"Maybe. Let's finish the pizza and get out of here. Here's the plan. The Fourth of July is just around the corner. You come up with this wonderful idea for a rafting trip down the New River in West Virginia, three days on the river, two nights camping out. Me and you and some of the old gang from Duquesne. A boys' weekend while we can still do it. The list there has ten names and e-mails, stuff you already have. It also has the name of an outfitter in Beckley, West Virginia. I've done all the homework."

Joey nodded as if nothing made sense.

Kyle pressed on. "The purpose of the trip is to shake the surveillance. Once we're on the river and in the mountains, there's no way they can follow me. We can talk and talk and not have to worry about being watched."

"This is crazy. You're crazy."

"Shut up, Joey. I'm not crazy. I'm dead serious. They watch me around the clock. They listen to my phone calls, and they've bugged my laptop."

"And they're not cops?"

"No, they're much scarier than cops. If we spend too much time together now, they'll become suspicious, and your life will get complicated. Eat some pizza."

"I'm not hungry."

There was a long gap in the conversation. Kyle kept eating. Joey kept watching the ESPN highlights. Springsteen kept singing.

After a few minutes, Kyle said, "Look, we need to go. I have a lot to tell you, but I can't do it now. If you'll plan the rafting trip, we can have some fun and I'll give you the full story."

"You ever been rafting?"

"Sure. You?"

"No. I don't like the water."

"They provide life jackets. Come on, Joey, have some fun. A year from now you'll be married and your life will be over."

"Thanks, pal."

"It's just a boys' trip down the river, a bunch of old friends from college. Shoot the e-mails and put it all together. Whatta you say?"

"Sure, Kyle. Whatever."

"But when you e-mail me, use the diversion."

"The diversion?"

"Yes, it's written down. In your e-mails to me we're headed for the Potomac River in western Maryland. We can't give these thugs too much notice."

"What are they gonna do, follow us down the river in a speedboat?"

"No. It's just a precaution. I don't want them anywhere around me."

"This is real strange, Kyle."

"It gets stranger."

Joey suddenly slid the pizza aside and leaned forward on his elbows. He glared at Kyle and said, "I'll do it, but you gotta give me a clue."

"Elaine's back, with her rape scenario."

Just as quickly as he had leaned forward, Joey shrunk back to his side of the booth and limply recoiled. Elaine who? He'd forgotten her last name, if in fact he'd ever known it. That was five, maybe six years ago, and the cops had not only closed the file but slammed the damned thing shut. And why? Because nothing happened. There was no rape. Intercourse maybe, but with that girl everything was consensual. He had a December wedding planned with the woman of his dreams, and nothing, absolutely nothing could screw it up. He had a career, a future, a good name. How could this nightmare be alive?

With so much to say, he managed to say nothing. He stared at Kyle, who couldn't help but feel sorry for him.

Is she awake? Joey asks.

No response from Baxter Tate. No response from the girl.

"This is something we can deal with, Joey. It's frightening, but we can handle it. We need to talk, for hours, but not here, not now. Let's get away."

"Sure. Whatever you say."

THAT NIGHT, Kyle met his father for dinner at a Greek place called the Athenian. They were joined by Joey Bernardo, who'd had a few drinks in preparation for the evening and was so mellow he was quite dull. Or maybe he was just stunned or scared or something else, but he was certainly preoccupied. John McAvoy downed two martinis before he touched a menu and was soon telling war stories about old trials and old cases. Joey matched him martini for martini, and the gin thickened his tongue but did not lighten his mood.

Kyle had invited him because he did not want his father to launch into a last-ditch effort to persuade him to resist the evils of corporate law and do something productive with his life. But after the second martini, and with Joey barely coherent, John McAvoy made such an effort. Kyle chose not to argue. He ate garlic crackers and hummus and listened. Red wine arrived, and his father told another story about representing some poor soul with a good case but no money, and of course he won, as is true with the vast majority of lawyers' tales. John McAvoy was the hero of all of his stories. The poor were saved. The weak were protected.

Kyle almost missed his mother.

Late that night, long after dinner, Kyle walked the Yale campus for the last time as a student. He was stunned at the speed at which the last three years had gone by, yet he was also tired of law school. He was tired of lectures and classrooms and exams and the meager existence on a student's budget. At twenty-five, he was now a fully grown man, nicely educated and all in one piece with no bad habits, no permanent damage.

At this point, the future should hold great promise and excitement.

Instead, he felt nothing but fear and apprehension. Seven years of school, great success as a student, and it was all coming down to this—the miserable life of an unwilling spy.

12

Of the two apartments Kyle was considering, Bennie preferred the one in the old meatpacking district, near the Gansevoort Hotel, in a building that was 120 years old and had been built for the sole purpose of slaughtering hogs and cows. But the carnage was now history, and the developer had done a splendid job of gutting the place and renovating it into a collection of boutiques on the first floor, hip offices on the second, and modern apartments from there upward. Bennie cared nothing about being hip or modern, and could not have cared less about the location. What impressed him was the fact that the apartment directly above 5D was also available as a sublet. Bennie grabbed it, 6D, at $5,200 a month for six months, then he waited for Kyle to lease 5D.

Kyle, though, was leaning toward a second-story walk-up on Beekman Street, near City Hall and the Brooklyn Bridge. It was smaller and cheaper at $3,800, still an obscene amount for the square footage. In New Haven, Kyle had been splitting $1,000 a month for a dump, but one that was three times as large as anything he'd seen in Manhattan.

Scully & Pershing had paid him a signing bonus of $25,000, and he was thinking of using it to secure a nice apartment early in the summer when more were available. He would lock himself away in his new digs, study nonstop for six weeks, and take the New York bar exam in late July.

When it became obvious to Bennie that Kyle was ready to lease the Beekman apartment, he arranged for one of his operatives to suddenly appear, badger the real estate agent, and offer more money. It worked, and Kyle was headed for the meatpacking district. When he verbally agreed to take 5D, for $5,100 a month for a year, beginning on June 15, Bennie dispatched a team of technicians to "decorate" the place two weeks before Kyle was scheduled to move in. Listening devices were planted in the walls of every room. The telephone and Internet lines were tapped and wired to receivers in computers located directly above in 6D. Four hidden cameras were installed—one each in the den, the kitchen, and the two bedrooms. Each could be withdrawn immediately in the event Kyle or someone else started poking around. They, too, were connected to computers in 6D, so Bennie and his boys could watch Kyle do everything except shower, shave, brush his teeth, and use the toilet. Some things should be kept private.

On June 2, Kyle loaded everything he owned into his Jeep Cherokee and left Yale and New Haven. For a few miles, he went through the usual nostalgia of saying goodbye to his student days, but by the time he passed through Bridgeport, he was thinking about the bar exam and what was waiting beyond it. He drove to Manhattan where he planned to spend a few days with friends, then move into his apartment on the fifteenth. He had yet to sign a lease, and the real estate agent was becoming irritated. He was ignoring her phone calls.

As scheduled, on June 3 he took a cab to the Peninsula hotel in midtown and found Bennie Wright in a tenth-floor suite. His handler was dressed in customary drab attire—dark suit, white shirt, boring tie, black shoes—but on June 3 he had an additional article or two. His suit coat was off, and Bennie had strapped around his shirt a shiny black leather holster with a nine-millimeter Beretta snug just below his left armpit. A quick move with the right hand, and the pistol was in play. Kyle ran through all the sarcastic remarks he might make in the presence of such weaponry, but decided at the last second to simply ignore it. It was obvious that Bennie wanted his Beretta to be noticed, maybe even mentioned.

Just ignore it.

Kyle sat as he always sat with Bennie—right ankle on his left knee, arms folded across his chest, wearing a look of complete contempt.

"Congratulations on your graduation," Bennie said, sipping coffee from a paper cup and standing by the window that overlooked Fifth Avenue. "Did things go well?"

You were there, you asshole. Your boys watched me and Joey eat a pizza. You know what my father had for dinner and how many martinis he knocked back. You saw Joey stagger out of the Greek place drunk as a skunk. When they took my photo in cap and gown, your goons were probably snapping away, too.

"Swell," Kyle said.

"That's great. Have you found an apartment?"

"I think so."

"Where?"

"Why do you care? I thought we agreed that you would stay away from me."

"Just trying to be polite, Kyle, that's all."

"Why? It really pisses me off when we get together and you start this happy horseshit like we're a couple of old pals. I'm not here because I want to be. I'm not chitchatting with you because I choose to. I'd rather be anywhere else in the world right now. I'm here because you're blackmailing me. I despise you, okay. Don't ever forget that. And stop trying to be polite. It goes against your personality."

"Oh, I can be a prick."

"You are a prick!"

Bennie sipped his coffee and kept smiling. "Well, moving right along. May I ask when you take the bar exam?"

"No, because you know precisely when I take the bar exam. What am I here for, Bennie? What's the purpose of this meeting?"

"Just a friendly hello. Welcome to New York. Congrats on finishing law school. How's the family? That kind of stuff."

"I'm touched."

Bennie set down his coffee cup and picked up a thick notebook. He handed it to Kyle. "These are the latest filings in the Trylon-Bartin lawsuit. Motion to dismiss, supporting affidavits, supporting exhibits, briefs in support of, and briefs in opposition to. Order overruling said motion. Answer filed by the defendant, Bartin, and so on. As you know, the file is sealed, so what you're holding there is unauthorized."

"How'd you get it?" Kyle asked.

Bennie responded with the same silly smirk he always gave when Kyle asked a question that could not be answered. "When you're not studying for the bar exam, you can bone up on the lawsuit."

"A question. It seems to me that it's a long shot for Scully & Pershing to assign me to the litigation section that happens to be handling this case, and it's even more of a stretch to believe they would allow a green associate to get anywhere near it. I'm sure you've thought about this."

"And the question is . . . ?"

"What happens if I'm nowhere near this case?"

"Your class will have about a hundred rookie associates, same as last year and the year before. Roughly 10 percent will be assigned to litigation. The others will go into everything else—mergers, acquisitions, tax, antitrust, transactions, securities, finance, estates, and all the other wonderful services the firm provides. You'll be the star of the litigation rookies because you're the brightest and you'll work eighteen hours a day, seven days a week, and you'll suck up and kiss ass and backstab and do all the right things it takes to succeed in a big law firm. You'll want to work on this case, you'll demand it, and because it's the biggest lawsuit in the firm, you'll eventually be assigned to it."

"Sorry I asked."

"And while you're worming your way onto this case, you'll be providing us with other valuable information."

"Like what?"

"It's too early to discuss. Right now you need to concentrate on the bar exam."

"Bless you. I hadn't thought about it."

They sniped for another ten minutes, then Kyle left in a huff, as usual. From the backseat of a taxi, he called the realtor and said he'd changed his mind about living in the meatpacking district. The realtor was upset but managed to keep her cool. Kyle had signed nothing, and she had no legal ammo to launch. He promised to give her a call in a few days, and they would resume their search, for something smaller and cheaper.

Kyle moved his junk into a spare room in the SoHo apartment of Charles and Charles, two Yale Law grads who'd finished a year earlier and were now working for different mega-firms. They had played lacrosse at Hopkins, and were probably a couple, though they'd kept things quiet, at least at Yale. Kyle had no interest in their relationship. He needed a bed for a while and a place to store his possessions. And he needed to keep Bennie honest, if that was possible. The Charleses offered him their junk room for free, but Kyle insisted on paying $200 a week. The apartment would be a great place to study because the Charleses were seldom there. Both were being thrashed by hundred-hour workweeks.

WHEN IT BECAME clear that Bennie's operation had just been stiffed for six months' rent at $5,200 per, for apartment 6D in the slaughterhouse, plus the costly "decoration" of 5D below it, plus $4,100 a month for a year for the apartment on Beekman, Bennie fumed but did not panic. The wasted money was not a factor. What bothered him was the unpredictability of it. For the past four months, Kyle had done little to surprise them. The surveillance had been effortless. The trip to Pittsburgh in February had been dissected and no longer concerned them. But now Kyle was in the city, where watching him was more challenging. A civilian subject is usually easy because of predictable thoughts and patterns. Why would he try to shake surveillance if he didn't know it was there? But how much did Kyle know or suspect? How predictable was he?

Bennie licked his wounds for an hour, then began planning his next project—research on Charles and Charles and a quick inspection of their apartment.

THE SECOND detoxification of Baxter Tate began with a knock on his front door. Then another. He had not answered his cell phone. He had been driven home by a cab at four in the morning from a trendy nightclub in Beverly Hills. The driver helped him into his condo.

After the fourth knock, the door was quietly opened with no effort because Baxter hadn't bothered to lock it. The two men, specialists in retrieving wayward family members with addiction problems, found Baxter on his bed, still dressed in last night's getup—white linen shirt stained with some strain of liquor, black linen Zegna sport coat, bleached designer jeans, Bragano loafers, no socks over his very tanned ankles. He was comatose, breathing heavy but not snoring. Still alive but not for long, not at the rate he was going.

They quickly searched the bedroom and adjoining bathroom for weapons. Both men were armed, but their handguns were hidden under their jackets. Then they radioed to a waiting car, and another man entered the condo. He was Baxter's uncle, a man named Walter Tate. Uncle Wally, brother to Baxter's father, the only one of five siblings who had accomplished anything in life. The family banking fortune was now three generations old and declining at a steady, but not alarming, rate. The last time Walter had seen his nephew he was in a lawyer's office in Pittsburgh cleaning up after another drunk-driving episode.

Because his four siblings were unable to make even the most basic decisions in life, Walter had long since assumed the role of the family boss. He watched the investments, met with the lawyers, handled the press when necessary, and reluctantly intervened when one of his nieces or nephews flamed out. His own son had been killed hang gliding.

This was his second intervention with Baxter, and it would be the last. The first had been two years earlier, also in L.A., and they had shipped the boy off to a ranch in Montana where he sobered up, rode horses, made new friends, saw the light. Sobriety lasted all of two weeks after he returned to his worthless career in Hollywood. Walter's limit was two rehabs. After that, they could kill themselves for all he cared.

Baxter had been dead to the world for about nine hours when Uncle Wally shook his leg long enough and hard enough to rouse him from his drunkenness. The sight of three strange men standing by his bed startled him. He backed away from them, scrambling to the other end of the bed, then he recognized Uncle Wally. He'd lost some hair, put on a few pounds. How long had it been? The family never got together; in fact, the family strove mightily to avoid one another.

Baxter rubbed his eyes, then his temples. A skull-cracking headache arrived suddenly. He looked at Uncle Wally, then at the two strangers. "Well, well," he said. "How's Aunt Rochelle?"

Rochelle had been the first of Walter's wives, but she was the only one Baxter ever remembered. She had terrified him as a child, and he would always despise her.

"She died last year," Walter said.

"That's just awful. What brings you to L.A.?" He kicked off his loafers and wrapped his arms around a pillow. It was now obvious where this was going.

"We're taking a trip, Baxter. The four of us. We're gonna check you into another clinic, sober you up, then see if they can put you back together."

"So this is an intervention?"

"Yes."

"Groovy. Happens all the time out here. It's a miracle a single movie ever gets made with all the damned intervening that goes on in Hollywood. Everybody's always getting asked to help with an intervention. I mean, look, you're not going to believe this, but two months ago I took part in an intervention. A link, that's what I was called, but I guess you guys know all about that. Can you imagine? I'm sitting in a hotel room with these other links, some I know, some I don't, and poor Jimmy walks in, beer in hand, and gets absolutely ambushed. His brother sits him down, then we go around the room and tell the poor boy what a miserable piece of shit he is. Made him cry, but then they always cry, don't they? I cried, didn't I? Now I remember. You should've heard me lecturing Jimmy about the evils of vodka and cocaine. If he hadn't been crying so hard, he would've come after me. Could I have a glass of water? Who are you?"

"They're with me," Uncle Wally said.

"I figured."

One of the specialists handed Baxter a bottle of water. He drained it in one long, noisy slurp with water splashing down his chin. "Got any painkillers?" he said desperately. They handed over some pills and another bottle of water. When he had consumed it all, he said, "Where we going this time?"

"Nevada. There's a clinic near Reno, in the mountains, spectacular country."

"It's not a dude ranch, is it? I can't take another thirty days on a horse. My ass is still raw from the last detox."

Uncle Wally was still standing at the foot of the bed. He had not moved a step. "No horses this time. It's a different kind of place."

"Oh, really. I hear they're all the same. Folks here are always talking about their latest rehab. Always comparing notes. Great way to pick up girls in a bar." He spoke with his eyes closed tightly as the pain rippled through his head.

"No, this is different."

"How so?"

"It's a bit tougher, and you'll be there longer."

"Do tell. How long?"

"As long as it takes."

"Can I just promise to stop drinking right now and skip the whole damned thing?"

"No."

"And I'm assuming that since you're here and since you're the big chief of this sorry little tribe my participation is not exactly voluntary?"

"Right."

"Because if I say go to hell, get out of my house, I'm calling the police because the three of you broke in, and that there's no way I'm taking a trip with you—if I say all that, then you'll simply bring up the trust funds. Right?"

"Right."

The nausea hit like lightning. Baxter bolted from the bed, shedding his sport coat as he stumbled through the door to the bathroom. The vomiting was loud and long and mixed with waves of profanities. He washed his face, looked at his swollen red eyes in the mirror, and admitted that a few days of sobriety was not a bad idea. But he couldn't imagine a whole lifetime with no booze and no drugs.

The trust funds had been established by a great-grandfather who had no idea what he was doing. In the days before private jets and luxury yachts and cocaine and countless other ways to burn the family fortune, the prudent thing to do was to preserve the money for future generations. But Baxter's grandfather had seen the warning signs. He hired the lawyers and changed the trusts so that a board of advisers could exercise a measure of discretion. Some of the money arrived each month and allowed Baxter to survive quite comfortably without working. But the serious money could be turned off like a spigot, and Uncle Wally controlled it with an iron fist.

If Uncle Wally said you were going to rehab, then you were about to dry out.

Baxter stood in the bathroom door, leaning on the facing, and looked at the three. They had not budged. He looked at the specialist nearest to him and said, "You guys here to break my thumbs if I put up a fight?"

"No," came the reply.

"Let's go, Baxter," Walter said.

"Do I pack?"

"No."

"Your jet?"

"Yes."

"Last time I was allowed to get hammered."

"The clinic says you can drink all you want on the ride in. The bar is stocked."

"How long's the flight?"

"Ninety minutes."

"I'll have to drink fast."

"I'm sure you can handle that."

Baxter waved his arms and looked around his bedroom. "What about my place? The bills, the maid, the mail?"

"I'll take care of everything. Let's go."

Baxter brushed his teeth, combed his hair, changed his shirt, then followed Uncle Wally and the other two outside and into a black van. They rode in silence for a few minutes, but the tension was finally broken by the sounds of Baxter crying in the rear seat.

13

The bar review course was offered at Fordham University on Sixty-second Street, in a vast lecture hall that was filled with anxious former law students. From 9:30 until 1:30 each weekday, various professors from nearby law schools covered the intricacies of constitutional law, corporations, criminal law, property, evidence, contracts, and many other subjects. Since virtually every person in the room had just finished law school, the material was familiar and easily digested. But the volume was overwhelming. Three years of intense study would be reduced to a nightmare of an exam that ran for sixteen hours over a two-day period. Thirty percent of those taking it for the first time would not pass, and because of this there was little hesitation in forking over the $3,000 for the review course. Scully & Pershing picked up the bill for Kyle and its other new recruits.

The pressure was palpable the first time Kyle walked into the room at Fordham, and it never went away. By the third day he was sitting with a group of friends from Yale, and they soon formed a study group that met every afternoon and often worked into the night. During three years of law school, they had dreaded the day they would be forced to revisit the murky world of federal taxation or the tedium of the Uniform Commercial Code, but the day was at hand. The bar exam consumed them.

Scully & Pershing was typical in that it forgave the first flunking of the exam, but not the second. Two bad tests, and you're out. A few of the crueler firms had a one-strike policy, and there were a handful of more reasonable firms that would forgive twice if the associate was showing promise on all other fronts. Regardless, the fear of failure boiled just under the surface and often made it difficult to sleep.

Kyle found himself taking long walks around the city, at all hours, to break the monotony and clear his head. The walks were informative, and at times fascinating. He learned the streets, the subways, the bus system, the rules of the sidewalks. He knew which coffee shops stayed open all night and which bakeries had warm baguettes at 5:00 a.m. He found a wonderful old bookstore in the Village and resumed his rabid new interest in spy and espionage novels.

After three weeks in the city, he finally found a suitable apartment. At daybreak one morning, he was sitting on a stool in the window of a coffee shop on Seventh Avenue in Chelsea, sipping a double espresso and reading the *Times*, when he saw two men wrestle a sofa out of a door across the street. The men were obviously not professional movers, and they showed little patience with the sofa. They practically threw it into the back of a van, then disappeared through the door. A few minutes later they were back with a bulky leather chair that received the same treatment. The men were in a hurry, and the move did not appear to be a happy one. The door was next to a health food store, and two floors above it a sign in a window advertised an apartment available for a sublet. Kyle quickly crossed the street, stopped one of the men, then followed him upstairs for a look around. The apartment was one of four on the third floor. It had three small rooms and a narrow kitchen, and as he talked to the man, Steve somebody, he learned that Steve had the lease but was leaving town in a hurry. They shook hands on an eight-month sub at $2,500 per. That afternoon, they met again at the apartment to sign the paperwork and transfer the keys.

Kyle thanked Charles and Charles, reloaded his meager assets in his Jeep, and drove twenty minutes uptown to the corner of Seventh and West Twenty-sixth. His first purchase was a well-used bed and night table from a flea market. His second was a fifty-inch flat-screen television. There was no urgency in furnishing or decorating. Kyle doubted he would live there beyond the eight months and could not imagine having guests. It was an adequate place to start, then he would find something nicer.

Before leaving for West Virginia, he carefully set the traps. He cut several four-inch pieces of brown sewing thread, and with a dab of Vaseline stuck the threads to the bottoms of three interior doors. Standing and looking down, he could barely see the thread against the oak stain, but if anyone entered the apartment and opened the doors, they would leave a trail by displacing the threads. Along one wall in the den he had stacked textbooks, notebooks, files for this and that, generally useless stuff that he wasn't ready to part with. It was a haphazard pile, but Kyle arranged everything in careful order and photographed it all with a digital camera. Anyone looking through it would be tempted to toss things back into the collection, and if that happened, Kyle would know it. He informed his new neighbor, an elderly lady from Thailand, that he would be gone for four days and was not expecting any visitors. If she heard anything, call the cops. She agreed, but Kyle was not at all confident she understood a word he said.

His counterintelligence tactics were rudimentary, but the basics often worked just fine, according to the spy novels.

THE NEW RIVER runs through the Allegheny Mountains in southern West Virginia. It's fast in some places, slower in others, but on any stretch of it the scenery is beautiful. With Class IV rapids in some areas, it has long been a favorite of serious kayakers. And with miles and miles of slower water, it attracts thousands of rafters each year. Because of its popularity, there are several established outfitters. Kyle had found one near the town of Beckley.

They met there at a motel the first night. Joey, Kyle, and four other Beta brothers. They drank two cases of beer to celebrate the Fourth of July, and woke up with hangovers. Kyle, of course, stayed with diet soda and woke up pondering the mysteries of the bankruptcy code. One look at his five friends and he was proud of his sobriety.

Their guide was a rather rustic local named Clem, and Clem had a few rules for the twenty-four-foot rubber raft that was his livelihood. Helmets and life vests were mandatory. No smoking, period. No drinking was allowed in the "boat" while it was moving down the river. When it stopped, for lunch or for the night, they could drink all they wanted. Clem counted ten cases of beer and realized what he was facing. The first morning was uneventful. The sun was hot, and the crew was subdued, even suffering. By late afternoon, they were splashing water and began jumping in. By 5:00 p.m., they were parched, and Clem found a sandbar to settle into for the first night. After a couple of beers each, and one for Clem himself, they pitched four tents and set up camp. Clem cooked T-bones on a grill, and after dinner the crew ventured off to explore.

Kyle and Joey followed the river for half a mile, and when they were certain they could not be seen, they sat on a log with their feet in the backwater. "Let's have it," Joey said, cutting to the chase.

For weeks, even months, Kyle had struggled with the conversation they were about to have. He loathed the idea of upsetting his friend's life, but he had decided that he had no choice but to tell the story. All of it. He justified his decision by convincing himself that he would certainly want to know if things were reversed. If Joey had been the first to see the video and knew of its dangers, he, Kyle, would want to know. But the bigger reason, and one that made him feel selfish, was that Kyle needed help. He had worked on a rough draft of a plan, and it was more than he could handle himself, especially with Bennie lurking in the shadows. The plan could easily lead nowhere, and it could just as easily lead to something dangerous. It could be aborted at any time. It could also be rejected outright by Joey Bernardo. The first step involved Elaine Keenan.

Joey listened in rapt silence to Kyle's detailed replaying of the initial encounter with a man known as Bennie. He was sufficiently stunned by the existence of the video. He was thoroughly bewildered by the blackmail. He was terrified by the thought of some forgotten girl accusing him of rape and producing the evidence to back it up.

Kyle unloaded everything but the background on the lawsuit. He had not yet passed the bar and received a license to practice, but he had signed a contract with Scully & Pershing and felt an ethical obligation to protect firm business. This was silly in light of what he would be forced to do, but for the moment his career was unblemished and he felt rather ethical.

Joey's first reaction was a halfhearted attempt to deny any contact with Elaine, but Kyle waved him off. "You're on the video," Kyle said as sympathetically as possible. "You're having sex with a girl who's probably floating in and out of consciousness. In our apartment. Baxter goes first, then you. And I saw it on a twelve-inch laptop screen. If it's ever seen in court, it'll be on a big screen, a massive one. It'll be like sitting in the cinema with the images and sounds enhanced so that everybody there, especially the jurors, will have no doubt that it's you. I'm sorry, Joey, but you're there."

"Totally nude?"

"Not a stitch. Do you remember it?"

"It was five years ago, Kyle. I've worked hard to forget it."

"But you do remember?"

With great reluctance, Joey said, "Yeah, sure, but there was no rape. Hell, the sex was her idea."

"That's not real clear on the video."

"Well, the video is missing several important details. First, when the cops showed up that night, we scattered. Baxter and I ran next door and ducked into Thelo's apartment where there was a smaller and quieter party. Elaine was there, bombed as usual and having a good time. We hung around for a few minutes, waited for the cops to clear out, then Elaine tells me she wants to leave, wants to go back to our place for a "session," as she liked to call it. With Baxter and me. That's the way she was, Kyle, always on the prowl. She was the easiest lay at Duquesne. Everybody knew it. She was very cute and very easy."

"I remember well."

"I never saw a girl so promiscuous and so aggressive. That's why we were stunned when she cried rape."

"And it's why the police lost interest."

"Exactly. And there's something else, another little detail not on the video. The night before the party, you and Alan and some others went to a Pirates game, right?"

"Yes."

"Elaine was in the apartment, which was nothing new. And we had a three-way. Me, Baxter, and Elaine. Twenty-four hours later, same apartment, same guys, same everything, she passes out, wakes up, decides she was raped."

"I don't remember this."

"It was no big deal until she cried rape. Baxter and I talked about it and decided to keep it quiet because she might claim we raped her twice. So we buried it. When the police started squeezing us, we finally told them. That's when they packed up and went home. Case closed. No rape."

A small turtle stopped swimming by a log and seemed to stare at them. They stared back, and for a long time nothing was said.

"Do Baxter and Alan know about this?" Joey finally asked.

"No, not yet. It was hard enough telling you."

"Thanks for nothing."

"I'm sorry. I need a friend."

"To do what?"

"I don't know. Right now I just need someone to talk to."

"What do these guys want from you?"

"It's very simple. The scheme is to plant me as a spy in my law firm, where I can extract all sorts of secrets that the other side can use to win a big lawsuit."

"Simple enough. What happens if you get caught?"

"Disbarred, indicted, convicted, sentenced to five years in prison—state, not federal."

"Is that all?"

"Bankrupted, humiliated, it's a long list."

"You need more than friends."

The turtle crawled onto the sand and disappeared into the roots of a dead tree. "We'd better get back," Kyle said.

"We gotta talk some more. Let me think about this."

"We'll sneak away later."

They followed the river to the campsite. The sun had dropped below the mountains, and night was approaching quickly. Clem stoked the coals and added wood to the fire. The crew gathered around and opened beers, and the chatter began. Kyle asked if anyone had heard from Baxter. There was a rumor the family had locked him away in a high-security rehab unit, but this had not been confirmed. No one had heard from him in three weeks. They told Baxter stories for far too long.

Joey was notably quiet, obviously preoccupied. "You got girl trouble?" Clem asked at one point.

"Naw, just sleepy, that's all."

By 9:30 they were all sleepy. The beer and sun and red meat finally caught up with them. When Clem finished his third long joke in a row with a lame punch line, they were all ready for their sleeping bags. Kyle and Joey shared a tent, and as they were arranging two rather thin air mattresses, Clem yelled across the campsite, "Be sure and check for snakes." Then he laughed, and they assumed it was another attempt at humor. Ten minutes later they heard him snore. The sound of the river soon put them all to sleep.

At 3:20 a.m., Kyle checked his watch and saw the time. After three rough weeks of bar review, his nights were erratic. The fact that he was essentially sleeping on the ground didn't help matters.

"You awake?" Joey whispered.

"Yes. I assume you are too."

"I can't sleep. Let's go talk."

They quietly unzipped the front tent fly and eased away from the campsite. Kyle led with a flashlight, moving carefully, watching for snakes. The path led up to a rocky trail, and after a few minutes of tentative hiking they stopped near a huge boulder. Kyle turned off the flashlight, and their eyes began to focus in the darkness.

"One more time," Joey said. "Describe the video."

Since it was seared into Kyle's memory, he had no trouble replaying it—exact times, camera location, angle, the people involved, the arrival of the police, and the presence of Elaine Keenan. Joey absorbed it again without a word.

"Okay, Kyle," he said finally. "You've lived with this since February. You've had plenty of time to think. Right now I ain't thinking real clear. Tell me what we should do."

"The big decision has been made. I'm officially employed by Scully & Pershing, and at some point I'll get around to the dirty work. But there are two things I want to know. The first concerns Elaine. I know where she is, but I'd like to know who she is now. Is she capable of dragging this up again, or has she moved on? Does she have a life, or is she living in the past? According to Bennie, she has a lawyer and she still wants justice. Maybe so, maybe not, but I'd like to know the truth."

"Why?"

"Because Bennie is a liar by trade. If she's still angry, or if she's dreaming of squeezing money out of us, especially Baxter, it's important to know. It could impact what I do at the law firm."

"Where is she?"

"She lives in Scranton, but that's all I know. For about two thousand bucks we can hire a private investigator to do a background on her. I'll pay it, but I can't arrange it myself, because they're watching and listening."

"So you want me to do it?"

"Yes. But you have to be careful. No phones or e-mails. There's a reputable investigator in Pittsburgh, not too far from your office. I give you the cash, you give it to him, he does the snooping, gives us the report, and nobody will know about it."

"Then what?"

"I want to know who Bennie is and who he works for."

"Good luck."

"It's a long shot. He might work for an opposing law firm, or a client involved in a big lawsuit, or he might work for some intelligence operation, domestic or foreign. If I'm being forced to spy, I would like to know who I'm spying for."

"That's too dangerous."

"It's very dangerous, but it can be done."

"How?"

"I haven't got that far yet."

"Great. And I'm guessing that I'll be involved in this plan that has yet to be created."

"I need help, Joey. There's no one else."

"I got a better idea. Why don't you just go to the FBI and tell them everything? Tell them this creep is trying to blackmail you into stealing secrets from your law firm?"

"Oh, I've thought of that, believe me. I've spent hours upon hours walking through that scenario, but it's a bad idea. There's no doubt whatsoever that Bennie will use the video. He'll send a copy to the Pittsburgh police, a copy to Elaine, and a copy to her lawyer with clear instructions on how to use it to inflict as much misery as possible on me, you, Alan, and especially Baxter. He'll put it on the Internet. The video will become a big part of our lives. You want Blair to know about it?"

"No."

"This guy is ruthless, Joey. He's a professional, a corporate spy with an unlimited budget and plenty of manpower to do whatever he wants. He would watch us burn and have a good laugh, probably from someplace where the FBI can't touch him."

"A real prince. You'd better leave him alone."

"I'm not doing anything stupid. Look, Joey, there's an even chance that I can survive this. I'll do the dirty work for a few years, and when I'm no longer useful, Bennie will disappear. By then, I've violated every ethic in the book, and I've broken laws too numerous to mention, but I haven't been caught."

"That sounds awful."

And indeed it did. Kyle listened to his own words and was hit again by the folly of it all, and by the bleakness of his future.

They talked for two hours, until the sky began to change, and never once thought about returning to the tent. It was cooler on the ridge.

The old Joey would have jumped in with both feet, looking for a fight. This later version was much more cautious. He had a wedding to think about, a future with Blair. They had already bought a new condo together, and Joey, without the slightest trace of embarrassment, claimed that he was enjoying the decorating. Joey Bernardo, decorating?

Breakfast was scrambled eggs with hot sauce and bacon with onions. Clem cooked over the fire while his crew broke camp and loaded the raft. By eight o'clock, they were off, floating leisurely on the New River, headed nowhere in particular.

After a month in the city, Kyle savored the fresh air and open spaces. He envied Clem, a good ole boy from the mountains who earned little and needed even less. Clem had worked "these rivers" for twenty years and loved every minute of it. Such an uncomplicated life. Kyle would trade with him in an instant.

The thought of returning to New York made him ill. It was July 6. The bar exam was in three weeks. Scully & Pershing was two months away.

14

Tuesday morning, September 2, 8:00 sharp. A hundred and three nicely dressed and quite apprehensive new associates congregated on the law firm's forty-fourth-floor mezzanine for coffee and juice. After signing in and receiving name tags, they chatted nervously, introduced themselves, and looked for friendly faces. At 8:15 they began to file into the large meeting room, and on the way in each was handed a four-inch-thick notebook with the bold Scully & Pershing Gothic logo printed on the front. It was filled with the usual information—a history of the firm, a directory, pages and pages on firm policies, health insurance forms, and so on. In the "Diversity" section there was a breakdown of their class: Male, 71, Female, 32; Caucasian, 75, African-American, 13, Hispanic, 7, Asian, 5, Other, 3; Protestant, 58, Catholic, 22, Jewish, 9, Muslim, 2, Undeclared, 12. Each member had a small black-and-white photo with a one-paragraph bio. The Ivy League dominated, but there was fair representation from other top schools such as NYU, Georgetown, Stanford, Michigan, Texas, Chicago, North Carolina, Virginia, and Duke. There was no one from a second-tier school.

Kyle sat with a group from Yale and played with the numbers. Fourteen from Harvard, and though they were indistinguishable at the moment, it would not be long before the rest of the class knew who they were. Five from Yale. None from Princeton because Princeton had never established a law school. Nine from Columbia.

With 103 associates at a starting salary of $200,000, there was now more than $20 million in fresh legal talent sitting in the room. A lot of money, but over the next twelve months each would bill at least two thousand hours at $300–$400 an hour. The hours would vary, but it was safe to say that the rookie class would generate at least $75 million for the firm in the coming year. These numbers were not in the binder, but the math was easy.

Other numbers were missing, too. Of the 103, 15 percent would leave after the second year. Only 10 percent would survive and make partner in seven or eight years. The attrition was brutal, but Scully & Pershing did not care. There was an endless supply of disposable labor, even that of the Harvard and Yale variety.

At 8:30, several older men entered the room and sat in chairs along the narrow stage. The managing partner, Howard Meezer, stepped to the podium and began an elaborate welcoming speech, one he had no doubt memorized from years of use. After telling them how carefully they'd been chosen, he spent a few minutes touting the greatness of the firm. Then he outlined the rest of the week. The next two days would be spent in that room listening to various talks about all aspects of their new careers and life at good old Scully & Pershing. On Wednesday, they would spend a full day in computer and technology training. On Thursday, they would break down into smaller groups and begin brief orientations in specialized fields. The tedium was rapidly approaching.

The next speaker talked about compensation and benefits. Next was the firm's librarian, who spent a long hour on legal research. A psychologist talked about stress and pressure and in a nice way told them to remain single as long as possible. For those who were already married, the top ten law firms in New York currently had a 72 percent divorce rate among associates under the age of thirty. The monotony of the lectures was broken by the "tech team" when they handed out shiny new laptops for everyone. A lengthy tutorial followed. Once the laptops were warmed up, the next technical adviser handed out the dreaded FirmFone. It was similar to most of the current smartphones on the market, but it had been designed especially for the hardworking lawyers at Scully & Pershing—designed and built by a software and gadget company that the firm had taken public with great success a decade earlier. It came with contact and biographical information for every lawyer in the firm, in all thirty offices, plus every paralegal and secretary, almost five thousand people in New York alone. The database included detailed summaries of all S&P clients, a small library of the most commonly used research, recent state and federal appellate decisions, and a registry of all New York and New Jersey judges and court clerks. The phone was equipped with high-speed Internet access and a dizzying assortment of bells and whistles. It was valuable and invaluable, and if one was lost, stolen, or otherwise misplaced, bad things would happen to its owner. It was to be kept at hand twenty-four hours a day, seven days a week until further notice.

In other words, the fancy little FirmFone now controlled their lives. Mega-firm lore was replete with outrageous tales of cell phone and e-mail abuse.

There were snide comments and soft groans from the crowd, but nothing too loud. None of the class clowns wanted to get too cute.

Lunch was a quick buffet on the mezzanine. The afternoon

dragged on, but interest remained high. These were not boring law school lectures. These were important. The orientation ended at six, and as they hurried out, there was a lot of chatter about heading to the nearby bars.

ON WEDNESDAY, Kyle passed his first test. He and eleven others were assigned to the litigation practice group and led to a conference room on the thirty-first floor. They were greeted by Wilson Rush, the firm's leading litigator and attorney of record for Trylon Aeronautics in its case against Bartin Dynamics, though that lawsuit was not mentioned. Kyle had read so much background on Mr. Rush he felt as though he'd already met him. The great man told a few war stories, great trials from his illustrious career, then hurried away, no doubt off to sue another large corporation. More thick notebooks were passed out, and the next lecture was on the nuts and bolts of preparing lawsuits, responses, motions, and other filings that either pushed litigation along or tried to bog it down forever.

The first gunner appeared. There is at least one in every class, whether it's first-year contracts in law school or a group of fresh recruits on Wall Street. A gunner sits in the front row, asks complicated questions, sucks up to whoever happens to be at the podium, works every angle, cuts throats for better grades, stabs backs to make law review, interviews only at the top-rated firms regardless of how bad their reputations might be, and arrives at the firm with every intention of making partner before anyone else in his class. Gunners succeed magnificently; most make partner.

His name was Jeff Tabor, and they immediately knew where he was from because in the midst of his first question he managed to say, "Well, at Harvard, we were taught that not all known facts should be included in the initial lawsuit."

To which the fifth-year associate handling the lecture quickly retorted, "This ain't Kansas, Toto. It's our way or the highway." Everyone laughed but the gunner.

At 9:00 p.m. on Wednesday, the twelve new litigation associates met at a three-star restaurant in midtown for what was supposed to be a nice dinner with Doug Peckham, the partner who had supervised Kyle the previous summer. They waited in the bar and had a drink, and at 9:15 the first comment was made regarding Doug and his tardiness. All twelve had their FirmFones in their pockets. In fact, each had two phones. Kyle's old one was in the right pants pocket, the FirmFone was in the left. At 9:30, they began to debate the idea of calling Mr. Peckham, but decided against it. Then, at 9:40, he called Kyle with a quick apology. He'd been in trial, things had run late, and he was now back at the office tending to some urgent matter. The associates were to proceed with dinner and not worry about the bill.

The fact that a partner was working until 10:00 p.m. on a Wednesday night throttled the enthusiasm for a fine meal. It also set the tone of the conversation. As the wine flowed, they began telling the worst associate-abuse stories they'd heard. The contest was won by Tabor the Gunner, who when lubricated with alcohol was not the same asshole he'd been throughout the day. During a recruiting visit a year earlier, Tabor had dropped in on a friend he'd known in college. The friend was a second-year associate with another mega-firm and was perfectly miserable in his new profession. His office was tiny, and while they were chatting, Tabor's friend tried to shove a sleeping bag under his desk, out of view. Tabor, ever curious, had asked, "What's that for?" And as soon as he asked the question, he knew the answer. His friend sheepishly explained that he often found it necessary to catch a few hours of sleep during the night when he was overworked. Tabor pressed on and extracted the truth. The firm was a lousy place to work. Most of the rookies were on the same floor, and it was nicknamed "the Campsite."

ON THE NINETIETH day of Baxter's recovery at Washoe Retreat, Walter Tate entered the small conference room and shook hands with his nephew. Then he shook hands with Dr. Boone, Baxter's chief therapist. Walter had spoken with Boone several times by phone, but the two had not met.

Baxter was tanned, fit, and in relatively good spirits. He had gone ninety days with no booze or drugs, the longest stretch in at least ten years. Under the direction of Uncle Wally, he had reluctantly signed the paperwork that allowed the clinic to keep him locked away for up to six months. Now he was ready to leave. Uncle Wally, though, was not so sure.

The meeting belonged to Dr. Boone, and he went through a rather wordy summary of Baxter's progress. Once properly dried out, Baxter had proceeded nicely through the initial stages of therapy. He was aware of his problem. On day 23, he admitted he was an alcoholic and an abuser of drugs. However, he still would not admit to being physically addicted to cocaine, his favorite. At all times, he had been cooperative with his counselors, even helpful to other patients. He exercised strenuously each day and became fanatical about his diet. No coffee, tea, or sugar. In short, Baxter had been a model of good behavior. His rehab had been successful, so far.

"Is he ready to be released?" Uncle Wally asked.

Dr. Boone paused and stared at Baxter. "Are you?" he asked.

"Of course I am. I feel great. I'm enjoying the sober life."

"I've heard this before, Baxter," Walter said. "The last time you stayed clean for, what, two weeks?"

"Most addicts need more than one rehab," Dr. Boone added.

"That was different," Baxter said. "It was only thirty days, and I knew when I left that I'd start drinking again."

"You can't stay clean in L.A.," Walter said.

"I can stay clean anywhere."

"I doubt that."

"You doubt me?"

"Yes. I doubt you. You have a lot to prove, son."

Each took a breath and looked at Dr. Boone. It was time for judgment, for the sentencing, for a final word in this horribly expensive facility. "I want your frank opinion," Walter said.

Dr. Boone nodded, and without taking his eyes off Baxter, he began, "You're not ready. You're not ready, because you're not angry, Baxter. You must reach a point where you're angry at your old self, your old life, your addictions. You have to hate the way you were, and when this hatred and anger consumes you, then you'll have the determination not to go back there. I can see it in your eyes. You're not a believer. You'll go back to L.A., back to the same friends, and then parties, and then you'll take a drink. You'll tell yourself that one drink is okay. You can handle it, no problem. That's what happened before. You start with a couple of beers, then three or four, and then it spirals down. Booze at first, but the coke quickly follows. If you're lucky, you'll come back here and we'll try again. If you're unlucky, you'll kill yourself."

"I don't believe this," Baxter said.

"I've talked to the other counselors. We're all in agreement. If you leave now, there's a good chance you'll screw up again."

"There's no way."

"Then how much longer?" Walter asked.

"That depends on Baxter. We haven't broken through yet, because he's not angry at his old self." Dr. Boone's eyes met Baxter's. "You still have this fantasy of making it big in Hollywood. You want to be famous, a star, lots of girls, parties, magazine covers, big movies. Until you get that out of your system, you cannot stay clean."

"I'll find you a real job," Walter said.

"I don't want a real job."

"See what I mean?" Dr. Boone said, pouncing. "You're sitting here now, trying to talk your way out so you can hustle back to L.A. and take up where you left off. You're not the first Hollywood casualty I've seen, Baxter. I've been around the block a few times. If you go back there, you'll be at a party within a week."

"What if he goes somewhere else?" Walter asked.

"When he's finally discharged, we'll certainly recommend a new place of residence, away from his old friends. Of course there's booze everywhere, but it's the lifestyle that has to change."

"What about Pittsburgh?" Walter asked.

"Oh, hell no!" Baxter said. "My family's in Pittsburgh, and look at them. I'd rather die on skid row."

"Let's work here for another thirty days," Dr. Boone said. "Then we'll reevaluate."

At $1,500 a day, Walter had his limits. "What will you do for the next thirty days?" he asked.

"More intensive counseling. The longer Baxter stays here, the better his chances of success when he reenters."

" 'Reentry.' I love the term," Baxter said. "I can't believe you're doing this."

"Trust me, Baxter. We've spent hours together, and I know that you're not ready."

"I'm so ready. You don't know how ready I am."

"Trust me."

"All right then, let's meet again in thirty days," Walter said.

15

The orientation dragged on through Thursday and became as dull as most of the litigation files the new associates would soon be assigned to. On Friday, they finally got around to the issue that had been conspicuously ignored the entire week—office assignments. Real estate. There was little doubt that their space would be cramped, sparsely furnished, and hidden from view, and so the real question was, how bad will it be?

Litigation was concentrated on floors 32, 33, and 34, and somewhere in there, far away from the windows, were cubicles with the new names mounted on small plates and stuck to the movable walls. Kyle was shown to his on the thirty-third floor. His cube was divided into four equal shares by canvas partitions so that it was possible for him to sit at his desk, talk quietly on the phone, and use his laptop with some small measure of privacy. No one could actually see him; however, if Tabor to his right and Dr. Dale Armstrong to his left rolled their chairs back no more than two feet, then they could see Kyle and he could see them.

His desk had enough surface area for his laptop, a legal pad, the office phone, and not much else. A few shelves finished off the design scheme. He noted that there was barely enough room for a man to unroll his sleeping bag. By Friday afternoon, Kyle was already tired of the firm.

Dr. Dale was a female mathematics whiz who'd taught at the college level before deciding for some reason to become a lawyer. She was thirty, single, attractive, unsmiling, and frosty enough to be left alone. Tabor was the gunner from Harvard. The fourth member of their little cube was Tim Reynolds, a Penn man who'd been eyeing Dr. Dale since Wednesday. She did not seem at all interested. Among the torrent of firm policies and dos and don'ts that had been carped on all week, the one that rang loudest was a strict prohibition against interoffice romances. If a love affair blossomed, then one of the two had to go. If a casual affair was discovered, there would be punishment, though its exact nature was not spelled out in the handbook. There was already a hot rumor that a year earlier an unmarried associate had been fired while the married partner who'd been hounding her got sent to the office in Hong Kong.

A secretary was assigned to the four. Her name was Sandra, and she had been with the firm for eighteen long and stressful years. She had once made it to the major leagues as an executive secretary for a senior partner, but the pressure proved too much, and she had slowly been demoted down through the minors, all the way down to the rookie league, where she spent most of her time holding the hands of kids who were just students four months earlier.

Week one was finished. Kyle had not billed a single hour, though that would change come Monday. He found a cab and headed for the Mercer Hotel in SoHo. The traffic was slow, so he opened his briefcase and pulled out the FedEx envelope sent from a brokerage house in Pittsburgh. Joey's handwritten note read: "Here's the report. Not sure what it means. Drop me a line."

Kyle found it impossible to believe that Bennie could monitor the avalanche of mail in and out of Scully & Pershing every day—fifteen hundred lawyers cranking out paperwork because that's what they were supposed to do. The mail room was larger than a small-town post office. He and Joey had decided to play it safe with snail mail and overnight delivery.

The report had been prepared by a private security firm in Pittsburgh. It was eight pages long and cost $2,000. Its subject was Elaine Keenan, now age twenty-three, who currently lived in an apartment in Scranton, Pennsylvania, with another female. The first two pages covered her family, education, and employment history. She attended Duquesne for only one year, and a quick check of her birth date confirmed that she was not quite eighteen when the episode occurred. After Duquesne, she attended classes off and on at a couple of schools around Erie and Scranton, but had yet to finish her degree. During the previous spring semester she had taken some classes at the University of Scranton. She was a registered Democrat with two campaign stickers on the rear bumper of her 2004 Nissan, which was titled in her name. According to the available records, she did not own any real estate, firearms, or stock in foreign banks. There were two minor incidents with the law, both involving underage drinking and both handled expeditiously by the courts. The second scrape required counseling for alcohol and drug use. Her attorney had been a local female named Michelin Chiz, better known as Mike. This was notable since Elaine worked part-time in the law offices of Michelin Chiz & Associates. Ms. Mike Chiz had a reputation as a fierce divorce lawyer, always on the side of the wives, and always ready to castrate wayward husbands.

Elaine's full-time job was with the City of Scranton as an assistant director of parks and recreation. Salary, $24,000. She had been employed there for almost two years. Before that, she had bounced from one part-time job to another.

Her living arrangement was not clear. Her roommate was a

twenty-eight-year-old female who worked in a hospital, also took classes at a local college, had never been married, and had no criminal record. Elaine was observed off and on for thirty-six hours. After work the first day, she met her roommate in the parking lot near a bar favored by the alternative crowd. Upon meeting, the two roommates held hands briefly as they walked to the bar. Inside, they joined three other women at a table. Elaine had a diet soda, nothing stronger. She smoked skinny brown cigarettes. The women were very affectionate with each other, and, well, the obvious became more obvious.

Scranton had a women's shelter called Haven, and it advertised itself as a refuge and resource center for victims of domestic abuse and sexual assault. It was nonprofit, privately funded, and staffed by volunteers, many of whom claimed to have been victims.

Elaine Keenan was listed as a "counselor" on Haven's monthly newsletter. A female employee of the security firm used a pay phone in downtown Scranton, called Elaine at home, claimed to be the victim of a rape, and said she needed someone to talk to. She was afraid to come forward for all sorts of reasons. Someone at Haven had told her to call Elaine. They talked for almost thirty minutes, during which time Elaine admitted that she, too, was the victim of a rape and that the rapists (more than one) had never been brought to justice. She was eager to help, and they agreed to meet the following day at Haven's office. The entire conversation was recorded, and, of course, no meeting occurred the next day.

"Still the victim," Kyle mumbled to himself in the back of the cab. The night Kyle had sex with her, about a month before the alleged rape, he'd been in his own bed, sound asleep, when she crawled under the sheets naked and quickly got what she wanted.

The cab was at the Mercer. He returned the report to an inside pocket of his briefcase, paid the driver, and entered the hotel. Bennie was in a room on the fourth floor, waiting as usual with his customary purpose and appearing to have been there for hours. They did not exchange pleasantries.

"So how was the first week?" Bennie asked.

"Great. A lot of orientation. I got assigned to litigation," Kyle said as if he'd done something to be proud of. He had succeeded already.

"Very good news. Excellent. Any sign of the Trylon case?"

"No, we haven't been near a real case. We start work Monday. This week was just the warm-up."

"Of course. They give you a laptop?" Bennie asked.

"Yes."

"What kind?"

"I'm sure you already know."

"No, I do not. The technology changes every six months. I'd like to see it."

"I didn't bring it."

"Bring it next time."

"I'll think about it."

"What about a phone? A BlackBerry?"

"Something like that."

"I'd like to see it."

"I didn't bring it."

"But the firm requires you to keep it on at all times, is this not true?"

"True."

"Then why don't you have it?"

"For the same reason I didn't bring the laptop. Because you want to see them, and you're not going to see them until I'm ready. They are of no value to you at this point, and so the only reason you want them is to make sure I'm compromised, right, Bennie? As soon as I give something to you, then I've broken the law, violated the ethics, and you own me. I'm not stupid, Bennie. We're going slow here."

"We reached an agreement many months ago, Kyle. Have you forgotten? You have already agreed to break the law, violate the ethics, do whatever I want you to do. You will find the information and give it to me. And if I want something from the firm, then it's your job to get it. Now, I want the phone and I want the laptop."

"No. Not yet."

Bennie walked back to the window. After a long pause, he said, "Baxter Tate is in rehab, you know?"

"I know."

"For some time now."

"That's what I hear. Maybe he'll clean up and get a life."

Bennie turned and walked to within striking distance. "You need a reminder, Kyle, of who is in charge here. If you don't follow my orders, then I'll provide a little reminder. Right now I'm giving serious consideration to releasing the first half of the video. Plaster it around the Internet, notify all the folks who might find it interesting, have some fun with it."

Kyle shrugged. "It's just a bunch of drunk college kids."

"Right, no big deal. But do you really want it out there, Kyle, for the whole world to see? What would your new colleagues think at Scully & Pershing?"

"They'll probably think I was just another stupid drunk college kid, like many of them when they were younger."

"We'll see." Bennie picked up a thin file from the credenza, opened it, and pulled out a sheet of paper with a face on it. "You know this guy?" he asked, handing it to Kyle, who glanced at it and shook his head. No. White male, age thirty, coat and tie, at least from the shoulders up.

"Name's Gavin Meade, four years now at Scully & Pershing, litigation, one of about thirty associates toiling away on the case of Trylon versus Bartin. In the normal course of things you'd probably meet him in a few weeks, but Mr. Meade is about to be sacked."

Kyle was holding the sheet of paper, looking into the handsome face of Gavin Meade, and wondering what sin he'd committed.

"Seems he, too, has a little problem from the past," Bennie was saying, relishing the role of executioner. "Seems he, too, liked to get rough with the girls. Not rape, though."

"I didn't rape anybody and you know it."

"Maybe not."

"Got another video, Bennie? Been crawling through the gutter again, looking for someone else to ruin?"

"Nope, no video. Just some affidavits. Mr. Meade doesn't rape women; he just beats them. In college, ten years ago, he had a girlfriend who had a problem with bruises. One night he put her in the hospital. The police were finally invited in, things unraveled for Mr. Meade. He was arrested, jailed, formally charged, and facing trial. Then there was a settlement, money changed hands, the girl wanted no part of a trial, and everything was dropped. Meade walked away, but he's got this record now. No problem, he just lied about it. When he applied to law school at Michigan, he lied on his application. When he went through the background check at Scully, he lied again. Automatic termination."

"I'm so happy for you, Bennie. I know how much these little stories mean to you. Go get him. Ruin him. Attaboy."

"Everybody has secrets, Kyle. I can ruin anyone."

"You're the man." Kyle slammed the door and left the hotel.

AT NOON ON Saturday, three charter buses pulled away from the Scully & Pershing office building and left the city. They carried all 103 members of the first-year associate class. On board each bus was a full bar and plenty of snacks, and the drinking was fast and serious. Three hours later, they arrived at a yacht club in the Hamptons. The first party was under a tent near Montauk Beach. Dinner was under another tent on the hotel grounds. The second and last party was at the mansion of one of the Scully descendants. A reggae band played by the pool.

The "retreat" was designed to break the ice and make the recruits happy they'd come on board. Many of the firm's partners were there, and they got as drunk as the associates. The night went long, and the morning was not pleasant. After an early brunch, with gallons of coffee, they settled in a small ballroom to listen to the wise old men offer their secrets to a successful career. Several retired partners, legends at the firm, told war stories and cracked jokes and offered advice. The floor was open, and any question could be asked.

After the old goats were gone, a very diverse panel went to the front and continued with the storytelling. A black man, a white woman, a Hispanic, and a Korean—all partners—talked about the firm's commitment to tolerance and equal rights and so on.

Later in the day, they ate shrimp and oysters on a private beach, then the buses were reloaded and headed back to Manhattan. They arrived after dark, and the weary young lawyers headed home for a short night.

For them, the concept of exhaustion was about to be redefined.

16

Any hope of pursuing meaningful work was promptly crushed at 7:30 Monday morning when all twelve new litigation associates were sent into the abyss of Document Review. As far back as the first year of law school, Kyle had heard horror stories of bright and eager young associates being marched into some dreary basement, chained to a desk, and given a mountain of densely worded documents to read. And while he'd known that his first year would include a generous dose of this punishment, he simply wasn't prepared for it. He and Dale, who was looking better by the day but showing no signs of a personality, were assigned to a case involving a client that was being hammered in the financial press.

Their new boss for the day, a senior associate named Karleen, called them into her office and explained things. For the next few days they would review some crucial documents, billing at least eight hours a day at $300 an hour. That would be their rate until the bar results were made known in November, and, assuming they passed, their hourly rate would jump to $400.

There was no thought given to a quick word about what might happen if they did not pass the bar exam. Scully & Pershing associates posted a pass rate of 92 percent the previous year, and it was simply assumed that everyone had passed.

Eight hours was the minimum, at least for now, and with lunch and coffee thrown in, that meant, roughly, a ten-hour day. Start no later than 8:00 a.m., and nobody ever thought about leaving before 7:00 p.m.

In case they were curious, Karleen billed twenty-four hundred hours last year. She had been with the firm for five years and acted as though she were a lifer. A future partner. Kyle glanced around her well-appointed office and noticed a diploma from Columbia Law School. There was a photo of a younger Karleen on a horse, but none of her with a husband, boyfriend, or children.

She was explaining that there was a chance that a partner might need Kyle or Dale for a quick project, so be prepared. Document Review was certainly not glamorous, but it was the safety net for all new associates. "You can always go there and find work that can be billed," Karleen said. "Eight hours minimum, but there is no max."

How delightful, thought Kyle. If for some reason ten hours a day were not enough, the door to Document Review was always wide open for more.

Their first case involved a client with the slightly ludicrous name of Placid Mortgage—ludicrous in Kyle's opinion, but he kept his mouth shut as Karleen rattled off the more salient facts of the case. Starting in 2001, when a new wave of government regulators took over and adopted a less intrusive attitude, Placid and other huge home mortgage companies became aggressive in their pursuit of new loans. They advertised heavily, especially on the Internet, and convinced millions of lower- and middle-class Americans that they could indeed afford to buy homes that they actually could not afford. The bait was the old adjustable-rate mortgage, and in the hands of crooks like Placid it was adjusted in ways never before imagined. Placid sucked them in, went light on the paperwork, collected nice fees up front, then sold the crap in the secondary markets. The company was not holding the paper when the overheated real estate market finally crashed, home values plummeted, and foreclosures became rampant.

Karleen used much softer language in her summary, but Kyle had known for some time that his firm was representing Placid. He'd read a dozen stories about the mortgage meltdown and seen the name Scully & Pershing mentioned often, always in defense of Placid's latest setback.

Now the lawyers were trying to clean up the mess. Placid had been battered by lawsuits, but the worst one was a class action involving thirty-five thousand of its former borrowers. It had been filed in New York a year earlier.

Karleen led them to a long, dungeonlike room with no windows, a concrete floor, poor lighting, and neat stacks of white cardboard boxes with the words "Placid Mortgage" stamped on the end. It was the mountain Kyle had heard so much about. The boxes, as Karleen explained, contained the files of all thirty-five thousand plaintiffs. Each file had to be reviewed.

"You're not alone," Karleen said with a fake laugh, just as both Kyle and Dale were about to resign. "We have other associates and even some paralegals on this review." She opened a box, pulled out a file about an inch thick, and went through a quick summary of what the litigation team was looking for.

"Someday in court," she said gravely, "it will be crucial for our litigators to be able to tell the judge that we have examined *every* document in this case."

Kyle assumed it was also crucial for the firm to have clients who could pay through the nose for such useless work. He was suddenly dizzy with the realization that in just a few short minutes, he would punch in and begin charging $300 an hour for his time. He was worth nothing close to that. He wasn't even a lawyer.

Karleen left them there, her heels clicking on the polished concrete as she hustled out of the room. Kyle gawked at the boxes, then at Dale, who looked as stunned as he did. "You gotta be kidding," he said. But Dale was determined to prove something, so she grabbed a box, dropped it on the table, and yanked out some files. Kyle walked to the other end of the room, as far away as possible, and found himself some files.

He opened one and glanced at his watch—it was 7:50. Scully lawyers billed by tenths. A tenth of an hour is six minutes. Two-tenths is twelve, and so on. One point six hours is an hour and thirty-six minutes. Should he roll back the clock two minutes, to 7:48, and therefore be able to bill two-tenths before the hour of eight? Or should he stretch his arms, take a sip of coffee, get more situated, and wait until 7:54 to begin his first billable minute as a lawyer? It was a no-brainer. This was Wall Street, where everything was done with aggression. When in doubt, bill aggressively. If not, the next guy will, and then you won't catch him.

It took an hour to read every word in the file. One point two hours to be exact, and suddenly he had no reluctance in billing Placid for 1.2 hours, or $360 for the review. Not long ago, say about ninety minutes, he found it hard to believe he was worth $300 an hour. He hadn't even passed the bar! Now, though, he had been converted. Placid owed him the money because their sleaze had gotten them sued. Someone had to plow through their debris. He would aggressively bill the company out of revenge. Down the table, Dale worked diligently without any distraction.

Somewhere in the midst of the third file, Kyle paused long enough to ponder a few things. Still on the clock, he wondered where the Trylon-Bartin room was. Where were the highly classified documents, and how were they protected? What kind of vault were they stored in? This dungeon appeared to be security-free, but then who would spend money to protect a bunch of mortgage files gone bad? If Placid had dirty laundry, you could bet it wasn't buried where Kyle might find it.

He thought about his life. Here, in the third hour of his professional career, he was already questioning his sanity. What manner of man could sit here and pore over these meaningless pages for hours and days without going bonkers? What did he expect the life of a first-year associate to be? Would it be any better at another firm?

Dale left for ten minutes and returned. Probably a bathroom break. He bet she kept the meter running.

Lunch was in the firm cafeteria on the forty-third floor. Much had been made about the high quality of the food. Great chefs consulted, the freshest ingredients used, a dazzling menu of light dishes, and so on. They were free to leave the building and go to a restaurant, but few associates dared. The firm's policies were prominently published and distributed, but there were many unwritten rules; one was that the rookies ate in-house unless a client could be billed for a real lunch. Many of the partners used the cafeteria as well. It was important for them to be seen by their underlings, and to brag about the great food, and, most important, to eat in thirty minutes as an example of efficiency. The decor was art deco and nicely done, but the ambience was still reminiscent of a prison mess hall.

There was a clock on every wall, and you could almost hear them ticking.

Kyle and Dale joined Tim Reynolds at a small table near a vast window with a spectacular view of other tall buildings. Tim appeared to be shell-shocked—glazed eyes, vapid stare, weak voice. They swapped stories of the horrors of Document Review and began joking about their departures from the legal profession. The food was good, though lunch was not about eating. Lunch was now an excuse to get away from the documents.

But it didn't last long. They agreed to meet after work for a drink, Dale's first sign of life, then headed back to their respective dungeons. Two hours later, Kyle was hallucinating and flashing back to the glory days at Yale when he edited the prestigious law journal from his own office and managed dozens of other very bright students. His long hours led to a product, an important journal that was published eight times a year and read widely by lawyers and judges and scholars. His name was first on the masthead as editor in chief. Few students were so honored with such a title. For one year, he was the Man.

How had he fallen so fast and so hard?

It's just part of the boot camp, he kept telling himself. Basic training.

But what a waste! Placid, its shareholders, its creditors, and probably the American taxpayers would get stuck with the legal fees, fees being racked up in part by the now-halfhearted efforts of one Kyle McAvoy, who, after reviewing nine of the thirty-five thousand files, was convinced that his firm's client should be locked away in prison. The CEO, the managers, the board of directors—all of them. You can't jail a corporation, but an exception should be made for every employee who ever worked at Placid Mortgage.

What would John McAvoy think if he could see his son? Kyle laughed and shuddered at the thought. The verbal abuse would be funny and cruel, and at that moment Kyle would accept it without firing back. At that moment, his father was either in his office counseling a client through a problem or in a courtroom mixing it up with another lawyer. Regardless, he was with real people in real conversations, and life was anything but dull.

Dale was seated fifty feet away with her back to him. It was a nice back, as far as he could tell, trim and curvy. He could see nothing else at the moment but had already examined the other parts—slim legs, narrow waist, not much of a chest, but then you can't have everything. What would happen, he reckoned, if (1) he slowly, over the next few days and weeks, put the move on her, (2) he was successful, and (3) he made sure they got caught? He'd be bounced from the firm, which at that moment seemed like a great idea. What would Bennie say about that? An ugly, involuntary dismissal from Scully & Pershing? Every young man has the right to chase women, and if you get caught, well, so what? At least you got fired for something worthwhile.

Bennie would lose his spy. His spy would get the boot without getting disbarred.

Interesting.

Of course, with his luck, there would probably be another video, this one of Kyle and Dale, and Bennie would get his dirty hands on it, and, well, who knows?

Kyle mulled these things over at $300 an hour. He didn't think about turning off the meter, because he wanted Placid to bleed.

He had learned that Dale earned a Ph.D. in mathematics at the age of twenty-five, from MIT no less, and that she had taught for a few years before deciding that the classroom was boring. She studied law at Cornell. Why she thought she could make the transition from the classroom to the courtroom was not clear, at least not to Kyle. Right now a class of struggling geometry students would seem like a parade. She was thirty years old, never married, and he had just begun the task of trying to unravel her withdrawn and complicated personality.

He stood to go for a walk, something to get the blood pumping into his stultified brain. "You want some coffee?" he asked Dale.

"No, thanks," she said, and actually smiled.

Two cups of strong coffee did little to stimulate his mind, and by late afternoon Kyle began to worry about permanent brain damage.

To be on the safe side, he and Dale decided to wait until 7:00 p.m. before checking out. They left together, rode the elevator down without a word, both thinking the same thought—they were violating another of the unwritten rules by leaving so early. But they shook it off and walked four blocks to an Irish pub where Tim Reynolds had secured a booth and was almost finished with his first pint. He was with Everett, a first-year from NYU who'd been assigned to the commercial real estate practice group. After they sat down and got themselves situated, they pulled out their FirmFones. All four were on the table, much like loaded guns.

Dale ordered a martini. Kyle ordered a club soda, and when the waiter disappeared, Tim said, "You don't drink?"

"No. I had to quit in college." It was Kyle's standard line, and he knew all of the follow-ups it would provoke.

"You had to quit?"

"Yep. I was drinking too much, so I quit."

"Rehab, AA, all that stuff?" Everett asked.

"No. I saw a counselor, and he convinced me that the drinking would only get worse. I went cold turkey and have never looked back."

"That's awesome," Tim said as he drained the pint of ale.

"I don't drink either," Dale said. "But after today, I'm hitting the bottle." From someone with absolutely no sense of humor, this declaration was quite funny. After a good laugh, they settled into a rehash of their first day. Tim had billed 8.6 hours reading the legislative history of an old New York law aimed at discouraging class action lawsuits. Everett had billed 9 hours reading leases. But Kyle and Dale won the game with their descriptions of the dungeon and its thirty-five thousand files.

When their drinks arrived, they toasted Placid Mortgage and the 400,000 foreclosures it had precipitated. They toasted Tabor, who had vowed to stay at his desk until midnight. They toasted Scully &

Pershing and its wonderful beginning salaries. Halfway through the martini, the gin hit Dale's mushy brain and she began giggling. When she ordered a second, Kyle excused himself and walked home.

AT 5:30 ON Tuesday, Kyle was wrapping up his second day in the dungeon and mentally drafting his letter of resignation. He would happily tell Bennie to go to hell, and he would happily face Elaine and her rape claim in a courtroom in Pittsburgh. Anything would be better than what he was enduring.

He had survived the day by continually repeating the mantra "But they're paying me $200,000 a year."

But by 5:30, he didn't care what they were paying him. His FirmFone pinged with an e-mail, from Doug Peckham, and it read, "Kyle, need some help. My office. Now if possible."

He forgot his letter of resignation, jumped to his feet, and bolted for the door. To Dale he said as he dashed by, "Gotta run see Doug Peckham, a litigation partner. He's got a project." If this sounded cruel, then so be it. If it was boasting, he didn't care. She looked shocked and wounded, but he left her there, all alone in the Placid dungeon. He ran down two flights of stairs and was out of breath when he walked through Peckham's open door. The partner was on the phone, standing, fidgeting, and he waved Kyle into a fine leather chair across from his desk. When he signed off with a "You're a moron, Slade, a true moron," he looked at Kyle, forced a smile, and said, "So how's it going so far?"

"Document Review." Nothing else needed to be said.

"Sorry about that, but we all suffered through it. Look, I need a hand here. You up to it?" Peckham fell violently into his chair and began rocking, thrusting himself back and forth without taking his eyes off Kyle.

"Anything. Right now I'll shine your shoes."

"They're shined. Gotta case here in the Southern District of New York, a big one. We're defending Barx in a class action filed by some folks who took their heartworm pills and eventually croaked. Big, messy, complicated case that's raging in a number of states. We go before Judge Cafferty on Thursday morning. You know him?"

I've been here two days, Kyle almost blurted. I don't know anybody. "No."

"Caffeine Cafferty. He's got some chemical imbalance that keeps him up all night and all day, and when he's off his meds, he calls up lawyers and screams at them because the cases are moving so slowly. When he's on his meds, he yells, too, but doesn't swear as much. Anyway, his schedule is called the Rocket Docket because he moves things along. Good judge, but a real pain in the ass. Anyway, this case has dragged on, and now he's threatening to send it to another jurisdiction."

Kyle was scribbling notes as fast as possible. At the first break in the narrative, he said, "Heartworms?"

"Actually, it's a drug that eats away plaque in the major blood vessels, including the left and right ventricles. From a medical point of view, it's complicated and nothing you should worry about. We have two partners with medical degrees handling that aspect of the case. Four partners total, as well as ten associates. I'm lead counsel." He said this with far too much smugness. Then he jumped to his feet and lumbered over to the window for a quick look at the city. His white starched shirt was oversized and did a nice job of hiding his bulbous physique.

Bennie's summary had been typically to the point. Peckham's first marriage broke up thirteen months after he joined Scully & Pershing fresh out of Yale. His current wife was a lawyer who was a partner in a firm down the street. She, too, worked long hours. There were two small children. Their apartment on the Upper West Side was appraised for $3.5 million, and they owned the obligatory house in the

Hamptons. Last year Doug earned $1.3 million; his wife, $1.2 million. He was regarded as a top litigator whose specialty was defending big pharmaceuticals, though he rarely went to trial. Six years earlier he was on the losing end of a major case involving a painkiller that caused suicides, at least in the opinion of the jury. Scully & Pershing sent him to a spa in Italy for a two-week treatment.

"Cafferty wants to get rid of the case," he said, stretching a sore back. "We, of course, will fight that. But, truthfully, I would rather see it in another jurisdiction. There are four possibilities—Duval County, Florida; downtown Memphis; a rural county in Nebraska called Fillmore; or Des Plaines, Illinois. Your mission, should you choose to accept it, is to research these four jurisdictions." He fell into his chair again and began rocking. "I need to know what juries do there. What are the verdicts? How do big companies fare in these places? Now, there are several jury research outfits that sell their data, and we subscribe to all of it, but it's not always accurate. Lots of numbers but not a lot of useful info. You gotta dig and dig. You gotta call lawyers in these four places and find the dirt. Are you in, Kyle?"

As if he had a choice. "Sure. Sounds great."

"I wouldn't call it great. I need this by 7:30 Thursday morning. Have you pulled an all-nighter yet?"

"No. I've only been here for—"

"Right, right. Well, get to work. Memo form, but nothing fancy. We'll meet here at 7:30 on Thursday with two other associates. You'll have ten minutes to do your summary. Anything else?"

"Not right now."

"I'll be here until ten tonight, so zip me a note if you need something."

"Thanks, and thanks for getting me out of Document Review."

"What a waste."

The desk phone was ringing as Kyle hustled out of the office. He went straight to the cube, grabbed his laptop, and raced off to the firm's cavernous main library on the thirty-ninth floor. There were at least four smaller libraries scattered throughout, but Kyle had yet to find them.

He could not remember being so excited over a research project. It was a real case, with deadlines and an angry judge and strategic decisions in the air. The memo he was about to prepare would be read and relied on by real lawyers in the heat of battle.

Kyle almost felt sorry for the poor rookies left behind in Document Review. But he knew he'd be back there soon enough. He forgot dinner until almost 10:00 p.m., when he ate a cold sandwich from a machine while reading jury research. With no sleeping bag at hand, he left the library at midnight—there were at least twenty associates still there—and took a cab to his apartment. He slept four hours, then made the thirty-minute walk back to Broad Street in only twenty-two minutes. He was not about to start gaining weight. The firm's private gym on the fortieth floor was a joke because it was eternally empty. A few of the secretaries used it during lunch, but no lawyer would be caught dead there.

His meter began promptly at 5:00 a.m. By 9:00, he was calling trial lawyers and defense lawyers in Duval County, Florida, in and around Jacksonville. He had a long list of cases that had gone to trial, and he planned to talk to every lawyer he could get on the phone.

The more calls he made, the longer the list became. Lawyers in Florida, Memphis and western Tennessee, Lincoln and Omaha, and dozens in the Chicago area. He found more cases and more trials, and called more lawyers. He tracked every Barx trial in the past twenty years and compared their verdicts.

There was no word from Doug Peckham, no text message or e-mail on the FirmFone always lying on the table next to the legal pad. Kyle was delighted to be given such free rein, such discretion. Dale sent an e-mail and asked about lunch. He met her in the cafeteria for a quick salad at 1:00 p.m. She was still imprisoned in the Placid tomb, but mercifully three other rookies had been sent in to help with the grunt work. All three were thinking about quitting. She seemed genuinely pleased that someone she knew had been given a real task.

"Save me some Placid files," Kyle said as they left the cafeteria. "I'll be back tomorrow."

He left the library at midnight on Wednesday, after billing Barx for eighteen hours. Six the day before. He added two more early Thursday morning as he polished up the fifteen-page memo and rehearsed his ten-minute presentation to Peckham and a team of senior associates. At precisely 7:30, he approached the partner's door and saw that it was closed.

"He's expecting me at seven thirty," he said politely to a secretary.

"I'll let him know," she said without making a move toward the phone.

Five minutes passed as Kyle tried to settle his nerves and appear calm. He had a knot in his stomach, and there was sweat around his collar. Why? he kept asking himself. It's just a brief presentation before a friendly audience. We're on the same team, right? Ten minutes, fifteen. He could hear voices in Peckham's office. Finally, the door was opened by one of the associates, and Kyle walked in.

Peckham appeared surprised to see him. "Oh, yes, Kyle, I forgot," he said, snapping his fingers and frowning. "I should've e-mailed. The hearing's been postponed. You're off the hook. Keep the memo. I might need it later."

Kyle's mouth fell open and he glanced around. Two associates were huddled over a small worktable, papers everywhere. And two more were seated near the desk. All four seemed to be amused.

The False Deadline.

Kyle, of course, had heard of this little maneuver. The hapless associate is run through the grinder to produce a useless memo or brief that is time sensitive but will never be used. But the client will nonetheless get billed, and will pay, so even though the research is not needed, it is at least profitable.

Kyle had heard of the False Deadline, but didn't see this one coming. "Uh, sure, no problem," he said, backtracking.

"Thanks," Peckham said as he flipped the page of another document. "See you later."

"Sure."

Kyle was at the door when Peckham asked, "Say, Kyle, where's the best place for Barx to try the case?"

"Nebraska, Fillmore County," Kyle said eagerly.

Two of the associates laughed out loud, and the other two were highly entertained. One of them said, "Nebraska? No one tries cases in Nebraska."

"Thanks, Kyle," Peckham said, patronizing. "Nice work." And please get out of here.

For $200,000 a year, plus treats, the job would naturally have its moments of humiliation. You're getting paid for this, Kyle kept repeating as he slowly made his way up the stairs. Take it in stride. Be tough. Happens to everyone.

Back in the dungeon, he managed to smile. When Dale asked "How did it go?" he said, "It's hard to say." At the far end of the room two associates were plowing through mortgage files. Kyle nodded at them, then parked himself near Dale, arranged his pen, legal pad, and FirmFone. He opened a box, removed a file, and reentered the world of Placid Mortgage. It was known territory, and he felt oddly safe there. He would not be harmed or humiliated. A long career as a document reviewer would no doubt be dull, but it would also be much less hazardous than that of a litigator.

17

When Kyle left the office late Friday afternoon, he considered his first week to be a success, though a dismal one. He billed Placid thirty hours and Barx Biomed twenty-six, and though virtually all of this valuable time would eventually mean little to either client, he wasn't paid to worry about such things. He was there to do one thing—bill. If he kept up the pace and managed only fifty hours a week, he would hit twenty-five hundred for the year, a high number for a first-year and one that would catch the attention of the higher-ups.

For the week, Tabor the Gunner billed fifty hours. Dale, forty-four. Tim Reynolds, forty-three.

It was amazing how consumed they were with the clock after only five days on the job.

He walked to his apartment, changed into jeans, stuffed a phone in each pocket, and headed for the ballpark. The Mets were at home against the Pirates, who were already guaranteed another losing season. With seventeen games to go, the Mets were in first place, two games ahead of the Phillies, and primed for another choke in the stretch.

Kyle had paid cash for two tickets sold by a broker recommended by a paralegal at the firm. As he made his way to Shea Stadium, he picked up his surveillance as it was picking up him.

His seat was fifteen rows behind the third-base dugout. The night was hot; the Mets were in first; the place was packed. He timed his entrance perfectly and sat down just as the first pitch was thrown in the bottom of the first. To his right was a young boy holding a baseball glove and eating ice cream. To his left was a real fan with a Mets cap, Mets jersey, blue and orange sweatbands, even goofy Mets eyeglasses. Under the cap and behind the glasses was Joey Bernardo, who had spent his entire life in Pittsburgh and hated the Mets almost as much as he hated the Phillies.

"Do not acknowledge me," Kyle said as he watched the field.

"Don't worry. Right now I hate your guts. And I hate the Mets almost as much as I hate you."

"Thanks. I like the glasses."

"Can I take them off? I can't see a damned thing."

"No."

They were talking out of the corners of their mouths, just loud enough to hear each other. Shea was alive with every pitch, and there was little chance of being overheard.

Joey took a sip of a tall beer. "Are they really following you?"

"Oh, yes. Every day, everywhere."

"Do they know that you know?"

"I don't think so."

"But why?"

"Basic espionage tradecraft."

"Of course."

"Information is crucial. The more they watch and listen, the more they know about me. If they know what I eat, drink, wear, watch, listen to, and who I talk to and hang out with and where I like to shop and browse and sneak away to, then they might one day be able to use it all to their advantage. Sounds pretty dull to you and me, but not to these guys."

More beer as Joey absorbed this.

A ball bounced off the left-field wall, scoring a run, and the crowd was on its feet. Kyle and Joey acted like all the other fans. When things had settled down, Kyle continued: "For example, I've found this wonderful little store in midtown that sells all sorts of spy gadgets. Tiny cameras, hidden mikes, phone-tapping devices, and some high-tech stuff that the military has left behind. It's run by a couple of misfits who claim to be ex-CIA, but then people who are really ex-CIA don't talk about it. I found the store online, at the office, not at the apartment, and I've been there twice when I was able to shake surveillance. I might need the store one day, but if the goons knew I had discovered the place, they would really be interested."

"This is too weird."

A lady in front of Joey turned around and offered a curious glance. They did not speak for the rest of the first inning.

"How about the report on Elaine?" Joey whispered.

"It worries me."

"So what's next?"

"I think you should go see her."

"No way."

"It's easy. Just bump into her and see what happens."

"Right! Drive to Scranton, a town I can't recall seeing in the past ten years, somehow find her, recognize her, assume she'll recognize me, then what? Have a friendly little chat about the last time we were together? Have a laugh for old times' sake? Hell, Kyle, she accused me of rape."

"Shhhh," Kyle hissed softly. The word "rape" sort of hung in the thick air, but no one reacted to it.

"Sorry," Joey whispered, and they watched the game for a long time.

A ferocious argument erupted at first base after a close call, and all fifty thousand fans had an opinion. In the roar, Kyle said, "It would be an interesting meeting. To see how she reacts. Will she talk to you? Is she bitter, angry, full of vengeance? You take the high road and say that the encounter has always troubled you, that you want to talk about it. See if she'll meet you for a drink and a serious conversation. You're not going to admit anything, you just want to see how she feels. Maybe you want closure. What's there to lose?"

"What if she recognizes me, pulls out a gun, and bam!?"

"I'll take care of Blair." Kyle managed this with a grin, though the thought of spending any more time with Joey's girl was not pleasant.

"Thanks. She's pregnant, you know. Thanks for asking."

"Why is she pregnant?"

"Basic biology. But we're both surprised."

"Congratulations, Daddy."

"Getting married is one thing, but I'm not so sure about this fatherhood business."

"I thought her career was at full throttle."

"Yep. Me too. She said she was on the pill, but I don't know."

This was not a topic Kyle wanted to explore. The more they talked, the easier conversation became, and that was not wise. "I'm going to the restroom," Kyle said.

"Bring me a beer."

"No. I don't know you, remember?"

"Come on, Kyle. You think someone here is watching you?"

"With binoculars. At least two of them. They followed me here, probably bought tickets from a scalper outside the gates, and now they're watching."

"But why?"

"Basic surveillance, Joey. I'm a valuable asset, yet they don't trust me. You should read some spy novels."

"That's your problem. Too much fiction."

Kyle took his time between innings. He visited the men's room, then bought a diet soda and peanuts. When he returned to his seat, he struck up a conversation with the kid on his right, a loyal Met fan who knew every player and all their stats. His father was in advertising, and Kyle managed to seem intrigued with that career. He cracked peanuts, scattered the hulls at his feet, and ignored Joey for a long time.

Joey, still half-blinded by the oversized Mets eyeglasses, suffered in silence. The Pirates were down four runs after four innings, and he was ready to leave. Kyle eventually re-shifted, and began studying the scoreboard in center field. "Any word from Baxter?" he said without moving his jaws.

"Nothing. I think they've locked him in a cave."

"I know the feeling. I've been in a dungeon all week."

"I don't want to hear it. For the money they're paying you, no complaints."

"Okay, okay. They know that he's in rehab, and they probably know where he is," Kyle said as a long fly ball was caught on the warning track.

"They?"

"The goons. Their leader told me last week that he's in rehab."

"How often do you meet with this guy?"

"Too often."

"Have you handed over any secrets?"

"Nope. I have not been compromised."

Joey sipped his beer, swallowed slowly, and with the cup in front of his mouth said, "If they know about Baxter, are they keeping tabs on me?"

"It's possible. Play it safe. Vary your movements. Be careful with all correspondence."

"Oh, this is just great."

"My apartment is full of cameras and mikes. They come and go when they wish. I don't have an alarm system, don't want one, but I know when they've been there. Everything I do in my apartment is subject to being watched and recorded. But they don't know that I know, so I give them nothing of consequence."

"So you're outsmarting these professional intelligence agents?"

"I think so."

Another long pause in the conversation as the Pirates changed pitchers again.

"What's the endgame, Kyle?"

"I don't have one. I'm taking small, safe steps. Next, we make contact with the girl and see how bad things are there."

"Pretty bad, I'd guess."

"Let's see."

Kyle reached for his vibrating pocket and yanked out the Firm-Fone. He scrolled down, found the message, and felt like cursing. "What is it?" Joey asked, trying not to look at the phone.

"It's a partner. He's got a project. Wants me at the office at seven in the morning."

"Tomorrow's Saturday, Kyle."

"Just another day at the office."

"Are these guys crazy?"

"No, just greedy."

During the seventh-inning stretch, Kyle eased out of his seat and made his way to the gates. Joey stayed until the eighth, and finally he left as his beloved Pirates were losing their ninetieth game.

JEANS WERE ALLOWED on Saturdays and Sundays. The fact that there was a dress code for the weekend, however relaxed, said much about the practice of corporate law on Wall Street.

Why were they even there?

Kyle wore jeans, as did Dale, who looked spectacular in a pair of tight ones. Tim Reynolds wore starched khakis. All three were dazed at the reality of being in a small conference room on the thirty-fourth floor at 7:00 a.m. on the second Saturday of their fledgling careers. They joined four older associates, four young men Kyle had not had the pleasure of meeting or even seeing during his first two weeks on the job. Passing introductions were made, but only because they were expected.

The partner who had called the meeting was nowhere to be seen. His name was Tobias Roland, Toby behind his back, and of all the sizzling gossip Kyle had heard so far, the worst had been about Toby. Toby stories were abundant, and very few were even remotely flattering. Yale undergrad, Columbia Law, poor kid from a rough neighborhood with a gigantic chip on his shoulder. Brilliant, ruthless, conniving, he'd made partner in only five years, primarily because he worked harder than the rest of the workaholics and never relaxed. His idea of time off was a ten-minute tryst with a secretary on the sofa in his office. Most secretaries were terrified of him, too frightened to complain or file suit. Some, though, found him sexy enough for a quick romp. For fun he berated young associates, often cursing them in the foulest of language for the smallest of infractions. He intimidated the other partners because he was smarter and always better prepared. At the age of forty-four, he was the top-producing (billing) litigator in the firm and had not lost a jury trial in eight years. Toby was in demand by the in-house lawyers of many major corporations. A year earlier, Kyle had read and clipped an article in *Fortune* touting the greatness of Scully & Pershing's "fanciest litigator."

When Toby beckoned, you went running, albeit with a great deal of trepidation.

In his place that morning was a senior associate named Bronson, who, as he explained without a trace of enthusiasm, was standing in for Mr. Roland, who was just down the hall working on another aspect of the lawsuit at hand. He might pop in at any moment, and this prospect kept everyone wide awake.

Their client was a major oil company that was about to be sued by a Dutch firm over some disputed reserves in the Gulf of Mexico. The lawsuit was expected to be filed in New Orleans, but Mr. Roland had decided to file a preemptive lawsuit in New York. The plan was to file it first thing Monday morning. It was an ambush, a daring tactic that could backfire, the type of risky maneuver that Toby was famous for.

After a few minutes of listening to a lawsuit described in terms reminiscent of the D-day invasion, Kyle realized that his Saturday and Sunday were shot to hell and would be spent researching jurisdictional issues in the law library. He glanced at his FirmFone, scrolled down through the e-mails, and something caught his eye. At 7:30 on a Saturday morning, the firm was sending an e-mail to all lawyers announcing the resignation of Gavin Meade, a fourth-year associate in litigation. No details. No comments. Nothing but a quiet and quick exit.

Everybody has secrets, Bennie said. How did he do it? Perhaps an anonymous package mailed to someone in Human Resources. Affidavits, police records, the works. Poor Meade, ten years removed from his crime and hustling through the grind at $400,000 a year, when suddenly he gets a summons to a meeting with closed doors.

Bronson was rattling on about being the hub of a wooden wheel, with spokes running down and out to the seven associates below him, and several running upward to Mr. Roland and the other litigation partners. At the hub, he, Bronson, would direct traffic between the big boys and the rookies. He would organize the work, supervise the research, and handle correspondence with the partners. Everything crossed his desk.

Time was crucial. If word leaked, the Dutch firm and its lawyers might do all sorts of evil things. The nation's oil supply hung in the balance, perhaps even Western civilization.

Off they went to the library.

18

After a series of phone calls that became more and more tense, a deal was finally reached. Dr. Boone and Uncle Wally acquiesced, but managed to keep one string attached. Baxter would leave early, but spend three nights in a halfway house in Reno before "reentry" into the real world. A hundred and five days after arriving sloppy drunk, with a blood alcohol content of 0.28, and with significant residues of cocaine in his system, Baxter rode through the gates and left behind the safety of the Washoe Retreat. He was squeaky-clean and ten pounds lighter, and not only had he kicked booze and drugs, he had also quit smoking. He was fit, tanned, and clearheaded and thoroughly believed he had conquered his demons and would henceforth live the sober life. He was armed for battle with the teachings of Dr. Boone and the other counselors. He had confessed his sins and surrendered to a higher power, whatever and whoever that was. At the age of twenty-five, he was beginning a new life, and Baxter was both proud and apprehensive, even frightened. As the miles passed, he found himself more uncomfortable. His confidence was rapidly disappearing.

He had failed so many times in so many ways. It was a family tradition. Was it in his DNA?

An orderly drove him from the clinic in the Nightingale Mountains into Reno, a two-hour drive in which little was said. As they approached the city, they passed a splashy billboard advertising an imported beer in a cold green bottle. The slinky young woman holding it could entice any man to do almost anything. Fear hit Baxter harder. It consumed him, and beads of sweat lined his forehead. He wanted to turn around, to run back to the clinic, where there was no alcohol and no temptations. But he said nothing.

Hope Village was in a run-down section of Reno—abandoned buildings, cheap casinos, and bars. It was the domain of Brother Manny, the founder, pastor, and leader of Hope Village. He was waiting at the curb outside the church's front door when Baxter stepped onto the hot sidewalk. He grabbed Baxter's hand and shook it violently. "Mr. Tate, may I call you Baxter?"

The question suggested its own answer. He was Baxter, not Mr. Tate.

"Sure," Baxter said, his spine stiffened from this physical assault.

"I'm Brother Manny," he said, placing his thick left arm on Baxter's shoulder, completing a rather rough howdy do. "Welcome to Hope Village."

He was about fifty, Hispanic, bronze skin, gray hair pulled back tightly into a long ponytail that fell to his waist, warm eyes, big toothy smile, a small scar beside his left nostril and a larger one on his right cheek. His face was adorned with a soft white goatee that had been pampered for many years.

"Another escapee from Washoe Retreat," he said with a deep, melodious voice. "How is the good Dr. Boone doing up there?"

"Fine," Baxter said. Brother Manny's nose was about five inches from his. Close contact obviously did not bother him, but it made Baxter uncomfortable. "He sends his regards."

"A fine man. Come, I'll show you around. We have you for just three nights, as I understand."

"That's right."

They began walking slowly. Brother Manny kept one arm across Baxter's shoulders. He was a large man, with a thick barrel chest, and he wore dungarees and a white linen shirt—top two buttons open—with a long tail left out so that it swept behind him. Sandals, no socks.

The church had once belonged to an affluent white congregation that fled to the suburbs. As Baxter shuffled through the tour, he also got the backstory. Manny Lucera had found the Lord during his second term in prison—armed robbery, the proceeds from which were meant to buy drugs for personal consumption—and upon his parole he was led by the Spirit to Reno to start his ministry. Seventeen years ago, and the Lord had blessed him mightily. The church had grown and now housed a shelter for the homeless in the basement, a soup kitchen that fed anyone who showed up, a community center for the poor kids in the neighborhood, an intake center for women and children fleeing abusive men, and there were plans for an orphanage. The old buildings next door had been purchased and renovated. The complex was crawling with people—employees, volunteers, street people—and they almost bowed in deference when they saw Brother Manny.

They parked themselves on a picnic table in the shade and sipped canned lemonade. "What's your drug?" Manny asked.

"Coke, booze, but I didn't say no to anything," Baxter admitted. After fifteen weeks of baring his soul to people who already knew everything, he did not hesitate to tell the truth.

"For how long?"

"Started slow when I was about fourteen. Picked up steam as I got older. I'm twenty-five now, so eleven years."

"Where are you from?"

"Pittsburgh, originally."

"Background?"

"Privileged."

Brother Manny issued the questions and absorbed the answers with such ease that after fifteen minutes together, Kyle felt as though he could chat for hours and tell him everything.

"First rehab?"

"Second."

"I did every drug you can imagine, and some you've never heard of, for twenty years. I bought, sold, smuggled, and manufactured drugs. I got knifed four times, shot three, and went to prison twice for drugs. I lost my first wife and two children because of drugs and alcohol. I lost my chance for an education. I lost eight years because of prison. I almost lost my life. I know all about addictions because I've been there. I'm a certified drug and alcohol counselor, and I work with addicts every day. Are you an addict?"

"Yes."

"Bless you, brother. Do you know Christ?"

"I guess. My mother took me to church every Christmas."

Brother Manny smiled and slowly wiggled his large rear end off the table. "Let me show you your room. It's not the Ritz, but it'll do." The homeless shelter was a large basement room with a temporary partition dividing it—women on one side, men on the other. It was open, with rows of Army surplus cots in neat lines. "Most of these people work during the day. They're not bums," Brother Manny was saying. "They'll start drifting in around 6:00 p.m. Here's your room."

Near the showers, there were two small private rooms with nicer cots and portable fans. Brother Manny opened the door to one and said, "You can have this one. It's for a supervisor. To get a private room, you must have a job, so you'll help with the dinner preparation, then later, when everybody's tucked in, you'll help with security." He uttered these definitive statements in such a way that any thought of protest was immediately cut off and out of the question.

Baxter's world was spinning. He'd begun the day in the cushy confines of a four-star rehab ranch, and done so with giddy thoughts of finally leaving. Now he was in the hot basement of an old church that was home to fifty-two of the poorest souls in America, and he was expected to live with them for the next three days. And to cook their meals and break up their fights.

Baxter Tate, of the Pittsburgh Tate dynasty. Bankers, blue bloods who lived in mansions handed down from one miserable generation to the next, proud and arrogant people who married into other, similar clans, thus producing even shallower gene pools.

How had he reached this point in his young life?

Legally, he could leave anytime he wanted. Hit the door, find a cab, never look back. There was no court order restraining him. Uncle Wally might be disappointed, but that would be the extent of Baxter's worries if he fled.

"Are you okay?" Brother Manny asked.

"No." It was refreshing to be so honest.

"Take a nap. You look pale."

HE COULDN'T SLEEP because of the heat. After an hour, he sneaked away and found himself roaming downtown Reno. He had a late lunch in a diner—his first burger and fries in months. He had the money to get a hotel room for a day or two, and that plan consumed him as he zigzagged through the streets. He passed and repassed the casinos. He'd never been a gambler, but every casino had a bar, didn't it? Of course the bars were off-limits, but he couldn't stomach the thought of returning to Hope Village, at least not now.

At a blackjack table he pulled out five $20 bills, got some green chips, and played the $5 game for a few minutes. An aging cocktail waitress swept by, asked what he wanted to drink. "A bottle of water," he said without hesitation, then patted himself on the back. The only other player at the table was a cowboy, black hat and all, with a bottle of beer in front of him. Baxter drank his water, played his hands, and occasionally glanced at the bottle of beer. It looked so harmless. So beautiful.

When his chips had been taken by the dealer, he left the table and wandered around the casino floor. It was a dreadful place, sparsely filled with people who had no business being there, gambling with money they could not afford to lose. He walked by a sports bar, with wide screens showing old football games. The weekend's point spreads were posted. The bar was empty. He settled onto a stool and ordered water.

What would Dr. Boone say about this? Not six hours into "reentry" and he was already at a bar. Relax, Dr. Boone. It's just water. If I can resist the urge here at ground zero, then the next place will be easy. He sipped water and occasionally glanced at the rows of liquor bottles. Why were there so many different shapes and sizes? So many different types of spirits? One entire row was taken by flavored vodkas, delicious liquids he had consumed by the barrel back in the days when he was a drunk.

Thank God those days were over.

In the distance, across the floor somewhere, a siren squealed and bells erupted. A lucky slot player had hit a jackpot, and the racket was to remind everyone just how easy it was to win. The bartender filled a glass with a draft beer, then slammed it in front of Baxter. "On the house!" he proclaimed. "Super Slot Jackpot!"

Free drinks for everyone at the bar, which was nobody but Baxter. He almost said, "Hey, pal, take it away. I don't drink anymore." But the bartender was gone, plus it would sound silly. How many nondrinkers sidle up to a casino bar at three o'clock in the afternoon?

The glass was frosty, the beer ice-cold. It was darker in color, and Baxter looked at the tap. Nevada Pale Ale. One he'd never tried. His mouth was dry, so he sipped water. For 105 days he'd been hammered by Dr. Boone and the other pros at Washoe Retreat into believing that another drink would eventually lead him back to his addictions. He'd watched and listened as other patients, or guests as they were called, struggled through detox and told their stories of repeated failures. Don't ever be fooled, they warned repeatedly, you cannot handle a single drink. Total abstinence is required.

Maybe so.

Small bubbles of water formed on the glass, then began to run down to the napkin under it.

He was twenty-five years old, and he never truly believed, not even in his purest moment back at Washoe, that he would live the rest of his life without a drink. Somewhere deep down in his soul he knew he could find the willpower to have a drink, maybe a couple, then stop for the night before things got out of hand. If he planned to drink, why not start now? The last time he tortured himself for fourteen days before breaking down. For two weeks he lied to himself and especially to his friends about loving the life of sobriety, and every single moment he craved a drink. Why go through the misery again?

The beer was getting warm.

He heard the voices of his counselors. He remembered the tears and confessions of the other guests. He heard himself proclaim the gospel of the sober—"I am an alcoholic, weak and powerless, in need of strength from a higher being."

And they were weak, those other losers back at Washoe Retreat. But not Baxter. He could handle a few drinks because he was stronger. He rationalized that he would, under no circumstances, succumb to the romance and horror of cocaine. Nor would he indulge in hard liquor. Just a little beer, occasionally, and he might get serious about wine.

No big deal.

Still, he could not make himself reach forward and touch the glass. It was eighteen inches away, well within his grasp, just standing there like a coiled rattler ready to kill. Then it was a luscious treat that delivered a pleasant buzz. Back and forth, back and forth. Evil versus good.

"You need to make new friends," Dr. Boone had said repeatedly. "And you can't go back to your old haunts. Find some new places, new friends, new challenges, a different place to live."

Well, how about this, Dr. Boone? Sitting here for the very first time in a run-down Reno casino he couldn't remember the name of? Never been here before? Ha-ha.

Both hands were free, and at some point Baxter realized his right hand was shaking slightly. And his breathing was labored and heavy.

"You okay, buddy?" the bartender asked as he walked by.

Yes, no. Baxter nodded something but couldn't speak. His eyes were locked on the glass of beer. Where was he? What was he doing? Six hours after leaving rehab he was in a bar brawling with himself over whether he should take another drink. He was already a loser. Look where he was.

With his left hand, he reached forward, touched the glass, then slid it slowly toward him. He stopped when it was six inches away. He could smell the barley and hops. The glass was still cold, or cold enough.

The war shifted from good versus evil to run versus stay. He almost managed to shove himself away from the bar and sprint back through the slots to the front door. Almost. Oddly, it was Keefe who helped him make the decision. Keefe was his best friend at Washoe, and Keefe was from a wealthy family that was paying for the third rehab. The first two tanked when Keefe convinced himself that a little pot was harmless.

Baxter whispered to himself, "If I drink this beer now, and if things turn out badly, I can always go back to Washoe, and with two failures, I'll be convinced that total abstinence is required. Just like

Keefe. But right now I really want this beer." With both hands he clasped the glass, raised it slowly, sniffing as it grew closer. He smiled when the cold glass touched his lips. The first sip of Nevada Pale Ale was the most magnificent nectar he'd ever tasted. He savored it, eyes closed, face serene.

From over his right shoulder someone yelled loudly, "There you are, Baxter!"

He almost choked and he almost dropped the glass. He jerked around and there was Brother Manny, closing fast and obviously not happy. "What are you doing?" he demanded as he lowered a heavy hand on Baxter's shoulder and seemed ready to trade punches.

Baxter wasn't sure what he was doing. He was drinking a beer, one that was definitely off-limits, but he was so horrified at the moment he couldn't speak. Brother Manny delicately took the glass and slid it down the bar. "Get rid of this," he growled at the bartender, then he sat on the stool next to Baxter and moved in low until his nose was once again five inches away. "Listen to me, son," he said in a soft voice. "I cannot make you leave this place right now. That is your decision. But if you want me to help you, then say so. I'll get you out of here, take you back to my church, make some coffee, and we'll tell some stories."

Baxter's shoulders sagged and his chin dropped. The ale was still attacking his taste buds.

"This could be the most important decision of your life," Brother Manny said. "Right now, at this moment. Stay or go. If you stay, you'll be dead in five years. If you want to go, then say so and we'll leave together."

Baxter closed his eyes and said, "I'm so weak."

"Yes, but I'm not. Let me get you out of here."

"Please."

Brother Manny practically lifted him off the stool, then put a thick arm around his shoulders. They slowly made their way past the slot machines and empty roulette wheels, and they were almost to the front door when Brother Manny realized that Baxter was crying. The tears made him smile. An addict must hit the bottom before he starts his climb.

THE PASTOR'S OFFICE was a large cluttered room next to the sanctuary. The secretary, Brother Manny's wife, brought them a pot of strong coffee and two mismatched mugs. Baxter sat low in an old leather sofa and sipped furiously, as if he could rinse away the taste of the beer. The tears had stopped, for now.

Brother Manny sat close by on a wooden rocker, and as he talked, he moved slowly back and forth. "I was in prison in California," he was saying. "The second time around, in a gang, doing worse stuff on the inside than we did on the streets. I got careless one day, got away from my turf, and the rival gang jumped me. Woke up in the prison hospital with broken bones and cuts and such. Cracked skull. Terrible pain. I remember thinking death would be welcome. I was so sick of living, sick of my life, sick of the miserable person I was. I knew that if I survived and one day got paroled again, I'd end up on the streets, playing the same game. Where I grew up, you either went to prison or you died young. Sounds very different from the way you grew up, doesn't it, Baxter?"

He shrugged.

"In many ways it is, in many ways it is not. My life was all about myself, much like yours. I loved the bad things, just like you. Pleasure, selfishness, pride—that was my life, and it's been yours, I suppose."

"Oh, yes."

"It's all sin, and it all leads to the same end—misery, pain, destruction, ruin, then death. That's where you're headed, son, and you're in a hurry to get there."

Baxter nodded slightly. "So what happened?"

"I got lucky and lived, and not long afterward I met an inmate, a career criminal who would never be eligible for parole, and he was the gentlest, sweetest, happiest person I'd ever talked to. Had no worries, every day was beautiful, life was grand, and this from a man who'd spent fifteen years in max security. Through a prison ministry, he'd been exposed to the gospel of Christ, and he became a believer. He said he was praying for me, as he prayed for a lot of the bad guys in prison. He invited me to a Bible study one night, and I listened to other inmates tell their stories and praise God for his forgiveness and love and strength and promise of eternal salvation. Imagine, a bunch of hardened criminals locked away in a rotten prison singing songs of praise to their Lord. Pretty powerful stuff, and I needed some of it. I needed forgiveness, because there were lots of sins in my past. I needed peace, because I'd been at war my entire life. I needed love, because I hated everybody. I needed strength, because deep inside I knew how weak I was. I needed happiness, because I'd been miserable for so long. So we prayed together, me and those bad boys who were like little lambs, and I confessed to God that I was a sinner, and that I wanted salvation through Jesus Christ. My life changed in an instant, Baxter, a change so overwhelming I still can't believe it. The Holy Spirit entered my soul, and the old Manny Lucera died. A new one was born, one whose past was forgiven and his eternity secured."

"What about the drugs?"

"Forgotten. The power of the Holy Spirit is far greater than human desire. I've seen it a thousand times with addicts who try everything to quit—rehab clinics, state facilities, shrinks and doctors, fancy meds sold as substitutes. When you're an addict, you're powerless in the face of booze and drugs. Strength comes from somewhere else. For me, it comes from the power of the Holy Spirit."

"I don't feel very strong right now."

"You're not. Look at yourself. From Washoe Retreat to a cheap bar in a run-down casino in a few hours. That might be a record, Baxter."

"I didn't want to go to that bar."

"Of course not. But you did."

"Why?" His voice was soft, fading.

"Because you've never said no."

A tear rolled down Baxter's cheek, and he wiped it with the back of his hand. "I don't want to go back to L.A."

"You can't, son."

"Can you help me? I'm pretty shaky here, okay? I mean, I'm really scared."

"Let's pray together, Baxter."

"I'll try."

19

Six months after the Trylon-Bartin dispute went public with the filing of the lawsuit, the battleground had been defined and the troops were in place. Both sides had filed ponderous motions designed to capture the higher ground, but so far no advantage had been gained. They were of course haggling over deadlines, schedules, issues, discovery, and who got to see what documents, and when.

With the waves of lawyers working in sync, the case was plodding along. A trial was nowhere in sight, but then it was far too early. With monthly billings to Trylon averaging $5.5 million, why push the case to a conclusion?

On the other side, Bartin Dynamics was paying just as much for a vigorous and gold-plated defense coordinated by the bare-knuckle litigators at Agee, Poe & Epps. APE had committed forty lawyers to the case and, like Scully, had such a deep bench that it could send in another wave whenever necessary.

The hottest issue so far was no surprise to either set of litigators. When the forced marriage of Trylon and Bartin unraveled, when their clumsy joint venture blew up, there had been a virtual slugfest for the documents. Hundreds of thousands, perhaps millions of documents had been generated during the development of the B-10 HyperSonic Bomber. Researchers employed by Trylon grabbed all the documents they could. Researchers for Bartin did the same. Software was routed and rerouted, and some of it was destroyed. Hardware controlled by one company found its way to the other. Thousands of secured files disappeared. Crates of printed documents were hoarded and hidden. And throughout the melee each company accused the other of lying, espionage, outright thievery. When the dust settled, neither knew exactly what the other possessed.

Because of the supersensitive nature of the research, the Pentagon watched in horror as the two companies behaved outrageously. The Pentagon, as well as several intelligence agencies, leaned heavily on Trylon and Bartin to keep their dirty laundry private, but they were ultimately not successful. The fight was now controlled by the lawyers and the courts.

A major task for Mr. Wilson Rush and his Scully & Pershing team was to accumulate, index, copy, and store all documents in the possession of Trylon. A warehouse was leased in Wilmington, North Carolina, about a mile from the Trylon testing facility where most of the B-10 research had taken place. After it was leased, it was completely renovated and made fire-, wind-, and waterproof. All windows were removed and replaced with a six-inch cinder-block wall. A Washington security firm wired the warehouse with twenty closed-circuit cameras. The four large doors were equipped with infrared alarms and metal detectors. Armed guards patrolled the empty warehouse long before any of the documents arrived.

When they did arrive, they came in unmarked tractor-trailer rigs, complete with more armed guards. Dozens of deliveries were made over a two-week period in mid-September. The warehouse, nicknamed Fort Rush, came to life as ton after ton of paperwork was stacked neatly in white cardboard boxes, all waiting to be organized into a system understood only by the lawyers up in New York.

The warehouse was leased by Scully & Pershing. Every contract was signed by Wilson Rush—contracts for the renovations, security operations, transporting of documents, everything. Once the documents entered the warehouse, they were deemed AWP—Attorneys' Work Product—and thus subject to a different set of rules regarding disclosure to the other side.

Mr. Rush selected ten associates from his litigation team, ten of the brightest and most trusted. These unlucky souls were shipped to Wilmington and introduced to Fort Rush, a long, windowless hangar of a building with shiny concrete floors and a pungent industrial smell to it. In the center was the mountain of boxes. Along both sides were rows of empty folding tables, and beyond the tables were ten large, fierce-looking copy machines, with wires and cables running everywhere. The copiers were, of course, state-of-the-art color and capable of instant scanning, collating, even stapling.

Far away from their New York offices, the associates were allowed to wear jeans and running shoes, and they were promised bigger bonuses and other goodies. But nothing could compensate them for the dismal job of physically copying and scanning a million documents. And in Wilmington! Most were married, with spouses and children back home, though of the ten, four had already suffered through a divorce. And it was quite likely that Fort Rush would be the cause of even more marital problems.

They began their forbidding task under the direction of Mr. Rush himself. Every document was copied twice, in a split second, and instantly scanned into the firm's virtual library. Several weeks down the road, when the task was complete, the library would be accessible by a secured code, and once inside, a lawyer could locate any document in a matter of seconds. The firm's computer experts designed the library and were supremely confident that its security was impenetrable.

To impress upon the associates the gravity of their seemingly mindless work, Mr. Rush stayed for three days and was involved in the unpacking, sorting, scanning, copying, and repacking. When he left, two other litigation partners remained and directed traffic. Such mundane work was normally contracted out to a copying service and supervised by the firm's litigation support staff, but that was far too risky with these documents. They had to be handled by real lawyers who appreciated their importance. The real lawyers manning the copiers averaged about $400,000 in salary, and most had at least one degree from an Ivy League school. At no point in their graduate or postgraduate studies could they have pictured themselves running copiers, but after four or five years with Scully & Pershing they were shockproof.

The rotation began after the first week. Eight days in the warehouse, then four days in New York, then back to Wilmington. The assignments were staggered, and a total of fifteen associates were eventually used. All were forbidden to discuss any aspect of Fort Rush with anyone in New York. Security and confidentiality were paramount.

The first project took six weeks. Two point two million documents were copied, indexed, and added to the library. The associates were freed from Fort Rush and flown back to New York on a chartered jet.

By then, Bennie knew exactly where the warehouse was located and had a general idea of its security features, but his interest in these matters was only passing. What Bennie wanted, of course, was access to the virtual library, access only his spy could deliver.

20

For another $1,000, the security firm in Pittsburgh watched Elaine Keenan long enough to determine her daily routine. She usually had lunch with some co-workers at a sandwich shop not far from the parks and recreation complex where she worked.

A chance encounter would have to be believable, and Joey couldn't sell the idea of bumping into her in the lesbian bar she and her roommate occasionally frequented. He wasn't sure he could sell any encounter with Elaine. Aside from the casual sex five and a half years earlier, he'd never really known her. She had been one of several groupies around the Beta fraternity, and he'd tried to forget all of them.

The security firm provided three color photos. Joey had studied them for hours and was not convinced he'd ever met the girl. Kyle, however, had studied them and claimed to recall her vividly.

Now, at the age of twenty-three, her dark hair was tinted a deep red and worn very short. There was no makeup, no lipstick, nothing but matching tattoos around her forearms. If she had any interest in being attractive, it was not apparent. Somewhere under all the attitude was a cute girl, but sex appeal was unimportant.

Joey swallowed hard, cursed Kyle again, and entered the sandwich shop. He eased behind her as she waited in line to order, and after a few minutes, as the line moved slowly forward, managed to bump into her. "Sorry," he quickly said with a wide fake smile.

She smiled back, but said nothing. He moved a step closer and said, "Hey, you were at Duquesne a few years ago, weren't you?" Her two co-workers glanced back but were not interested.

"Briefly," she said, eyeing him carefully, searching for any clue.

He snapped his fingers as if trying to recall something. "Elaine? Right? Can't think of the last name."

"That's right. And who are you?"

"Joey Bernardo. I was in Beta."

A look of horror swept over her face, and she dropped her gaze to the floor. For a moment she was frozen, unable to speak, ready, it seemed, to erupt. Then she shuffled a step to keep pace in line. She turned her back on the man who once raped her, a man who walked away from the crime not only unpunished but completely vindicated. Joey watched her from the corner of an eye and felt uneasy for several reasons. First, she was obviously frightened by him, but since she considered herself the victim and him the rapist, this was not surprising. It was also uncomfortable being this close to someone he'd once had sex with, regardless of how casual or how uneventful it now seemed.

She turned halfway to him and hissed, "What are you doing here?"

"I'm eating lunch, same as you."

"Would you please leave?" Her voice was barely audible, but one of her co-workers turned around and glared at Joey.

"No. I'm just getting a sandwich."

Nothing else was said as they ordered and moved down to the pickup counter. Elaine hurried off to a distant table and ate quickly with her two friends. Joey ate alone at a small table near the front door. The note was already prepared. It read: "Elaine: I'd like to talk to you about what happened. Please call my cell at 412-866-0940. I'll be in Scranton until 9:00 tomorrow. Joey Bernardo." He hauled his tray back to the counter, then walked to her table, handed her the note without a word, and disappeared.

Two hours later, she called.

At 5:00 p.m. sharp, as agreed, Joey returned to the sandwich shop. He found Elaine at the same table she'd used for lunch, but instead of sitting with a couple of friends, she was accompanied by her attorney. Icy introductions were made, and Joey sat down across from them with a knot in his throat and a strong desire to maim Kyle McAvoy. Where the hell was Kyle anyway? He was the lawyer.

Elaine's lawyer was an attractive middle-aged woman. Everything was black—pantsuit, thick coral necklace, boots, eye shadow, and, worst of all, her mood. This woman went for the throat. The business card Joey was holding and glancing at proclaimed her to be Michelin "Mike" Chiz, Attorney & Counselor at Law. She began matter-of-factly: "My first question for you, Mr. Bernardo, is, what are you doing here?"

"How many questions do you have?" Joey asked in his finest smart-ass manner. He had been assured time after time by his psuedo-lawyer and near co-defendant, one Kyle McAvoy, that there was no danger in this chance meeting with Elaine Keenan. Any legal action she wanted to initiate could have been commenced long ago. Five and a half years had passed.

"Well, Mr. Bernardo, may I call you Joey?"

There was almost no chance that she would allow him to call her Mike, so he abruptly said no.

"Very well, Mr. Bernardo, I have just a few questions. I have represented Ms. Keenan here for some time now. She actually works part-time in my office, a fine paralegal, and I'm familiar with her story. Now, what are you doing here?"

"First of all, I don't have to explain a damned thing to you. But I'll try to be nice, at least for the next sixty seconds. I work for a brokerage firm in Pittsburgh, and we have some clients in Scranton. I'm here to see these clients. I got hungry around noon today. I chose this four-star restaurant at random, walked in, saw Ms. Keenan here, said hello, she freaked, I wanted to chat, and now I'm taking questions from her lawyer. Why, exactly, do you need a lawyer, Elaine?"

"You raped me, Joey," Elaine blurted. "You and Baxter Tate, and maybe Kyle McAvoy." By the time she finished, her eyes were moist. Her breathing was heavy, almost heaving, as if she might lunge at him at any moment.

"Maybe this, maybe that. You never got your story straight."

"Why did you want to talk to my client?" Ms. Chiz demanded.

"Because it was a misunderstanding, and I wanted to apologize for the misunderstanding. That's all. After she cried rape, we never saw her again. The cops investigated, found nothing because nothing happened, and by then Elaine had disappeared."

"You raped me, Joey, and you know it."

"There was no rape, Elaine. We had sex—me and you, you and Baxter, you and most of the other boys at Beta—but it was all very consensual."

Elaine closed her eyes and began shaking as if chills swept her body.

"Why does she need a lawyer?" Joey asked Ms. Chiz.

"She's suffered greatly."

"I don't know how much she's suffered, Ms. Chiz, but I do know that she suffered very little during her days at Duquesne. She was too busy partying to spend time suffering. Lots of booze, drugs, and sex, and there are lots of boys and girls perfectly capable of refreshing her memory. You'd better get to know your client before you pursue some bogus legal action. There's a lot of bad stuff back there."

"Shut up!" Elaine snarled.

"You want to apologize to her?" the lawyer said.

"Yes. Elaine, I apologize for the misunderstanding, whatever the hell it was. And I think you should apologize for accusing us of something that did not happen. And right now, I want to apologize for even being here." Joey sprang to his feet. "This was not a good idea. So long."

He walked quickly out of the deli, strolled to his car, and left Scranton. Driving back to Pittsburgh, when he wasn't cursing Kyle McAvoy, he was hearing her voice again and again. "You raped me, Joey." Her words were painful and free of doubt. She may not have known precisely what happened in their apartment five-and-a-half years earlier, but she certainly knew now.

He hadn't raped anyone. What began as consensual sex, at her suggestion nonetheless, had now been transformed into something far different, at least in her mind.

If a girl consents to sex, can she change her mind once things are underway? Or if she consents to sex, then blacks out halfway through the act, how can she later claim she'd changed her mind? Difficult questions, and Joey wrestled with them as he drove.

"You raped me, Joey."

The mere accusation carried a heavy dose of suspicion, and for the first time Joey questioned himself. Had he and Baxter taken advantage of her?

FOUR DAYS LATER, Kyle stopped by the mail room at Scully & Pershing and picked up a letter from Joey. It was a detailed summary of the encounter, complete with their choice of sandwiches and a description of Elaine's hair color and matching tattoos. After setting out the facts, Joey offered his opinions:

> EK has definitely convinced herself that she was raped by several of us, JB and BT for sure and "maybe" KM. She is weak, fragile, emotionally unstable, haunted, but at the same time carries a certain smugness in her victimhood. She has chosen the right attorney, a tough broad who believes in her and would not hesitate to start legal trouble if she could find any evidence. Her finger is on the trigger. If that little video is half as damaging as you say it is, then by all human means keep it locked away from these people. Elaine and her lawyer are two cobras, pissed and coiled and ready to strike.

He finished with: "I'm not sure what my next little project might be, but I'd rather not go near Elaine again. I don't like being called a rapist. The entire episode was unnerving, plus I had to lie to Blair to get out of town. I have two tickets to the Steelers-Giants game on October 26. Shall I call you with this news so your goons will know about it? I really think we should go to the game and hash out our next moves. Your faithful servant, Joey."

Kyle read the letter and summary in the main library while hiding between shelves of ancient law books. It confirmed his worst fears, but he had little time to dwell on it. He quietly tore the sheets of paper into a hundred pieces, then dropped them in a wastebasket as he left the library. Immediately destroy all written correspondence, he'd instructed Joey.

The hotel nearest his apartment was the Chelsea Garden, a fifteen-minute walk. At eleven that night, Kyle dragged himself along Seventh Avenue, looking for the hotel. Had he not been so exhausted, he might have enjoyed the cool autumn night with leaves sweeping across the sidewalk and half the city still awake and going somewhere. But Kyle was numb with fatigue and capable of only one thought at a time, and that was often too much.

Bennie was in a suite on the third floor, where he'd been waiting for two hours because his "asset" couldn't get away from the office. But Bennie didn't mind. His asset belonged at the office, and the more time he spent there, the quicker Bennie could get on with his work.

Regardless, though, Bennie opened up with a nasty "You're two hours late."

"Sue me." Kyle stretched out on the bed. This was their fourth meeting in New York since Kyle had moved there, and he had yet to hand over anything that Bennie wasn't supposed to have. His ethics were still intact. No laws had been broken.

So why did he feel like such a traitor?

Bennie was tapping a large white poster board mounted on an easel. "If I could have your attention, please," he said. "This won't take long. I have some coffee if you'd like."

Kyle wasn't about to concede an inch. He jumped to his feet, poured coffee in a paper cup, and sat on the edge of the bed. "Go."

"This is the Trylon team as it is now assembled. At the top here is Wilson Rush, and below him are eight litigation partners—Mason, Bradley, Weems, Cochran, Green, Abbott, Etheridge, and Wittenberg. How many have you met?"

Kyle studied the eight squares with the names scrawled inside them, and thought for a second. "Wilson Rush spoke to us during orientation, but I haven't seen him since. I did a memo for Abbott on a securities case, met him briefly, and I had lunch one day in the cafeteria with Wittenberg. I've seen Bradley, Weems, maybe Etheridge, but I can't say I've met them. It's a big firm." Kyle was still amazed at the unknown faces he encountered every day in the halls and elevators, the cafeteria and libraries and coffee rooms. He tried to socialize and at least say hello, but the clock was always ticking and billing was much more important.

His supervising partner was Doug Peckham, and he was relieved Peckham's name was not on the board.

There were a bunch of smaller squares under the partners. Bennie tapped an index finger near them. "There are sixteen senior associates, and under them another sixteen younger ones. The names are in that binder over there. You need to memorize them."

"Sure, Bennie." Kyle glanced at the binder, this one a two-inch blue one. The last three were black and thicker. Then he studied the names on the board.

"How many of these associates have you worked with?"

"Five, six, maybe seven," he said with no effort at being accurate. How would Bennie know whom he'd worked with? And how Bennie knew the names of all forty-one lawyers assigned to the Trylon case was a question Kyle didn't even want to consider. A few of the names would appear in the court file, but only the big boys. How many sources did he have?

He pointed to a smaller box. "This is a senior associate named Sherry Abney. You met her?"

"No."

"A rising star, fast track to partnership. Two degrees from Harvard and a federal clerkship. She reports to Partner Mason, who's in charge of discovery. Under her is a second-year associate by the name of Jack McDougle. McDougle has a cocaine problem. No one at the firm knows it, but he's about to get busted, so everybody will know it. His departure will be quick."

Kyle stared at the box with McDougle's name and thought of so many questions he didn't know where to start. How did Bennie know this?

"And you want me to take his place?"

"I want you to schmooze it up with Sherry Abney. Check her out, get to know her. She's thirty years old, single but committed to an investment banker at Chase who works as many hours as she does, so they have no time for any fun. No wedding date, as of now, at least nothing that has been announced. She likes to play squash, when she can find the time, and as you know, the firm has two courts on the fortieth floor beside the gym. You play squash?"

"I guess I do now." Kyle had played several times at Yale. "Not sure when I'll find the time."

"You figure it out. She just might be your entrée onto the Trylon team."

Go, team, go. Kyle planned to avoid Trylon and its litigation team as diligently as possible. "Small problem here, Bennie," Kyle said. "Nice homework, but you're missing the obvious. There are no first-year grunts anywhere near this case. A couple of reasons. First, we don't know anything—five months ago we were still in law school—and, second, the smart boys at Trylon probably told their lawyers to keep the rookies away from this case. That happens, you know. Not all of our clients are stupid enough to pay $300 an hour for a bunch of kids to stick it to them. So, Bennie, where is plan B?"

"It takes patience, Kyle. And politics. You start angling for the Trylon case, networking with the upper associates, kissing the right asses, and we might get a lucky break."

Kyle wasn't finished with the discussion about McDougle. He was determined to pursue it, when another man suddenly appeared from the sitting room adjacent to the bedroom. Kyle was so startled he almost dropped the half-filled cup of coffee. "This is Nigel," Bennie was saying. "He'll spend a few minutes on systems." Nigel was in his face, thrusting forward a hand to shake. "A pleasure," he sang in a cheery British way. He then moved to the tripod and mounted his own display.

The sitting room was twelve by twelve. Kyle looked through the open double doors into it. Nigel had been hiding in there and listening to every word.

"Scully & Pershing uses a litigation support system called Jury Box," he began quickly. All movements were rapid and precise.

British, but with a strange accent. Forty years old. Five feet ten inches, 150 pounds. Short dark hair, half gray. Eyes, brown. No remarkable features but slightly elevated cheekbones. Thin lips. No eyeglasses.

"How much have they taught you about Jury Box?" Nigel wanted to know.

"The basics. I've used it on several occasions." Kyle was still reeling from Nigel's unexpected appearance.

"It's your typical litigation support system. All discovery is scanned into a virtual library that can be accessed by all lawyers working on the case. Quick retrieval of documents. Super-quick search of keywords, phrases, contract language, anything, really. You're up to speed?"

"Yes."

"It's fairly secure, pretty standard stuff these days. And like all smart law firms, Scully also uses a more secure system for sensitive files and cases. It's called Barrister. You in on this one?"

"No."

"Not surprised. They keep it quiet. Works pretty much like Jury Box, but much harder to access, or to hack into. Keep your ears open for it."

Kyle nodded as if he would do precisely as he was being told. Since February, on that awful night when he'd been ambushed after a youth-league basketball game on the cold streets of New Haven, he had met only with Bennie Wright. Or whoever he really was. He had assumed, without really thinking about it, that Bennie, as his handler, would be the only face of the operation. There were other faces, to be sure; in particular, a couple of the street pounders who followed him night and day and who'd made enough mistakes so that Kyle could now spot them. But it had not occurred to him that he would actually be introduced to someone else with a bogus name who worked for the operation.

And why was he? Bennie was certainly capable of handling Nigel's little presentation.

"And then you have the Trylon case," Nigel was singing. "A completely different matter, I'm afraid. Much more complicated and secure. Whole different batch of software, really. Probably written just for this one lawsuit. Got the docs locked up in a warehouse down south with Uzis at every door. But we've made progress." He stopped long enough to allow himself a quick approving smile at Bennie.

Aren't we clever?

"We know that the program is code-named Sonic, as in B-10 HyperSonic Bomber, not very creative if you ask me, but then they didn't, did they? Ha-ha. Sonic cannot be accessed by the nice little laptop they gave you greenies on day one, no sir. No laptop can have a peek at Sonic."

Nigel bounced to the other side of the tripod. "There is a secret room on the eighteenth floor of your building, heavily secured, mind you, with a bank of desktop computers, some really fancy stuff, and there is where you will find Sonic. Pass codes change every week. Passwords every day, sometimes twice a day. Must have the proper ID before logging in, and if you log out without quitting to a tee, they'll write you up and maybe show you the door."

Show me the door, Kyle almost said.

"Sonic is probably a bastardized version of Barrister, so it will be incumbent upon you to master Barrister as soon as you're given the opportunity."

Can't wait, Kyle almost said.

Slowly, through the shock and the fatigue, it was sinking in that Kyle was crossing the line, and doing it in a way he had not envisioned. His nightmare was to walk out of Scully & Pershing with secrets he was not supposed to have, and deliver them like Judas to Bennie for thirty pieces of silver. Now, though, he was receiving firm secrets from an outside source. He had yet to steal anything, but he damned sure wasn't supposed to know about Sonic and the hidden room on the eighteenth floor. Perhaps it wasn't criminal and maybe it wasn't a violation of the canons of ethics, but it certainly felt wrong.

"That's enough for now," Bennie was saying. "You look exhausted. Get some rest."

"Oh, thank you."

Back on Seventh Avenue, Kyle glanced at his watch. It was almost midnight.

21

At 5:00 a.m., the usual hour now, the alarm clock exploded at full volume and Kyle slapped it twice before it shut off. He hurried through the shower and the shave, and fifteen minutes later he was on the sidewalk, fashionably dressed because he could certainly afford fine clothes. His life had quickly become a harried, fatigued mess, but he was determined to look nice as he stumbled through the day. He bought a coffee, a bagel, and a copy of the *Times* at his favorite all-night deli, then caught a cab at the corner of Twenty-fourth and Seventh. Ten minutes later, he'd finished breakfast, scanned the newspaper, and gulped half the coffee. He walked into the Broad Street entrance of his office building at 6:00, on schedule. Regardless of the hour, he was never alone during the elevator ride up. There were usually two or three other bleary-eyed and gaunt-faced associates, all sleep deprived, all avoiding eye contact as the elevator hummed and rocked gently upward and they asked themselves several questions.

What was I thinking when I chose law school?

How long will I last in this meat grinder?

What fool designed this method of practicing law?

There was seldom a word because there was nothing to say. Like prisoners riding to the gallows, they chose to meditate and put things in perspective.

At the cube, Kyle was not surprised to see another young lawyer. Tim Reynolds had been the first to sneak in a sleeping bag—a new, thermally insulated Eddie Bauer special that he claimed he'd owned for years and taken all over the country. But it had a new smell to it. Tim—without shoes, tie, shirt, or jacket, and wearing an old T-shirt—was partially curled under his small desk, inside the sleeping bag, dead to the world. Kyle kicked his feet, woke him up, and began with a pleasant "You look like crap."

"Good morning," Tim said, scrambling to his feet and reaching for his shoes. "What time is it?"

"Six ten. What time did you go to sleep?"

"I don't remember. Sometime after two." He was pulling on his shirt quickly, as if a dreaded partner might appear any second and issue demerits. "I have a memo due for Toby Roland at seven and I have no idea what I'm doing."

"Just keep billing," Kyle said without a trace of sympathy as he unpacked his briefcase and pulled out his laptop. Tim finished dressing and grabbed a file. "I'll be in the library," he said, already a wreck.

"Don't forget to brush your teeth," Kyle said.

When Reynolds was gone, Kyle went online, to a Web site called QuickFace.com. There were several sites that allowed amateur sleuths to put together composite sketches of faces, and Kyle had studied them all. QuickFace was by far the most detailed and accurate. He began with Nigel's eyes, always the most important feature. Get the eyes right, and half the identification is over. The site offered over two hundred different types of eyes—every race, color, origin, and blend. Kyle went through them quickly, found the closest set, and began his face. Nose, thin and pointed. Eyebrows, moderately thick and a bit long down the sides. Lips, very thin. Cheekbones, higher and wider. Chin, not long but very flat, no dimple. Ears, oval and stuck close to the skull. After he added the hair, he went back to the eyes, tried another pair, then another. The ears were too high, so he lowered them. He tinkered and sculpted until 6:30—a half hour unbilled and wasted unless he chose to pad a bit during the day—and when Nigel was properly put together and easily identified from forty feet away, Kyle printed the face and hustled off to the library, carrying a thick file because everyone carried a thick file into the library. His private spot was a dead end in a dark corner on the third level of stacked tiers, a lonesome place where they stored thick tomes of annotations no one had used in decades. On the second shelf from the bottom, he lifted three of the books and removed an unmarked manila envelope, letter-sized. He opened it and pulled out three other composites—a splendid rendering of his archenemy, Bennie, and two others of the goons who were stalking him around New York City. To his knowledge, he had not been within fifty feet of them, and had never made eye contact, but he'd seen both on several occasions and was confident that his artwork was at least a decent starting point. The addition of Nigel's dreadful face to the collection did nothing to improve its overall attractiveness.

He hid the envelope and returned to the cube, where Tabor the Gunner was busy making his usual noisy preparations for the day. The issue of whose career held the most promise had been settled weeks earlier. Tabor was the man, the star, the fast-tracked partner-to-be, and everyone else could get out of the way. He'd proven his talents by billing twenty-one hours in a single day. He'd shown his skill by billing more the first month than all other litigation rookies, though Kyle was only four hours behind. He volunteered for projects and worked the cafeteria like an old Irish ward boss.

"Slept in the library last night," he said as soon as he saw Kyle.

"Good morning, Tabor."

"The carpet in the main library is thinner than the carpet in the twenty-third library, did you know that, Kyle? I much prefer sleeping on the twenty-third, but it does have more noise. Which do you prefer?"

"We're all cracking up, Tabor."

"Yes, we are."

"Tim used his sleeping bag last night."

"For what? He and Dr. Dale finally getting it on?"

"Don't know about that. I woke him up an hour ago."

"So you went home? Slept in your own bed?"

"Oh, yes."

"Well, I have two projects due at noon today, both extremely important and urgent, and I can't afford the luxury of sleep."

"You're the greatest, Tabor. Go, Superman."

And with that Tabor was gone.

DALE ARMSTRONG arrived promptly at seven, her usual time, and though she looked a bit sleepy, she was put together as always. Evidently, the bulk of her fat salary was being spent on designer clothing, and Kyle, along with Tim and Tabor, looked forward to the daily fashion statement.

"You look great today," Kyle said with a smile.

"Thank you."

"Prada?"

"Dolce & Gabbana."

"Killer shoes. Blahniks?"

"Jimmy Choo."

"Five hundred bucks?"

"Don't ask."

Admiring her each day, Kyle was quickly learning the names of the high priests of female clothing. It was one of the few topics she cared to discuss. After six weeks of shared space in the cube, he still knew very little about her. When she talked, which was not very often, it was always about law firm business and the miserable life of a first-year associate. If there was a boyfriend, he had yet to be mentioned. She had dropped her guard twice and agreed to drinks after work, but she usually declined. And while every rookie was openly grousing about the hours and the pressure, Dale Armstrong seemed to be feeling the strain more than most.

"What are you doing for lunch?" Kyle asked.

"I haven't had breakfast yet," she replied coolly and withdrew into her little section of the cube.

22

The lights in the shelter came on each morning at six, and most of the homeless awoke and began making preparations for another day. The rules did not allow them to stay past eight o'clock. Many had jobs, but those who didn't were expected to be on the streets looking for employment. Brother Manny and his staff were very successful in placing their "friends," even if the work was often part-time and minimum wage.

Breakfast was served upstairs in the fellowship hall, where volunteers manned the small kitchen and prepared eggs, toast, oatmeal, and cereal. And it was served with a smile, a warm "Good morning" for everyone, and a quick prayer of thanks once they were all seated. Brother Manny, a notorious late sleeper, preferred to delegate the early-morning duties at his compound. For the past month, the kitchen had been organized and supervised by Baxter Tate, a smiling young man who'd never boiled water in his previous life. Baxter scrambled eggs by the dozen, toasted loaves of white bread, prepared the oatmeal—real, not instant—and also restocked the supplies, washed the dishes, and he, Baxter Tate, often said the prayer. He encouraged the other volunteers, had a kind word for everyone, and knew the names of most of the homeless he graciously served. After they had eaten, he loaded them into three old church vans, drove one himself, and delivered them to their various jobs around Reno. He picked them up late in the afternoon.

Alcoholics Anonymous met three times each week at Hope Village—Monday and Thursday nights and at noon on Wednesday. Baxter never missed a meeting. He was warmly received by his fellow addicts, and quietly marveled at the groups' compositions. All races, ages, male and female, professionals and homeless, rich and poor. Alcoholism cut a wide, jagged path through every class, every segment. There were old, confident drunks who boasted of being sober for decades, and new ones like himself who freely admitted that they were still afraid. They were comforted, though, by the veterans. Baxter had made a mess of his life, but his history was a cakewalk compared to that of some of the others. Their stories were compelling, often shocking, especially those of the ex-convicts.

During his third AA meeting, with Brother Manny watching from the rear, he walked to the front of the group, cleared his throat, and said, "My name is Baxter Tate, and I'm an alcoholic from Pittsburgh." After he uttered those words, he wiped tears from his cheeks and listened to the applause.

Following the Twelve Steps to recovery, he made a list of all the people he had harmed and then made plans to make amends. It wasn't a long list and was heavily focused on his family. He did not, however, look forward to a return to Pittsburgh. He'd talked to Uncle Wally. The family knew he was still sober, and that was all that mattered.

After a month, he began to grow restless. He did not relish the thought of leaving the safety of Hope Village, but he knew the time was coming. Brother Manny encouraged him to make his plans. He was too young and smart and gifted to spend his life in a homeless shelter. "God has big plans for you," Brother Manny said. "Just trust him and they will be revealed."

WHEN IT LOOKED as if they might escape at a decent hour on Friday night, Tim Reynolds and others quickly organized a drinking party and hurried out of the building. Saturday was to be a rare day off. No member of the litigation group at Scully & Pershing could be seen at work on Saturday because it was the annual family picnic in Central Park. Thus, Friday night was cleared for serious drinking.

Kyle declined, as did Dale. Around 7:00 p.m., as they were both wrapping up the last details of an endless week, and with no one else around, she leaned around the canvas partition that separated their tight cubicles and said, "What about dinner?"

"Great idea," Kyle said without hesitation. "Any place in particular?"

"My place. We can relax and talk and do whatever. You like Chinese?"

"Love it." The word "whatever" was bouncing around his addled brain. Dale was thirty, single, attractive, apparently straight, a pretty lady alone in the big city. At some point, she had to think about sex, though Kyle was depressed at how little he thought about it.

Was she picking him up? It was a startling idea. Dale was so shy and reserved it was hard to believe she would put the move on anyone.

"Why don't you pick up some Chinese and bring it over?" she said.

"Great idea."

She lived alone in Greenwich Village, in a fourth-floor walk-up. They discussed various take-out restaurants in the neighborhood, then left the office together. An hour later, Kyle climbed the stairs with a sack of shrimp-and-chicken fried rice and knocked on the door. Dale opened it, with a smile, and welcomed him to her apartment.

Two rooms, a den-kitchen combo, and one bedroom. It was small but nicely decorated, a minimalist theme with leather and chrome and black-and-white photos on the wall. She, too, was well-appointed and pursuing the less-is-more approach. Her white cotton skirt was extremely short and revealed more of the slender legs Kyle and the other vultures had been admiring. Her shoes were short heels, open toe, no straps, red leather, high-class-tart stuff. Kyle glanced at them and said, "Jimmy Choos?"

"Prada."

The black cotton sweater was tight, without a bra under it. For the first time in far too many weeks, Kyle began to feel the excitement of sexual arousal.

"Nice place," he said, looking at a photograph.

"Four thousand a month, can you believe it?" She was opening the fridge, one about the size of a large desktop computer. She removed a bottle of white wine.

"Yes, I can believe it. It's New York. But no one made us come here."

She was holding the bottle of chardonnay. "I'm sorry, but I don't have any club soda. It's either wine or water."

"I'll have some wine," he said, with only a slight hesitation. And he decided on the spot that he would not torment himself by arguing back and forth about whether he should take a drink after five and a half years of sobriety. He'd never been to rehab, never been forced to detox, never considered himself an alcoholic. He had simply stopped drinking because he was drinking too much, and now he wanted a glass of wine.

They ate on a small square table, their knees almost touching. Even at home and completely relaxed, conversation did not come easily for Dale, the mathematician. He could not imagine her in a classroom in front of fifty students. And he certainly couldn't picture her in a courtroom in front of a jury.

"Let's agree that we will not talk about work," Kyle said, taking the lead. He took his fourth sip of wine.

"Agreed, but first there's some great gossip."

"Let's have it."

"Have you heard about the split?"

"No."

"There's a rumor, I heard it twice today, that Toby Roland and four other partners, all in litigation, are about to split and open their own firm. They may take as many as twenty associates."

"Why?"

"A fee dispute. The usual." Law firms are famous for exploding, imploding, merging, and spinning off in all directions. The fact that some unhappy partners wanted their own show was no surprise, either at Scully or at any other firm.

"Does that mean more work for the rest of us?" he asked.

"I sure hope so."

"Have you met Toby?"

"Yes. And I hope the rumor is true."

"Who's the biggest prick you've met so far?"

She took a sip of wine and thought about the question. "That's a tough one. So many contenders."

"Too many. Let's talk about something else."

Kyle managed to shift the conversation around to her. Background, education, childhood, family, college. She had never been married. One bad romance still stung. After one glass of wine she poured another, and the alcohol loosened her up. He noticed that she ate almost nothing. He, though, devoured everything in sight. She pushed the topics back to his side of the table, and he talked about Duquesne and Yale. Occasionally, the law firm would get mentioned, and they would find themselves wrapped up in it.

When the wine and food were gone, she said, "Let's watch a movie."

"Great idea," Kyle said. As she looked through her DVDs, he glanced at his watch. Ten twenty. In the past six days he'd pulled two all-nighters—he now owned a sleeping bag—and averaged four hours of sleep each night. He was physically and mentally exhausted, and the two and a half glasses of quite delicious wine he'd just consumed were thoroughly soaking whatever brain he had left.

"Romance, action, comedy?" she called out as she flipped through what appeared to be an extensive collection. She was on her knees, the skirt barely covering her rear. Kyle stretched out on the sofa because he didn't like the looks of either chair.

"Anything but a chick flick."

"How about *Beetlejuice*?"

"Perfect."

She inserted the disc, then kicked off her heels, grabbed a quilt, and joined Kyle on the sofa. She wedged and wiggled and snuggled and pulled the quilt over them, and when she was finally situated, there was a lot of contact. And then there was touching. Kyle sniffed her hair and thought how easy this was.

"Doesn't the firm have a rule against this sort of thing?" he said.

"We're just watching a movie."

And they watched it. Warmed by the quilt, the wine, and each other's bodies, they watched the movie for all of ten minutes. Later, they could not determine who fell asleep first. Dale woke up long after the movie was over. She spread the quilt over him, then went to bed. Kyle woke up at 9:30 on Saturday morning to an empty apartment. There was a note saying she was around the corner at a coffee shop reading the newspapers, so stop by if he was hungry.

THEY RODE THE subway together to Central Park, arriving around noon. The litigation section of the firm threw a family picnic on the third Saturday of each October, near the boathouse. The main event was a softball tournament, but there were also horseshoes, croquet, bocce, and games for the kids. A caterer barbecued ribs and chicken. A rap band made its noise. There was an entire row of iced kegs of Heineken.

The picnic was to promote camaraderie and to prove that the firm did indeed believe in having fun. Attendance was mandatory. No phones allowed. For most associates, though, the time could've been better spent sleeping. At least they were not subject to being dragged into the office for another all-nighter. Only Christmas, New Year's, Thanksgiving, Rosh Hashanah, and Yom Kippur afforded the same protection.

The day was clear, the weather perfect, and the weary lawyers shook off their fatigue and were soon playing hard and drinking even harder. Kyle and Dale, anxious to avoid even the possibility of gossip, soon separated and got lost in the crowd.

Within minutes, Kyle heard the news that Jack McDougle, a second-year associate from Duke, had been arrested the night before when a narc team kicked in the door of his apartment in SoHo and found a substantial stash of cocaine. He was still in jail and likely to remain there over the weekend until bail could be arranged on Monday. The firm was pulling strings to get him out, but the firm's involvement on his behalf would only go so far. Scully & Pershing took a hard line on such behavior. McDougle would be laid off pending the charges. If the gossip turned out to be true, he would find himself unemployed in a few weeks.

Kyle paused for a few minutes and thought about Bennie. His chilling prediction had come true.

LITIGATION HAD 28 partners and 130 associates. Two-thirds were married, and there was no shortage of young, well-dressed children running around. The softball tournament began with Mr. Wilson

Rush, senior of all seniors, announcing the brackets and the rules and declaring himself the acting commissioner. Several lawyers had the guts to boo him, but then anything was permitted on this fine day. Kyle had elected to play—it was optional—and he found himself on a ragtag team with two people he'd met and seven he had not. Their coach was a partner named Cecil Abbott (of Team Trylon), who was wearing a Yankees cap and a Derek Jeter jersey, and it was soon evident that Coach Abbott had never run to first base in his life. With a cold Heineken in hand, he prepared a lineup that couldn't beat a decent T-ball team, but then who cared? Kyle, easily the best athlete, was stuck in right field. In center was Sherry Abney, the fifth-year associate Bennie was stalking as Kyle's entrée into the Trylon-Bartin case. As they came to bat in the first inning, Kyle introduced himself and chatted her up. She was visibly upset by the McDougle arrest. They had worked together for two years. No, she had no idea he had a drug problem.

Mingling was encouraged, and after Coach Abbott's team was finally saved by the mercy rule in the fourth inning, Kyle plunged into the crowd and said hello to every strange face he encountered. Many of the names were familiar. He had, after all, been studying the bios for six weeks. A notorious partner, Birch Mason, also clad in Yankee garb and half-drunk by 2:00 p.m., grabbed Kyle like an old friend and introduced him to his wife and two teenage children. Doug Peckham took him around to meet some of the partners. The conversations were all the same—where'd you go to school, how's it going so far, bet you're worried about the bar exam results, life gets better after the first year, and so on.

And, "Can you believe McDougle?"

The tournament was double elimination, and Kyle's team distinguished itself by becoming the first to lose two games. He found Dale playing bocce, and they headed for the food tent. With plates of barbecue and bottles of water, they joined Tabor and his rather homely girlfriend at a table under a shade tree. Tabor, of course, was on a team that was undefeated, and he'd driven in the most runs so far. He had urgent work at the office and planned to be there at six the following morning.

You win, Kyle wanted to say. You win. Why don't they just go ahead and declare you a partner?

Late in the afternoon, with the sun fading behind the towering apartment buildings on Central Park West, Kyle eased away from the party and found a park bench on a knoll under an oak. Golden leaves dropped around him. He watched the game in the distance, listened to the happy voices, smelled the last of the smoke from the grills. If he really tried, he could almost convince himself that he belonged at that party, that he was just another of the many successful lawyers taking a quick break from their hectic lives.

But reality was never far away. If he got lucky, he would commit a heinous crime against the firm and not get caught. But if luck went against him, then one day during this family picnic they would be talking about him the way they were talking now about McDougle.

23

Sunday, with most of the litigators nursing hangovers, Kyle was up early with a clear head, a tall coffee, walking shoes, and five hours to do nothing but hike the city. The FirmFone was in his pocket, but the FirmFone would not be ringing, because the Sunday after the picnic was a day off as well. A few of the gunners and diehards would be at the office, but most of the firm's litigators would savor another beautiful autumn day without billing an hour.

He worked his way south, through the Village and into Tribeca, then east into the frenzy of Chinatown. In SoHo, he managed to get a seat at the bar at Balthazar, a popular restaurant modeled after a Parisian bistro and raved about in all the guides. He had eggs Benedict and tomato juice, and was thoroughly entertained by the rowdy crowd. Then he found the Brooklyn Bridge, climbed to the top, to the promenade, and hiked across the East River to Brooklyn. It took forty minutes, and then forty minutes back into Manhattan, where he made his way to Broadway and followed it through the garment district, the theater district, Times Square, and on to Columbus Circle.

Brunch was at eleven thirty, at the Upper West Side apartment of Doug and Shelly Peckham. It was an old building on Sixty-third, two blocks off Central Park, and as Kyle rode the stuffy elevator to the third floor, he caught himself doing what most New Yorkers do in their spare time and even while they're working. He pondered real estate. Doug Peckham, as a forty-one-year-old full equity partner in the firm, earned $1.3 million the previous year. His income was no secret. Scully & Pershing, like most mega-firms, published their numbers. Peckham could expect to earn at least that much for the rest of his career, so he could afford a nice place. But $1.3 million a year in New York was not exactly in the big leagues. Not even close. The heavy hitters were the investment bankers, hedge fund whizzes, high-tech entrepreneurs, and corporate executives who were worth billions and thought nothing of dropping $20 million for a midtown apartment. And of course each had the obligatory weekend home in the Hamptons for the summer and one in Palm Beach for weekends in the winter.

The Peckhams had a place in East Hampton. Kyle hoped Shelly and the kids enjoyed the summer house because he knew Doug certainly did not. He was at the office most Saturdays and often on Sundays.

Shelly greeted him with a hug, another old friend now, and welcomed him into their open and unpretentious apartment. Doug was in jeans, sockless, unshaven, and pushing Bloody Marys on his guests. Four other associates were present, all under the supervision of Partner Peckham. The brunch was another effort by him and the firm to soften the edges and make Scully seem like a humane place after all. The goal of the get-together was to talk. Doug wanted to hear their problems and concerns, their ideas and plans, their impressions, and their goals. He also wanted to hurry up and finish brunch so they could watch the Giants versus the 49ers and drink beer, kickoff at 1:00.

Shelly did the cooking herself, and Doug helped serve and pour the wine. After an hour of useless chatter about the same boring lawsuits they'd slaved over all last week, it was time for the Giants. Kyle, the only first-year associate at the table, contributed less than anyone. Halfway through brunch he was already planning his return hike downtown. After dessert, they gathered in the den, where a small fire made things cozy and Doug fiddled with the controls to his high-def, flat-screen TV. In an effort to liven up a dying party, Kyle claimed to be an avid 49ers fan, a hater of the Giants, and this succeeded in generating some trash talk. Two of the older associates were asleep by the end of the first quarter. Doug began to nod off, too, and at halftime Kyle made a clumsy exit and hit the streets.

At five on Monday morning, he was at the office, digging in for another long week.

THE GIANTS' next game was on the road, at Pittsburgh, and two hours before game time Kyle and Joey Bernardo settled into their seats at the forty-yard line and tried to stay warm. A cold front had chased away autumn and a freezing mist hovered above the new stadium. It didn't matter. As die-hard Steelers fans, they had shivered through many games at Three Rivers Stadium, the old place that was gone now. They welcomed the cold. This was real football weather.

Mercifully, Blair had little interest in football. Now five months pregnant, she had gained an enormous amount of weight and was not handling prospective motherhood too well. Joey was having second thoughts about marriage, but for some reason felt trapped. Kyle had little useful advice. If she wasn't pregnant, he would tell his friend to run. But you can't abandon a pregnant fiancée, can you? It just didn't seem right. What did he know about such matters?

As the crowd settled in and the teams warmed up, Kyle was ready to talk. "Speak softly, and tell me about Elaine Keenan," he said.

Joey had a flask filled with vodka, his antifreeze. He took a swig, grimaced as if it tasted awful, and said, "Nothing but trouble."

Their only correspondence about Elaine had been Joey's written summary of his encounter. Kyle needed all the details, and they needed a plan.

"She is one bitter young woman," Joey said. "But she's not nearly as mean as her lawyer."

"Start at the beginning, and tell me everything as it happened."

Another swig, a good smacking of the lips, a glance around to make sure no one cared, and then Joey launched into a slow, thoughtful, detailed reenactment of his trip to Scranton. Kyle interrupted with questions, but the narrative moved along. Just before the coin toss, with the stadium packed and rocking, Joey finally finished with the admonition, "If they have the slightest opening, they'll attack us with a fury. Don't give them the opening. Let's just bury this little episode."

They watched the game for a while and talked about nothing but football. During a time-out, Joey said, "So what's the plan?"

"Can you come to New York next weekend? Steelers–Jets. Four o'clock Sunday at the Meadowlands. I'll get tickets."

"Oh, boy. I don't know." The problem was Blair, with money also a concern. Joey made a nice salary with commissions, but he wasn't getting rich. Now he had a baby on the way and a wife sometime after that, or vice versa, they couldn't decide. One day Blair wanted to postpone the wedding until the baby arrived so she could regain her figure. The next day she wanted to hurry up and get married so the birth wouldn't be out of wedlock. Joey was just straddling the fence, hanging on by his fingernails, and getting whipsawed from both sides. They were now paying for an expensive new condo. He couldn't afford to spend too much watching football.

"Why do you want me in New York?" he asked.

"Because I want to try to get a photo of Bennie."

"And why do you want a photo of this guy? These people are dangerous, right?"

"Oh, yes. Lethal."

"So why are we messing with them?"

"I want to know who they are."

Joey shook his head and looked away, toward the scoreboard, then he took a sip and leaned close to Kyle. "I say we leave them alone. I say you do what they want you to do, play their games, don't get caught, keep the damned video buried, and life will be good for all of us."

"Maybe. Can you come to New York?"

"I don't know. I'll have to figure it out."

"It's very important. Please."

"How, old buddy, do you plan to get a picture of this guy Bennie? He's a professional operative, right?"

"Something like that."

"You're a lawyer, I'm a stockbroker. We have no idea what we're doing, and we could easily get ourselves in trouble."

"Yes, we could."

Kyle took a small package from a pocket of his bulky black and gold Steelers parka. "Take this," he said, keeping it low so that no one could see it. Joey took it and stuffed it into a pocket of his own black and gold Steelers parka. "What is it?"

"It's a video camera."

"Doesn't feel like a video camera."

"It's a video camera, but not one you're likely to see in a store window."

The Steelers scored on a long pass, the game's first touchdown, and the crowd celebrated for five minutes. During the ensuing timeout, Kyle continued: "It's not much larger than an ink pen. It goes in the pocket of either a shirt or a jacket, with a thin wire running to a control switch in your left hand. You can talk to someone face-to-face and video the conversation without their knowledge."

"So I just walk up to Bennie, who's probably heavily armed and has several other heavily armed pals nearby, and introduce myself and ask him to smile."

"No. There's a better way. But this week you need to practice with it."

"Does it have a name?"

"It's all there in the paperwork—specs, instructions, all that stuff. Just bone up on it this week and learn how to use it. If things go perfectly, you'll have about three seconds to video Bennie."

"And if they don't go perfectly?"

"I'll rescue you."

"Great." A long, nervous swig from the flask. "So, Kyle, let's say we get Bennie on video. How do you, not me, but you, go about identifying him?"

"I haven't figured that out."

"There's a lot you haven't figured out."

"I'll e-mail you Tuesday, tell you I've got tickets, the usual drill. Are you in, Joey, old pal?"

"I don't know. I think you're crazy, and you're making me crazy."

"Come on. You need to have some fun while you can."

KYLE WAS hard at work in the main library when the FirmFone rattled softly at four on Thursday afternoon. The e-mail described itself as urgent and commanded the first-year associates to congregate immediately on the forty-fourth-floor mezzanine, the largest gathering place at Scully & Pershing. The message meant only one thing—the bar exam results were in. And the fact that Kyle was being summoned meant that he had passed.

For weeks they had labored against the clock and suffered the often unbearable pressure of adjusting to life in the big firm, and added to that misery was the bar exam hanging over them like a dark cloud. It was always there, seldom discussed because the exam was over and talking about it only made life worse. But it woke them up when they desperately needed sleep. It followed them to the table and could ruin a meal in an instant. The bar exam. What if they flunked the bar exam?

The ritual varied from firm to firm, but Scully & Pershing had a rather pleasant way of breaking the news. They gathered the lucky ones together and threw a party. Though it was supposed to be a surprise, by the second week of September every new associate knew the drill. The cruel part of the festivities was that the unlucky ones were simply not invited. They were left to retreat, to sneak out of the building and go wander the streets for the rest of the day.

As Kyle ran up the stairs and raced along the hallways, he searched for his friends. There were high fives, yelps for joy, people running in shoes that were not meant for running. He saw Dale and gave her a hug, and they walked quickly together. Once on the mezzanine, the crowd was already in a raucous mood before Mr. Howard Meezer, the firm's managing partner, stepped to a small podium and said, "Congratulations. Let's have a party. Not another hour can be billed today."

Champagne corks were soon flying. Bartenders were busy, and waiters began passing delicious antipasto. The general feeling was one of euphoria, even giddiness, because the nightmare was over and they were now lawyers forever.

Kyle was enjoying a glass of champagne with Dale and a few others when the conversation shifted to their less fortunate colleagues. "Does anybody see Garwood?" And they began searching the party for Garwood, who was unaccounted for and soon presumed to be on the other list.

Tim Reynolds approached them with a nasty smile, a drink in one hand and a printout in the other. “Tabor flunked,” he announced proudly. “Can you believe it? A Harvard casualty.” Kyle wasn’t as pleased. Sure, Tabor was obnoxious and opportunistic, but he was their cube mate, and flunking the bar would kill him. He wasn’t a bad guy.

Word spread; the body count rose. In all, there were 8 failures out of 103, a pass rate of 92 percent, an excellent number for any class at any firm. Once again it was clear that they were the brightest stars and were now destined for even greater things.

They got as drunk as possible, then rode home in private sedans arranged by the firm. Kyle had only two drinks and walked to Chelsea. Along the way, he called his father with the wonderful news.

24

His appointment at noon Friday with Doug Peckham was described as a working lunch to review some discovery, but when Kyle arrived ten minutes early, the partner said, "Let's celebrate." They left the building and crawled into the back of a Lincoln sedan, one of the innumerable "black cars" that roam the city and keep the professionals out of the yellow cabs. The firm had a fleet of black cars on call.

"Been to Eleven Madison Park?" Doug asked.

"No. I don't get out much these days, Doug, because I'm a first-year associate and I'm either usually too tired to eat, or I don't have time, or I simply forget."

"Whining, are we?"

"Of course not."

"Congrats on passing the bar."

"Thank you."

"You'll like this place. Great food, beautiful dining room. Let's have a long lunch, with some wine. I know just the client we can stick it to."

Kyle nodded. Two months in, and he was still uncomfortable with the notion of sticking it to clients. Padding the file. Overbilling. Racking up expenses. He wanted to ask what, exactly, the client was about to get stuck for. Just the lunch, which was a certainty, or would the client also get billed for two hours of his time and two hours of Peckham's? But he didn't ask.

The restaurant was in the lobby of the old Metropolitan Life Building, with views of Madison Square Park. The decor was contemporary, with high ceilings and wide windows. Doug, of course, claimed to know the chef and the maître d' and the sommelier, and Kyle was not surprised when they were seated at a choice table looking at the park.

"Let's get your evaluation out of the way," Doug said, snapping a bread stick and sending crumbs across the pristine white tablecloth.

"Evaluation?"

"Yes, it's my job as your supervising partner to evaluate you after the bar results. Obviously, if you'd flunked, we wouldn't be here, and I wouldn't have nice things to say. We'd probably be stopping by one of those carts pushed by a street vendor, selecting a greasy kielbasa, taking a walk, and having a bad conversation. But you passed, so I'm going to be nice."

"Thank you."

The waiter presented menus while the water was poured. Doug chomped on a bread stick, more crumbs flying across the table. "Your billing is above average; in fact, it's very impressive."

"Thanks." No surprise that any evaluation at Scully & Pershing would begin with how much money one was raking in.

"I've had nothing but positive comments from other partners and senior associates."

"Drinks? Something to start with?" the waiter asked.

"We'll order some wine with lunch," Doug said, almost rudely, and the waiter disappeared.

"At times, though, you seem to lack commitment, as if you're not fully on board. Fair?"

Kyle shook his head and thought about a response. Doug was a no-nonsense type, so why not level with him? "I live, eat, and sleep at the firm, like every other first-year associate, because that's the business model some guy came up with years ago. The same way medical residents go twenty hours a day to prove their mettle. Thank God we're not treating sick people. I don't know what else I can do to prove my commitment."

"Good point," Doug said, suddenly much more concerned with the menu. The waiter hovered, waiting.

"You ready?" Doug said. "I'm starving."

Kyle had yet to look at the menu and was still stinging from the criticism of his commitment. "Sure," he said. Everything looked delicious. They ordered, the waiter approved, and the sommelier appeared. At some point during the serious wine discussion that followed, Doug mentioned a "first bottle" and a "second bottle."

The first was a white burgundy. "You'll love it," Doug said. "One of my favorites."

"I'm sure."

"Any problems, complaints?" Doug asked, as if he were clicking off the items on the evaluation checklist.

With perfect timing, Kyle's FirmFone vibrated. "Funny you should mention it," he said as he pulled it from his coat pocket and looked at the e-mail. "It's Karleen Sanborn, looking for a few hours of light lifting in the Placid Mortgage mess. What shall I tell her?"

"You're having lunch with me."

Kyle typed the e-mail, sent it, then asked, "Can I turn this off?"

"Of course." The wine was being presented. Doug sampled it and rolled his eyes, and two glasses were poured.

Kyle pressed on. "My complaint is this damned phone. It has become my life. When you were an associate fifteen years ago, they didn't have cell phones and smartphones and FirmFones, and so—"

"We worked just as hard," Doug interrupted with a wave of dismissal. Stop complaining. Get tough. With his other hand he was raising his wineglass to inspect its contents. He finally took a sip, then nodded his approval.

"Well, my complaint is this phone."

"Okay, anything else?" Another check mark in another box.

"No, just the usual complaints of associate abuse. You've heard them before, and you don't want to hear them now."

"You're right, Kyle, I don't want to hear it. Look, as partners we know what's going on. We're not oblivious. We survived it, and now we reap the rewards. It's a bad business model because everybody's miserable. You think I want to push myself out of bed at five every morning so I can spend twelve crazy hours at the office so, at the end of the year, we can divide the spoils and be at the top of the rankings? Last year APE's partners averaged $1.4 million. We were at $1.3 million, and everybody panicked. We gotta cut costs! We gotta bill more! We gotta hire more associates and grind them into the concrete because we're the biggest! It's crazy. No one ever stops and says, 'Hey, you know, I can live on a million bucks a year and spend more time with my kids, or more time at the beach.' No sir. We gotta be No. 1."

"I'll take a million bucks a year."

"You'll get there. Evaluation's over."

"One quick question."

"Shoot."

"There's a cute first-year associate, and I'm growing rather fond of her. How big a deal is it?"

"Strict prohibition. How cute?"

"Getting cuter by the day."

"Name?"

"Sorry."

"You gonna do it at the office?"

"Haven't got that far yet. There are plenty of sleeping bags."

Doug took a breath and leaned forward on his elbows. "There's a lot of sex around the place. Come on, it's an office. You put five thousand men and women together and it happens. The unwritten rule is this: Don't screw around with the employees. Secretaries, paralegals, support staff, clerks, those who are considered somewhat below us. We call them the nonlawyers. As for your fellow associates, or partners for that matter, no one really cares as long as you don't get caught."

"I've heard some great stories."

"They're probably true. Careers have been ruined. Last year two partners, both married to other people, started a hot affair, got caught, and were kicked out. They're still looking for jobs."

"But for two unmarried associates, come on."

"Just don't get caught."

The first courses arrived and sex was forgotten. Kyle had a leek and cheese tart. Doug went a bit heavier with a salad of Maine lobster with fennel and black trumpet mushrooms. Kyle drank less wine and more water. Doug was determined to polish off the first bottle and get to the second.

"A bit of a shake-up is coming down," Doug said between bites. "I'm sure you've heard."

Kyle nodded with a mouth full.

"It's probably going to happen. Five of our litigation partners are leaving with a bunch of associates and several clients. The mutiny is being led by Toby Roland, and it's not pretty."

"How many associates?" Kyle asked.

"Twenty-six as of this morning. It's a free-for-all. They're waving money and twisting arms and no one knows how many will eventually leave, but it will knock a hole in litigation. We'll survive."

"How do we fill the gap?"

"We'll probably raid another firm. They didn't teach you this in law school?"

They both laughed and returned to their food for a moment.

"Will this increase the workload for those left behind?" Kyle asked between bites.

Doug shrugged as if to say yes. "Maybe. It's too early to tell. They're taking some big clients with some big lawsuits. In fact, that's why they're leaving."

"Is Trylon leaving or staying?"

"Trylon is an old client, and it's firmly within the protective custody of Mr. Wilson Rush. What do you know about Trylon?" Doug was eyeing him closely, as if they were moving into territory that was off-limits.

"Just what I've read in the newspapers and magazines. You ever worked for them?"

"Sure, several times."

Kyle decided to push on, just a little. A waiter removed their plates. Another poured more wine.

"What's this Bartin dispute all about? The *Journal* said the court file is locked away because the issues are so sensitive."

"Military secrets. Huge sums of money involved. The Pentagon is all over it. They tried like hell to stop the companies from fighting, but it blew up anyway. There's a lot of technology involved, not to mention a few hundred billion dollars."

"Are you working on it?"

"No. I passed. There's quite a team, though."

Fresh bread arrived to cleanse the palate. The first bottle was empty, and Doug ordered a second. Kyle was carefully pacing himself.

"The partners and associates who are leaving," Kyle said, "how many are working on the Bartin lawsuit?"

"I don't know. Why are you so interested?"

"Because I don't want to work on it."

"Why not?"

"Because I think Trylon is a rogue defense contractor with a rotten history of making cheap products, screwing the government and the taxpayers, dumping dirty weapons around the world, killing innocent people, promoting war, and propping up nasty little dictators, all in an effort to increase the bottom line and have something to show the shareholders."

"Anything else?"

"Lots."

"You don't like Trylon?"

"No."

"The company is an extremely valuable client."

"Good. Let someone else work for them."

"Associates are not allowed to choose who they work for."

"I know. I'm just sharing my opinion."

"Well, keep it to yourself, okay. That kind of language will get you a lousy reputation."

"Don't worry. I'll do the work that's assigned to me. But as a favor, as my supervising partner, I'm asking that you keep me busy elsewhere."

"I'll see what I can do, but Mr. Rush makes the final decisions."

The second wine was a pinot noir from South Africa, and it, too, caused Doug's eyes to roll around. Their entrées—braised pork shoulder and aged prime rib of beef—were not far behind, and they got serious about eating.

"You know your rate now goes to four hundred an hour," Doug said, chewing.

"Are you still at eight hundred?"

"Yes."

Kyle was not sure he had the spine to bill a client, regardless of how large the corporation might be, $400 for an hour of his inexperienced legal work. Not that he had a choice.

"On the subject of billing," Doug said. "For the month of October, I need you to estimate my hours on the Ontario Bank case. I got busy and lost track."

Kyle managed to keep chewing a small bite of braised pork, but he almost choked. Did he say "Estimate my hours"? He certainly did, and this was something new. There had been nothing at orientation, nothing in the handbook, nothing anywhere about "estimating" hours. Just the opposite. They had been trained to treat billing as the most important aspect of their practice. Pick up a file, look at the clock. Make a phone call, record the time. Sit through a meeting, count the minutes. Every hour had to be accounted for, and the billing was done on the spot. It was never to be delayed, and it had to be precise.

"How does one estimate hours?" Kyle asked carefully.

"Look at the file. Check the hours you billed on it. Look at my work, then estimate my time for the month of October. It's no big deal."

At $800 an hour it was indeed a big deal.

"And don't underestimate," Doug said, swirling his wine in the goblet.

Of course not. If we're going to guess here, let's be damned sure we land on the high side. "Is this a common practice?" Kyle asked.

Doug snorted in disbelief and swallowed a hunk of beef. Don't be stupid, boy. It happens all the time. "And since we're now talking about Ontario Bank," he said, meat visible between his teeth, "bill 'em for this lunch."

"I was planning on getting the check," Kyle said, a lame effort at humor.

"Of course not. I'll put it on a credit card and bill the bank. I'm talking about our time. Two hours for you, now at four hundred, and two for me. The bank had record earnings last year."

That was nice to hear. They would need healthy earnings to continue their relationship with Scully & Pershing. Twenty-four hundred dollars for lunch, and that did not include food, wine, or tip.

"And now that you've passed the bar," Doug said as he took another bite, "you are entitled to use the black cars and bill clients for dinner. The rule goes like this: If you work until eight o'clock at night, then call a car. I'll give you the number and code, and be sure the client gets billed for the car. And if you choose, you can go to a restaurant, spend no more than a hundred bucks on yourself, and also bill the client."

"You gotta be kidding."

"Why?"

"Because I'm at the office almost every night until eight, and if somebody else is buying dinner, then I'll be damned sure I stay until eight."

"Attaboy."

"Seems kinda rich, doesn't it?"

"What?"

"Billing the client for expensive dinners and lunches and cars."

A swirl of the pinot, a thoughtful stare at the red liquid, a long pull. "Kyle, my boy, look at it this way. Our biggest client is BXL, the seventh-largest company in the world, sales last year of $200 billion. Very smart businessmen who have a budget for everything. They live by budgets. They are fanatics about budgets. Last year their budget for legal fees was one percent of their total sales, or about $2 billion. We didn't get all of that, because they use twenty different law firms around the world, but we got our share. Guess what happens if they don't spend the amount they budget, if their legal fees fall short? Their in-house lawyers monitor our billings, and if our numbers are low, they call up and raise hell. What are we, the lawyers, doing wrong?

Aren't we properly protecting them? The point is, they expect to spend the money. If we don't take it, then it screws up their budgets, they get worried, and maybe they start looking around for another firm, one that will work harder at billing them. You follow?"

Yes, Kyle followed. It was beginning to make sense. Expensive meals were necessary not only to keep the hungry lawyers going but also to properly balance their clients' financial statements. Now it seemed almost prudent.

"Yes," Kyle said, and for the first time the wine warmed his brain and made him relax.

Doug spread his arms and looked around. "And look at where we are, Kyle. Wall Street. The absolute pinnacle of success in America. We're here, we're on top, we're smart and tough and talented, and we make a boatload of money to prove it. We are entitled, Kyle, and don't forget it. Our clients pay us because they need us and we offer the best legal advice money can buy. Never forget that."

John McAvoy had lunch every day at the same table at an old café on Queen Street in York, and from the time Kyle was ten years old and hanging around the office, he loved having lunch with his father. The café's special was a vegetable plate that varied each day and cost little, with homemade rolls and iced tea, no sugar. The café attracted lawyers, bankers, and judges, but there were also mechanics and bricklayers. The gossip roared and the bantering was nonstop. The lawyers always joked, "Who's paying for lunch?" and boasted of wealthy clients who they'd stick with a $3.99 check.

Kyle doubted that his father ever gave a passing thought to billing a client for lunch.

Doug insisted on dessert. Two hours after entering the restaurant, they pushed themselves out the door and into the black car. Both nodded off during the fifteen-minute ride back to the office.

25

For the first time in the nine-month life of the operation, Kyle contacted Bennie and suggested they meet. All prior meetings had been prompted by the handler, not the asset. Kyle gave no reason for wanting to meet, but then none was necessary. It was assumed that Kyle finally had something valuable to pass along. It was almost 6:00 p.m. on Friday, and Kyle was working in the main library on the thirty-ninth floor. By e-mail, Bennie suggested the hotel 60 Thompson in SoHo, and Kyle agreed. Kyle always agreed because he was not allowed to disagree or suggest another meeting place. It didn't matter; he had no intention of showing up, not that Friday night. Joey wasn't in town yet.

Four hours later, Kyle was hiding in the Placid Mortgage tomb mindlessly flipping through foreclosure files—now at $400 an hour—when he e-mailed Bennie with the sad news that he wouldn't be leaving the office anytime soon. Could be an all-nighter. Although he loathed the work and hated the tomb, and found it hard to believe he was still at the office so late on a Friday night, he was slightly amused at the image of Bennie waiting impatiently in the hotel room for a meeting that would not take place because his asset was holed up in the office and wouldn't come out. The handler couldn't complain if the asset was hard at work.

Kyle suggested a meeting late Saturday afternoon, and Bennie took the bait. Within minutes he e-mailed the instructions: 7:00 p.m., Saturday, room 42, Wooster Hotel in SoHo. So far, a different hotel had been used for each meeting.

On a desk phone, Kyle called Joey's new cell number and passed along the details. His flight from Pittsburgh would arrive at LaGuardia at 2:30 on Saturday afternoon. He would take a cab to the Mercer Hotel, check into his room, and kill time while his friend practiced law. He would roam the streets, walk in the front doors of bars and out the back, browse through bookstores, dart here and there in cabs, and when he was certain he was not being followed, he would drop in at the Wooster Hotel and mill around the lobby. He had in his pocket a copy of the Bennie Wright composite Kyle had been perfecting for weeks. Joey had studied it for hours and was confident he could spot the man anywhere. Now Kyle wanted Bennie in complete digital color.

At 7:30, Kyle walked through the hotel lobby and took the elevator to the fourth floor. Bennie had a small room, no suite this time. As Kyle tossed his trench coat and briefcase on the bed, he glanced into the bathroom. "Just looking for Nigel, or perhaps another surprise," he said as he flipped on a light switch.

"Just me this time," Bennie said. He was relaxing in a velvet chair. "You passed the bar. Congratulations."

"Thanks." The inspection over, Kyle sat on the edge of the bed. The inspection had revealed no one but Bennie, but it had also revealed no luggage, no shaving kit, nothing to indicate Bennie would stay in the room after Kyle left.

"You're putting in the hours," Bennie said, again making an attempt at small talk.

"I'm a full-blown lawyer now, so evidently I'm expected to work even more." He noted the shirt—light blue cotton, no pattern, no buttons on the collar, no necktie. The slacks were dark brown, wool, pleated. The jacket was evidently in the closet next to the bathroom, and Kyle cursed himself for not noticing it. Dark socks, no distinguishable color. Black scuffed shoes, quite ugly.

"Here's the scoop," Kyle said. "Five litigation partners are splitting off—Abraham, DeVere, Hanrahan, Roland, and Bradley. They're opening up their own shop and stealing at least three clients in the process. As of last count, twenty-six associates are jumping with them. Of the partners, Bradley is the only one working on the Trylon-Bartin case. However, at least seven of the associates are assigned to the lawsuit."

"I'm sure you have a memo."

Kyle pulled out a single sheet of paper, tri-folded, and handed it over. It was a summary of the names of all the Scully & Pershing lawyers who were leaving. He knew Bennie would want it in writing, something to preserve in the file and keep as evidence of his treachery. There. He'd finally done it. He'd handed over firm secrets, and now there was no turning back.

Except that it was not exactly accurate. The gossip was changing by the hour, and no one seemed to know precisely who was planning to leave. Kyle had taken a few liberties with the names, especially those of the associates. Nor was it highly confidential information that he was passing along. The *New York Lawyer*, the trade daily, had carried at least two brief stories about the spin-off in the litigation section of Scully & Pershing. Given the ever-shifting nature of law firm personnel, it was not headline news. And besides, Bennie already knew as much as Kyle. And Kyle knew he knew.

The memo gave no details about the business of any client. In fact, it did not mention a client by name. While it appeared to have been put together in a hurry, Kyle had spent time on it and was convinced it was not a violation of ethics.

Bennie unfolded the sheet of paper and studied it carefully. Kyle watched him for a moment, then said, "I need to use the bathroom."

"In there," Bennie said, pointing without looking.

As Kyle walked to the bathroom, he passed the closet, its door half-open, and hanging on a rack was a cheap navy sport coat and a dark gray trench coat.

"I'm not sure this means anything," Kyle said when he returned. "Trylon's in-house attorneys are hands-on, and they prefer the more experienced associates. Those who are leaving will likely be replaced with third- and fourth-year people. I'm still a long shot."

"Who'll take Bradley's place?"

"Not a clue. There are a lot of rumors."

"Have you met Sherry Abney?"

"Yes, we played softball together at the picnic in Central Park. We hit it off, but she's not in charge of which associates are assigned to the case. That decision rests with Mr. Wilson Rush."

"Patience, Kyle, patience. Good intelligence is based on long-term placement and relationships. You'll get there."

"I'm sure I will, especially if you keep picking off the associates ahead of me. How'd you get rid of McDougle? Plant the drugs in his apartment?"

"Come on, Kyle. The young man had a serious problem with cocaine."

"He didn't need your help."

"He's on the road to recovery."

"You asshole! He's on the road to prison."

"He was dealing coke, Kyle. A menace to society."

"What do you care about society?"

Kyle stood and began gathering his things. "Gotta run. My old pal Joey Bernardo is in from Pittsburgh for the Jets game tomorrow."

"How nice," Bennie said, getting to his feet. He knew Joey's flight numbers, coming and going, and he knew their section and seat numbers for tomorrow's game.

"You remember Joey? The second one in your little video?"

"It's not my video, Kyle. I didn't take it. I just found it."

"But you couldn't leave it alone, could you? Later." Kyle slammed the door behind him and hurried down the hallway. He ran down four flights of stairs and entered the lobby not far from the elevators. He made eye contact with Joey, then went straight to the men's room around the corner. There were three urinals to the right. He straddled the center one, waited about ten seconds, then was joined by Joey on the left. There was no one else in the men's room.

"Light blue shirt, no tie, navy sport coat, all under a dark gray trench coat. Black-rimmed reading glasses that come and go, probably will not be wearing them when he comes down. No sign of a briefcase, hat, umbrella, or anything else. He should be alone. He is not staying for the night, so I expect him to be down shortly. Good luck." Kyle pulled the flush handle, left the room, and left the hotel. Joey waited two minutes, then returned to the lobby, where he picked up his newspaper from a chair and sat down. His dark hair had been cut short the day before and was almost entirely gray. He wore fake eyeglasses with thick black frames. The camera, slightly larger than a disposable pen but practically indistinguishable from one, was in the pocket of his brown corduroy jacket, next to a red pocket square.

A hotel security agent in a smart black suit watched him closely, though his curiosity had more to do with the relative inactivity of the lobby than with any real suspicion. Thirty minutes earlier, Joey had explained to the agent that he was waiting on a friend who was upstairs. Two clerks behind the reception desk went about their business with their heads down, seeing nothing but missing little.

Ten minutes passed, then fifteen. Each time an elevator door opened, Joey tensed slightly. He kept the newspaper low, on his knees, so that he could appear to be reading while the camera had a clear shot at the target.

A bell, the door to the elevator on the left opened, and Bennie the Handler was there all by himself in a long gray trench coat. The composite of his face was remarkably accurate—slick bald head, a few strands of black hair greased down about the ears, long narrow nose, square jaw, heavy eyebrows over dark eyes. Joey swallowed hard, his head down, and squeezed the "on" button in his left hand. For eight steps, Bennie walked directly toward him, then veered with the marble walkway toward the front door and was gone. Joey twisted his upper body slightly so the camera could follow, then he switched it off, breathed deeply, and became engrossed in his newspaper. He looked up each time the elevator opened, and after ten long minutes stood and walked back to the men's room. After lingering for half an hour, he feigned frustration with his tardy friend upstairs and stomped out of the hotel. No one followed.

Joey plunged into the Saturday night chaos of lower Manhattan, strolling aimlessly with the thick foot traffic, window-shopping, ducking into music stores and coffee shops. He was convinced he'd lost his tail two hours earlier, but he took no chances. He hurried around corners and cut through narrow streets. At a used bookshop he'd scoped out late in the afternoon, he locked himself in the tiny toilet and washed his hair with a cleansing rinse that took out much of the gray. What was left was covered with a black Steelers cap. He dropped the fake eyeglasses in the wastebasket. The video recorder was stuck deep in his right front pocket.

KYLE WAITED nervously at the bar in the Gotham Bar and Grill on Twelfth Street. He sipped a glass of white wine and chatted occasionally with the bartender. Their reservation was for 9:00 p.m.

The worst-case scenario, indeed the only way they could screw up the operation, was for Bennie to recognize Joey and confront him in the lobby of the Wooster Hotel. It was a long shot, though. Bennie knew Joey was in the city, but he would not recognize him in disguise, nor would he expect him to be anywhere near the hotel. Kyle was assuming that since it was Saturday night, and since he had done little if anything in two months to arouse suspicions, Bennie would be traveling light with a skeleton crew on the streets.

Joey arrived promptly at nine. His hair was almost natural; in fact, as he walked through the front door, Kyle could not see a hint of gray. He had somehow exchanged the well-used brown corduroy jacket for a more stylish black one. His smile told the story. "Got him," he said as he took a stool and began looking for a drink.

"So?" Kyle said softly as he watched the door for anything suspicious.

"Double Absolut on the rocks," Joey said to the bartender. Then to Kyle, much lower, he said, "I think I nailed him. He waited sixteen minutes, used the elevator, and I shot him for at least five seconds before he passed by me."

"Did he look at you?"

"I don't know. I was reading the newspaper. No eye contact, remember. But he never slowed down."

"No trouble recognizing him?"

"No. Your composite is terrific."

They drank for a few moments as Kyle continued to watch the front door and as much of the sidewalk as he could see without being obvious. The maître d' fetched them and led them to a table in the rear of the restaurant. After the menus were presented, Joey handed over the camera. "When can we see it?" he asked.

"A few days. I'll use a computer at the office."

"Don't e-mail me the video," Joey said.

"Don't worry. I'll make a copy and send it snail mail."

"Now what?"

"Good work, pal. Now we enjoy a fine meal, with wine, as you'll notice—"

"Proud of you."

"And tomorrow we watch the Steelers kill the Jets."

They clinked glasses and savored their triumph.

BENNIE YELLED at the three operatives who'd lost Joey after his arrival in the city. They had first lost him late in the afternoon, not long after he had checked in at the Mercer and hit the streets. They'd found him in the Village before dark, then lost him again. Now he was having dinner with Kyle at the Gotham Bar and Grill, but that was exactly where he was supposed to be. The operatives swore he moved as if he knew he was being followed. He had deliberately tried to shake them. "And did a damned fine job, didn't he?" Bennie yelled.

Two straight football games, one in Pittsburgh, now one in New York. More e-mail chatter between the two. Joey was the only friend from college Kyle was now regularly in touch with. The warning signs were there. Something was being planned.

Bennie decided to beef up surveillance on Mr. Joey Bernardo.

They were also watching Baxter Tate and his remarkable transformation.

26

At 4:30 on Monday morning, Kyle hurried off the elevator, alone, on the thirty-third floor and walked to his cube. As usual, lights were on, doors were open, coffee was brewed, someone was working. Someone was always working, regardless of the day or hour. The receptionists, secretaries, and clerks weren't due until 9:00, but then they only worked a forty-hour week. The partners averaged around seventy. It was not unusual for an associate occasionally to hit a hundred.

"Good morning, Mr. McAvoy." It was Alfredo, one of the plainclothes security agents who roamed the hallways during the weird hours.

"Good morning, Alfredo," Kyle said as he wadded his trench coat and tossed it in a corner, next to his sleeping bag.

"How 'bout those Jets?" Alfredo asked.

"I'd rather not discuss it," Kyle shot back. Twelve hours earlier, the Jets had drubbed the Steelers by three touchdowns in heavy rain.

"Have a nice day," Alfredo said happily as he walked away, his day obviously made better because his team had slaughtered the Steelers and, more important, he'd found a place to rub it in. New York sports fans, Kyle mumbled as he unlocked his drawer and pulled out his laptop. As he waited for it to power up, he glanced around to make sure he was alone. Dale refused to punch in before 6:00. Tim Reynolds hated mornings and preferred to arrive around 8:00 and make up for it at midnight. Poor Tabor. The gunner had flunked the bar exam and had not been seen since. He'd called in sick last Friday, the day after the results were published, and evidently his sickness had continued throughout the weekend. But there was no time to worry about Tabor. He could take care of himself.

Working quickly, Kyle slid the tiny T-Klip from the video camera into an adapter, which he plugged into his laptop. He waited a few seconds, clicked twice, then froze as the image appeared: Bennie in perfect color, standing at the elevator door, waiting patiently for it to open completely, then walking forward, the steady, confident walk of a man with no fears, no hurries, four steps over the marble floor, then a long glance down at Joey but no connection; five more steps and he disappeared from view. Screen blank. Rewind, watch it again and again, slower and slower. After the fourth step, when Bennie looked casually at Joey, Kyle stopped the action and studied Bennie's face. The shot was clear, the best of the video. He clicked on "print" and quickly made five copies.

He had his man, at least on tape. How about this little video, Bennie? Guess you're not the only one who can play games with hidden cameras. Kyle quickly fetched the copies from the printer beside Sandra's desk. All printing was supposed to be logged in and charged to a client, but no questions were asked by the secretary if a few pages were used for personal reasons. Kyle held the five copies and patted himself on the back. He stared at the face of his tormentor, his blackmailer, the rotten little son of a bitch who was currently in charge of his life.

He thanked Joey for such a superb job. A master of disguise, too quick for the bloodhounds behind him, and a brilliant cameraman.

There was a voice somewhere nearby, and Kyle put away his laptop, hid the T-Klip, and walked up six flights to the main library on the thirty-ninth floor. There, lost among the stacked tiers, he added four of the prints to his hidden file. The fifth he would mail to Joey with a note of congratulations.

From an upper-level balcony, he looked down at the central floor of the library. Rows of tables and study carrels, piles of books scattered around urgent projects. He counted eight associates hard at work, lost in a world of research for memos and briefs and motions that were past due. Five o'clock on a Monday morning in early November. What a way to start the week.

The next step in his scheme had not yet been determined. He wasn't certain there was a next step. But for the moment, Kyle was content to take a breath, savor a small victory, and tell himself there was a way out.

JUST MINUTES AFTER the markets opened Monday, Joey was chatting with a client who wanted to dump some more oil stocks when his second desk phone rang. He routinely carried on more than one phone conversation at the same time, but when the second caller said, "Hey, Joey, it's Baxter. How are you?" Joey got rid of the client.

"Where are you?" Joey asked. Baxter had left Pittsburgh three years earlier, after they graduated from Duquesne, and he seldom returned. When he did, though, he rounded up the old gang, those who could not avoid him, and threw some wild drunken party that killed a weekend. The longer he stayed in L.A. and pursued his acting career, the more insufferable he became when he was back home.

"Here, in Pittsburgh," he said. "Clean and sober for 160 days now."

"That's great, Baxter. Wonderful. I knew you were in rehab."

"Yes, Uncle Wally again. God bless him. You got time for a quick lunch? I need to talk to you about something."

They had never had lunch, not since college. Lunch was too civilized for Baxter. When he met friends, it was always at a bar with a long night ahead of them.

"Sure. What's up?"

"Nothing much. Just want to say hello. Grab a sandwich and meet me down at Point State Park. I'd like to sit outdoors and watch the boats."

"Sure, Baxter." Since it was all so obviously planned, Joey was becoming suspicious.

"Noon okay?"

"See you then."

At noon, Baxter showed up with nothing to eat, nothing but a bottle of water. He was thinner and dressed in old dungarees, a faded navy sweater, and a pair of black combat boots, all selected from the secondhand shop above Brother Manny's shelter for the homeless. Long gone were the designer jeans, Armani jackets, and crocodile loafers. The old Baxter was history.

They embraced and swapped insults, and found an empty bench near the point where the Allegheny and Monongahela rivers merge. A large fountain spewed water behind them.

"You're not eating," Joey said.

"Not hungry. Go ahead."

Joey set aside his deli sandwich and studied the combat boots.

"You seen Kyle?" Baxter asked, and they spent a few minutes catching up about Kyle, Alan Strock, and a few of the other fraternity brothers. When Baxter spoke, he did so softly and slowly and he gazed across the rivers, as if his tongue were working but his mind were engaged elsewhere. When Joey spoke, Baxter listened but did not really hear.

"You seem detached," Joey said, blunt as ever.

"It's just weird being back, you know. Plus, it's so different now that I'm sober. I'm an alcoholic, Joey, a full-blown raging alcoholic, and now that I've stopped drinking and all of that poison is out of my system, I look at things differently. I'm never going to drink again, Joey."

"If you say so."

"I'm no longer the Baxter Tate you once knew."

"Good for you, but the old Baxter wasn't such a bad guy."

"The old Baxter was a selfish, pompous, egotistical, drunken pig, and you know it."

"True."

"He would've been dead in five years."

An old barge inched along the river, and they watched it for a few minutes. Joey slowly unwrapped his turkey on rye and began eating.

"I'm working my way through recovery," Baxter announced quietly. "Are you familiar with the process in Alcoholics Anonymous?"

"Sort of. I had an uncle who sobered up a few years ago and is still active in AA. It's a great program."

"My counselor and pastor is an ex-con known affectionately as Brother Manny. He found me in a bar in a Reno casino six hours after I left the rehab clinic."

"Now that's the old Baxter."

"Indeed. He's led me through the Twelve Steps recovery process. Under his direction, I've made a list of all the people I harmed along the way. Talk about frightening. I had to sit at a table and think of all the people I've hurt because I was drunk."

"And I'm on the list?"

"No, you didn't make it. Sorry."

"Darn."

"It's mainly family members. They're on my list, and I'd probably be on their lists if they ever got serious about life. Now that I've made the list, the next step is to make amends. That's even more frightening. Brother Manny beat his first wife before he went to prison. She divorced him, and years later when he sobered up, he tracked her down to say he was sorry. She had a scar above her lip, thanks to him, and when she finally agreed to meet with him, he begged for forgiveness. She kept pointing to the scar. She was crying, he was crying, sounds horrible, doesn't it?"

"It does."

"I assaulted a girl one time. She's on my list."

The turkey on rye froze halfway down the esophagus. Joey kept chewing, but the food wasn't moving. "You don't say."

"Elaine Keenan, remember her? She claimed we raped her at a party in our apartment."

"How could I forget?"

"Do you ever think about her, Joey? She went to the police. Scared the hell out of us. We almost hired lawyers. I tried my best to forget about it, and I almost did. But now that I'm sober and my mind is clear, I'm remembering things better. We took advantage of that girl, Joey."

Joey placed the sandwich aside. "Maybe your memory is not as sharp as you think. What I remember is a wild girl who loved to party, loved to drink and snort coke, but what she loved the most was random sex. We did not take advantage of anyone. At least I did not. If you want to revise history, then go ahead, but don't include me."

"She passed out. I went first, and while I was doing it, I realized she'd blacked out. Then I remember you walked up to the sofa and you said something like 'Is she awake?' Do you remember any of this, Joey?"

"No." Portions of it were familiar, but Joey wasn't sure anymore. He'd worked so hard to forget the episode, then he'd been shocked back to reality when Kyle described the video.

"She claimed she was raped. Maybe she was right."

"No way, Baxter. Allow me to refresh your memory. You and I had sex with her the night before. Evidently she liked it, because on the night in question we bumped into her again and she said, 'Let's go.' She consented before we got back to our apartment."

Another long pause as each tried to anticipate what was next.

"You thinking about having a little chat with Elaine?" Joey asked.

"Maybe. I need to do something, Joey. I don't feel right about what happened."

"Come on, Baxter, we were all drunk out of our minds. The whole night was a blur."

"Oh, the wonders of alcohol. We do things we don't remember. We hurt others because of our selfishness. And when we finally sober up, we are compelled to at least apologize."

"Apologize? Let me tell you a quick story, Brother Baxter. I bumped into Elaine a few weeks ago. She lives in Scranton. I was passing through on business, saw her in a deli during lunch. I tried to be civil, she freaked out on me, called me a rapist. I suggested we get together a few hours later for a polite cup of coffee. She showed up with her lawyer, a real tough broad who thinks all men are scum. So let's say you go over to Scranton, find her, and tell her you're sorry because there's a good chance she was telling the truth after all, and you want to feel better about yourself because now you're sober and you have this desire to be a good little alcoholic. Know what'll happen, Baxter? Indictments, arrests, trials, lawsuits, prison—all of the above. And not just for you, Brother Baxter, but for some of your friends as well."

A brief gap as Joey caught his breath. He had Baxter on the ropes, time to finish him off. "Her lawyer explained that the statute of limitations on rape is twelve years in Pennsylvania, so time has not expired. We got a long way to go. You get near her with some half-baked, feel-good apology and you'll find out what rape is all about when they lock you away."

Joey jumped to his feet, walked across the boardwalk, and spat at the rivers. He returned to the bench but didn't sit down. Baxter hadn't moved, but he was shaking his head.

"She wanted the sex, Baxter, and we were happy to accommodate her. You're blowing this way out of proportion."

"I've got to talk to her."

"Hell no! You're not going near her until the four of us—me, you, Kyle, and Alan—have a long discussion. That'll be ugly, won't it?"

"I need to talk to Kyle. He has more sense than the rest of us."

"Yes, he does, but he has a crushing workload. Tremendous stress." Joey tried to imagine such a meeting between the two. Kyle, thinking about the video, while Baxter and his amazing new memory confirm the details. It would be a disaster.

"I'll go to New York," Baxter said.

"Don't do it."

"Why not? I'd like to see Kyle."

"Okay, but if you talk to Kyle, then talk to Alan, too. Everybody talks for a good long time before you go blundering into Scranton and screw up our lives. I'm telling you, Baxter, this girl is out for blood and her lawyer has a nose for it."

Another long gap in the conversation. Joey finally sat down and thumped his pal on the knee. Just a couple of old frat brothers who still cared for each other. "You can't do this, Baxter," Joey said with as much conviction as he could muster. At the moment, he was thinking about his own skin. How would he tell Blair, who was now five months pregnant? "*Hey, babes, just got a phone call. Seems they want me downtown, something about a rape charge. Could be serious. Might not be home for dinner. Someone said reporters are waiting. Catch it on Channel 4. Later. Hugs and kisses.*"

"I'm not sure about what happened, Joey," Baxter said, softly and slowly as ever. "But I know what I did was wrong."

"My uncle, the alcoholic, when he went through AA, he made a list, too. He had stolen a rifle from my father, and he saved his money until he could buy another one. Brought it to the house one night, big surprise, big scene. But if I remember correctly, you, as the alcoholic working your way through the Twelve Steps process, cannot make amends if doing so will harm others. Isn't that right?"

"That's correct."

"Then there's your answer. If you approach her and beg forgiveness, she and her lawyer will go nuts and drag in me and probably Kyle and Alan as well. You can't do it, because it will harm us."

"If you did nothing wrong, you have nothing to worry about. I'm confronting what I did, and what I did was wrong."

"This is crazy, Baxter. Look, you're clean and sober and full of the gospel, good for you. I'm very proud of you. The future looks great, yet you're willing to throw it all away and risk twenty years in prison. Come on! This is madness."

"Then what should I do?"

"Get your ass back to Reno or somewhere far away and forget about this. Go live a great life out there. Just leave us alone."

Two policemen walked by, laughing, and Joey stared at the handcuffs on their belts.

"You can't do this, Baxter," he said. "Give it some time. Pray about it. Talk to your minister."

"I have already."

"And what did he say?"

"He said to be cautious."

"Smart guy. Look, you're in a state of transition right now. Everything is unsettled. You're out of L.A., you're clean and sober. All good stuff. Again, I'm proud of you. But it's a mistake to rush off and do something foolish."

"Let's walk," Baxter said and slowly rose to his feet. They strolled along the river, saying little, watching the boats.

"I really want to see Kyle," Baxter finally said.

27

In the four and a half months Kyle had lived in his grim little apartment, he had managed to avoid having guests. Dale had asked about it a few times, then let the matter drop. Kyle described his place as a dump with almost no furnishings, lukewarm water, bugs, and uninsulated walls. He claimed to be looking for something much nicer, but then what first-year associate had time to look for an apartment? The truth was that he wanted a dump for that very reason—he could keep guests away, and in doing so avoid the risks of having their conversations listened to and recorded. Though he had not attempted to rid the place of mikes and electronic bugs, he knew they were there. He suspected there were cameras, always watching, and since he had lulled them into believing that he was clueless about their surveillance, he went through the motions each day of living pretty much like a hermit. Intruders came and went, at least one per week, but there were no invited guests.

Dale was content to meet at her place. She had a fear of bugs. If you only knew, thought Kyle. My apartment has every kind of bug known to the covert world.

They eventually managed to sleep together without actually falling asleep beforehand. Both collapsed shortly afterward. They had violated firm policy on at least four occasions and had no plans to stop.

When Baxter called and asked if he could crash at Kyle's for a few days, Kyle was ready with a string of lies that were mildly convincing. Joey had sent a Mayday call from his desk phone to Kyle's just minutes after he'd said goodbye to Baxter. "We gotta do something," Joey said over and over until Kyle told him to shut up.

The idea of Baxter lounging around his apartment and talking at length about the Elaine episode was almost too much to imagine. Kyle could see Bennie with his technicians, clutching his headphones, listening to Baxter preach about the need to confront the past, admit everything, and so on. If the Elaine episode blew up back in Pittsburgh, Kyle would be dragged into it at some level, and Bennie would risk losing his leverage in New York.

"Sorry, Bax," Kyle said happily on his cell phone. "I have only one bedroom, if you can call it that, and my cousin has been sleeping on the sofa for a month. She's in New York looking for a job, and, well, I gotta say, the place is cramped."

Baxter checked into the Soho Grand. They met for a late pizza at an all-night joint on Bleecker Street in the Village. Kyle picked the place because he'd been there before and, as always, had taken notes on its suitability for future use. One door in and out, large front windows that faced the sidewalk, lots of noise, and it was too small for one of the bloodhounds to enter without being noticed. Kyle arrived at 9:45, fifteen minutes early so he could secure a booth and sit facing the door. He pretended to be engrossed in a thick document, the tireless associate ever dedicated to his work.

Baxter was wearing the same dungarees, sweater, and combat

boots Joey had described. They embraced, then fell into the booth talking nonstop. They ordered soft drinks, and Kyle said, "I talked to Joey. Congrats on the rehab. You look great."

"Thanks. I've thought about you a lot in the past few months. You quit drinking during our sophomore year, right?"

"Right."

"I can't remember why."

"A counselor told me that the drinking would only get worse. I didn't have a serious problem, but one was definitely foreseeable. So I quit. Didn't touch a drop until a few weeks ago, when I had some wine. So far, so good. If I get worried, I'll quit again."

"I had three bleeding ulcers when they took me in. I thought about suicide, but I didn't really want to do it because I'd miss the vodka and cocaine. I was a mess."

They ordered a pizza and talked for a long time about the past, primarily Baxter's. He unloaded story after story about the last three years in L.A.—trying to break into the movie business, the parties, the drug scene, the gorgeous young girls from every small town in America doing everything physically possible to either get a break or marry rich. Kyle listened intently while keeping an eye on the front door and the front windows. Nothing.

They talked about their old friends, Kyle's new job, Baxter's new life. After an hour, when the pizza was gone, they eventually got around to more pressing matters. "I guess Joey told you about Elaine," Baxter said.

"Of course he did. It's a bad idea, Baxter. I understand the law, and you don't. You're walking into quicksand and you could take us with you."

"But you did nothing. Why are you worried?"

"Here's a scenario," Kyle said, leaning closer, eager to unveil a narrative he'd thought about for hours. "You go see Elaine, looking for some type of redemption, forgiveness, whatever you think you might find there. You apologize to someone you once hurt. Maybe she turns the other cheek and accepts your apology, and you two have a nice hug and say goodbye. That probably will not happen. What is much more likely to happen is that she chooses not to take the Christian approach, doesn't give a rip about this cheek-turning business, and decides, with the advice of a pretty nasty lawyer, that what she really wants is justice. She wants vindication. She cried rape once and nobody listened. You, with the best intentions, will vindicate her with your awkward apology. She feels violated now, and she likes being the victim. Her lawyer starts to push, and things unravel quickly. There's a prosecutor in Pittsburgh who, not surprisingly, likes to see his face on the front page. Like all prosecutors, he's tired of the mundane, the gang shootings, the daily street crime. Suddenly he has a chance to go after four white boys from Duquesne, and one just happens to be a Tate. Not only a Great White Defendant, but four of them! Talk about headlines, press conferences, interviews. He'll be the hero, and we'll be the criminals. Of course we are entitled to a trial, but that's a year away, a year of absolutely terrifying hell. You can't do it, Baxter. You'll hurt too many people."

"What if I offer her money? A deal with only two parties, me and her?"

"It might work. I'm sure she and her lawyer would enjoy those discussions. But offering money implies guilt, an admission of some sort. I don't know Elaine, and neither do you, but given Joey's encounter, it's safe to say she is not too stable. We can't predict how she will react. It's too risky."

"I can't live with myself until I talk to her, Kyle. I feel like I harmed her in some way."

"Got that. It sounds great in the AA handbook, but it's a different matter when other people are involved. You have to forget about this and put it behind you."

"I'm not sure I can."

"There's an element of selfishness here, Baxter. You want to do something that you think will make you feel better. Well, good for you. What about the rest of us? Your life will be more complete, our lives could be ruined. You're dead wrong here. Leave this girl alone."

"I can apologize to Elaine without admitting I committed a crime. I'll just say that I was wrong and want to apologize."

"Her lawyer is not stupid, and her lawyer will be sitting there with a tape recorder, probably a video camera." Kyle took a sip of a diet soda and had a quick flashback to the first video. If Baxter saw it now, saw himself tag-teaming with Joey while Elaine was motionless, his guilt would crush him.

"I have to do something."

"No, you don't," Kyle said, raising his voice for the first time. He was surprised at the stubbornness across the table. "You don't have the right to ruin our lives."

"I'm not ruining your life, Kyle. You did nothing wrong."

Is she awake? Joey asks. The words rattle around the courtroom. The jurors scowl at the four defendants. Maybe they feel compassion for Kyle and Alan because there is no evidence that they violated the girl, and find them not guilty. Maybe they're sick of the whole bunch and send them all to prison.

"I'll take all the blame," Baxter said.

"Why are you so determined to get yourself into more trouble than you can imagine? You're toying with prison here, Baxter. Wake up, man!"

"I'll take the blame," he repeated, very much the martyr now. "You guys will walk."

"You're not listening to me, Baxter. This is far more complicated than you realize."

A shrug. "Maybe so."

"Listen to me, dammit!"

"I'm listening to you, Kyle, but I'm also listening to the Lord."

"Well, I can't compete—"

"And he's leading me to Elaine. To forgiveness. And I believe she will listen, and she will forgive, and she will forget." He was firm, and pious, and Kyle realized he had little else to throw at Baxter.

"Let it sit for a month," Kyle said. "Don't do anything hasty. Joey, Alan, and I should have a say in the matter."

"Let's go. I'm tired of sitting here."

They roamed the Village for half an hour before Kyle, exhausted, finally said good night.

He was dead to the world when his cell phone rang three hours later. It was Baxter. "I talked to Elaine," he announced proudly. "Tracked her down, called her, woke her up, and we talked for a few minutes."

"You idiot," Kyle blurted before he could stop himself.

"It went pretty well, actually."

"What did you say?" Kyle was in the bathroom, splashing water on his face with one hand and holding his phone with the other.

"Told her I've never felt right about what happened. I didn't admit to anything other than some misgivings."

Thank God for that. "What did she say?"

"She thanked me for calling, then she cried and said no one has ever believed her. She still feels like she was raped. She's always known it was Joey and me, with you and Alan somewhere close by watching the action."

"That's not true."

"We're gonna meet in a couple of days, have lunch, just the two of us, in Scranton."

"Don't do it, Baxter, please don't do it. You will regret it forever."

"I know what I'm doing, Kyle. I've prayed about this for hours, and I'm trusting God to get me through it. She promised not to tell her lawyer. You gotta have faith."

"She works for her lawyer, part-time, did she tell you that, Baxter? No, she did not. You'll walk into a trap and your life will be over."

"My life is just beginning, old pal. Faith, Kyle, faith. Good night." The phone snapped shut; the connection was dead.

BAXTER FLEW BACK to Pittsburgh the following morning, retrieved his car—a Porsche he planned to sell—from the long-term parking area, and checked into a motel by the airport. Credit card records revealed that he spent two nights in the motel and never checked out. His cell phone records showed numerous incoming calls and text messages from both Joey Bernardo and Kyle McAvoy, with no outgoing calls in return. He had two long conversations with Brother Manny in Reno, and some short ones with his parents and his brother in Pittsburgh. There were two calls to Elaine Keenan.

On the last day of his life, he left Pittsburgh before sunrise, headed for Scranton, a drive that would cover three hundred miles in about five hours. According to the credit card trail, he stopped for gas at a Shell station near the intersection of I-79 and I-80, about ninety minutes north of Pittsburgh. He then headed due east on I-80 and traveled two hours until his journey came to an end. Near the small town of Snow Shoe, he stopped at a rest area and went to the men's room. It was approximately 10:40 a.m. on a Friday in mid-November. Traffic was light, and there were only a few other vehicles at the rest area.

Mr. Dwight Nowoski, a retiree from Dayton who was traveling to Vermont with his wife, who was already in the ladies' room, discovered Baxter not long after he had been shot. He was still alive but dying quickly from a gunshot to the head. Mr. Nowoski found him on the floor by the urinals, his jeans unzipped, the floor covered with blood and urine. The young man was gasping and whimpering and thrashing about like a deer hit by a car. There was no one else in the men's room when Mr. Nowoski walked in and stumbled upon the horrible scene.

Evidently, the murderer followed Baxter into the toilet, took a look around to make sure they were alone, then quickly placed a nine-millimeter pistol, a Beretta according to the lab, at the base of Baxter's skull and fired once. A silencer muffled the gunshot. The rest area was not equipped with surveillance cameras.

The Pennsylvania State Police closed the rest stop and sealed the area around it. Six travelers, including Mr. and Mrs. Nowoski, were questioned at length at the crime scene. One gentleman remembered a yellow Penske rental truck coming and going, but he had no idea how long it was there. The group estimated that another four or five vehicles had left the rest area after the body was discovered but before the police arrived. No one could recall seeing Baxter enter the men's room, nor did anyone see the murderer follow him in. A lady from Rhode Island recalled noticing a man standing by the door to the men's room when she entered the ladies', and upon further reflection she agreed that it was possible he might have been a lookout. He was not going in, nor was he coming out. Regardless, he was long gone, and her description was limited to: male white, somewhere between the ages of thirty and forty-five, at least five feet eight but no more than six feet four, wearing a dark jacket that could have been leather, linen, wool, cotton, anything. Along with the lab reports and autopsy, her description was the extent of the physical evidence.

Baxter's wallet, cash fold, and watch were untouched. The police inventoried his pockets and found nothing but a few coins, his car keys, and a tube of lip balm. The lab would later report that there was no trace of alcohol or illegal drugs in his system, on his clothing, or in his car.

The pathologist did note a remarkable degree of liver damage for a twenty-five-year-old.

Robbery was immediately ruled out for the obvious reasons—nothing was taken, unless the victim was carrying something valuable that no one knew about. But why would an armed thief leave behind $513 in cash and eight credit cards? Wouldn't a thief consider stealing the Porsche while he had the chance? There was no evidence that the crime had anything to do with sex. It could've been a drug hit, but that seemed unlikely. Those were usually much messier.

With sex, robbery, and drugs ruled out, the investigators began scratching their heads. They watched the bagged body disappear into the rear of an ambulance for the ride back to Pittsburgh, and they knew they had a problem. The apparent randomness of the act, plus the silent gunshot and the clean getaway, led them to conclude, at least at the scene, that they were dealing with professionals.

THE CONFIRMATION that a member of such a noted family had met such a strange and brutal end brightened up a dull news day in Pittsburgh. Television crews scampered to the Tate estate in Shadyside, only to be met by private security personnel. For generations the Tate family had offered "No comment" to every inquiry, and this tragedy was no different. A family lawyer issued a terse response and asked for prayers, consideration, and respect for privacy. Uncle Wally once again took charge and issued orders.

Kyle was at his cube, chatting with Dale about their plans for the evening, when the call came from Joey. It was almost 5:00 p.m. on Friday. He had eaten a pizza with Baxter late on Tuesday night, then chatted with him a few hours later, but had not spoken to him since. As far as he and Joey could tell, Baxter had disappeared, or at least he was ignoring his phone.

"What's the matter?" Dale asked as she noticed the look of shock. But Kyle did not respond. He kept the phone to his ear and began walking away, down the hall, past the front desk, listening as Joey unloaded all the details now being splashed across the television. He lost him in the elevator, and once outside the building he called Joey back and kept listening. The sidewalks along Broad were packed with the late-afternoon rush. Kyle plodded along, without a coat to layer against the chill, without a clue as to where he might be going.

"They killed him," he finally said to Joey.

"Who?"

"I think you know."

28

"A funeral lasts for two hours," Doug Peckham was saying as he glared at Kyle. "I don't understand why you need to take two days off."

"The funeral is in Pittsburgh. I have to fly there, then fly back. He was a fraternity brother. I'm a pallbearer. I'll need to see the family. Come on, Doug."

"I've done funerals!"

"For a twenty-five-year-old roommate shot in the head?"

"I get all that, but two days?"

"Yes. Call it vacation. Call it personal time. Don't we get a few personal days a year?"

"Sure, it's somewhere in the handbook, but no one takes them."

"Then I'm taking them. Fire me, I don't give a damn."

A deep breath on both sides of the desk, and Doug said calmly, "Okay, okay. When is the funeral?"

"Two o'clock, Wednesday afternoon."

"Then leave late tomorrow afternoon, and meet me here at five-thirty Thursday morning. I gotta tell you, Kyle, this place is a powder keg. This Toby Roland split is getting nastier, and larger, and those of us who stay behind are about to get dumped on."

"He was my roommate."

"And I'm sorry."

"Oh, thank you."

Doug waved off the last comment, picked up a thick file, and thrust it across the desk. "Can you read this on the airplane?" While phrased like a question, it was an outright command.

Kyle took the file and locked his jaws to keep from saying, Sure, Doug, I'll give it a look on the plane and I'll sneak a peek at the wake and I'll analyze the damned thing during the service and review my thoughts at the burial when they lower Baxter into his grave, and then, when I'm flying back to LaGuardia, I'll flip through it again, and for every minute I'm even remotely thinking about this file, I'll bill, or double bill, or maybe even triple bill the poor client who made the mistake of selecting this full-service sweatshop for its legal needs.

"You okay?" Doug asked.

"No."

"Look, I'm sorry. I don't know what else to say."

"There's nothing to say."

"Any clue as to who pulled the trigger?" Doug shifted his weight as he attempted a bit of small talk. He feigned, badly, interest in what had happened.

"No." If you only knew, Kyle thought.

"I'm sorry," Doug said again, and his effort at showing interest was gone.

Kyle started for the door, but stopped when he heard, "I asked you to estimate my hours for the Ontario Bank case, didn't I? Over lunch, remember? I need the hours."

Estimate your own damned hours, Kyle ached to say, or, better yet, Just keep up with your time like everybody else.

"Almost done," Kyle said and made it through the door without further abuse.

THE INTERMENT of Baxter Farnsworth Tate took place on a damp and overcast day at the family burial plot in Homewood Cemetery, in central Pittsburgh. It followed a staid and by-the-book Episcopal service that was closed to the public and especially closed to the media. Baxter left a brother, who attended the service, and a sister, who did not. Over the weekend the brother made a gallant effort to restructure the funeral into a "celebration" of Baxter's life, an idea that fell flat with the ultimate realization that there was so little to celebrate. The brother yielded to the rector, who led them through the standard rituals of remembering someone whom he, the rector, had never met. Ollie Guice, a Beta from Cleveland who had lived with Baxter for two of their years at Duquesne, struggled through a eulogy that evoked a few smiles. Of the eight surviving members of their pledge class, seven were present. There was also a respectable showing from old Pittsburgh—some childhood friends and those required to attend because they came from the upper crust. There were four long-forgotten pals from the second-tier boarding school the Tates had shipped Baxter to when he was fourteen years old.

Unknown to Kyle and the others, Elaine Keenan had attempted to enter the church but was turned away because her name was not on the list.

No one from Hollywood made it to the funeral. Not a single soul from L.A. Baxter's C-list agent sent flowers. A former female roommate e-mailed the rector a brief eulogy that she insisted be read by someone in attendance. She was "on the set" and couldn't get away. Her eulogy made references to the Buddha and Tibet and was not well received in Pittsburgh. The rector tossed it without a word to the family.

Brother Manny managed to talk his way into the church, but only after Joey Bernardo convinced the family that Baxter had spoken highly of his pastor in Reno. The family, along with all the other mourners, eyed Brother Manny with some suspicion. He wore his standard white uniform—baggy bleached dungarees and flowing shirttail—and layered it with a garment that was probably a robe of some variety but looked more like a white bedsheet. His only concession to the solemnity of the occasion was a black leather beret that adorned his tumbling gray locks and gave him an odd resemblance to an aging Che Guevara. He wept throughout the service, shedding more tears than the rest of the hidebound and stoic collection combined.

Kyle shed no tears, though he was deeply saddened by such a wasted life. As he stood next to the grave and stared at the oak casket, he was unable to dwell on the good times they had shared. He was too consumed with the raging internal debate over what he should have done differently. In particular, should he have told Baxter about the video, about Bennie and the boys, about everything? If he had done so, would Baxter have appreciated the danger and behaved differently? Maybe. Maybe not. In his zeal to clean up his past, Baxter might have gone nuts if he knew he'd actually been filmed doing whatever he did to Elaine. He might have confessed under oath and said to hell with everybody else. It was impossible to predict because Baxter was not thinking rationally. And it was impossible to second-guess now, because Kyle did not foresee the extent of the danger.

But he certainly saw it now.

There were about a hundred mourners huddled around the grave site, all pressing close together to hear the final words from the rector. A few cold raindrops hurried things along. A crimson tent provided shelter for the casket and the family seated near it. Kyle glanced away, at the rows of tombstones where the old money was buried, and beyond them to the stone gate at the cemetery's entrance. On the other side of the entrance was a large pack of media types, waiting like vultures for a glimpse of something newsworthy. Ready with cameras, lights, and microphones, they had been kept away from the church by the police and private guards, but they had dogged the procession like kids at a parade, and now they were desperate for a shot of the casket or the mother collapsing as she said goodbye. Somewhere in their midst was at least one of Bennie's boys, maybe two or three. Kyle wondered if they had a camera, not for a shot of the casket but to record which of Baxter's friends had bothered to attend. Useless information, really, but then so much of what they did made no sense.

They knew how to kill, though. There was little doubt about that. The state police had nothing to say so far, and as the days passed, it was becoming evident that their silence was not necessarily of their choosing. There was simply no evidence. A clean hit, a silent bullet, a quick getaway, and no motive whatsoever.

Brother Manny wailed loudly from the edge of the tent, and this rattled everyone else. The rector missed a beat, then droned on.

Kyle stared at the horde in the distance, too far away for any one face to be recognized. He knew they were there, watching, waiting, curious about his movements and those of Joey and Alan Strock, who'd driven in from med school at Ohio State. The four roommates, now reduced to three.

As the rector wound down, a few sobs could be heard. Then the crowd began backing away from the crimson tent, inching away from the grave site. The burial was over, and Baxter's parents and brother wasted no time in leaving. Kyle and Joey held back, and for a moment stood near the tombstone of another Tate.

"This will be our last conversation for a long time," Joey said softly but firmly. "You're messing around with the wrong people, Kyle. Just leave me out of it."

Kyle looked at the pile of fresh dirt about to be packed on top of Baxter.

Joey kept on, his lips barely moving as if bugs were close by. "Count me out, okay? I've got my hands full here. I've got a life with a wedding and a baby in the future. No more of your silly spy games. You keep playing if you want, but not me."

"Sure, Joey."

"No more e-mails, packages, phone calls. No more trips to New York. I can't keep you out of Pittsburgh, but if you visit here, don't call me. One of us will be next, Kyle, and it won't be you. You're too valuable. You're the one they need. So for our next mistake, guess who gets the bullet."

"We didn't cause his death."

"Are you sure about that?"

"No."

"These guys are around for a reason, and that reason is you."

"Thanks, Joey."

"Don't mention it. I'm going now. Please keep me out of it, Kyle. And be damned sure nobody sees that video. So long."

Kyle allowed him to walk ahead, then he followed.

29

At 6:30 on Thursday morning, Kyle walked into Doug Peckham's office and reported for duty. Doug was standing at his desk, which resembled, as always, a landfill. "How was the funeral?" he asked without looking up from whatever he was holding.

"It was a funeral," Kyle said. He handed over a single sheet of paper. "Here is an estimate of your hours on the Ontario Bank case." Doug snatched it, scanned it, disapproved of it, and said, "Only thirty hours?"

"At the most."

"You're way off. Double it and let's call it sixty."

Kyle shrugged. Call it whatever you want. You're the partner. If the client could pay $24,000 for work that wasn't performed, then the client could certainly pay another $24,000 on top of that.

"We have a hearing in federal court at nine. We'll leave here at eight thirty. Finish the Rule 10 memo and be here at eight."

The prospect of a litigation associate getting near a courtroom during his or her first year was unheard-of, and for Kyle a gloomy day suddenly improved. Of the twelve in his class, no one, at least to his knowledge, had seen live action. He hurried to his cube and was checking e-mails when Tabor appeared with a tall coffee and a haggard look. Since flunking the bar, he had slowly managed to put himself back together, and though he was initially humbled, the cockiness was returning.

"Sorry about your friend," he said, flinging his overcoat and briefcase.

"Thanks," Kyle said. Tabor was still standing, slurping coffee and anxious to talk.

"Have you met H. W. Prewitt, litigation partner two floors up?" he asked.

"No," Kyle answered, still pecking away.

"He's about fifty, big Texan. They call him Harvey Wayne behind his back. Get it? Harvey Wayne, from Texas, double first name?"

"Got it."

"They also call him Texas Slim because he weighs about four hundred pounds. Mean as hell. Went to a community college, then A&M, then Texas Law and hates anybody from Harvard. He's been stalking me, caught me two days ago and gave me a project that any part-time secretary could handle. I spent six hours Tuesday night taking apart exhibit binders for a big deposition yesterday. Took them apart, then reconfigured them just the way Harvey Wayne wanted. There were a dozen binders, couple of hundred pages each, a ton of paperwork. At nine yesterday morning I put them on a cart, raced them down to a conference room where about a hundred lawyers are gathering for this depo, and what did Harvey Wayne do?"

"What?"

"There's this door that leads to another conference room and it won't stay shut, sort of swings back and forth, and so Harvey Wayne, fat ass, tells me to stack the binders on the floor and use them as a doorstop. I do what he tells me, and as I'm leaving the room, I hear him say something like 'Those Harvard boys make the best paralegals.' "

"How much coffee have you had?"

"Second cup."

"I'm on my first, and I really need to crank out this memo."

"Sorry. Look, have you seen Dale?"

"No. I left Tuesday afternoon for the funeral yesterday. Something the matter?"

"She got nailed with some heinous project Tuesday night, and I don't think she's slept at all. Let's keep an eye on her."

"Will do."

At 8:30, Kyle left the office with Doug Peckham and a senior associate named Noel Bard. They walked hurriedly to a parking garage a few blocks away, and when the attendant pulled up in Bard's late-model Jaguar, Peckham said, "Kyle, you drive. We're going to Foley Square."

Kyle wanted to protest but said nothing. Bard and Peckham climbed into the rear seat, leaving Kyle, the chauffeur, alone in the front.

"I'm not sure of the best route," Kyle admitted, with a flash of fear at what would happen if he got lost and the two big shots in the back were late for court.

"Stay on Broad until it becomes Nassau. Take it all the way to Foley Square," Bard said, as if he made the drive every day. "And be careful. This little baby is brand-new and cost me a hundred grand. It's my wife's."

Kyle could not remember being so nervous behind the wheel. He finally found the mirror-adjustment scheme and eased into traffic, cutting his eyes in all directions. To make matters worse, Peckham wanted to talk. "Kyle, a couple of names, all first-years. Darren Bartkowski?"

Without glancing at Peckham in the rearview mirror, Kyle waited and finally said, "So?"

"You know him?"

"Sure. I know all of the first-year litigation associates."

"What about him? Have you worked with him? Good, bad, talk to me, Kyle. How would you evaluate him?"

"Uh, well, nice guy, I knew him at Yale."

"His work, Kyle, his work?"

"I haven't worked with him yet."

"The word is he's a slacker. Ducks the partners, late with projects, lazy with the billing."

I wonder if he estimates his hours, Kyle thought but kept his concentration on the yellow cabs passing, darting, turning abruptly, violating every known rule of the road.

"Have you heard he's a slacker, Kyle?"

"Yes," Kyle said reluctantly. It was the truth.

Bard decided to help thrash poor Bartkowski. "He's billed the fewest hours so far of anyone in your class."

Talking about colleagues was a contact sport at the firm, and the partners were as bad as the associates. An associate who cut corners or ducked projects was labeled a slacker, and the tag was permanent. Most slackers didn't mind. They worked less, got the same salary, and ran almost no risk of being fired unless they stole money from a client or got caught in a sex scandal. Their bonuses were small, but who needs a bonus when you have a fat paycheck? Career slackers could slide for six or seven years at a firm before being informed they would not make partner and shown the door.

"What about Jeff Tabor?" Doug asked.

"I know him well. Definitely not a slacker."

"He has the reputation of being a gunner," Doug said.

"Yes, and that's accurate. He's competitive, but he's not a cutthroat."

"You like him, Kyle?"

"Yes. Tabor's a good guy. Smart as hell."

"Evidently not smart enough," Bard said. "That bar exam problem."

Kyle had no comment, and no comment was necessary because a yellow cab swerved in front of them, cutting off the Jaguar and forcing Kyle to slam on the brakes and hit the horn at the same time. A fist shot out from the driver's window, then an angry middle finger, and Kyle received his first bird. Be cool, he said to himself.

"You gotta watch these idiots," Doug said.

The sound of important papers being extracted crackled from the backseat, and Kyle knew something was being reviewed. "Will we get Judge Hennessy or his magistrate?" Doug asked Bard. Kyle was shut out of the conversation, which was fine with him. He preferred to concentrate on the street in front of him, and he had no interest in assessing the performance of his colleagues.

After ten minutes of downtown traffic, Kyle was wet under the collar and breathing heavy. "There's a lot at the corner of Nassau and Chambers, two blocks from the courthouse," Bard announced. Kyle nodded nervously. He found the lot but it was full, and this caused all manner of cursing in the rear seat.

Peckham took charge. "Look, Kyle, we're in a hurry. Just drop us off in front of the courthouse at Foley Square, then circle the block until you find a spot on the street."

"A spot on which street?"

Doug was stuffing papers back into his briefcase. Bard suddenly had business on the phone. "I don't care. Any street, and if you can't find a spot, then just keep making the block. Let us out here."

Kyle cut to the curb, and a horn erupted somewhere behind them. Both lawyers scrambled out of the rear seat. Peckham's final words were "Just keep moving, okay. You'll find something."

Bard managed to tear himself away from his phone conversation long enough to say, "And be careful. It's my wife's."

Alone, Kyle eased away and tried to relax. He headed north on Centre Street, drove four blocks, then turned left on Leonard and headed west. Every inch of available space was packed with vehicles and motorbikes. An amazing abundance of signs warned against parking anywhere near a potential space. Kyle had never noticed so many threatening signs. He passed no parking garages, but he did pass several traffic cops working the streets, slapping tickets on windshields. After a long, slow block, he turned left on Broadway, and the traffic was even heavier. He inched along for six blocks, then turned left onto Chambers. Two blocks later he was back at the courthouse in which he was supposed to be making his debut as a litigator, if only as a reserve.

Left on Centre, left on Leonard, left on Broadway, left on Chambers, back at the courthouse. Ever concerned about billing, he noted the time. The second loop ate seventeen minutes of the clock, and along the way Kyle again saw nowhere to park. He saw the same signs, same traffic cops, same street bums, same drug dealer sitting on a bench working his cell phone.

Nine o'clock came and went without a call from Peckham, not even a quick "Where the hell are you?" The hearing was under way, but without Kyle the litigator. Kyle the chauffeur, though, was hard at work. After three loops, he was bored with the route and added extra blocks to the north and west. He thought about stopping for a coffee to go, but decided against it out of fear of spilling something onto the fine beige leather of Bard's wife's new Jaguar. He had settled into the leather and was comfortable behind the wheel. It was a very nice car. A hundred thousand dollars and no doubt worth every penny. The gas tank was half-full, and this was worrying him. The stop-and-go driving was a strain on such a large engine. The hearing that he was missing was an important one, no doubt requiring the presence of many high-powered lawyers, all anxious to plead their positions, and things might drag on for a long time. It was obvious that every legal parking spot in lower Manhattan was taken, and with clear instructions to "just keep moving," Kyle accepted the fact that he had no choice but to burn fuel. He began to look for a gas station. He'd fill the tank, bill the client, and score a few points with Bard.

Once the tank was full, he began to ponder other ways to score points. A quick car wash? A quick lube job? When he passed the courthouse for the seventh or eighth time, a street vendor selling soft pretzels looked at him, spread his arms, and said something like "Are you crazy, man?" But Kyle was unperturbed. He decided against a wash or oil change.

Now confident in traffic, he picked up his phone and called Dale. She answered on the third ring and in a hushed voice said, "I'm in the library."

"Are you okay?"

"Yes."

"That's not what I hear."

A pause. "I haven't slept in two nights. I think I'm delirious."

"You sound terrible."

"Where are you?"

"Right now I'm on Leonard Street, driving Noel Bard's wife's new Jaguar. What do you think I'm doing?"

"Sorry I asked. How was the funeral?"

"Terrible. Let's do dinner tonight. I need to unload on someone."

"I'm going home tonight, to bed, to sleep."

"You have to eat. I'll grab some Chinese, we'll have a glass of wine, then sleep together. No sex whatsoever. We've done it before."

"We'll see. I gotta get out of here. Later."

"Are you gonna make it?"

"I doubt it."

At 11:00 a.m., Kyle congratulated himself because he could now bill the client $800 for driving in circles. Then he laughed at himself. Editor in chief of the *Yale Law Journal* behind the wheel here, making perfect turns, clean stops and goes, taking in the sights, dodging the cabs, ah, the life of a big-time Wall Street lawyer.

If his father could see him now.

The call came at 11:40. Bard said, "We're leaving the courtroom. What happened to you?"

"I couldn't find a parking space."

"Where are you?"

"Two blocks from the courthouse."

"Pick us up where you dropped us off."

"My pleasure."

Minutes later, Kyle wheeled to the curb like a veteran driver, and his two passengers jumped into the rear seat. He pulled away and said, "Where to?"

"The office," came the terse reply from Peckham, and for several minutes nothing was said. Kyle expected to be grilled about what he'd been doing for the past few hours. Where were you, Kyle? Why did you miss the hearing, Kyle? But nothing. Sadly, he began to realize that he had not been missed at all. To create some noise, he finally asked, "So how'd the hearing go?"

"It didn't," said Peckham.

"What hearing?" said Bard.

"What have you been doing since 9:00 a.m.?" Kyle asked.

"Waiting for the Honorable Theodore Hennessy to shake off his hangover and grace us with his presence," Bard said.

"It was postponed for two weeks," Peckham said.

AS THEY STEPPED off the elevator on the thirty-second floor, Kyle's phone vibrated. A text message from Tabor read: "Hurry to cube. Problem."

Tabor met him at the stairs. "So how was court?"

"Great. I love litigation. What's the problem?" They were walking quickly through the hall, past Sandra the secretary.

"It's Dale," Tabor whispered. "She fainted, collapsed, passed out, something."

"Where is she?"

"I've hidden the body."

At the cube, Dale was lying peacefully on a sleeping bag partially hidden under Tabor's desk. Her eyes were open, she seemed alert, but her face was very pale.

"She woke up at five Tuesday morning, and she hasn't slept since. That's about fifty-five hours, which might be a record."

Kyle knelt beside her, gently took her wrist, and said, "You okay?"

She nodded yes, but was not convincing.

Tabor, the lookout, glanced around and kept talking: "She doesn't want anyone to know, okay. I say we call the nurse. She says no. What do you say, Kyle?"

"Don't tell anyone," Dale said, her voice low and raspy. "I fainted, that's all. I'm fine."

"Your pulse is good," Kyle said. "Can you walk?"

"I think so."

"Then the three of us will slip out for a quick lunch," Kyle said. "I'll take you home, and you're going to rest. Tabor, call a car."

With a hand under each arm, they slowly pulled her up. She stood, took deep breaths, and said, "I can walk."

"We're right beside you," Kyle said.

They caught a curious glance or two as they left the building—one petite, well-dressed young associate, with very pale skin, arm in arm with two of her colleagues, off for a quick lunch, no doubt, but no one cared. Tabor helped her into the car, then returned to the cube to cover their trails if necessary.

Kyle half-carried her up the three flights to her apartment, then helped her undress and tucked her in. He kissed her forehead, turned off the lights, and closed the door. She did not move for hours.

In the den, he took off his coat, tie, and shoes. He covered the small kitchen table with his laptop, FirmFone, and a file full of research for a memo he'd been neglecting. Once he was fully situated, his eyelids became heavier and heavier until he walked to the sofa for a quick nap. Tabor called an hour later and woke him up. Kyle assured him Dale was sleeping well and would be fine after a long rest.

"There's an announcement coming at 4:00 p.m.," Tabor said. "Big news about the split. Watch your e-mails."

At exactly 4:00 p.m., Scully & Pershing sent an e-mail to all of its lawyers announcing the departure of six partners and thirty-one associates from its litigation practice group. The names were listed. The departures were effective as of 5:00 p.m. that day. The bulletin then proceeded with the standard drivel touting the greatness of the firm and assuring everyone that the split would have no impact on the firm's ability to fully service the needs of its many wonderful and valuable clients.

Kyle peeked through the bedroom door. The patient was breathing nicely and had not changed positions.

He dimmed the lights in the den and stretched out on the sofa. Forget the memo, forget the billing. To hell with the firm, at least for a few stolen moments. How often would he have the chance to relax like this on a Thursday afternoon? The funeral seemed like a month ago. Pittsburgh was in another galaxy. Baxter was gone but not forgotten. He needed Joey, but Joey was gone, too.

The vibration of the phone woke him again. The e-mail was from Doug Peckham, and it read: "Kyle: Major realignment in litigation. I've been added to the Trylon case. So have you. Office of Wilson Rush, 7:00 a.m. sharp tomorrow."

30

For the senior litigation partner, and member of the firm's management committee, the cost of square footage was not a concern. Wilson Rush's office was spread over a large corner on the thirty-first floor, an area at least four times larger than any Kyle had yet seen. Mr. Rush evidently liked boats. His polished and gleaming oak desk was mounted on four rudders from old sailing yachts. A long credenza behind it held a collection of intricate models of sleek clippers and schooners. Every painting depicted a grand vessel at sea. As Kyle walked in and did a quick scan, he caught himself almost waiting for the floor to rock and the salt water to splash across his feet. But he forgot about the decor when Mr. Rush said, "Good morning, Kyle. Over here."

The great man was rising from a large conference table at the far end of his office. A crowd had already gathered there and heavy lifting was under way. Kyle sat next to Doug Peckham. Quick introductions were made. There were nine others present, excluding Mr. Rush and Mr. Peckham, and Kyle recognized most of the faces, including that of

Sherry Abney, the senior associate Bennie had been shadowing. She smiled. Kyle smiled back.

Mr. Rush, seated at the head of the table, launched into a quick review of the current upheaval. Two of the partners who'd mutinied with Toby Roland, and seven of the thirty-one associates, had been assigned to the Trylon versus Bartin case—"much more about that in a minute"—and it was imperative that the firm's manpower be shuffled immediately because the client, Trylon, was important and demanding. Therefore, two partners, Doug Peckham and a woman named Isabelle Gaffney, were entering the fray, along with eight associates.

Mr. Rush was explaining how uneasy the in-house boys at Trylon were with the defections and how necessary it was to shore up the troops, to literally throw more lawyers at APE and Bartin Dynamics.

Isabelle, or Izzy behind her back, was somewhat notorious because she had once required two associates to wait in the delivery room while she was temporarily sidetracked giving birth to a child. Firm lore held that no one had ever seen her smile. And she wasn't about to smile as Mr. Rush went on about the reshuffling and realigning and deft maneuvering of the unlimited legal talent at his disposal.

Two first-year associates were being added, Kyle and a mysterious young man from Penn named Atwater. Of the twelve litigation rookies, Atwater was by far the quietest and loneliest. Dale was a distant second, but she had warmed up nicely, at least in Kyle's opinion. He'd spent the night on her sofa again, alone, while she was dead to the world. He'd slept little. There was too much to consider. The shock of being assigned to the Trylon case caused him to stare at the ceiling and mumble to himself. The horror of Baxter's murder, the images of the funeral and burial, the harsh words of Joey Bernardo—who could sleep with such nightmares rattling around?

Late that night, Kyle had called Peckham and picked and probed to find out why he had been selected to a case he had been rather vocal in trying to avoid. Peckham had no sympathy and was not in the mood to talk. The decision had been made by Wilson Rush. End of conversation.

Mr. Rush was now going through the basics of the lawsuit, material Kyle had committed to memory weeks and months earlier. Binders were passed around. A half hour dragged by and Kyle began to wonder how a person as dull and methodical as Wilson Rush could be so successful in the courtroom. Discovery was under way, with both parties at war over the documents. At least twenty depositions had been scheduled.

Kyle took notes because everyone else was taking notes, but he was thinking about Bennie. Did Bennie already know that Kyle had landed the prize position? Bennie had known every member of the Trylon team. He knew that Sherry Abney supervised Jack McDougle. Was there another spy in the firm? Another victim of Bennie and his blackmail? If so, was this person watching Kyle and reporting to Bennie?

Though he hated every meeting with Bennie, their next encounter would be the biggest challenge. Kyle would go through the motions and engage in somewhat civilized conversation with the man responsible for the murder of Baxter Tate, and he would be forced to do so without a hint that he was remotely suspicious.

"Any questions?" Mr. Rush asked.

Sure, Kyle thought, more questions than you can possibly answer.

After a full hour of update and review, Kyle, Atwater, and the other six new associates were led by Sherry Abney to the secret room on the eighteenth floor. Secret to some, but Bennie and Nigel certainly knew about it. Along the way they were introduced to a nonlawyer named Gant, a security expert of some variety. Gant stopped them at the door and explained that it was the only door. One way in and one way out and a coded plastic strip smaller than a credit card was required for entry and exit. Each lawyer was given a card, and every time the lawyer came or went, it was recorded. Gant nodded at the ceiling and informed them that there were video cameras watching everything.

Inside, the room was about the size of Wilson Rush's office. No windows, bare walls, drab olive carpet. There was nothing in the room but ten square tables with a large computer on each one.

Sherry Abney took charge. "This case now has over four million documents, and they're all right here in our virtual warehouse," she said, patting a computer like a proud mother. "The actual paperwork is in secured storage in a facility in Wilmington, but you can access it all from one of these. The main server is locked up in a room next door." She kept patting. "These are pretty fancy computers, custom made by a company you've never heard of and never will. Do not, under any circumstances, attempt to repair, examine, or just plain fiddle with the hardware.

"The software is called Sonic, and it, too, is customized for this case. It's really just some home brew that our computer folks put together, a variation of Barrister with some bells and whistles added for security reasons. Pass code changes every week. Password changes every day, sometimes twice a day. When it changes, you will receive a coded e-mail. If you try to access with the wrong code or password, then all manner of hell breaks loose. You could be fired."

She looked around with as much menace as possible, then continued, "This system is self-contained and cannot be accessed anywhere else within the firm, or outside the firm. It's online, you just can't get to it. This is the only place, the only room in which you are able to access the documents, and this room is closed from 10:00 p.m. until 6:00 a.m. Sorry, no all-nighters in here, but it is open seven days a week."

At her direction, each associate sat down before a computer and was given a pass code and password. There was nothing on the screen to indicate who manufactured the computer or who wrote the software.

Sherry walked from lawyer to lawyer, looking at the monitors and chatting like a college professor. "There's an extensive tutorial at the beginning, and I strongly suggest you go through it today. Pull up the index. The documents are classified in three basic groups, with a hundred subgroups. Category A contains all the harmless junk that Bartin has already been given—letters, e-mails, office memos, the list is endless. Category B has important materials that are discoverable, though we have not handed all of them over. Category R, for 'Restricted,' is where you'll find the good stuff, about a million documents dealing with the technological research that is the heart of this little dispute. It's top secret, classified, and no one but the judge knows if it will ever be shown to Bartin. Mr. Rush thinks not. Category R is privileged, confidential, Attorneys' Work Product. When you enter Category R, a record of your entry automatically registers with Mr. Gant's computer right next door. Any questions?"

All eight associates stared at their monitors, all thinking the same thing—there are four million documents in there, and someone has to examine them.

"Sonic is amazing," Sherry said. "Once you master it, you will be able to find a document or group of documents within seconds. I'll be here for the rest of the day for a workshop. The sooner you learn your way around our virtual library, the easier your life will be."

AT 4:20 ON Friday afternoon, Kyle received an e-mail from Bennie. It read: "Let's meet tonight at 9:00. Details to follow. BW."

Kyle responded: "I can't."

Bennie responded: "Tomorrow afternoon, say 5:00 or 6:00?"

Kyle: "I can't."

Bennie: "Sunday night, 10:00 p.m.?"

Kyle: "I can't."

KYLE WAS SLEEPING when someone rapped on the door of his apartment at ten minutes after seven on Saturday morning. "Who is it?" he yelled as he stumbled through his cluttered den.

"Bennie," came the reply.

"What do you want?" Kyle demanded at the door.

"I've brought you some coffee."

Kyle unlocked and unchained the door, and Bennie walked by him quickly. He was holding two tall paper cups of coffee. He placed them on the counter and looked around. "What a dump," he said. "I thought you were making some money."

"What do you want?" Kyle snapped.

"I don't like being ignored," Bennie snapped back as he jerked around, ready to pounce. His face was taut and his eyes were hot. He pointed a finger that came within inches of Kyle's face. "You do not ignore me, understand?" he hissed. It was the first real display of temper Kyle had seen from him.

"Be cool."

Kyle brushed by him, their shoulders touching solidly, and walked to the bedroom, where he found a T-shirt. When he returned to the den, Bennie was removing the tops from the cups. "I want an update."

The nearest weapon was a cheap ceramic table lamp Kyle had found at a secondhand store. He took the coffee without saying thanks. He glanced at the lamp and thought how nicely it would crack over Bennie's bald head, how wonderful it would be to hear them break into pieces, both lamp and skull, and how easily he could pound away until the little bastard was dead but still bleeding on the cheap rug. Greetings from my old pal Baxter. Kyle took a sip, then took a breath. Both men were still standing. Bennie was wearing his gray trench coat. Kyle was decked out in red boxers and a wrinkled T-shirt.

"I got assigned to the Trylon case yesterday. Big news, huh, or did you already know this?"

Bennie's eyes revealed nothing. He took a sip, then said, "And the secret room on the eighteenth floor? Tell me about it."

Kyle described it.

"What about the computers?"

"Manufacturer unknown. Basic desktop models but supposedly custom built for the project, all linked to a server locked away next door. Lots of memory, all the bells and whistles. Video cameras everywhere and a security expert next door monitoring everything. It's a dead end if you ask me. There's no way to steal anything."

To which Bennie offered a grunt and a smart-ass smirk. "We've cracked much bigger vaults, I assure you of that. Everything can be stolen. Let us worry about that. Sonic is the software?"

"Yes."

"Have you mastered it?"

"Not yet. I'll go in later this morning for another lesson."

"How many documents?"

"Over four million."

That brought the only smile of the morning. "What about access to the room?"

"Open seven days a week but closed from ten at night until six in the morning. There's only one door, and there are at least three cameras watching it."

"Does someone check you in?"

"I don't think so. But the key leaves a record of each entry and exit."

"Let me see the key."

Kyle reluctantly got the key from his room and handed it over. Bennie examined it like a surgeon, then gave it back. "I want you to visit the room as often as possible over the next few days, but don't arouse any suspicions. Go at different hours, watch everything. We'll meet at ten on Tuesday night, room 1780, Four Seasons Hotel on Fifty-seventh. Got it?"

"Sure."

"No surprises."

"Yes, sir."

31

With seventy-eight thousand lawyers in Manhattan, the selection of one should not have been so difficult. Kyle narrowed his list, did more research, added names, and deleted names. He had begun the secret project not long after he arrived in the city, and had abandoned it several times. He was never sure he would actually hire a lawyer, but wanted the name of a good one just in case. Baxter's murder changed everything. Kyle not only wanted protection; now he wanted justice.

Roy Benedict was a criminal defense lawyer with a two-hundred-man firm located in a tall building one block east of Scully & Pershing. The location of the chosen lawyer was crucial, given the attention paid to Kyle's movements. Benedict measured up in other important areas as well. He had worked for the FBI before law school at NYU and after graduation spent six years with the Department of Justice. He had contacts, old friends, people on the other side of the street now, but people he could trust. Crime was his specialty. He was ranked in the top one hundred of the city's white-collar defense specialists, but not in the top ten. Kyle needed solid advice, but he couldn't afford an ego. Benedict's firm was often listed as opposing counsel in lawsuits involving Scully & Pershing. The icing on the cake was his basketball career at Duquesne some twenty-five years earlier. On the phone, he seemed to have little time for small talk and said he wasn't taking any new cases, but the basketball angle opened the door.

The appointment was at 2:00 p.m. on Monday, and Kyle arrived early. He found it impossible to walk through the law firm without comparing it with his. It was smaller, and it spent less trying to impress visitors with abstract art and designer furniture. The receptionists were not as cute.

In his briefcase he had a file on Roy Benedict—old stats and photos from Duquesne, bios from legal directories, newspaper stories about two of his more notorious cases. He was forty-seven, six feet six, and appeared to be in great shape, ready for a pickup game. His office was busy, smaller than most of the partners' at Scully, but nicely appointed. Benedict was cordial and genuinely pleased to meet another New York lawyer who'd played for the Dukes.

Kyle explained that he didn't play much. The basketball talk dragged on, and Kyle cut things off by saying, "Look, Mr. Benedict—"

"It's Roy."

"Okay, Roy, I can't spend too much time here because I'm being followed."

A few seconds passed as Roy allowed this to sink in. "And why is a first-year associate at the biggest law firm in the world being followed?"

"I have a few problems. It's complicated, and I think I need a lawyer."

"I do nothing but white-collar crime, Kyle. Have you screwed up in that area?"

"Not yet. But I'm being pressured to commit a whole list of crimes."

Roy bounced a pencil on his desk, tried to think of how to proceed.

"I really need a lawyer," Kyle said.

"My initial retainer is fifty grand," Roy said and watched carefully for a response. He knew within $10,000 how much Kyle was earning as a first-year associate. His firm didn't try to compete with Scully & Pershing, but it came close.

"I can't pay that much. I have five thousand in cash." Kyle yanked an envelope from his pocket and tossed it on the desk. "Give me some time, and I'll get the rest."

"What does this case involve?"

"Rape, murder, theft, wiretapping, extortion, blackmail, and a few others. I can't give you the details until we reach an agreement."

Roy nodded, then smiled. "There's someone following you now?"

"Oh, yes. I've been under surveillance since early February, back at Yale."

"Is your life in danger?"

Kyle thought for a moment. "Yes, I believe so."

The air was thick with unanswered questions, and Roy's curiosity got the best of him. He opened a drawer and withdrew some papers. He scanned them quickly—three sheets stapled together—added some notes with a pen, then slid them across. "This is a contract for legal services."

Kyle read it hurriedly. The initial retainer had been reduced to $5,000. The hourly rate cut in half, from $800 to $400. Kyle had just recently accepted the fact that he charged $400 an hour. Now he would be the client paying that much. He signed his name and said, "Thanks."

Roy took the envelope and placed it in the drawer. "Where do we begin?" he asked, and Kyle sank deeper into his chair. A huge weight was leaving him. He wasn't sure if the nightmare was coming to an end or if he was digging a deeper hole, but the fact that he had someone to talk to was beyond comforting.

Kyle closed his eyes and said, "I don't know. There's so much ground to cover."

"Who's following you? Government agents of some sort?"

"No. Private thugs. Very good ones. And I have no idea who they are."

"Why don't we start at the beginning?"

"Okay."

Kyle began with Elaine, the party, the accusations of rape, the investigation. He introduced Bennie and his boys, his blackmail, the video, his covert mission to steal documents from Scully & Pershing. He produced a file and spread out the photos of Bennie, along with the composites of Nigel and two of the street thugs who'd been following him.

"Bennie Wright is just an alias. The guy probably has twenty names. He speaks with a slight accent that's probably eastern European. Just a guess."

Roy studied the photo of Bennie.

"Is there a way to identify him?" Kyle asked.

"I don't know. Do you know where he is?"

"Here, in New York. I saw him on Saturday, and I'll meet him again tomorrow night. He's my handler. I'm his asset."

"Keep talking."

Kyle removed another file and went through the basics of the Trylon-Bartin war, and in doing so discussed only the facts that had been published in news stories. Even though Roy was his lawyer and sworn to confidentiality, Kyle was a lawyer, too, and his client expected the same. "It's the largest Pentagon contract in history, so it's potentially the biggest lawsuit ever filed."

Roy spent a few minutes scanning the articles, then said, "I've heard of it. Keep talking."

Kyle described the surveillance and eavesdropping, and Roy forgot about Trylon and Bartin. "Wiretapping carries five years, federal," he said.

"Wiretapping is nothing. What about murder?"

"Who got murdered?"

Kyle raced through Joey's involvement, then the surprising arrival of Baxter and his desire to reach out to the girl. He handed over a dozen newspaper reports on the random shooting of Baxter Tate.

"I saw something about this in the news," Roy said.

"I was a pallbearer at his funeral last Wednesday," Kyle said.

"I'm sorry."

"Thanks. The cops have no clue. I'm sure Bennie ordered the hit, but the killers have vanished."

"Why would Bennie kill Baxter Tate?" Roy alternated between scribbling notes, looking at the face of Bennie Wright, and picking through the file, but for the most part he just shook his head in confusion and disbelief.

"He had no choice," Kyle said. "If Baxter succeeded in making some harebrained confession to Elaine, which certainly appeared likely, then the events that follow are out of control. I think the girl goes nuts, cries rape again, and I'm dragged back to Pittsburgh along with Joey and Alan Strock. My life is derailed. I leave the firm, leave New York, and Bennie loses his asset."

"But with Baxter dead, doesn't the rape case lose some steam?"

"Yes, but the video is still out there. And believe me, we want no part of it. It's brutal."

"But it doesn't implicate you?"

"Only for being a drunken idiot. When the sex begins, I'm nowhere to be seen. I don't even remember it."

"And you have no idea how Bennie got the video?"

"That's the greatest question of all, one that I've asked myself every hour for the past nine months. The fact that he somehow heard of the video, then stole it or bought it, is something I cannot comprehend. I don't know which is more terrifying—the video itself or the fact that Bennie got his hands on it."

Roy was shaking his head again. He stood and unfolded his gangly frame. He stretched and kept shaking his head. "How many interns did Scully & Pershing hire the summer before last?"

"Around a hundred."

"So Bennie and his group get the names of a hundred summer interns, and they investigate them, looking for an Achilles' heel. When they get to your name on the list, they snoop around Pittsburgh and Duquesne. They probably hear about the rape, lean on someone in the police department, get the rape file, and decide to dig even deeper. The file is closed, so the cops talk more than they should. There was the rumor about a video, but the cops could never find it. Somehow, Bennie does."

"Yep."

"He's got plenty of money and plenty of people."

"Obviously, so who's he working for?"

Roy glanced at his watch, frowned, and said, "I have a meeting at three." He grabbed his desk phone, waited, then barked, "Cancel my three o'clock. And no interruptions." He fell into his chair and rubbed his chin with his knuckles.

"I doubt if he works for APE. I cannot believe that a rival law firm would spend this kind of money to break so many laws. It's inconceivable."

"Bartin?"

"Much more probable. Plenty of money, plenty of motive. I'm sure Bartin is convinced the documents were stolen from them, so why not steal them back?"

"Any other suspects?"

"Oh, please, Kyle. We're talking about military technology. The Chinese and the Russians prefer to steal what they can't develop.

That's the nature of the game. We dazzle with the research, they just steal it."

"But using a law firm?"

"The law firm is probably just one piece of the puzzle. They have spies in other places, and there are more people like Bennie, who have no name and no home and ten passports. He's probably a well-trained former intelligence pro who now hires himself out for a zillion dollars to do exactly what he's doing."

"He killed Baxter."

Roy shrugged. "Killing doesn't bother this guy."

"Great. Just when I was starting to feel better."

Roy smiled, but the wrinkles never left his forehead. "Look, give me a few days to digest this."

"We need to move fast. I now have access to the documents, and Bennie's much more excited."

"You'll see him tomorrow night?"

"Yes. At the Four Seasons Hotel on Fifty-seventh. Care to join the party?"

"Thanks. How long do these little meetings last?"

"Ten minutes if I'm lucky. We bitch and bark, and then I slam the door on the way out. I act tough, but the whole time I'm scared to death. I need help, Roy."

"You've come to the right place."

"Thanks. I gotta go. Doofus is waiting."

"Doofus?"

Kyle stood and reached across the desk. He picked out a composite and laid it on top of the pile. "Meet Doofus, probably the worst of the street crawlers who've shadowed me for the past nine months. His buddy there is Rufus. He's bad, too, but not as bad as Doofus. I have become so adept at appearing to be so clueless that these clowns think they can follow me in their sleep. They make a lot of mistakes."

They shook hands and said goodbye, and long after Kyle was

gone, Roy stared at his window and tried to absorb it all. A twenty-five-year-old former editor in chief of the *Yale Law Journal* being stalked on the streets of New York City by a deadly group of professional operatives who are blackmailing him into spying on his own law firm.

Roy was awestruck by the scenario. He smiled and reminded himself of how much he loved his job.

THERE WERE A few bright spots in the ugly split among the firm's litigators. More partners would be needed, and sooner. Advancement opportunities were created with all those gaps to fill. And, most crucial to the first-year associates, offices had been emptied. The jockeying began as soon as the malcontents fled. Over the weekend, Tabor nailed down a place of his own and had moved his junk by Sunday night.

Kyle gave little thought to a move. He'd grown accustomed to his little cubicle, and he enjoyed having Dale close by. They groped occasionally when they were completely safe. He looked forward to her daily appearance and expected a full rundown on what she was wearing and who designed it. Discussing her clothes was almost as much fun as removing them.

He was surprised when Sherry Abney dropped by late Monday afternoon and asked him to follow her. They took the stairs one floor up to the thirty-fourth, and, after walking past a dozen doors, she stopped, stepped in, and said, "This is yours."

It was a twelve-by-twelve square room, with a glass desk, leather chairs, handsome rug, and a window that faced south and allowed real sunlight to pass through. Kyle was overwhelmed. Why me? he wanted to ask. But he pretended to take it in stride.

"Compliments of Wilson Rush," she said.

"Nice," Kyle said, stepping to the window.

"You share a secretary with Cunningham next door. I'm just down the hall if you need anything. I'd get myself moved in because Mr. Rush might stop by for a quick inspection."

Moving took fifteen minutes. Kyle made four trips back and forth, and during his last one Dale carried his sleeping bag and laptop. She was genuinely happy for him, and even passed along a few decorating ideas. "Too bad you don't have a sofa," she said.

"Not at the office, dear."

"Then where and when?"

"I take it you're in the mood."

"I need to be loved, or at least lusted after."

"How about dinner, then a quickie?"

"How about a marathon, then a quick dinner?"

"Oh, boy."

They sneaked out of the building at 7:00 p.m. and took a cab to her apartment. Kyle was unbuttoning his shirt when his FirmFone buzzed with an e-mail sent by an unknown partner to about a dozen grunts. All hands were needed on deck immediately for an urgent orgy of work that was absolutely critical to the future of the firm. Kyle ignored it and turned off the lights.

32

For no reason other than sheer obstinacy, Kyle arrived forty-five minutes late for the Tuesday night meeting at the Four Seasons. He expected to see Nigel, so he was not surprised when Bennie's sidekick met him at the door and pretended to be pleased to see him. "Kyle, old boy, how have you been?" he chirped with a fake smile.

"Marvelous. And your name is?"

"Nigel."

"Oh, yeah, I forgot. Last name?"

"Sorry, old boy."

"Do you have a last name, or do you have so many you can't remember which one fits right now?"

"Good evening, Kyle," Bennie said, rising to his feet, folding a newspaper.

"So nice to see you, Bennie." Kyle placed his briefcase on the bed but did not remove his trench coat. "Now, who called this meeting?" he asked.

"Tell us about the room on the eighteenth floor," Bennie said, abandoning any more preliminaries.

"I've already described it."

Nigel fired away: "Ten monitors on ten tables, right, Kyle?"

"Yes."

"And where are the computers themselves?"

"On the tables, next to the monitors."

"The computers, Kyle, tall and thin, short and fat? Give us a hint here!"

"More of a square box, to the right of each monitor."

On the dresser next to the television there was a thin notebook, already opened. Nigel lunged for it and said, "Take a look at these computers, Kyle. All shapes and sizes, various makes from around the world. See anything remotely similar?"

Kyle methodically flipped through it. Each page had color photos of eight computers, ten pages in all, eighty machines that varied wildly in design and construction. He settled on one that looked more like a color jet printer than a computer.

"Yes, rather square," Nigel observed. "How many disc drives?"

"None."

"None? Are you certain, Kyle?"

"Yes. These were custom built for maximum security. There are no disc drives, no ports, no way to transfer the data."

"Control panel? Switches, buttons, lights, anything, Kyle?"

"Nothing. Plain-vanilla box."

"And the server?"

"Locked up next door. Out of sight."

"Interesting. And the monitors, Kyle?"

"Basic LCD flat screens."

"Let's take a peek," Nigel said as he opened the notebook to another section, this one filled with an assortment of monitors. "Size, Kyle?"

"Fourteen inches."

"Full-color display I'm sure?"

"Yes." Kyle stopped on the third page and pointed. "This one is very close."

"Excellent, Kyle."

"And printers?"

"None."

"Nowhere in the room? Not a single printer?"

"None."

Nigel paused to scratch his face and ponder this. "Suppose you're working on a brief or a memo. When it's time to produce it, what happens?"

"You notify your supervisor, who then enters the room, pulls it up, reviews it, and so on. If it is to be submitted to the court, or to the opposing attorneys, it's printed."

"Where? I thought there were no printers."

"There's a machine in a room next door with a paralegal who monitors the printing. Every sheet of paper that's printed is coded and duplicated. It's impossible to print anything without leaving a trail."

"Quite nice, really." With that, Nigel took a sharp step back and relaxed. Bennie took over. "Kyle, how many times have you entered the room?"

"Once a day for the last five days."

"And how many people are normally in the room?"

"It varies. Sunday afternoon I was alone for about an hour. This morning there were five or six others."

"Have you been there late at night when they close the room?"

"No, not yet."

"Do it, okay. Be there at ten one night."

"I can't go there just to hang out, Bennie. It's not a coffee room. Surveillance is constant, cameras watching and all that. There has to be a reason to be there, other than casing the joint."

"Does anyone notice when you come and go?"

"There's not a guard at the door. The key makes a record of each entry and exit, and I'm sure it's all recorded by closed circuit."

"Do you take your briefcase in with you?"

"No."

"Are briefcases forbidden?"

"No."

"Do you wear your jacket?"

"No. Jackets are not required around the office."

Bennie and Nigel studied each other for a minute or so, both minds hard at work.

"Will you go there tomorrow?" Bennie asked.

"Maybe. I'm not sure right now. It depends on what I'm asked to do in the morning."

"I want you to enter the room tomorrow, carrying your briefcase and wearing your jacket. As soon as you're settled in, take off your jacket. Keep the briefcase under the table."

"Will this work, Kyle?" Nigel piled on quickly.

"Oh, sure. Why not? Anything else? And what if I haul in a box of tacos and drop cheddar crumbs on the keyboard? Where is this going?"

"Just trust us here, Kyle," Nigel said gently. "We know what we're doing."

"You're the last person I'd trust."

"Now, Kyle."

"Look, I'm tired. I'd really like to go—"

"What are your plans for the next few days?" Bennie asked.

"I'll work tomorrow, leave the office around five, take the train to Philly, rent a car, and drive to York. I'm having Thanksgiving dinner with my father on Thursday. I'll be back in the city late Friday afternoon, and back at the office early Saturday. Good enough?"

"We'll meet Sunday night," Bennie said.

"Your place or mine?"

"I'll pass along the details."

"Happy Thanksgiving, boys," Kyle said as he left the room.

ON HIS NEW office door, Kyle hung two waterproof, all-purpose trench coats, one black and the other one a light brown. The black one he wore every day, to and from work and when moving around the city. The brown one was used rarely, only on those occasions when Kyle really didn't want to be followed. At 2:30 on Wednesday, he draped it over his arm and rode the elevator to the second floor. From there, he took a service elevator to the basement, put on the trench coat, and ducked through the rows of thick plumbing pipes and electrical cables and heating units until he came to a metal stairway. He spoke to a technician, one he'd spoken to on several occasions. He saw daylight in a narrow alley that barely separated his building from the fifty story edifice next door. Ten minutes later, he walked into the office of Roy Benedict.

They had chatted briefly on the phone, and Kyle was uneasy about the plan.

Roy was not at all uneasy. He had studied the file, analyzed the facts and issues, weighed the predicament, and was ready to move. "I have a friend with the FBI," he began. "A friend I trust completely. We worked together years ago before I became a lawyer, and even though we are now on opposite sides of the street, I trust him even more. He's a heavyweight here in the New York office."

Kyle flashed back to his last encounter with the FBI. Fake names, fake badges, a long night in a hotel room with Bennie. "I'm listening," Kyle said with skepticism.

"I want to meet with him and lay everything on the table. Everything."

"What will he do?"

"Crimes have been committed. Crimes are in process. Crimes are being planned. And not small crimes. I suspect he will be as shocked as I am. I suspect the FBI will get involved."

"So Bennie gets nabbed by the feds?"

"Sure. Don't you want him locked up?"

"For life. But he has a vast network out there in the shadows."

"The FBI knows how to lay its traps. They screw up occasionally, but their record is very good. I deal with them all the time, Kyle. I know how smart these guys are. If I talk to them now, they'll move in quietly and lay the groundwork. When they want to, they can throw a whole army at the enemy. Right now you need an army."

"Thanks."

"I need your permission to talk to the FBI."

"Is there a chance they'll take a look and let it pass?"

"Yes, but I doubt it."

"When will you talk to your friend?"

"Maybe as early as this afternoon."

Kyle barely hesitated. "Let's do it," he said.

33

It was almost midnight when Kyle quietly slipped through the unlocked kitchen door of his family home in York. All lights were off. His father knew he would be arriving late, but John McAvoy let nothing interfere with a night's sleep. Zack, the ancient border collie who'd never met an intruder he didn't like, managed to rouse himself from his pillow in the breakfast nook and say hello. Kyle rubbed his head, thankful to see the dog one more time. Zack's age and exact lineage had never been clear. He was a gift from a client, partial payment on a fee, and he liked to spend his days under the desk of John McAvoy, sleeping through all sorts of legal problems. He usually ate lunch in the firm's kitchen with one of the secretaries.

Kyle kicked off his loafers, sneaked up the stairs to his bedroom, and within minutes was under the covers and dreaming.

Less than five hours later, John practically kicked in the door and boomed, "Let's go, knucklehead. You can sleep when you're dead."

In a drawer, Kyle found an old set of his thermal underwear and a pair of wool socks, and in the closet, among a collection of dusty old clothes that dated back to high school, he pulled out his hunting overalls. Without a woman in the house, the dust and spiderwebs and unused garments were accumulating. His boots were precisely where he'd left them a year earlier, last Thanksgiving.

John was at the kitchen table preparing for war. Three rifles with scopes were laid out, next to several boxes of ammo. Kyle, who'd learned the art and rules of hunting as a child, knew his father had thoroughly cleaned the rifles the night before.

"Good morning," John said. "You ready?"

"Yep. Where's the coffee?"

"In the thermos. What time did you get in?"

"Just a few hours ago."

"You're young. Let's go."

They loaded the gear into the late-model Ford pickup, four-wheel drive, John's preferred means of transportation in and around York. Fifteen minutes after crawling out of bed, Kyle was riding through the darkness of a frigid Thanksgiving morning, sipping black coffee and nibbling on a granola bar. The town was soon behind them. The roads became narrower.

John was working a cigarette, the smoke drifting through a small crack in the driver's window. He usually said little in the mornings. For a man whose day was spent in the midst of a busy small-town law office, with phones ringing and clients waiting and secretaries scurrying about, John needed the solitude of the early hours.

Kyle, though still sleepy, was almost numb with the shock of open spaces, empty roads, no people, the great outdoors. What, exactly, had been the attraction of a big city? They stopped at a gate. Kyle opened it and John drove through, then they continued deeper into the hills. There was still no trace of sun in the east.

"So how's the romance?" Kyle said, finally attempting conversation. His father had mentioned a new girlfriend, a serious one.

"Off and on. She's cooking dinner tonight."

"And her name is?"

"Zoe."

"Zoe?"

"Zoe. It's Greek."

"Is she Greek?"

"Her mother is Greek. Her father is an Anglo mix. She's a mutt, like the rest of us."

"Is she cute?"

John thumped ashes out the window. "You think I'd date her if she wasn't cute?"

"Yes. I remember Rhoda. What a dog."

"Rhoda was hot. You just didn't appreciate her beauty." The truck hit a rough section of gravel road and bounced them around.

"Where's Zoe from?"

"Reading. Why all the questions?"

"How old is she?"

"Forty-nine, and hot."

"You gonna marry her?"

"I don't know. We've talked about it."

The road went from gravel to dirt. At the edge of a field, John parked and turned off the lights. "Whose property is this?" Kyle asked softly as they gathered their rifles.

"It used to be owned by Zoe's ex-husband's family. She got it in the divorce. Two hundred acres, crawling with deer."

"Come on."

"True. All legal and aboveboard."

"And you handled the divorce?"

"Five years ago. But I didn't start dating her until last year. Maybe it was the year before, I really can't remember."

"We're hunting on Zoe's property?"

"Yes, but she doesn't care."

Ah, the small-town practice of law, Kyle thought to himself. For twenty minutes they hiked along the edge of the woods, without a word. They stopped under an elm tree just as the first hint of light fell across the small valley before them.

"Bill Henry killed an eight-point last week just over that ridge there," John said, pointing. "There are some big bucks in here. If he can get one, anybody can."

A deer stand had been built in the elm, twenty feet up, with a rickety ladder leading to it. "You take this stand," John said. "I'll be a hundred yards that way in another one. Nothing but bucks, okay?"

"Got it."

"Is your hunting license current?"

"I don't think so."

"No big deal. Lester's still the game warden. I kept his son out of jail last month. A drug head. Meth."

John walked away, and as he disappeared into the darkness, he said, "You stay awake, now."

Kyle tucked the rifle over his shoulder and crawled up the ladder. The deer stand was a small platform made of planks and two-by-fours anchored into the elm, and like all deer stands it was constructed with little thought to comfort. He twisted one way, then another, and finally situated himself with his rear on the planks, his back to the bark, his feet dangling. He'd been in deer stands since he was five years old, and had learned the lessons of complete stillness. A soft breeze rustled a few leaves. The sun was rising fast. The deer would soon quietly ease from the woods to the edge of the field in search of fescue and field corn.

The rifle was a Remington 30.06, a gift for his fourteenth birthday. He tucked it firmly across his chest and promptly dozed off.

The crack of a gunshot jolted him from his nap, and he swung the rifle around, ready to fire. He glanced at his watch—a forty-minute nap. To his left, in the direction of his father, he saw several white tails bouncing in a rapid getaway. Ten minutes passed with no word from John. He'd obviously missed with his first shot and was still in the stand.

An hour passed without a sighting, and Kyle fought to stay awake.

Thanksgiving Day. The offices of Scully & Pershing were officially closed, but he knew that a few of the gunners were there, casually dressed in jeans and boots and billing away. There were a few partners hard at work, all with deadlines screaming at them. He shook his head.

Sounds were approaching, footsteps unconcerned with making noise. John was soon near the elm. "Let's go," he said. "There's a creek just beyond the field, a favorite watering hole."

Kyle lowered himself carefully, and when his feet were on the ground, John said, "You didn't see that buck?"

"Nope."

"I don't know how you missed it. It ran right in front of you."

"The one you shot at?"

"Yeah, at least a ten-pointer."

"I guess you missed it, too."

They returned to the truck and went for the thermos. As they sat on the tailgate, sipping strong coffee from paper cups and finishing the last of the granola bars, Kyle said, "Dad, I don't want to hunt anymore. We need to talk."

HIS FATHER LISTENED calmly at first, then lit a cigarette. As Kyle plowed through the rape investigation, he expected an eruption, a series of sharp and painful questions about why he had not called his father. But John listened intently without a word, as if he knew this story and had been expecting the confession.

The first flash of anger came when Bennie entered the narrative. "They blackmailed you," he said, then lit another cigarette. "Son of a bitch."

"Just listen, okay," Kyle pleaded and went full speed ahead. The details came in torrents, and several times he raised his hand to keep from being interrupted. After a while, John became stoic, absorbing it all in disbelief but saying nothing. The video, Joey, Baxter, the murder, Trylon and Bartin and the secret room on the eighteenth floor. The meetings with Bennie, Nigel, the plan to filch the documents and hand them to the enemy. And finally, the hiring of Roy Benedict and the appearance of the FBI.

Kyle apologized repeatedly for not trusting his father. He admitted his mistakes, too numerous to recall at that moment. He laid open his soul, and when he finished, hours later it seemed, the sun was well into the sky, the coffee was long gone, the deer long forgotten.

"I think I need some help," Kyle said.

"You need your ass kicked for not telling me."

"Yes, I do."

"Good Lord, son. What a mess."

"I had no choice. I was terrified of the video, and the thought of another rape investigation was just too much. If you saw the video, you'd understand."

They left the rifles in the truck and went for a long hike along a narrow trail through the woods.

THE FEAST OF turkey, dressing, and all the trimmings had been prepared by a deli that sold the whole package to those who preferred not to be troubled. As John set the dining room table, Kyle left to fetch his mother.

Patty answered her door with a smile and a long hug. She was up, and properly medicated. She escorted Kyle through her apartment and couldn't wait to show off her latest masterpieces. He eventually led her back to the door and down to his rental car, and they enjoyed a quick drive through York. She was wearing lipstick, makeup, and a pretty orange dress that Kyle remembered from his teenage years, and her hair was clean, neat, and almost white. She chattered nonstop with news about locals she'd known years ago, bouncing from one subject to another with a randomness that would have been comical under other circumstances.

Kyle was relieved. There'd been an even chance she would be off her meds and out of her mind. His parents greeted each other with a polite hug, and the small struggling family worked its way through the gossip about the twin daughters, neither of whom had been back to York in over a year. One was in Santa Monica, the other in Portland. They called both and passed around the phone. The television was on in the den, muted, a football game waiting to be watched. At the dining table, Kyle poured three glasses of wine, though his mother wouldn't touch it.

"You're drinking wine these days," John said to Kyle as he sat the small turkey on the table.

"Not much."

The two men served Patty, fussed over her, worked hard to make her comfortable. She prattled on about her art and about events in York that happened years earlier. She managed to ask a few questions about Kyle and his career in New York, and he made his life sound enviable. The strain from events in New York was palpable, but Patty did not notice. She ate almost nothing, but her son and ex-husband devoured the lunch as quickly as possible. After pecan pie and coffee, she announced she wanted to go home, to her work. She was tired, she said, and Kyle wasted no time loading her up for the ten-minute drive.

ONE FOOTBALL GAME blurred into another. Kyle, on the sofa, and John, in a recliner, watched the games between naps, and said little. The air was heavy with things unsaid, questions that came and went, plans that needed to be discussed. The father wanted to lecture and yell, but the son was too vulnerable, too dependent at that moment.

"Let's go for a walk," Kyle said when it was almost dark.

"Walk where?"

"Around the block. I need to talk."

"Can't we talk here?"

"Let's walk."

They bundled up and put Zack on a leash. They were on the sidewalk when Kyle said, "I'm sorry, but I don't like to have serious conversations indoors."

John lit a cigarette with the ease of a longtime smoker, perfect coordination without missing a step. "I'm almost afraid to ask why not."

"Bugs, mikes, nasty little twerps listening to conversations."

"Let me get this straight. You think that my house might be bugged by these thugs?"

They were strolling along the street Kyle had roamed as a child. He knew the owner of every home, at least the owners back then, and every home had a story. He nodded at one and asked, "Whatever happened to Mr. Polk?"

"Dead, finally. Lived in a wheelchair for almost fifty years. Very sad. Back to my question. We're not walking down memory lane here, okay?"

"No, I don't think your house is bugged, nor your office, but there's a chance. These guys believe in surveillance and have an unlimited budget. Bugging is easy. Ask me, I'm an expert. I could make a homemade listening device in half an hour with a few items from RadioShack."

"And how did you acquire such knowledge?"

"Books. Manuals. There's a great little spy store in Manhattan and I drop in occasionally, when I'm able to lose my tail."

"This is unbelievable, Kyle. If I didn't know better, I'd say you're cracking up. You sound schizophrenic, like a few of my clients."

"I'm not crazy yet, but I've learned to play it safe and have the serious conversations outdoors."

"Your apartment is bugged?"

"Oh, yes. I know of at least three listening devices hidden in the place. One is in the AC vent above the sofa in the den. There's one hidden in the bedroom wall, just above the chest of drawers, and there's one in the kitchen in a door facing. I can't really examine them, because there are also three tiny cameras, at least three, that watch me continuously when I'm in the apartment, which is not very often. I've managed to locate these devices by pretending to do all sorts of routine chores around the place, cleaning vents, washing windows, scrubbing floors. The place is a dump, but it's pretty clean."

"And your phone?"

"I still have the old one from law school, and they're listening. That's why I haven't switched. I know they're listening, and so I give them enough harmless crap to make them happy. I installed a landline in the apartment, and I'm sure it's bugged. I haven't been able to inspect it, though, because the cameras are watching. I use it just for harmless stuff—ordering a pizza, bitching at my landlord, calling a car service." Kyle pulled out the FirmFone and glanced at it. "This is one the firm gave us on day one. I'm pretty sure this one is bug-free."

"The question is, why is it in your pocket on Thanksgiving Day?"

"Habit. It's turned off. For serious stuff I use the desk phone in my office. I figure that if they can bug the office phones, then we're all really screwed."

"Oh, you're screwed, there's no doubt about that. You should've told me months ago."

"I know. I should've done a lot of things differently, but I didn't have the benefit of hindsight. I was scared. Still am."

Zack stopped at a fire hydrant. John needed another smoke. The wind had picked up and leaves were blowing and landing around them. It was dark, and they still had dinner at Zoe's.

They made the block and talked about the future.

34

The associates who'd dared to slack off by leaving for the short holiday break returned with a vengeance early Saturday morning. The time away was refreshing, though the strain of frenzied travel left them even more exhausted. And time off also meant no billing.

Kyle punched his clock at 8:00 a.m. sharp when he entered the secret room on the eighteenth floor and settled himself at one of the workstations. Four other members of Team Trylon were there, lost in a virtual world of endless research. He nodded to a couple, but no one spoke. He wore jeans and a wool sport coat, and he hauled in his black Bally briefcase, six inches thick and showing some wear. He'd bought it at a shop on Fifth Avenue a week before orientation. All briefcases at the firm were black.

He placed it on the floor beside him, partially under the table, directly under the plain-vanilla computer that had so captivated dear Nigel. He withdrew a legal pad, then a file, and before long his workstation looked authentic. After a few minutes, he took off his jacket, hung it on the back of his chair, and rolled up his sleeves. Trylon was now paying old Scully an additional four hundred bucks an hour.

A quick look around the room revealed one other briefcase. All other jackets and coats had been left upstairs in the offices. The hours began to drag by as Kyle lost himself in the futuristic world of the B-10 HyperSonic Bomber and the people who designed it.

The only good thing about the secret room was the prohibition against cell phones. After a few hours, Kyle needed a break, and he wanted to check his messages. Specifically, he was waiting to hear from Dale, who hadn't bothered to show up on such a beautiful morning. He walked to his office, closed the door, which was a minor violation of firm policy, and called her private cell phone. As a refuge from the much-hated FirmFone, every associate carried a private one as well.

"Yes," she answered.

"Where are you?"

"I'm still in Providence."

"Are you coming back to New York?"

"I'm not sure."

"Need I remind you, young lady, that this is the third consecutive day in which you have not billed a single hour."

"I take it you're at the office."

"Yes, racking up hours along with every other first-year grunt. Everyone's here but you."

"Fire me. Sue me. I don't care."

"You'll never make partner with that attitude."

"Promise?"

"I was thinking about dinner tonight. There's a new restaurant in the East Village that just got two stars from Frank Bruni."

"Are you asking me out for a date?"

"Please. We can split the check since we work for a gender-neutral firm."

"You're so romantic."

"We could do the romance later."

"So that's what you're really after."

"Always."

"I get in around seven. I'll call you then."

KYLE CLIPPED TRYLON for twelve hours, then called a sedan for the ride to dinner. The restaurant had twenty tables, a Turkish menu, and no dress requirement, though jeans were preferred. After the two-star review by the *Times* the place was crowded. Kyle got a table only because there had been a cancellation.

Dale was at the bar sipping white wine and looking almost serene. They kissed, a peck on each cheek, then squeezed together and started talking about their Thanksgiving holidays as if they'd just had a month at the beach. Both of her parents taught mathematics at Providence College, and, though wonderful people, they had a rather dull existence. Dale's gift for math led to a relatively quick Ph.D., but she began to fear she'd wind up much like her parents. The law beckoned her. The law, as portrayed in film and on television as nonstop excitement. The law, as the cornerstone of democracy and the front lines for so many social conflicts. She had excelled at law school, received offers from the top firms, and now, after three months of practice, she sorely missed mathematics.

Later, at their table and still sipping wine, she was quick to confess some exciting news. "I had a job interview this morning."

"I thought you had a job."

"Yes, but it sucks. There's a boutique firm in Providence, downtown in a beautiful old building. I got a job there one summer when I was in college, making copies and coffee and doing the general gofer routine. About twenty lawyers, half women, a general practice. I talked them into an interview on a Saturday morning."

"But you have a cherished associate's position with the largest firm in the world. What more could you want?"

"A life. The same thing you want."

"I want to be a partner so I can sleep until 5:00 a.m. every day until I die at fifty. That's what I want."

"Look around, Kyle. Very few stay more than three years. The smart ones are gone after two. The crazy ones make a career out of it."

"So you're leaving?"

"I'm not cut out for this. I thought I was pretty tough, but you can have it."

The waiter took their orders and poured more wine. They were side by side, in a narrow half booth with a view of the restaurant. Kyle's hand was between her knees under the table.

"When are you leaving?" he asked.

"As soon as humanly possible. I practically begged for a job this morning. If I don't get an offer, I'll keep knocking. This is madness, Kyle, and I'm checking out."

"Congratulations. You'll be the envy of our class."

"What about you?"

"I have no idea. I feel as though I just got here. We're all in shock, but it'll wear off. It's boot camp, and we're still sore from the initial bruising."

"No more bruises for me. I've collapsed once. It won't happen again. I'm slacking off to fifty hours a week and I dare them to say something."

"Go, girl."

A platter of olives and goat cheese arrived, and they toyed with it. "How was York?" she asked.

"The same. I had lunch with my real mother and dinner with my next one, a quick deer hunt that killed nothing, and some long talks with my dad."

"About what?"

"The usual. Life. The past. The future."

NIGEL WAS PRESENT for the second meeting in a row, and long before Kyle arrived in the hotel suite, preparations had been under way. On a small desk, Nigel had set up a computer that looked very similar to those on the eighteenth floor. Next to it was a monitor that was identical to the one Kyle had stared at for twelve hours the day before.

"Are we close here, Kyle?" Nigel was singing away as he proudly revealed his copycat workstation. "Please have a seat."

Kyle sat at the desk, with Bennie and Nigel watching every move.

"It looks very similar," Kyle said.

"Just the hardware here, Kyle, as you know. Not crucial, but we're trying to pinpoint the manufacturer, that's all. Only the software matters, we know that. Are we off the mark?"

Neither the computer nor the monitor had markings or names or models or makers. They were as blandly generic as the ones they were trying to imitate.

"These are very close," Kyle said.

"Look hard, man, and find something different," Nigel pressed. He was beside Kyle, bent and staring at the screen.

"The computer is slightly darker in color, almost a gray, and it's sixteen inches wide and twenty inches tall."

"You measured, Kyle?"

"Obviously. I used a fifteen-inch legal pad."

"Bloody brilliant," Nigel exclaimed and seemed ready to hug Kyle. Bennie couldn't hide a smile.

"It has to be a Fargo," Nigel said.

"A what?"

"Fargo, Kyle, a specialty computer company in San Diego, big on government and military machines, tons of work for the CIA, big stout computers with more security and more gadgets than you can believe, I assure you of that. You won't see one at the local mall, no sir. And Fargo is owned by Deene, a client of you know who. Old Scully protects its ass at a thousand bucks an hour."

As Nigel chirped away, he hit a button on the keyboard. The screen became a page unlike any Kyle had ever seen. Nothing from Microsoft or Apple.

"Now, Kyle, tell me what the first page looks like. Anything remotely similar here?"

"No, not even close. The home page has one icon for the tutorial, but that's it—no other icons, message boards, edit bands, format options, nothing but an index to the documents. You turn the computer on, get through the pass codes and passwords, then wait about ten seconds, and, presto, you're into the library. No system profiles, no spec sheets, no home page."

"Fascinating," Nigel said, still staring at the monitor. "And the index, Kyle?"

"The index is a real challenge. It starts with broad divisions of documents, then it breaks down into subcategories and subgroups and sub-this and sub-that. It takes some work to find the batch of documents you're looking for."

Nigel took a step back and stretched. Bennie moved closer and said, "Suppose you wanted to locate the research materials relating to the B-10's air-breathing engines and the various types of hydrogen fuel that were tested. How would you get there?"

"I don't know. I haven't been there yet. I've seen nothing about air-breathing engines." The statement was true, but Kyle decided to draw a line at this point. With over four million documents in play, he could easily claim he had not seen whatever they were curious about.

"But you could find these materials?"

"I could find them quickly, once I knew where to look. The Sonic program is pretty fast, but there's a ton of paper to sift through."

Bennie's movements were quick, his words a little more urgent than usual. Nigel was downright giddy with Kyle's information. It was obvious that his progress had them agitated.

"You were in the room yesterday?" Bennie asked.

"Yes, all day."

"With a briefcase and a jacket?"

"Yes, both, no problem. There was one other briefcase. No one checks them."

"When will you return to the room?" Bennie asked.

"The team meets in the morning, and there's a good chance I'll get another assignment. Monday or Tuesday for sure."

"Let's meet Tuesday night."

"Can't wait."

35

Now that he was an official member of Team Trylon, Kyle had the honor of beginning each week with a 7:00 a.m. Monday chalk talk in a huge conference room he'd never seen before. After three months in the building, he still marveled at the meeting areas and balconies and tucked-away mezzanines and small libraries he was stumbling upon for the first time. The firm needed its own guidebook.

The room was on the forty-first floor and large enough to house many smaller law firms. The table in the center seemed as long as a bowling alley. Forty lawyers, give or take a few, crowded around it, gulping coffee and settling in for another long week. Wilson Rush stood at the far end and cleared his throat, and everyone shut up and froze. "Good morning. We'll have our weekly session. Keep your comments brief. This meeting will last for one hour only."

There was no doubt that they would leave at exactly 8:00 a.m.

Kyle was as far from Rush as possible. He kept his head low and took furious notes that no one, not even himself, could have read afterward. Each of the eight partners stood in turn and gave succinct updates on such gripping topics as the latest motions filed in the case, the latest haggling over documents and experts, the latest moves by APE and Bartin. Doug Peckham presented his first report on a complicated discovery motion. It almost put Kyle and the others to sleep.

But Kyle stayed awake, and while scribbling on a legal pad, he kept telling himself not to smile at the absurdity of the moment. He was a spy, perfectly planted by his handler, and now within reach of secrets that were so important he could not comprehend their value. They were certainly valuable enough to cause men to commit murder.

Kyle glanced up as Isabelle Gaffney took her turn on the floor, and ignoring her words, he looked at the far end of the bowling lane, where Wilson Rush seemed to be glaring at him. Maybe not, there was so much distance between them, and the old man was wearing reading glasses, so it was hard to tell exactly whom he was frowning at.

What would Mr. Rush do if he knew the truth? What would Team Trylon and the hundreds of other Scully partners and associates do when they learned the truth about young Kyle McAvoy, former editor in chief of the *Yale Law Journal*?

The consequences were horrifying. The magnitude of the conspiracy caused Kyle's heart to hammer away. His mouth became dry and he sipped lukewarm coffee. He wanted to leap for the door, sprint down forty-one flights of stairs, and run through the streets of New York like a madman.

DURING LUNCH he used the basement exit ploy and hustled over to the office of Roy Benedict. They chatted for a minute or two, then Roy said there were two people Kyle should meet. The first was his contact in the FBI, the second was a senior lawyer in the Department of Justice. Kyle nervously agreed, and they walked next door to a meeting room.

The FBI supervisor was Joe Bullington, an affable sort with a big toothy smile and hearty handshake. The man from Justice was Drew Wingate, a sour-faced sort who acted as though he preferred not to shake hands at all. The four sat at a small conference table, Kyle and Roy on one side, the government guys on the other.

It was Roy's meeting, and he took charge. "First of all, Kyle, how much time do you have?"

"About an hour."

"I've laid it all on the table. I've had a dozen conversations with Mr. Bullington and Mr. Wingate, and it's important now for us to review where we are. Joe, talk about the background on Mr. Bennie Wright."

Always smiling, Bullington squeezed his hands together and began, "Yes, right, well, we ran the photo of this guy through our system. I won't bore you with the details, but we have some very sophisticated computers that store facial images of millions of people. When we feed in a suspect, the computers search and scan, and in general do their thing. With Mr. Wright, or whoever he is, we came up with nothing. No hit. No clue. We then sent it to the CIA, and they conducted a similar search, different computers, different software, same result. Nothing. We're surprised, frankly. We were pretty confident we could identify this guy."

Kyle was not surprised, but he was disappointed. He'd read about the supercomputers used by the intelligence services, and after a lifetime of living with Bennie, he really wanted to know who he was.

Bullington brightened a bit and went on: "Nigel might be a different story. We placed your composite of him into our system and came up empty. But the CIA got a probable hit." Bullington opened a file, pulled out an eight-by-ten black and white, and handed it to Kyle, who immediately said, "That's him."

"Good. His real name is Derry Hobart, born in South Africa, raised in Liverpool, trained as a techie in the British intelligence services, got bounced ten years ago for hacking into the confidential files of some rich folks in Switzerland, generally regarded as one of the most brilliant hackers in the world. Brilliant, but a real rogue, a hired gun, warrants outstanding in at least three countries."

"How much have you told these people?" Wingate asked. It was more of an accusation than a question. Kyle looked at his lawyer, who nodded and said, "Go ahead, Kyle. You're not under any type of investigation. You've done nothing wrong."

"I've given them the layout of the computer room, general stuff like that. Enough to keep them happy, but no data whatsoever."

"Anyway," Bullington said, "the other two composites turned up nothing. If I understand things, these two boys are just part of the surveillance and not that important."

"That's right," Kyle said.

"Your composite of Mr. Hobert is remarkable, Kyle," Bullington said.

"It's from a Web site. QuickFace.com. Anybody could do it."

"What's your next step?" Wingate asked.

"We meet tomorrow night for an update. The plan is for me to somehow hack into the system, either download or divert the documents, and hand them over. I have no idea how this is supposed to be done. The computer system looks completely secure."

"When is this supposed to happen?"

"They haven't told me, but I get the impression it will be soon. I have a question for you."

Neither Bullington nor Wingate offered to take the question, so Kyle plunged ahead. "Who are these guys? Who are they working for?"

Bullington flashed all of his teeth and said with a boyish shrug, "We honestly don't know, Kyle. Hobart is a whore who travels the world selling himself. We have no clue where Bennie comes from. You say he's not American."

"He doesn't sound like it."

"Without an idea as to who he is, we can't even begin to guess who he's working for."

"There were at least five agents involved in the first encounter, back in February, the night I first met Bennie. All five were definitely Americans."

Bullington was shaking his head. "Probably hired guns, Kyle, thugs brought in for the job, paid, turned loose. There's a whole dark world out there of former cops and agents and former soldiers and intelligence types who got shoved out for a multitude of reasons. Most are misfits. They were trained in the shadows, and that's where they work. They'll hire on with anyone who'll pay them. Those five probably had no idea what Bennie was up to."

"What are the chances of catching the ones who killed Baxter Tate?"

The smile went away for a moment. Both government faces looked sad and perplexed. Bullington finally said, "First we have to catch Bennie, then we work our way up to the big boys who are paying him, then we'll work our way down to the street thugs who do his dirty work. If he's a pro, though, and it's quite obvious that he is, the chances of squeezing him for names are pretty slim."

"How do you catch Bennie?"

"That's the easy part. You'll lead us to him."

"And you arrest him?"

"Oh, yes. We'll have enough warrants to arrest him ten times—wiretapping, extortion, conspiracy, take your pick. We'll throw him under the jail, with Hobart as well, and no federal judge in the world will bond him out. We'll probably move him to a secured facility far away from New York so we can begin the interrogation."

The image of Bennie chained to a chair as a couple of pit bulls screamed at him was rather pleasant.

Roy cleared his throat, glanced at his watch, and said, "If you'll excuse us, I need to talk to Kyle. I'll call you later." And with that Kyle stood, shook their hands again, and followed his lawyer back to his office. Roy closed the door and said, "What do you think?"

"You trust those guys?" Kyle shot back.

"Yes. You don't?"

"Would you trust them with your life?"

"Yes."

"Try this scenario. Currently there are at least eighteen intelligence outfits in this country, and those are just the ones on paper. There are probably a few more we know nothing about. What if Bennie works for one of them? Suppose his project is just one of several to procure and protect all the secrets? What if the supercomputers couldn't find his face because they weren't supposed to?"

"That's a pretty ridiculous scenario, Kyle. A rogue operative working for the United States, spying on a U.S. law firm, killing U.S. citizens? I don't think so."

"Sure it's ridiculous, but when your skull might be the next target, it does wonders for the imagination."

"Take it easy. This is your only way out."

"There's no way out."

"Yes, there is. Let's take it one step at a time. Don't panic."

"I haven't panicked in nine months, but I'm getting close."

"No, you're not. Be cool. We have to trust those guys."

"I'll call you tomorrow." Kyle grabbed his brown trench coat and left the office.

36

The Cessna 182 was owned by a retired doctor who flew it only in clear weather and never at night. He had known John McAvoy for over forty years and had flown him several times around the state for legal matters. Their little trips were as much pleasure as business, with John wearing a headset and taking the controls and thoroughly enjoying his time as the pilot. They always haggled over the rate. John wanted to pay more than just the fuel costs, and the doctor demanded less because flying was his hobby and he didn't need the money. Once they agreed on the cost of the trip, $250, they met at the York airport early on Tuesday morning and took off in perfect weather. Seventy-one minutes later they landed in Scranton. John rented a car, and the doctor left in the Cessna to drop in on his son in Williamsport.

The law office of Michelin Chiz was on the second floor of an old building on Spruce Street in downtown Scranton. John walked in promptly at 9:00 a.m. and was greeted coolly by a secretary. He had never met Ms. Chiz, never heard of her, but that was not unusual in a state with over sixty thousand lawyers. A Scranton lawyer he did know had told him that she ran an all-woman shop with a couple of associates, a couple of paralegals, and the usual assortment of secretaries and part-time help. No men need apply. Ms. Chiz specialized in divorce, custody, sexual harrassment, and employment discrimination, all from the female side, and had a busy practice. Her reputation was solid. She was a tough advocate for her clients, a good negotiator, and not afraid of the courtroom. Not bad looking either, the lawyer had informed John.

And he was right about that. Ms. Chiz was waiting in her office when John walked in and said good morning. She was wearing a black leather skirt, not too short, with a tight purple sweater and a pair of black and purple spiked-heeled platform sling backs that most hookers would shy away from. She was in her mid-forties, with, according to John's source, at least two divorces under her belt. She wore a lot of jewelry and makeup, far too much for John's taste, but he wasn't there to evaluate the talent.

For his part, he was wearing a boring gray wool suit and a plain red tie, nothing anyone would remember.

They settled around a small worktable in a room adjacent to her office, and the secretary was sent for coffee. They played a few minutes of who-do-you-know, kicking around the names of lawyers from Philadelphia to Erie. After the coffee was served and the door was closed, Ms. Chiz said, "Let's get down to business."

"Great idea," Mr. McAvoy said. "Please call me John."

"Sure, and I'm Mike. Don't know if that's the correct nickname for Michelin, but it stuck a long time ago."

"Mike it is." So far she had exuded nothing but charm and hospitality, but John could already tell that just behind the smile was a very tough lawyer. "Would you like to go first?" John asked.

"No. You called me. You traveled here. There's something you want, so let's have it."

"Very well. My client is my son, not the best arrangement in the world, but that's the way it is. As you know, he works for a law firm in New York. Law school at Yale, undergrad at Duquesne. I'm sure you know the details of the alleged rape."

"Indeed I do. Elaine works here part-time, and we're very close. She wants to go to law school someday."

"I hope she succeeds. As you know, the police in Pittsburgh closed the investigation not long after they opened it. Frankly, I knew nothing about it until very recently."

Her surprise was obvious, and John continued. "No, Kyle did not tell me when it happened. He was planning to, but the investigation was closed. This is upsetting because we are very close, but it's not important. I understand that you and Ms. Keenan met with Joey Bernardo here in Scranton a few weeks back, and the meeting did not go well, according to Joey's version. I also know that Baxter Tate contacted your client, and was evidently on his way here to talk to her when he was murdered."

"That's correct."

"They were planning to meet?"

"Yes."

"So, it appears, Mike, that the episode five and a half years ago will not go away. My client would like to resolve things, to close this matter. It's a dark cloud hanging over these kids, and I'm here to explore ways to get rid of it. I'm representing only my son. The others know nothing of this meeting. The Tate family, of course, has no clue, and you can imagine what they're going through right now. Joey has a child on the way and is about to get married. Alan Strock, as far as we know, has forgotten the episode."

Mike had yet to lift a pen. She listened intently as she softly tapped all ten fingertips together. Most fingers were adorned with rings, and both wrists were laden with inexpensive bangles. Her hard hazel eyes did not blink. "I'm sure you have something in mind," she said, content to listen.

"I'm not sure what your client wants. She might be thrilled if all three surviving roommates admitted there was a rape, got themselves convicted, and were sent off to prison. She might be satisfied with a quiet apology. Or she might entertain the idea of a financial settlement. Perhaps you could help me here."

Mike licked her lipstick and rattled some bracelets. "I've known Elaine for two years. She has a troubled past. She's frail, vulnerable, and at times subject to some very dark moods. It might be depression. She's been sober for almost a year, but she's fighting those demons. She has become almost like a daughter to me, and she has insisted from day one that she was raped. I believe her. She is convinced that the Tate family got involved, leaned on their friends, who leaned on the cops, who quickly backed off."

John was shaking his head. "That's not true. None of the four boys told their parents."

"Maybe, but we don't know that for sure. Regardless, many of Elaine's problems stem from that episode. She was a healthy, fun-loving, vibrant coed who loved college and had big plans. Shortly after the rape, she dropped out and has been struggling ever since."

"Have you seen her grades from Duquesne?"

"No."

"Her first semester, she flunked one course, dropped out of another, and made horrible grades in the other three."

"How did you gain access to her student records?"

"She improved slightly the second semester and made straight Cs. She took all four exams after the alleged rape, then went home and never returned to Duquesne."

Mike's eyebrows arched and her spine stiffened. "How did you gain access to her student records?" she snarled again. Ah, the woman had a temper after all.

"I didn't, and it's not important. How often do your clients tell you the entire truth?"

"Are you suggesting Elaine is lying?"

"The truth is a moving target here, Mike. But what's certain is that we'll never really know for sure what happened that night. These kids had been drinking and smoking pot for eight straight hours, and they were far more promiscuous than we'd like to believe. Your client was known to sleep around."

"They were all sleeping around. That's no excuse for rape."

"Of course not."

Money was in the air. There were a few other obstacles to clear, but both lawyers knew they would eventually discuss the possibility of a "financial settlement."

"What does your client say about the episode?" Mike asked, her tone cool again. The flash of anger was gone, but there was a lot more where that came from.

"They had been by the pool all afternoon, then the party moved indoors, into the apartment. There were about fifteen kids, more boys than girls, but Elaine was not in the group. Evidently, she was next door at a different party. Around eleven thirty, the cops showed up and the party ended. Nobody was arrested, the cops gave them a break."

Mike nodded patiently. This was all in the police report.

"After the cops left," John continued, "Elaine showed up. She and Baxter started making out on the sofa, and one thing led to another. My client was watching television in the same room, as was Alan Strock. My client was intoxicated, to say the least, and at some point he passed out. He is certain he did not have sex with Elaine that night, and at the time he was not certain if anyone else did either. He was too drunk to remember much the next morning, and, as you well know, no accusation was made by your client until four days later. The police investigated the matter. All four boys were on the verge of talking to their parents, but the investigators soon realized that they simply could not put together a case. In recent weeks, my client has talked to Baxter Tate and to Joey Bernardo, and both boys admitted to having sex with your client on the evening in question. Both are, were, adamant that it was consensual."

"Then why was Baxter so anxious to apologize?"

"I can't answer that. I don't speak for Baxter."

"Why did Joey apologize? He did so in my presence, you know?"

"Did Joey apologize for raping Elaine, or did he apologize for the misunderstanding?"

"He apologized. That's what's important."

"There's still no case, and his apology adds nothing to the evidence. There's no way to prove rape occurred. There was sex, sure, but you can't prove anything else."

She finally wrote something. Lavender legal pad, elegant strokes, noisy wrists. She took a deep breath and seemed to gaze out the window for a moment.

For Team McAvoy, it was time for the biggest gamble. They would never reveal every fact because successful negotiation does not hinge on full disclosure. But the one bomb that could wreck any deal had to be addressed.

"Have you talked to the detectives in Pittsburgh?" John asked.

"No, but I've read the entire file."

"Anything mentioned about a video?"

"Yes, there were notes in the file. But the cops couldn't find one. Elaine even heard the rumor."

"It's not a rumor. There is such a video."

She took this without the slightest flinch. Nothing in her eyes, hands, or body registered surprise. What a great poker face, John admitted quickly. She simply waited.

"I haven't seen it," he said. "But my client saw it in February of this year. Don't know where it is now and don't know how many others have seen it, probably very few. There's a chance it might surface, perhaps on the Internet, perhaps in your mailbox."

"And what would this video prove?"

"It would prove that your client was drunk and smoking pot when she sat down on the sofa with Baxter Tate and began kissing and groping. The angle of the camera does not allow a full picture of the two engaged in sex, but it's obvious from the knees down that they're having a fine time. Baxter is followed by Joey. At times Elaine is not active; at other times she's obviously engaged. My client thinks it proves that she was in and out of consciousness, but he's not certain. Nothing is certain, except that neither he nor Alan Strock had sex with her."

"Where is the video?"

"I do not know."

"Does your client?"

"No."

"Who has the video?"

"I do not know."

"Okay, who showed it to your client?"

"He does not know the person's real name. He had never met the person until the person showed him the video."

"Gotcha. I take it there's a complicated story behind this."

"Extremely complicated."

"A stranger pops up, shows your son the video, then disappears?"

"Right, except for the disappearance part. The stranger is still in contact."

"Extortion?"

"Something close."

"Is that why you're here? Your client is scared of the video? You wanna make peace with us so the extortion scheme goes away?"

"You're very astute." She still had not blinked. She seemed to be reading his mind at this point.

"Must be a helluva video," she said.

"My client found it troublesome, though he was not present during the sex portion of it. The video clearly shows your client happily getting involved in a good romp on a sofa. Whether she blacked out at some point is not clear, at least on the video."

"She is seen walking and talking and moving around?"

"Clearly. These boys didn't drag her in off the street, Mike. She had been in their apartment many times, drunk and sober."

"Poor thing," Mike said, her first false move.

"Poor thing was having a wonderful time. She carried a purse full of drugs, along with her collection of fake IDs, and she was always looking for a party."

Mike slowly stood and said, "Excuse me for a moment." She walked into her office, and John admired the black leather every step of the way. He heard her low voice, probably on the phone, and then she was back with a forced smile.

"We could debate this for hours," she said. "And not settle anything."

"I agree. Baxter was in New York three weeks ago today to see my client. In the course of a long discussion about what happened, he told my client that he believed that he had forced himself on Elaine. The guilt was heavy. Maybe there was a sexual assault."

"And the rapist is dead."

"Exactly. However, my client was there when it happened. It was his apartment, his friends, his party, and his booze. He wants this thing off his back, Mike."

"How much?"

John managed a nervous laugh. Such bluntness. She, however, did not crack a smile.

He made a note and asked, "Is it possible to reach a financial settlement and have your client release all civil claims and agree not to prosecute?"

"Yes, assuming the settlement is sufficient."

A pause as John made some more notes, then, "My client does not have a lot of money."

"I know how much your client earns. I've been practicing law for twenty years, and he earns more than me."

"And me, after thirty-five years. But he has student loans, and it's not cheap living in New York City. I'll probably need to chip in a little, and I'm not a wealthy man. I don't owe anything, but a busy street practice in downtown York is not the road to riches."

His honesty disarmed her for a moment, and she smiled and seemed to relax. They enjoyed a nice diversion swapping stories about the challenges of practicing law in small-town America. When the time was up, John said warmly, "Tell me about Elaine. Job, salary, finances, family, and so on."

"Well, as I said, she works part-time here for peanuts. She makes $24,000 a year as an assistant director of parks and rec for the city, not exactly a career job. She rents a modest apartment that she shares with her companion, Beverly, and drives a Nissan with a monthly note. Her family is from Erie, and I don't know how prosperous they once were, but things have taken a bad turn. She's on her own, twenty-three years old, surviving. She still has dreams of something beyond where she is now."

John made a few notes, then said, "Yesterday, I spoke with an attorney for the Tate family, big firm in Pittsburgh. Baxter had a trust that sent him six thousand a month, which was never enough. That sum would increase over time, but all the Tate trusts are now tightly controlled by an uncle who has a rather heavy hand. Baxter's trust folded when he died. There's very little in his estate, so any contribution from his family would fall under the category of charitable giving. These people are not known for their charity, and it's hard to imagine them entertaining notions of writing checks to Baxter's old girlfriends."

Mike was nodding in agreement. "What about Joey?" she asked.

"He's working hard, trying to provide for a growing family. He's probably strapped, and will be for the rest of his life. My client would like to keep both Joey and Alan Strock out of this."

"That's admirable."

"We propose two payments. One now, and one in seven years, when the statute of limitations expires on the rape charge. If your client puts this behind her, gives up the idea of pursuing these guys, then she gets a nice payment at the end. Twenty-five thousand now, and for the next seven years my client will add ten grand to an investment account that will render $100,000 when Elaine is thirty years old."

Same poker face. "Twenty-five up front is ridiculous," she said.

"He doesn't have twenty-five thousand. It'll come from me."

"We're not too concerned about where it comes from. We're much more interested in the amount."

"Well, right now you have zero, and if we don't reach an agreement, then it's very likely you'll stay at zero. Your chances of recovery are slim at best."

"Then why are you offering anything?"

"Peace of mind. Mike, come on, let's put this baby to sleep so these kids can get on with their lives. Kyle had almost forgotten the incident, hell, he's working a hundred hours a week, then Joey bumps into Elaine, then Baxter shows up all consumed with guilt because he remembers more now than he did before. This is crazy. They were just a bunch of drunk kids."

Yes, they were, and Mike couldn't argue the point. She recrossed her legs, and John was compelled to glance at the high heels, just a quick down and up, but she noticed it.

"Let me talk to Elaine, and we'll make a counteroffer," she said.

"Fine, but there's not much wiggle room here, Mike. The up-front money will be a loan from me to my client, and he is obviously nervous about taking on a seven-year obligation. He's twenty-five and can't see three years down the road."

"I'll call Elaine, and she'll probably want to run over and discuss this face-to-face."

"I'm not leaving town until we have a deal. I'll just walk down to the coffee shop and kill some time."

AN HOUR LATER he was back. They took their same positions, picked up their pens, and continued the negotiations.

"I assume you're not taking our offer," John said.

"Yes and no. The seven-year scheme is okay, but Elaine needs more up front. She is two years away from her degree at the University of Scranton. Her dream is law school, and without some help it will be impossible."

"How much help?"

"A hundred thousand now."

Shock, disbelief, amazement, rejection. John grimaced and squirmed and allowed a lungful of air to whistle over his teeth. It was all an act, the long-practiced pretense of utter incredulity when the other side puts its first demand on the table. Exasperation, near defeat. "Look, Mike, we're trying to reach an agreement here. You guys are trying to rob a bank."

"In two years, Elaine will still be earning $24,000 a year. Your client, on the other hand, will be earning about $400,000, with guaranteed increases. This is not a stretch for him."

John stood as if he were leaving, end of negotiations. "I need to call him."

"Sure. I'll wait."

John walked outside the building, put a cell phone to his head, and called no one. The amount they would pay had less to do with what Elaine needed and much more to do with keeping her quiet. A hundred thousand dollars was a bargain, under the circumstances.

"We'll go seventy-five grand, and that's it," John said, back at the table.

Her right hand rattled pleasantly as it came across. "Deal," she said. They shook on their agreement, then spent two hours haggling over the paperwork. When it was finished, he offered to buy lunch and she readily accepted.

37

Nigel's latest workstation had been hastily assembled on a fine mahogany desk in the center of the sitting room in a spacious suite at the Waldorf-Astoria on Park Avenue. The computer was a sixteen-by-twenty-inch exact replica of the ten models on the eighteenth floor. The monitor, too, was a perfect match. Next to it was an ominous navy blue box the size of a larger laptop.

As Nigel proudly went through a detailed description of the various cords and cables, the spaghetti, as he called it, Bennie and Kyle watched without a word. There was a power cord, audio, monitor, and printing cables. "Audio, Kyle? Do we have noise from these bad little boys?"

"No, no audio," Kyle replied, and Nigel carefully rolled up the audio cable and put it away. He bent low behind the computer and pointed to the magic spot. "Here we are, Kyle, the promised land, the USB port. Almost hidden, but I know it's there because I have a contact with Fargo. It has to be there, trust me."

Kyle grunted but said nothing.

"Here's the plan, Kyle," he said excitedly, thoroughly enthralled by his work. From his neat little hacker's high-tech tool kit he produced two small devices, identical in shape and length, three-quarters of an inch wide and about an inch and a half long. "This is the wireless USB transmitter, hot off the press, state of the art, not yet available to the public, no sir," he said, then quickly plugged it into the port that was under the power inlet. Once it was inserted, about a half an inch could be seen. "You plug it in just so, and, presto, we're in business. It's virtually invisible." He waved the other and explained, "And this little bugger is the USB receiver that goes in the blue box there. With me, Kyle?"

"Got it."

"The blue box goes inside your briefcase. You park the briefcase on the floor, directly under the computer, flip a switch, and the docs get themselves downloaded in a jiffy."

"How fast?"

"Sixty megabytes per second, about a thousand documents, assuming you get the receiver within three meters of the transmitter, which should be easy. The closer, the better, Kyle. Are you with me?"

"Hell no," Kyle said as he sat in the chair in front of the monitor. "I'm supposed to somehow reach behind the computer, plug in the transmitter, leave it there, download, et cetera, while there are other people in the room and the video cameras are watching. How, exactly, do I pull that off?"

"Drop a pen," Bennie said. "Spill some coffee. Throw some papers around. Create a diversion. Go when the place is empty, and keep your back to the camera."

Kyle was shaking his head. "It's too risky. These people are not stupid, you know. There's a security tech on duty in a room next door. Name's Gant."

"But does he work sixteen hours a day?"

"I don't know when he works. That's the point. You never know who's in there watching."

"We know security, Kyle, and the grunts who are paid to watch closed-circuit screens all day are usually half-asleep. It's terribly boring work."

"This is not a coffee room, Bennie. I'm supposed to be working in there. Stealing may be a priority for you boys, but the firm expects me to be plowing through the documents. I'll have a project due and a partner waiting on it."

Nigel charged in. "It could be over in two hours, Kyle, assuming you can find the documents quickly."

Bennie shook off all concerns. "Priority one is the air-breathing engines that Trylon and Bartin developed together. The technology is so sophisticated that the Pentagon is still orgasmic. Priority two is the fuel mix. Do a search for 'cryogenic hydrogen fuel' and follow it up with one for 'scramjet.' There should be a ton of research in the files. Priority three is called 'waveriders.' Do a search. These are aerodynamic designs used to increase the B-10's lift-to-drag ratio. Here's a memo." Bennie handed over a two-page summary.

"Any of this sound familiar, Kyle?" Nigel pleaded.

"No."

"It's there," Bennie insisted. "It's the heart of the research, the crux of the lawsuit, and you can find it, Kyle."

"Oh, thank you."

For practice, Nigel withdrew the transmitter and handed it to Kyle. "Let's see you do it." Kyle slowly got to his feet, leaned over the computer, shoved away some cables, and with some effort finally managed to insert the transmitter into the USB port. He sat down and said, "There's no way."

"Of course there is," Bennie scoffed. "Use your brain."

"It's dead."

Nigel bounced around to the blue box. "The software is some of my home brew. When you have inserted the transmitter, you reach down and flip this little switch, and the script automatically locates the computer and begins downloading the database. It will happen very quickly, Kyle, and if you like, you can take a break, leave the room, go for a pee, act like nothing at all is happening, and all the while my little gizmo is sucking up the documents."

"Bloody brilliant," Kyle said.

Bennie produced a black Bally briefcase identical to Kyle's, a stand-up model with a short leather flap that latched on one side. There were three compartments, with the middle one padded for a laptop. The substitute was complete with a few scuff marks and Kyle's Scully & Pershing business card firmly in the leather tag. "You'll use this," he said as Nigel carefully lifted the blue box and placed it in the center compartment of the briefcase. "When you unzip this divide," Nigel said, "the receiver will already be in place. If for some reason you need to abort, just close the case and punch this button, and it locks automatically."

"Abort?"

"Just in case, Kyle."

"Let me get this straight. Something goes wrong, somebody notices me, maybe some alarm goes off in a supercomputer we know nothing about as soon as I start dickering with the database, and your plan is then for me to lock the flap on the briefcase, grab the transmitter that's almost hidden, and then do what? Sprint from the room like a shoplifter who's been caught? Where do I go, Nigel? Any help here, Bennie?"

"Relax, Kyle," Bennie said with a fake smile. "This is a piece of cake. You'll do fine."

"No alarms, Kyle," Nigel said. "My software is too good for that. Trust me."

"Would you please stop saying that?"

Kyle walked to a window and looked out at the Manhattan skyline. It was almost 9:30 on Tuesday night. He had not eaten since he and Tabor had enjoyed a fifteen-minute lunch in the firm cafeteria at 11:30. Hunger, though, was only a minor concern on a long, sad list.

"Are you ready, Kyle?" Bennie called from across the room. Not a question, but a challenge.

"As ready as I'll ever be," he answered without turning around.

"When?"

"As soon as possible. I want to get it over with. I'll stop by the room a few times tomorrow, check the traffic. My best guess is that it'll be about eight tomorrow night, late in the day but with enough time to download, assuming I don't get shot."

"Any questions about the equipment, Kyle?" Nigel asked.

Kyle walked stiffly back to the workstation and stared at the machines. He finally shrugged and said, "No, it's pretty straightforward."

"Super. One last thing, Kyle. The blue box has a wireless signal so that I know precisely when you're downloading."

"Why is that necessary?"

"Monitoring. We'll be very close by."

Another shrug. "Whatever."

The blue box was still in the center compartment, with Nigel handling it as if it were a bomb. Kyle then added the materials from his own briefcase, and when he grabbed the handle and lifted it off the table, he was surprised at the weight.

"A bit heavier, Kyle?" Nigel quizzed, watching every move.

"Yes, quite a bit."

"Not to worry. We've reinforced the bottom of the Bally. It's not going to drop out as you're walking along Broad Street."

"I like the other one better. When do I get it back?"

"Soon, Kyle, soon."

Kyle pulled on his trench coat and made his way to the door. Bennie followed and said, "Good luck, Kyle. It's all come down to this. We believe in you."

"Go to hell," Kyle said, and left the room.

38

The briefcase grew heavier during the short, sleepless night, and when Kyle lugged it out of the rear of the taxi early Wednesday morning, he half-wished the bottom would indeed fall out, the blue box would crash onto Broad Street in a thousand pieces, and Nigel's precious home brew would be sent down the gutter. He wasn't sure what would happen after that, but any scenario was far better than what was planned.

Twenty minutes after he rode the elevator to the thirty-fourth floor, Roy Benedict entered the same elevator with two young men who were undoubtedly associates at Scully & Pershing. The signs were obvious. They were under thirty. It was 6:35 in the morning. They appeared to be fatigued and miserable, but they wore expensive clothes and carried handsome briefcases, black. He was prepared to see a familiar face, though felt it unlikely. It was not at all unusual to see attorneys from other firms in the building. Roy knew half a dozen partners at Scully, but with fifteen hundred lawyers arriving for work, he figured the odds were slim. And he was right. The two zombies riding up with him were just a couple of faceless souls who would be gone in a year or so.

The briefcase in Roy's hand was also a black Bally, identical to the one Kyle bought back in August, the third one required for this mission. He left the elevator alone on the thirty-fourth floor and walked past the vacant reception desk, down a hall to the right, four, five, six doors, and there was his client, sitting at his desk, sipping coffee, waiting. The exchange was brief. Roy swapped briefcases and was ready to go.

"Where are the feds?" Kyle asked, very softly, though no one was in the hall and the secretaries were just getting out of bed.

"Around the corner in a van. They'll do a quick scan to make sure there are no tracking devices. If they find one, I'll bring it back in a sprint and we'll concoct a story. If not, then they'll take it to their lab in Queens. This thing is heavy."

"The blue box. Specially designed by some evil geniuses."

"When do you need it?"

"Let's say 7:00 p.m. That's twelve hours. Should be enough, right?"

"That's what they say. According to Bullington, they have a small army of geeks just itching to unwrap it."

"They can't screw it up."

"They won't. You good?"

"Great. Do they have arrest warrants?"

"Oh, yes. Wiretapping, extortion, conspiracy, lots of good stuff. They're just waiting on you."

"If Bennie is about to be arrested, then I'm a motivated young man."

"Good luck."

Roy was gone, leaving behind the Bally with the same scuff marks and name tag. Kyle quickly stuffed it with files and legal pads and pens and went to find more coffee.

TWELVE LONG HOURS later, Roy was back with the second briefcase. He took a seat as Kyle closed the door. "So?" he said.

"It is what it is. It's a customized computer built along the lines of those used by the military, everything is heavy-duty. Designed for nothing but downloading. Two hard drives, with 750 gigabytes each. Basically, enough memory to store everything in this building and the three next door. Highly sophisticated software that the FBI geeks have never seen before. These guys are good, Kyle."

"Tell me about it."

"And there is indeed a wireless signal so they can monitor you."

"Dammit. So I have to download something?"

"I'm afraid so. The wireless signal cannot indicate what you are downloading, or how much. It just lets them know that you're inside and that you've started moving the database."

"Shit!"

"You can do it, Kyle."

"That seems to be the consensus."

"Do you know where you'll meet these guys?"

"No. It'll be a last-second notice. Assuming I download without setting off alarms, I'll call Bennie with the happy news, and he'll tell me where to meet. I'm going to the room in an hour, and I plan to quit at nine, regardless of the download. So, by nine fifteen, if I'm lucky, I should be on the street."

"I'll stay at my office. If you get a chance, please call. Pretty exciting stuff, Kyle."

"Exciting? How about terrifying?"

"You're the man." With that, Roy exchanged briefcases again and disappeared.

For sixty minutes, Kyle stared at the clock, did nothing but bill Trylon for an hour, and finally made a move. He loosened his tie, rolled up his sleeves, tried to look as casual as possible, and took the elevator to the eighteenth floor.

Sherry Abney was in the room, and he had to say hello. From the looks of her table, she'd been there for hours and the research had not gone well. Kyle chose a station as far away from her as possible. Her back was to him.

Despite his bitching and moaning, he foresaw little danger of being noticed by another member of Team Trylon. All ten chairs faced the outside walls, away from the center, so that while doing research, he could see nothing but the monitor, the computer, and the wall behind it. The danger was up above, lurking in the lenses of the video cameras. Still, he preferred to have the room to himself.

After fifteen minutes, he decided to visit the men's room. On the way out, he asked Sherry, "Can I get you a coffee?"

"No, thanks. I'm leaving soon."

Perfect. She left at 8:30, a nice breaking point that always made billing easier. Kyle placed a legal pad on top of the computer, then a couple of pens, things that could roll and slide and need retrieving. He scattered a couple of files beside the monitor and in general made a mess of things. At 8:40, he knocked on the locked metal door that led to the small printing room, and there was no answer. Then he tried a second metal door that led to places unknown, but he suspected it was the room where Gant hung out and secured things. He saw Gant occasionally and figured he worked close by. There was no answer. At 8:45, Kyle decided to plunge ahead before another associate arrived for one last hour of work. He walked to his table and bumped the legal pad on top of the computer, sending the pens flying against the wall. He threw up an arm, said "Shit!" as loudly as possible, then leaned over as if to retrieve things. He found one pen, couldn't find the other, but kept searching. On the floor, behind the monitor, under the chair, then again behind the computer, where he deftly inserted the tiny transmitter into the USB port just as he found the missing pen and held it up so the cameras could see it. Settled down now, composed, not cursing, he took his seat and began clicking away at the keyboard.

He slid the briefcase closer under the table, directly under the computer now, then he flipped the switch.

No alarms. No virus warnings screaming from the screen. No sudden entry by Gant with armed guards. Nothing. Kyle the hacker was downloading files, stealing at a dizzying rate of speed. In nine minutes, he transferred all Category A documents—letters, memos, a hundred different varieties of harmless information that had already been submitted to APE and Bartin. When he was finished with the Category A documents, he repeated the process and downloaded them again. And again, and again.

An hour after he entered the room, he again went through the charade of searching for lost pens, and while bumbling about, he plucked the transmitter from the USB port. Then he cleaned up his mess and left. He hurried to his office, got his jacket and trench coat, and made it to the elevators without seeing another person. As he rode down without a single stop, he realized that this was the moment he had always feared. He was leaving the office as a thief, with enough stolen files in his briefcase to get him convicted of numerous crimes and disbarred for life.

As he stepped into the raw December night, he immediately called Bennie. "Mission accomplished!" he said proudly.

"Great, Kyle. Oxford Hotel, corner of Lex and Thirty-fifth. Room 551, fifteen minutes away."

"I'm on the way." Kyle walked to a black sedan, one duly registered to a well-known car company in Brooklyn, and jumped into the backseat. The small Asian driver said, "Where to?"

"And your name is?"

"Al Capone."

"Where were you born, Al?"

"Tutwiler, Texas."

"You're the man, Al. Oxford Hotel, room 551."

Al the Agent immediately called someone and repeated the information. He listened for a few minutes, drove very slowly, then said, "Here's the plan, Mr. McAvoy. We have a team on the move, and they should be at the hotel in ten minutes. We'll take our time here. When the supervisor is in the hotel, he will call me with more instructions. Would you like a vest?"

"A what?"

"A vest, bulletproof. There's one in the trunk if you'd like."

Kyle had been too preoccupied with his thievery to contemplate the actual events surrounding the arrest of Bennie, and hopefully Nigel, too. He was sure he would lead the FBI to his handler, but he had not given much thought to the details of his betrayal. Why, exactly, might he need a bulletproof vest?

To stop bullets, of course. Baxter flashed through his overheated brain.

"I'll pass," Kyle said, realizing how ill equipped he was to make such decisions.

"Yes, sir."

Al looked for traffic, for detours, anything to burn some clock. His cell phone rang and he listened, then said, "Okay, Mr. McAvoy. I'll stop in front of the hotel, and you'll walk into the lobby alone. Go to the elevators to the right, and punch the button for the fourth floor. Get off on the fourth, turn left, walk to the door leading to the stairs. In the stairwell, you will meet Mr. Bullington and several other agents. They will take over from there."

"Sounds like fun."

"Good luck, Mr. McAvoy."

Five minutes later Kyle walked into the lobby of the Oxford Hotel and followed his instructions. In the stairwell between the fourth and the fifth floors, he met Joe Bullington and two other agents, all dressed exactly like the ones who'd snatched him some ten months earlier after a youth basketball game in New Haven. Except these were real, and he had no desire to inspect their credentials. Tensions were high, and Kyle's weary heart was pounding furiously.

"I'm Agent Booth, this is Agent Hardy," one said, and Kyle was impressed with how large they were.

"Go to the door of 551," Booth said. "The second it starts to open, kick it very hard, then jump back out of the way. We'll be right behind you. We do not anticipate gunfire. We assume they're armed, but they're not expecting trouble. Once we're inside, you'll be removed from the scene."

What! No gunfire! Kyle started to crack a funny, but his knees were suddenly weak.

"Got it?" Booth growled at him.

"Got it. Let's go."

Kyle entered the hall and walked with as much confidence as possible to room 551. He pressed the button, took a deep breath, and glanced around. Booth and Hardy were fifteen feet away, ready to spring, shiny black pistols drawn. From the other end of the hall, two other agents were approaching, also with guns visible.

Maybe I should've opted for the vest, Kyle thought.

He pressed the button again. Nothing. Not a voice from within, not a sound.

His lungs had ceased working, and his stomach was a mess. The briefcase weighed a ton, much heavier now that it contained the stolen files.

He frowned at Booth, who looked perplexed as well. Kyle pressed the button for the third time, then tapped on the door and yelled, "Hey, Bennie. It's Kyle."

Nothing. He rang the doorbell for the fourth time, then fifth.

"It's a single room," Booth whispered. Then he motioned for some type of well-rehearsed formation and said to Kyle, "Please step aside. Go right down there and wait." Hardy whipped out an electronic room key and inserted it. The green light came on, and the four FBI agents stormed in, high and low, right and left, barking, guns aimed in all directions. Joe Bullington was running toward them, and behind him were more agents.

The room was empty, of suspects anyway, and if anyone had been there recently, he'd left nothing behind. Bullington reappeared in the hall and commanded "Lock the building!" into a phone or walkie-talkie. He shot Kyle a look of complete astonishment, and Kyle began to fade. Agents hustled about, frantic with indecision and confusion. Some ran to the stairs, others to the elevators.

An old woman in 562 stepped into the hall and shouted, "Quiet!" but quickly lost her spunk when two frowning agents spun around with weapons. She retreated quickly, unharmed but awake for the night.

"Kyle, here please," Bullington said, waving him into room 551. Kyle clutched the briefcase and entered the room. "Stay here for a few minutes," Bullington said. "These two will remain with you."

Kyle sat on the edge of the bed, briefcase between his feet, as his two guards closed the door and put away their guns. Minutes passed as he thought of a hundred scenes and scenarios, none particularly appealing. He thought of Roy, and called him. He was still at his office, waiting for the news.

"They got away," Kyle said, his voice slow and weak.

"Whatta you mean?"

"We're in the hotel room, and it's empty. They're gone, Roy."

"Where are you?"

"Room 551, Oxford Hotel, under guard, I guess. The FBI is searching the hotel, but they won't find anybody."

"I'll be there in fifteen minutes."

WHILE THE HOTEL was being searched, three FBI agents entered Kyle's apartment in Chelsea. Using his key, they entered quietly and began a sweep that would take four hours and produce three hidden cameras, a wiretap on his wall phone, and six other eavesdropping devices. Plenty of evidence to support indictments. A strong case for the feds, but what they really needed was some suspects.

39

Roy arrived at 11:00 p.m. He was met by Joe Bullington at the front door and escorted through the lobby. The hotel was still locked down, a room-by-room search under way with lots of unhappy guests, and the front desk was chaos.

Roy's first question was "How's Kyle?"

"Pretty rattled," Bullington said. "Let's take the stairs. The elevators have been stopped. Hell, we're all rattled."

The second question was the most obvious one. "What happened?"

"I do not know, Roy. It's confusing."

Kyle was seated on the edge of the bed, briefcase still between his feet, trench coat still on, staring blankly at the floor and ignoring the two agents who were guarding him. Roy put a hand on his shoulder, then knelt down to face level and said, "Kyle, you okay?"

"Sure." It was somewhat helpful to see a trusted face.

Bullington was on the phone. He slapped it shut and said, "Look, there's a suite on the second floor. It's easier to secure and much larger. Let's make a move."

As they filed out, Kyle mumbled to his lawyer, "Did you hear that, Roy? Easier to secure. I'm being protected now."

"It's okay, Kyle."

The suite had three rooms, one of which would work well as an office—desk, fax, wireless Internet, several comfortable chairs, and a small conference area at the far end. "This'll do," Bullington said as he ripped off his trench coat, then his jacket, as if they would be there for some time, and Kyle and Roy did the same. They took their seats and settled in. Two younger agents stayed by the door.

"Here's what we know so far," Bullington began, very much the special agent in charge. "The room was reserved this afternoon by a Mr. Randall Kerr, who used both a bogus name and a bogus credit card. Around 8:45, Mr. Kerr shows up to check in, alone, one small carry-on and a black briefcase, and in chatting up the desk clerk tells her that he just flew in from Mexico City. We've watched the video. It's Bennie, with no effort at disguise. He went to his room, and according to the electronic entry grid he opened the door to room 551 at 8:58. He opened it again eighteen minutes later, leaving evidently, because the door was never used again. No one remembers seeing him exit the building. There are some video cameras in the hallways and lobby, but so far nothing. He's vanished."

"Of course he's vanished," Kyle said. "You won't find him."

"We're trying."

"What did you download, Kyle?" Roy asked.

"The Category A documents. Five or six times. I didn't touch anything else."

"And this went smoothly?"

"As far as I know. There were no problems inside the room."

"What time did you start downloading?" Bullington asked.

"About 8:45."

"And what time did you call Bennie?"

"Just before 10:00."

Bullington thought for a second, then stated the obvious. "So Bennie waited until they got your signal, and once he knew you were downloading, he checked into the room. Eighteen minutes later he fled. That doesn't make sense."

"It does if you know Bennie," Kyle said.

"I don't follow," Bullington said.

"Someone informed Bennie of our little plan, that much is obvious. It wasn't me. It wasn't my lawyer. And the only other parties involved would be you, Mr. Bullington, the FBI, and Mr. Wingate and his gang over at Justice. We have no idea at this point, and we probably never will. Regardless, Bennie got the tip and decided to have some fun. He knew I would lead you here to catch him, so this is all a setup. Bennie's probably down the street watching a hundred FBI agents swarm around the hotel and laughing his balls off."

Bullington's cheeks turned a dark red. He suddenly had a call to make and left the room.

"Take it easy, Kyle," Roy said softly. Kyle locked his fingers behind his head and bent over. The briefcase was still wedged between his feet. He closed his eyes and tried to control his thoughts, but that was impossible. Roy watched him but said nothing. He went to the minibar and pulled out two bottles of water.

"We should talk," Roy said, handing a bottle to Kyle. "We'll have to make some quick decisions."

"Okay. What do we do with this damned thing?" Kyle asked, patting the briefcase. "Scully doesn't need it, because the documents are not confidential. I just stole a copy. They haven't lost anything yet. Their files will appear to be untouched."

"I'm sure the FBI will want it for evidence."

"Evidence against who?"

"Bennie."

"Bennie? Bennie's gone, Roy, listen to me. They'll never find Bennie, because he's a helluva lot smarter than they are. Bennie won't be arrested. Bennie won't go to trial. Bennie's on an airplane right now, probably a private one, looking at his fifteen passports and deciding which one to use next."

"Don't be so sure."

"And why not? Bennie outfoxed us tonight, didn't he? Bennie has pals in high places, maybe not here in New York, maybe in Washington. Too many people got involved, Roy. The FBI, the Department of Justice, and the network of gossip spread. Plans here, authorizations there, meetings at high levels, more and more intelligence people in the loop. It was a mistake."

"You had no choice."

"My choices were limited. Looks like I made the wrong one."

"What about the law firm?"

"I'm sure I'll screw that up, too. What's your advice? God knows I'm paying for it, if even at a discount." Both managed smiles, but very brief ones.

Roy gulped his water, wiped his lips with a shirtsleeve, and leaned even closer. The two guards were still in the sitting room, within earshot. "You could say nothing. Just report tomorrow for duty and act like none of this happened. The files are safe. Nothing has been compromised. Look, Kyle, you never planned to hand over anything to Bennie. You were forced to download some stuff to facilitate his arrest. The arrest didn't happen. The firm has no clue. Assuming there won't be a prosecution, the firm will never know."

"But the plan was to bust Bennie, tell the firm everything, and beg for mercy. Sort of like the bank robber who brings back the cash and says he's sorry, can't we just forget about it. With a few more twists, of course."

"Do you want to stay at the firm, Kyle?"

"My exit from Scully & Pershing was a foregone conclusion the day I walked into your office."

"There might be a way to save the job."

"I took the job because Bennie had a gun to my head. That gun has now been replaced by a different one, but at least the threat of blackmail is gone. There's a chance the video may still cause some embarrassment, but nothing more. I'd like to get out of here."

A radio squawked in the sitting room, jolting the agents. It came and went with no further news.

Kyle finally abandoned the briefcase and stretched his legs. He looked at his lawyer and said, "You're a big partner in a big firm. What would you do if an associate pulled this stunt?"

"Fire him immediately."

"Exactly. On the spot, with little patience for a lot of talk. How can the firm ever trust me again? There are a thousand rookies out there ready to replace me. And there's something else here, Roy, something that Scully needs to know." Kyle glanced at the sitting room, where his bodyguards were now watching TV.

"I'm not the only spy. Bennie knew too much. Someone else is planted there, passing along information to Bennie. I have to tell them."

There was a commotion at the door, and the two guards quickly muted the television and hopped to attention. Kyle and Roy stood as Bullington swept in with a small, important group, the center of which was a man of about sixty with short gray hair, a fine suit, and the air of someone in complete control of all things around him. Bullington introduced him as Mr. Mario Delano, director in charge of the New York office of the FBI.

He addressed both Kyle and Roy: "Gentlemen, Mr. Bennie Wright has obviously left the building, and we have a serious problem. I have no idea where the leak was, but I assure you it was not my office. I doubt that's very comforting right now. We are searching frantically around the city—train stations, airports, subways, heliports, toll roads. Every agent under my authority is on the streets."

If Kyle was supposed to be impressed, he was not. He simply shrugged as if to say, "Big deal. The least you could do."

Delano pressed on. "It's urgent that you get out of town, Mr. McAvoy. I suggest that we take you into protective custody for a few days, let the dust settle, give us some time to track down Bennie Wright."

"And if you don't find him?" Kyle asked.

"Let's talk about that later. We have a small jet waiting at Teterboro Airport. We'll have you there in thirty minutes. You'll have protection around the clock until something changes." The crisp precision of Delano's plans left no doubt that the dangers were indeed substantial. Kyle could not argue. He was now the double agent, as well as the government's star witness in the event Bennie got caught. If they would murder Baxter to keep him away from Elaine, it was hard to imagine what they would do to Kyle.

"Let's go," Delano said.

"I need a minute with my client," Roy said.

"Certainly," said Delano as he snapped his fingers and the room emptied. Roy closed the door, and when they were alone, he said, "I'll call Scully and put them off."

Kyle withdrew his FirmFone and said, "No need. I'll check in with Doug Peckham and tell him I'm sick. Bennie never got his hands on my little phone here."

"Fine. It's best if I keep the briefcase and the computer."

"Just don't let the FBI have it."

"I won't."

They shook hands. Roy said, "You did the right thing."

"Right or wrong, it didn't work."

"You didn't hand over anything, Kyle. You didn't breach a client's confidence."

"Let's argue later."

"Be safe."

40

John McAvoy was enjoying a peaceful Thursday morning at his desk when a secretary rang in with the news that two gentlemen from the FBI had dropped by for a surprise visit. They were quickly shown in. Introductions were made, badges flashed, coffee declined. "Is he all right?" John asked.

"He's fine," the agent named Halsey said. The one named Murdock agreed, nodding with smug assurance.

"What's happened?"

"Kyle has informed us that you are aware of the plans he had to help apprehend his handler," Halsey said.

"Yes. I know the background and I know what he had in mind. What's happened?"

Both agents shifted weight. Murdock took over. "Well, things didn't go as planned. Kyle secured the documents, and he was supposed to meet the handler around ten last night in a midtown hotel. The handler didn't show, fled at the last moment. As of now, we have not apprehended him."

John closed his eyes, removed his reading glasses, and lit a cigarette. "Where's Kyle?"

"He's with us, in protective custody. He's safe, and he's anxious to talk to you. That will not be possible at this moment."

A blast of blue smoke escaped from John's side of the desk. "Protective custody?" he repeated. The smoke drifted over and began settling on Halsey and Murdock.

"Afraid so. He could be in danger."

"Who botched the operation?"

"Not sure it was botched, or how or why. Let's just say there is a lot of investigating going on right now."

"When can I talk to him?"

"Soon," Halsey said.

"We're out of Philly," Murdock said. "But we're here in York for the next few days. Our job is to relay messages to you." Both agents withdrew business cards. "Cell numbers on the back. Please don't hesitate to call."

KYLE SLEPT LATE into the morning, and awoke to the sounds of waves rolling onto a beach. He was adrift in the clouds—a thick white comforter, puffy white pillows, a thick white bedspread piled at his feet. The queen-sized bed was topped with a white canopy. He knew where he was, but it took a few minutes to convince himself he was really there.

The walls were adorned with cheap pastels of beach scenes. The floor was painted wood. He listened to the ocean and heard the distant calls of seagulls. There were no other sounds, quite a contrast to the early bustle of Chelsea. No alarm clock startling him at some obscene hour. No rush to shower and dress and hurry through the frantic rituals of getting to the office. None of that, at least not today.

This was not an unpleasant way to begin the rest of his life.

The bedroom was one of three in a modest two-story beach rental an hour east of Destin, Florida, on the Gulf, two hours and forty-eight minutes by Learjet from Teterboro Airport in New Jersey. They, he and his new friends, had landed at Destin just before 4:00 a.m. A van with armed drivers had scooped them up and raced along Highway 98, passing miles of empty condos and beach houses and small hotels. There were a few vacationers, judging by the parking lots, and many of the cars had Canadian license plates.

The two windows were half-open and the breeze blew the curtains. It was a full three minutes before Kyle thought about Bennie, but he fought the temptation and concentrated on the distant squawking of the seagulls. There was a slight knock at the door. "Yes," Kyle answered with a scratchy voice.

It opened slightly, and Todd, his new best friend, wedged through his chubby face and said, "You wanted a ten o'clock wake-up call."

"Thanks."

"You okay?"

"Sure."

Todd had joined the escape in Destin and was now assigned to guard their witness or snitch or whatever Kyle was considered to be. He was from the Pensacola office, went to Auburn, was only two years older than Kyle himself, and talked far more than any other FBI agent, real or fake, that he'd met so far in this ordeal.

Kyle, in boxers only, left the softness of the clouds and went next door to the large kitchen-den combo. Todd had been to the grocery store. The counter was covered with boxes of cereal, breakfast snacks, cookies, chips, all manner of boxed foods. "Coffee?" Todd asked.

"Sure."

There were a few items of folded clothing on the kitchen table. Kyle's other new best friend was Barry, an older, quieter type with premature gray hair and more wrinkles than any forty-year-old should have. Barry said, "Good morning. We've been shopping. Bought you a couple of T-shirts, shorts, a pair of khakis, deck shoes. Really nice stuff from the local Kmart. Don't worry, Uncle Sam paid the bill."

"I'm sure I'll look fabulous," Kyle said, taking a cup of coffee from Todd. Todd and Barry, both in khakis and polos, were unarmed but not far from their weapons. There was also a Nick and a Matthew somewhere close by.

"I gotta call the office," Kyle said. "Check in, you know, tell them I'm sick and can't work today. By now they're already looking for me."

Todd produced the FirmFone and said, "Be our guest. We're told it's secure. Just don't give a hint as to where you are. Agreed?"

"Where am I?"

"Western Hemisphere."

"Close enough."

With his coffee and his phone, Kyle stepped outside onto a wide deck that looked over some dunes. The beach was long and beautiful, and deserted. The air was light, brisk, but far warmer than frigid New York. With great reluctance he looked at the phone. E-mails, texts, and voice mails from Doug Peckham, Dale, Sherry Abney, Tim Reynolds, Tabor, and a few others, but nothing to alarm him. He scanned them quickly, just the usual daily barrage of communications from very wired people with too much access to each other. Dale asked twice if he was okay.

He called Doug Peckham, got his voice mail, and reported that he was down with the flu, flat on his back, sick as a dog, and so on. Then he called Dale, who was in a meeting. He left the same message. One useless advantage of working with workaholics was that they had no time to worry about each other's minor ailments. Got the flu—take some pills and sleep it off, but do not spread your germs at the office.

Roy Benedict seemed to be waiting by the phone. "Where are you, Kyle?" he asked, almost in a pant.

"Western Hemisphere. I'm doing well. How about you?"

"Fine. You're safe?"

"Safe. I'm hidden, stashed away, and I'm guarded by a posse of at least four, all anxious to shoot someone. Any news on our man Bennie?"

"No. They'll have indictments by noon, and they're adding one for murder. They'll splash these around the world and hope for a break. You were right. Your apartment had more bugs than a landfill. Good stuff, too, the latest in wiretapping technology."

"I'm honored."

"And they found a transmitter in the rear bumper of your Jeep."

"I never thought of that."

"Anyway, all this is being presented to the grand jury as we speak, so at least Bennie will have a thick indictment on record should he ever make a mistake."

"Don't bet on that."

"Have you talked to the law firm?"

"I left a message with Peckham, the flu routine. He'll buy it for a couple of days."

"No alarms, nothing strange."

"No. It's weird, Roy. I'm a thousand miles away now, and looking back, I can't believe how easy it was to walk in with the right gear and walk out with the files. I could've taken every single document in the database, four million plus, and handed them over to Bennie or another thug. And I could've gone back into my office this morning as if nothing happened. Scully has got to be warned."

"So who tells them?"

"I do. I have a few things to get off my chest."

"Let's talk about that tomorrow. I've been on the phone with Bullington all morning. Twice he's mentioned the witness protection program. The FBI is pushing it hard. They are pretty nervous about you, Kyle."

"I'm nervous about me, too, but witness protection?"

"Sure. You're convinced they can't find Bennie. They're convinced they can. If they do, and they haul him back for a trial, with an incredible list of charges, then you're the star. If you're not around to testify, then the government's case falls flat."

A pleasant morning at the beach was becoming complicated. And why not? Nothing had been simple for a long time now.

"That'll take some serious thought and consideration," Kyle said.

"Then start thinking."

"I'll call you later."

Kyle dressed in the khakis and a T-shirt, not a bad fit, then ate two bowls of cereal. He read the *Pensacola News Journal* and the *New York Times.* The *Times* had nothing about last night's excitement at the Oxford Hotel. Of course not, Kyle said to himself. It happened far too late, and it was far too clandestine. Then why was he looking for it?

After breakfast and the papers, Todd joined him at the kitchen table. "We have a few rules," he said with a jovial face but a hard smile.

"What a surprise."

"You can make calls, obviously, but only on that phone. Can't reveal your whereabouts. You can walk on the beach, but we have to follow, at a distance."

"You're kidding? I'm walking down the beach, and there's a guy with a machine gun tagging along. How relaxing."

Todd caught the humor and enjoyed a laugh. "No machine gun, and we won't be conspicuous."

"You're all conspicuous. I can spot an agent a mile away."

"Anyway, stay close to the house."

"How long will I be here?"

Todd shrugged and said, "I have no idea."

"Am I in protective custody or witness protection?"

"Custody, I think."

"You don't know, Todd? Come on. Custody implies that I'm a suspect of some variety, doesn't it, Todd?"

Another shrug.

"But I'm not a suspect. I'm a witness, but I have not agreed to enter the witness protection program. So, according to my lawyer, the one I just talked to, I'm free to walk out that door anytime I want. Whatta you think about that, Todd?"

"That machine gun you just mentioned? We have at least six on the premises."

"So I should stay here, right?"

"Right."

"Okay, it's noon. What are we going to do?"

Barry had been hovering nearby, not missing a word. He walked to the table with a large basket of the usual board games the owners of all beach rentals leave behind. Barry said, "We have Monopoly, Risk, Rook, Scrabble, Chinese checkers, your call, Kyle."

Kyle studied the basket. "Scrabble."

41

The flu raged unabated into Friday. Doug Peckham, while claiming to be sympathetic, was curious about any "improvement." They were getting hammered with motions in the Trylon case, and everyone was needed. His sympathy did not extend to a curiosity about where Kyle was staying, who, if anyone, was tending to him, what medications he was taking, and so on. Part of Kyle's ruse was the forbidding diagnosis that his particular strain of the flu was "hotly contagious." Since New York was going through its annual December flu warning, his story was easily digestible. Dale believed it, too, though she was much more sympathetic.

The temperature hit eighty degrees in the early afternoon, and Kyle was bored with the beach house. He said to Todd, "I'd like to take a walk. Would you please prepare the beach?"

"My pleasure. Which way are you going?"

"East, toward Miami."

"I'll round up the gang. They're getting bored with you."

Kyle walked for an hour, and passed fewer than ten beachcombers going the opposite way. Thirty yards behind him were two of his guardians, a male and a female, a happy couple with receivers in their ears and handguns in their pockets.

He heard music, and saw a small crowd under a fake thatched roof. It was the Gator Hotel, a 1950s-style mom-and-pop motel with a small pool and low rates, a depressing little place, but it had the only action on the beach. Just for the hell of it, and to torment his followers, he sauntered away from the water, walked between two small dunes, and pulled up a chair at Pedro's Bar. Jimmy Buffett was singing softly about life in a banana republic. The bartender was mixing rum punch specials. The crowd numbered seven, all over the age of sixty, all overweight, all chatting in crisp northern accents. The early snowbirds.

Kyle sipped a rum punch and ordered a cigar. Between the dunes he saw his trailing couple stop and gawk and try to figure out what to do. Within minutes, another agent appeared from the front of the motel. He walked through the open bar, winked at Kyle, and kept going. We're here, buddy.

He drank and smoked for a while, and tried to convince himself that he was relaxed. No worries. Just another overworked professional enjoying a few days at the beach.

But there was too much unfinished business in New York.

AFTER THREE DAYS of thorough protection, Kyle was fed up. The Lear landed at Teterboro just after 6:00 p.m. on Saturday, December 6. At Kyle's insistence, he was booked into a suite at the Tribeca Grand Hotel, between Walker and White, near the Village. And at his request, all FBI agents remained below, in the lobby and atrium. He was tired of their overkill and silly rules—silly in his opinion.

Dale arrived promptly at eight. She was driven over by two agents and sneaked in through a service entrance. When they were alone,

Kyle started with the fake flu and worked his way backward. It was a long journey, and she listened with the same disbelief that had been shared by Roy Benedict and John McAvoy. They ordered room service, lobster and a fine white burgundy, compliments of the government, and kept talking. He was leaving the firm, and not sure where he was headed. She was leaving the firm, a nice lateral transfer to a better life in downtown Providence. He wanted to talk about her future, but she was determined to finish up with his past. She found it fascinating, incredulous, frightening, and said over and over, "Why didn't you tell me?" The best response he could offer was "I didn't tell anyone."

They talked until well past midnight. The back-and-forth was more a conversation between two good friends than between two casual lovers. They said goodbye with a long kiss and a serious promise to meet in a few weeks, as soon as Kyle settled some issues.

At 1:00 a.m., he called downstairs and informed the boys that he was going to sleep.

KYLE MCAVOY entered the opulent offices of Scully & Pershing for the last time at noon on Sunday. He was accompanied by Roy Benedict, Mr. Mario Delano of the FBI, and Mr. Drew Wingate with the Department of Justice. They were led to a conference room on the thirty-fifth floor, yet another room Kyle had never seen. They were met by half a dozen of the firm's partners, all with very somber faces. All offered stiff introductions. Only Doug Peckham showed the slightest trace of warmth to Kyle, and only for a second. They took seats on opposite sides of the table like enemies glaring across the battlefield: Howard Meezer, the managing partner; Peckham; Wilson Rush, who looked particularly upset; a retired legend named Abraham Kintz; and two slightly younger partners from the firm's management committee, men Kyle had never laid eyes on.

Late Saturday evening, Roy Benedict had sent them a twenty-five-page, detailed summary of Kyle's big adventure, and there was little doubt that every word had been read more than once by all six of the partners. Attached to the narrative was Kyle's letter of resignation.

Meezer kicked things off with a pleasant "Mr. McAvoy, your resignation is unanimously accepted."

Not just accepted, but unanimously so. Kyle nodded but said nothing.

"We've read the summary prepared by your lawyer," Meezer said slowly, methodically. "It is fascinating, and troubling, and it raises a number of questions. I suggest we address them in order of priority."

Fine, fine, yes, agreed all around the table.

"The first issue is what to do with you, Mr. McAvoy. We understand the reasons behind your theft, but it was a theft nonetheless. You took the confidential files of a valuable client for purposes that had not been authorized by this firm. A criminal prosecution is in order, do you agree?"

Kyle had been told to keep his mouth shut unless Roy approved a response.

"A criminal prosecution is possible," Roy admitted. "But there is nothing to be gained. The firm lost nothing."

"Loss is not a requirement, Mr. Benedict."

"Agreed, technically. But let's be practical. Kyle had no intention of turning over the documents once he'd taken them. He did so only to stop a conspiracy to seriously harm this firm and its client."

"The FBI will not cooperate in a criminal prosecution, Mr. Meezer," Delano said, the heavy hand of the federal government.

"Nor will the Department of Justice," added Wingate.

"Thank you," Meezer said. "But we don't need your help. Theft can be a state charge, and we have some nice contacts with the authorities here in the city. However, we are not inclined to pursue this as a criminal matter." Heavy emphasis on the word "criminal." "There is little to be gained and much to be lost. We don't want our clients worried about confidentiality, and this little episode would make a wonderful story in the press."

Wilson Rush was glaring at Kyle, but Doug occupied himself with a legal pad. He was there because Kyle fell under his immediate supervision, and because the firm needed bodies, a grim show of force at this unfortunate moment. Kyle watched Doug, ignored Rush, and wondered how many of the six partners over there were billing Trylon at a double rate since they'd been dragged in on a Sunday.

Billing. Billing. He hoped he never saw another time sheet, never again glanced at his watch and divided an hour into tenths, never again tallied things up at the end of the month to make sure he'd gone over two hundred hours, padding here and there if he came up a few hours short.

"As to the matter of ethics," Meezer was saying, "this is a serious breach of a client's confidence. The state disciplinary committee should be notified."

He paused long enough for someone on the other side to respond. "I thought you were trying to avoid publicity," Roy said. "These matters are supposed to be private, but we know that they're often leaked. And if Kyle gets reprimanded or disbarred, it becomes public record. A Scully & Pershing associate disbarred for taking confidential files. Is that the story you want splashed in the *New York Lawyer*?"

At least four of the six were slowly shaking their heads, and it dawned on Kyle that they were as nervous as he was. Their vaunted reputation was on the line. A major client might pull its business. Others could follow. Scully's competitors would use the breach of security as a piece of delicious gossip to spread all over Wall Street.

"Do you plan to stay in New York, Mr. McAvoy?" Meezer asked.

Roy nodded, and Kyle said, "No, I can't."

"Very well. If you agree to forgo the practice of law in the state of New York, we will agree to forget the ethical violations."

"Agreed," Kyle said, and maybe a bit too quickly because he couldn't wait to leave the city.

Meezer shuffled through some notes as if there were a dozen tough topics to cover, but the meeting was practically over. The meeting was important so that the firm could officially dismiss Kyle, perhaps flog him a bit, listen to his apology, and then both sides could say good riddance.

"Where is this blue box?" Wilson Rush asked.

"Locked in my office," Roy said.

"And it has nothing but the Category A files?"

"That's correct," Roy said.

"I'd like for our security people to see it."

"Anytime."

"But we would like to be present," Delano added. "If this Bennie character is caught, the box is exhibit No. 1."

"Any progress on the search?" Meezer asked, veering off script.

Delano could never say there was no progress when searching for a suspect, so he gave the standard "We are pursuing leads. We're still confident."

In other words, no.

More shuffling of paper, more shifting of rear ends. "In your summary, Mr. McAvoy, you allude to additional security issues within Scully & Pershing. Care to expand on this?"

A nod from Roy, and Kyle began, "Yes, but first I want to apologize for my actions. I hope you understand the reasons behind what I did, but I was still wrong. And I apologize. As far as security, I met with these thugs ten times while I was in New York. The first meeting was in February, the tenth meeting was last Tuesday night. I took meticulous notes of each meeting—dates, places, duration, who was present, what was said, everything I could remember afterward. My attorney has these notes. The FBI has a copy. On three occasions, I was given information that could only be known by someone within this firm. I think there's another spy. For example, Bennie, and I hate to use that name because it's just an alias, but it's all we have, but Bennie knew about the warehouse full of documents, down south, as he said. During one meeting he and Nigel, another alias, hinted that they were making progress in breaching the security of the warehouse. They knew about the secret room on the eighteenth floor. Bennie knew every name of every partner and associate assigned to the lawsuit. Bennie knew that a young lawyer named McDougle was leaving, that he worked under a senior associate named Sherry Abney on the Trylon case, and Bennie told me to start playing squash because Sherry enjoyed the game. Bennie handed me copies of pleadings, motions, rulings—I have over six hundred pages of the court file that, as you know, is locked away and kept from the public."

Three of the six jaws had dropped on the other side, not down to their chests, not the kick-me-in-the-gut shock of sudden, horrific news, but a stunning blow nonetheless. The nightmare of one lowly associate tapping into their impenetrable defenses was bad enough. Now there might be another?

And just to give them more heartburn, Kyle added something he truly believed, but couldn't prove. "And I don't think it's an associate," he said, then withdrew from the fray and settled back into his chair.

All six partners had the same thought. If it's not an associate, then it must be a partner.

Doug Peckham swallowed hard, cleared his throat, and attempted to speak. "Are you saying—"

Next to him, Wilson Rush quickly raised his right hand, partially in Doug's space. Like a king calling for silence, a quick lifting of the hand, and all was quiet for the moment.

Roy finally said, "Anything else?"

"I believe that's all," Meezer said. After an awkward few seconds, Roy stood, followed by Kyle and Delano and Wingate. The six partners did not budge. They sat frozen, with matching scowls, as Kyle and his little entourage left the room.

42

In the lobby of the building, they were met by the same three large young men who'd brought Kyle from the hotel. The group made it safely outside, onto Broad Street, then walked one block east to the building next door, where Roy worked, sixteen floors up. The three agents, bodyguards really, camped in a reception area and began waiting again. Inside Roy's office, Drew Wingate decided that his job was over. He excused himself and promised to help in any way possible. After he left, Kyle, Roy, and Delano gathered around Roy's small conference table. Some poor secretary, beckoned on a Sunday, served them coffee with a smile.

"What are your plans, Kyle?" Delano asked.

"Well, looks like I won't be practicing law in the state of New York, that's for sure. I'll go home for a few weeks, take some time off, enjoy the holidays."

"I'm not sure that's a wise thing to do."

"Thank you, Mr. Delano. I appreciate your concern, but I'm not about to go into hiding. Thanks for the offer to enter the dark little world of witness protection, but no thanks. I'm twenty-five years old, stumbling but not falling, and I'll do just fine on my own."

Roy's coffee cup froze in midair, halfway to his mouth. "Kyle, you can't be serious."

"Dead serious, Roy. No pun intended. I've just survived three days of protection, guards all around me, hiding and watching for bad guys. No thanks. There's more to my future than fake names and non-stop Scrabble."

"Scrabble?"

"Don't go there. Listen, I've been under surveillance for the last ten months. You know what that does to you? You get real paranoid. You suspect everyone. You seize upon every new face because it might belong to a bad guy. You notice every corner, alley, every bum on a park bench, every guy wearing a dark trench coat. You pick up a phone and you wonder who's listening. You send an e-mail and change the wording because the wrong eyes might see it. In your own apartment you change clothes in a hurry, back to the camera, trying to hide your crotch. You walk in a coffee shop and go straight to the front window to see who's on the sidewalk behind you. You learn all sorts of stupid little tricks because the more you know, the more you might need to know. And the walls close in. The world becomes a small place because somebody is always watching. I'm sick of it. I'm not going to live on the run."

"These guys killed Baxter Tate without the slightest hesitation," Roy said. "What makes you think they won't do the same to you?"

"The operation was still hot when Baxter came barging in. The operation, at least that part that involves me, is now over. Bennie's gone. The operation failed. He might return with another plan—"

"I'm sure he will," Delano said.

"But it won't involve me. What does Bennie gain by taking me out?"

"He takes out a material witness," Roy said.

"Only if he's caught, which I seriously doubt. If Bennie gets hauled back for a trial, then we can talk about hiding."

"Oh, it'll be too late then, Kyle," Delano said. "Believe me. The moment Bennie gets nabbed, there'll be a few guys headed your way."

"Bring 'em on. We have at least five deer rifles at home. I'll carry a Luger in my briefcase. If they show up, we'll have a regular gunfight."

"Get serious, Kyle," Roy pleaded.

"The decision has been made. The FBI cannot force me into witness protection, and so I hereby officially, and respectfully, say no. Thank you, Mr. Delano, but the answer is no."

"I hope you don't regret this," Delano said.

"So do I," Kyle said. "And please don't follow me around. I might go berserk and shoot the next person I see lurking in the shadows."

"Oh, don't worry. We have plenty of work elsewhere." Delano stood and all hands were shaken. He said to Roy, "I'll check in once a week with an update."

Roy walked him to the door, and the FBI left Kyle's life. With the door closed, Roy took his seat and looked at Kyle as if he couldn't believe it. "You're awfully brave," he said.

"Brave or stupid. The line is often blurred."

"Why not disappear for a few months, maybe a year? Let everything cool off."

"A year means nothing. These guys have long memories. If Bennie wants revenge, he'll find me sooner or later, and it won't matter where I happen to be."

"You don't trust the FBI?"

"No. I trust you, me, my father, a girl named Dale, and that's about it."

"So it was an inside job?"

"We'll never know, will we? I have a hunch that Bennie works for the same government you and I send our taxes to. That's how he got away. That's why he'll never be found."

"I still don't believe that."

Kyle shrugged, and for a long time nothing was said.

Finally, Kyle glanced at his watch. "Look, Roy, it's Sunday afternoon and you have a family. Go home."

"What about you?"

"Me? I'm walking out the door, taking a long hike to my apartment, not once looking over my shoulder, and when I get there, I'll load up my clothes and as much junk as possible, cram all of it into my Jeep that has 200,000 miles on the odometer, and drive home. I should get there in time for a late dinner with my father. Tomorrow he and I will draw up a partnership agreement—McAvoy & McAvoy, Attorneys-at-Law—and I'll make partner faster than any graduate in the history of the Yale Law School."

"I like it. The editor in chief of the *Yale Law Journal* practicing law on Main Street in York, Pennsylvania."

"I like it, too. Real clients. Real people. Real cases. Deer hunting on Saturdays, Steelers on Sundays. A real life."

"You're not kidding, are you?"

"I have never been more serious."

"Come on. I'll walk you out."

They rode the elevator to the lobby and walked out of the building. They shook hands and said goodbye, and Roy watched his client stride nonchalantly along Broad Street and disappear around a corner.